THE WORLD HAD EVERYTHING TO OFFER . . .

Mary-Ellen

A statuesque American goddess men showered with riches. She'd take two of everything . . . and never be poor again.

Holly

A perfect Irish angel. Her wanton cravings answered every man's fantasies.

Arlette

A cool and clever French beauty. She plotted her course to settle down with a wealthy duke before her looks faded.

Sarah

She came from a quiet English village, but a childhood of hell had made her tough. A dangerous love in Paris made her tougher . . . and smarter.

HELENE MANSFIELD

AVON
PUBLISHERS OF BARD, CAMELOT, DISCUS AND FLARE BOOKS

SOME WOMEN DANCE is an original publication of Avon Books. This work has never before appeared in book form. This work is a novel. Any similarity to actual persons or events is purely coincidental.

AVON BOOKS
A division of
The Hearst Corporation
1790 Broadway
New York, New York 10019

First Avon Printing, December 1985

AVON TRADEMARK REG. U. S. PAT. OFF. AND IN
OTHER COUNTRIES, MARCA REGISTRADA, HECHO EN
U. S. A.

Printed in the U. S. A.

WFH 10 9 8 7 6 5 4 3 2 1

PROLOGUE

The Trans-Europa Express came into the station at precisely noon. Porters rushed to help passengers with their luggage, studiously avoiding those whose clothes betrayed a lack of money, preferring cigar-smoking businessmen with hard, choleric faces and pampered women enfolded in mink far too warm for the sunny spring day.

Sarah adored trains. From the earliest days of childhood, she had loved the excitement of getting aboard and going somewhere special, of imagining the surprises that lay in store. She glanced around the sleeping compartment with its stylish mahogany paneling and Edwardian advertisements for Vichy Celestins. Then she picked up the purse, shoulder bag, and Loewe briefcase and moved along the corridor toward the station's concourse. As she hurried along the platform, she scanned the waiting masses for Davington, the chauffeur she had engaged primarily because she longed to hear someone speak perfect English rather than the voluble cadences of Umberto's Sicilian *compadres*. She also needed someone who was her employee and not her lover's. Sarah smiled as Davington's stately figure came into view, his suit perfectly pressed, his eyes alert. She knew he was a fifty-two-year-old widower with a military background, fond of weight lifting, judo, and tap dancing. He was six feet

1

three, fair, blue eyed, and weighed one hundred and ninety pounds. Apart from that, Sarah knew nothing at all, except that he was lonely, devoted to her, and the perfect man of all work.

Overjoyed to be back in Paris, Sarah thought that this was going to be a very special day, the day of her long-awaited rendezvous with the three friends who had started their careers with her in the Tour of the Ballet Rose in Paris. They had planned this reunion ten years earlier. She handed her ticket to the collector and her bags to Davington.

"It's good to see you, Davington."

"Welcome home, madame. I'm glad to see you. The house is lonely without you. The neighbors haven't learned a word of English and I'm sure they never will."

"You've been in Paris for years. You must learn to speak French."

"It wouldn't do, madame. I'm English to the bone."

As he opened the trunk of the car to put away the luggage, Sarah recalled the night when Davington had not been on his dignity as the perfect English servant. That night, as she left the house, a drunk had teetered toward her, his arms outstretched, his befuddled voice roaring out a bawdy tune. Davington had responded by lifting the man as if he were a flea and depositing him on a traffic island in the center of a busy intersection. He had then driven her to the club without even mentioning the incident.

Sarah looked thoughtfully at the boulevards of Paris, the dove-gray of the stone buildings, the evanescent mist on the river. There were gray statues in a tiny park full of poplar trees and gray lamps on a bridge over the Seine. The delicate monotones of the landscape were enlivened by pink and white horse chestnuts in full spring bloom, green-leafed willows, and abundant cascades of lilac. Flower sellers sat on stools by stalls ablaze with lilies and marguerites, broom and tight red roses.

Sarah sighed at the memories the flowers evoked. Roses had been Mary-Ellen's favorite flower and the dressing room had always been full of them, dozens and dozens of scarlet roses swathed in cellophane, sent by men who needed a goddess to adore. Sarah thought of Mary-Ellen's exquisite looks and statuesque body, her trunks full of beautiful clothes, gifts, jewels, furs and the mischievous smile that came when she admitted she had bought two of everything "in case I run out." Childhood years in a Nebraska orphanage had left Mary-Ellen with a morbid fear of "running out." But why had she so rarely been in contact these past ten years? Again and again Sarah had sought a reason for her friend's silence. Was it possible that Mary-Ellen had simply wanted to forget the past?

Sarah's mind turned to Holly, the pure and perfect Irish girl, whose dedication to work had so pleased the show's director. Would she have changed much in these intervening years? Would the nights of decadence and humiliation have left their mark?

And what of Arlette? Sarah fell to thinking of the oldest member of the group—the only one who had known what she wanted from life. Arlette had decided at twelve, with much prompting from her mother, that she would marry a duke, live in a chateau, and be rich beyond her dreams. She had indeed married a duke, had a son, and was still living, as far as Sarah knew, in her chateau. Was she happy? Or did she still worry constantly about keeping her looks? Sarah shook her head as she recalled how Arlette had burst into tears at the very mention of aging. There was something daunting about these memories, about meeting old friends after ten years. It made her conscious of how much she had changed, how much of her innocence had been lost.

Davington's voice broke into Sarah's thoughts.

"Mr. di Castelli's chauffeur is following us, as usual. I wonder he doesn't tire of being a human bloodhound."

"To hell with him."

"Yes, madame. Shall I leave you at the Ritz and return at three-thirty, or might the meeting be cut short?"

Sarah appreciated Davington's diplomacy, conscious that he worried she might be upset at meeting her friends again.

"Come at three-thirty, Davington. We're going to have a drink and lunch and then we'll stay in the grill and talk. That's about it."

"I hope there won't be any unfortunate surprises, madame. Reunions are not in my opinion a good idea. Damn the fellow, what's he doing? Mr. di Castelli's chauffeur is signaling me to stop."

"Perhaps he has a message from Umberto."

Davington pulled to a halt. He gazed impassively at the Sicilian, who hurried over to hand Sarah a note and a box from Van Cleef and Arpels. The young man was apologetic.

"Signor di Castelli ask that I give you this before you arrive at the Ritz, madame. I came late to the station, please forgive me."

Sarah opened the box and found a posy of flowers made of amethysts, diamonds, and pearls, their emerald leaves shimmering in the sunlight. Then she read the note.

Today I too remember our first meeting. You carried a posy of violets and white daisies pink at the edge. I ask the jeweler to copy for you as a memento. I never forget the violets, because they match the color of your eyes. I am jealous of your friends because they lunch with you and keep us apart.

Umberto

Davington gazed through the mirror at Sarah, admiring the elegant St. Laurent suit in fine pin-striped gray wool, the trench coat tightly belted around the tiny waist. She had removed her owllike glasses to read the note. Davington smiled at the heart-shaped face, the huge eyes with their surrounding lashes that were thick and black. The long, corn-blonde hair dropped like a sheet of satin on either side of her face, swirling when Sarah tossed her head. Davington thought her the most beautiful creature he had ever seen and the most elegant. She was far too good for the man who loved her obsessively, pursued her persistently, and had her followed day and night. He noted that Sarah did not put on the pin. Di Castelli's day was long over, though he seemed not to know it.

As they reached the Vendôme entrance to the Ritz, Sarah stepped out of the car.

"See you soon, Davington."

"Have a very nice lunch, madame, and don't let anything upset you. Young women can be jealous, and your great success might have affected them that way. I'll be parked under the arches from two-thirty on if you wish to leave early."

"You're a lovely fellow, but you worry too much."

"Pessimism has always been one of my faults—that and the violent streak in my nature."

Arlette was in a chauffeur-driven Rolls, stuck in traffic on the Champs Elysées. She was wearing an Imperial sable cloak and a pink silk dress from Dior. A Leclerc triple-strand pearl choker was around her neck, and two heavy gold and ruby bracelets adorned her wrists. She gazed at her reflection in the mirror for the tenth time, enjoying the sight of the new gamine haircut her husband hated. Charles had been a tyrant from the day of their marriage and it was sometimes a relief to defy him. She took out a lip brush and redefined her mouth, annoyed because her hand was trembling. Though she longed to see her old friends again, she half wished she had not agreed to come. She was terrified that she might, while reliving for a brief moment the happiest days of her life, reveal her present, prevalent misery. Closing her eyes, she tried not to think of the scene at the chateau that morning, when she had discovered Charles and his young mistress breakfasting on the terrace, Ernestine sitting in *her* place. Arlette sighed wearily. She would be thirty-five in December, getting old and losing her looks and power and everything she needed most in life. A solitary tear ran down her cheek and she pulled out the mirror again, aghast at the black streak of mascara that stained her cheek.

"Can't you turn off and take the Faubourg Saint Honoré, Gaston? We're going to be late and Sarah will be furious."

"It's closed for repair, madame. We have no option but to wait."

Arlette repaired the makeup and redid the lashes. She was wondering about her friends and their lives. Mary-Ellen, whose beauty she had always envied, would probably arrive in a ten-strand diamond necklace with a string of millionaires panting behind her. Holly would appear in virginal white, to be cast off when darkness came and she transformed herself into the creature of every man's fantasy. And what of Sarah? Arlette was puzzled.

Sarah had always been the mystery, brought up in poverty by a half-mad, hate-filled mother. It had taken a long time for Arlette to learn anything about Sarah. The English girl had revealed little of herself. She would mention in passing her delicate lungs, her childhood bouts with asthma and pneumonia. There were also stories of walking to school in the dead of winter, making her way through the wet countryside with flimsy shoes that the child padded with cardboard to keep out the dampness. Sarah's mother seemed to have delighted in tormenting the child, pushing her to do things that would exacerbate her health problems. Sarah only spoke of her mother in terms of those childhood cruelties. Whatever love she felt for her mother had been destroyed—or else it had been transformed into Sarah's ambition. Arlette knew that whatever success her friend had had—and she had read a great deal in the newspapers about Sarah's growing business empire—was due entirely to willpower and grim dedication no doubt born in those early days in England. Arlette wondered how Sarah the woman was faring. Would she remain trapped in the golden cocoon of Umberto di Castelli's passion? Arlette shuddered at the thought of being loved by a man like him, with his soulless, saturnine eyes, his false bonhomie, and his black Sicilian soul.

Holly arrived on the flight from Dublin, then took a bus to the terminal and a taxi to the Ritz. She was thrilled to be in Paris and ecstatic at the thought of seeing her friends again. The quayside bookstalls by the Seine were busy, and from a nearby building Holly heard the concièrge's eternal cry—*"Monsieur, vous allez où?"* Paris had a smell like no other city, an elusive scent of *pastis* and Gauloises, gasoline and perfume, with occasional tempting odors when the door of a restaurant was opened. Holly felt her heart quickening as the taxi drew to the curb outside the Ritz, because the two men were still following her. They were surely French security officers. Holly walked into the hotel, her face thoughtful as she glanced at her reflection in the glass of the door. Her dress was gray with a starched white collar; her blue eyes were wide and innocent. She smiled enigmatically. This was a special day, a very special day, and nothing must be allowed to spoil it.

Mary-Ellen hurried across the Pont Neuf, her hair blowing in all directions. She was close to exhaustion, after the long journey, but Sarah hated tardiness, and Mary-Ellen was desperately anxious to please her friend. As she hastened through crowds of tourists near the Louvre and then on to the rue de Rivoli, she came upon an old house that had a motto engraved in the cornice: *May the joy of thy dwelling live here forever.* Tears burned her eyes and Mary-Ellen blew her nose loudly on a paper tissue. The joy of thy dwelling indeed! There had not been much joy in any house where she had dwelled—certainly not in the orphanage of her childhood or now in the deserted house in the bare Castilian countryside. The happiest days of her life had been those with the Tour of the Ballet Rose, the most glamorous and spectacular show in Europe. Mary-Ellen thought of the theaters they had played in Seville, Nice, Palermo, and Vienna. What days those had been and what adventures they had all had! Now, at last, the four special friends were going to meet again after ten years. Mary-Ellen ran into the Place Vendôme, finding one last burst of energy. In a few minutes she would be with the girls again.

Sarah was in the bar when Arlette appeared and hurried to her side, trailing her sable cloak on a cloud of Patou's Joy. She rose and kissed Arlette's cheeks.

"It's good to see you again."

"My dear Sarah, you look extremely rich. Saint Laurent, I presume?"

"Correct. How's life at the chateau?"

"Good and not good, both at the same time. I've been married for nearly ten years, my son is seven, and my husband is about to throw me out because he's in love with his twenty-four-year-old mistress." Arlette's face was miserable. "Ernestine started life as a peasant on a farm in Normandy and has been at the chateau since she was a child. The gutter has finally called the gutter." Arlette's fingertips fluttered to her eyes, blotting any tears that might fall.

"See my lawyer. He'll know how to handle everything."

"Ah, Sarah. Always so realistic."

"Here's Holly."

"Dear God, she's more beautiful than ever. Don't either of you ever age?"

Sarah turned to Holly and shook her hand.

"Did you hear what Arlette said?"

"I did and it's not true, but say it again. Oh, I'm so glad to be here! I've been dreaming of Paris for weeks and walking around Dublin like a leprechaun with its head in the clouds."

Holly looked behind her at the two men who were watching from the hall. Then she smiled reassuringly at her friends.

"Carlos is an arms dealer, so I usually get followed when I leave Ireland."

Sarah and Arlette exchanged silent, apprehensive glances. They ordered drinks from a passing waiter—a Bellini for Sarah, a crème-de-menthe frappé for Arlette, an Irish whiskey on the rocks for Holly. They were appraising each other, and laughing about the night when two grandees had threatened to fight a duel over Mary-Ellen, when a commotion broke out in the hall of the hotel. As they turned toward the noise, Mary-Ellen ran into the bar a few feet ahead of the burly doorman and the head porter.

Sarah, Arlette, and Holly stared in shock as she called out in desperation:

"For Christ's sake, *do* something, will you! He wouldn't let me in! He said I was improperly dressed."

Sarah looked at the dirty blue jeans, the darned sweater, the grimy, dust-stained feet in their plastic sandals. Then she stepped forward and whispered to the doorman, who relinquished his hold on Mary-Ellen and withdrew from the bar. Sarah turned to the concièrge and spoke with more calm than she was feeling.

"Madame Alarcon needs a room. Arrange it at once, please."

While the others sat in stunned silence, staring at Mary-Ellen's broken nails and strawlike hair, Sarah led her friend out of the bar to the reception area and then upstairs to the room. There, she made a phone call while Mary-Ellen took a shower. A few minutes later a large black box was delivered from an adjacent boutique. The porter spoke discreetly to Sarah.

"Madame Kirstina sent this for you, Miss Hallam. She says if you need anything else she will have it delivered immediately."

Sarah knocked on the door of the bathroom and handed in a dove-gray cashmere dress, a pair of soft leather pumps, and a set of silk underwear in cerulean blue.

"Put these on and you'll feel better in seconds."

Mary-Ellen reappeared, her face haggard, her body skeletally thin. Only the pleasure in her eyes hinted at the effervescent personality of years past.

"It's almost like old times to see myself in clothes like these, Sarah."

"You look wonderful, but you're too thin. We used to be the same size, remember?"

"I remember. I haven't forgotten a single day of the Tour of the Ballet Rose. I have no money to pay for this stuff, Sarah."

"Don't think of money." Sarah waved her toward the door. "I'm famished. Let's go down and join the others."

Sarah held out her hand and they hurried back to the bar, where an awkward silence enveloped the friends. Holly kept looking at Sarah, and Arlette could not stop gazing in horror at Mary-Ellen. Each one knew that something catastrophic had transformed Mary-Ellen from one of the most beautiful women in Europe to this soiled, pathetic wraith. Holly closed her eyes and murmured a brief prayer. Arlette worried that any of her husband's influential friends might have seen the incident that accompanied Mary-Ellen's entrance. Sarah was both furious at the damage nine years of marriage had wrought and eager to resurrect the legendary creature everyone had once admired. Realizing that the others needed time to adjust to the new Mary-Ellen, Sarah rose and led the way to the grill, linking arms with her friend, who looked terribly uneasy.

"How did you get here?" Sarah asked her.

"I took the bus from the house to the border at San Sebastien, then I hitched to Bordeaux and took the night train to Paris. I've been on the road for a week, and I know I smelled like it. I'm sorry I let you all down by arriving dressed like that. Things are pretty bad for me, but I was determined to keep the date. I've been saving for a whole year for this moment."

Suddenly tears began to course down Holly's cheeks and she put her arms around Mary-Ellen, who sobbed quietly. The women were shown to a table in a far corner of the Grill, where they could be alone with their memories. After a few minutes, Arlette passed Mary-Ellen a small leather makeup case. Mary-Ellen smiled at her friend and excused herself. When she had disappeared to the powder room, Arlette turned to Sarah.

"I never expected her to be a failure."

Sarah spoke tersely, annoyed by the callousness of the remark. "She'll make it. Mary-Ellen's a survivor."

"She's too far gone. She's lost hope."

"We'll give it back to her."

"And who will give *us* hope, tell me that?"

"We find it inside ourselves, Arlette, somewhere deep down. If we're lucky we find hate. Hate's the best cure for being miserable."

Arlette's eyes widened in response to her friend's vehemence.

"You're always so sure of yourself, Sarah."

"I'm sure of nothing, except that I have to live my life, get through each day, and raise my child."

Sarah ordered for them all, as she always had, a soufflé

d'homard with Dom Perignon, tournedos Rossini with a
bottle of Chateau Latour, and fresh raspberries with a bottle
of Perrier Jouët rosé. Then she turned to her companions.

"Well, we all got here. Let's drink to the next ten years.
If we've been unhappy since our last meeting, we'll drink to
happiness and hope. If we're content, we'll hope to stay that
way. To us and to the future."

Mary-Ellen gazed at Sarah and felt calm for the first time
in weeks. To her, Sarah was a source of enormous comfort.
She raised her glass and hoped for the first time in months
that she could indeed make a future for herself and her children.

Sarah looked at the pearls around Arlette's neck, the emerald on her finger, and the despair in her eyes. The haughti-
ness of her early days had gone, and at thirty-five Arlette
was facing the dread knowledge that she was no longer
young. Sarah turned then to Mary-Ellen, recalling the day
ten years earlier when they had met for the first time. They
had been young, green, eager to see the world and to taste
life. Sarah drank the champagne and motioned for a waiter
to pour another glass for them all. Then she voiced her
thoughts for the others.

"You know what I did when I first arrived in Paris? I sat
on my suitcase and cried on platform six of the Gare du
Nord. I was so scared I couldn't speak a word of French, despite having studied it for years at school. God, I was frightened! I felt as if I'd plunged into a hundred-foot-deep pool
without first learning to swim."

Mary-Ellen held Sarah's hand as she spoke, watching the
others across the table as memories of the past began to fill
their minds. It all seemed so very long ago. Was it possible
it was only ten years? Since then, the ones who had seemed
destined winners had lost and the quiet one had become a
woman of power. Mary-Ellen wondered which of them
would really stay the course. In another five or ten years, at

the next rendezvous, who would be wrapped in sable and who would have given up hope, submerged in the hidden snares that beauty brings?

Sarah's voice was soothing, and suddenly the amber lamps of the Ritz faded and they were all there, at the Théâtre de l'Empire, to rehearse for the opening of the show that would change their lives.

Part I

OVERTURE AND BEGINNERS

She is very clever, too clever for a woman. She lacks the indefinable charm of weakness.

—Oscar Wilde
The Picture of Dorian Grey

CHAPTER ONE

Paris, March 1967

On the first day of rehearsal it snowed. Sarah stood at the hotel window, looking out at people with pinched faces struggling home in a blizzard. Some children on their way to school stopped for a snow battle, hitting a passing postman more often than they pelted each other. Sarah scratched at the icy patterns on the inside of the window of the bathroom, where the heating was out of order. Then she sealed the letter to her mother, looking hard at the address and trying to still the irrational homesickness that kept welling up inside her. Sarah thought of the house in England, overlooking fields of brown cows munching meadowsweet. Then she looked again out the window, at statues green with age and covered with a layer of snow. For years she had longed to get away from home, to travel, to grow into a sophisticated woman. Since her arrival in Paris, all she had longed for was to be back in England. Suddenly she was terrified of everything. She was afraid she wouldn't learn the new routines fast enough, that the crippling homesickness would be unshakable, that she would not be able to say anything in the suddenly incomprehensible foreign language.

It was all ridiculous and Sarah knew she must control her rising panic. She was twenty years old and had lived a cloistered life, working near home so she could care for her

17

mother after her father's death, never letting herself think of what she really wanted to do. Then, suddenly, her mother had remarried. With characteristic cruelty she had informed her daughter that she was no longer needed about the house and should look for a job immediately, preferably one that took her out of the country. After twenty years as her mother's companion, slave, and occasional whipping boy, Sarah had at last found herself free.

Her mind went back to the earliest days of childhood and the morning when an elegant man had arrived at the house in a sleek black limousine. Sarah had been four years old and sitting on her grandmother's knee in the kitchen. Mother had welcomed the stranger, blushing furiously at Enid's presence. Left alone while her grandmother went to the garden to pick peas for lunch, Sarah had peeked around the door of the drawing room, fascinated to see the stranger kissing her mother passionately. She still remembered her apprehension lest Enid return. She also remembered the moment of parting, when the man had looked gravely down at her and told her to take good care of Anna, her mother.

After that, there had been incessant rows between her parents. Mama had changed suddenly and irrevocably, and the love once lavished on Sarah had disappeared. Schooldays had been a nightmare, because she lived under the constant threat of being given to the orphanage if she did not succeed. Evenings were worse. As Anna began to descend into a mental breakdown, the threats of suicide increased and Sarah recalled the tortured hours spent trying to persuade the deranged woman not to cut her wrists or run away. She sighed, remembering the other strange and twisted facets of Anna's personality: the desire to be famous, the detestation of doctors and intellectuals, the obsessive longing to inflict pain or fear.

Sarah recalled with a shiver of apprehension the night of her eighth birthday when her mother came into her bed-

room, looked into Sarah's eyes and chortled with a gleeful
smile, "When you go to sleep the rats will come and eat
your face!" Nearly twelve years later, Sarah could still recall that malevolent glee, remember the demented quality of
her mother's laughter as she peered into Sarah's eyes and
pinched at her face with the tips of her fingers. She had
never slept through the night since and she knew she never
would.

Despite everything, after her father's death, Sarah had
cared for her mother, the alternative being an asylum for
Anna and the orphanage for her. She had escaped the horrors of her home in daily ballet classes, aware that she was
only allowed to have them because her mother had once
dreamed of being a famous ballerina. But there had been no
career for Anna. Instead, she had sunk into depressive illness, a negative, occasionally violent or hypermanic creature, who sat at the window gazing with vacant eyes at her
garden and the street beyond. She ignored filth, squalor and
reality. It was only when Sarah found time from school, ballet lessons, extra music tuition and a course in typing that
any housework was done. The kitchen was begrimed with
the grease of many months. The sink was home to sky-
scraper piles of filthy crockery. Anna's bedroom was piled
high with the newspapers she had hoarded for years. Only
Sarah's pink room, with its crocheted cushions, was clean
and in perfect order. Whenever Anna was in a savage mood,
Sarah took refuge there, locking the door and daydreaming
about a beautiful home full of pure white carpets and arctic
fox bedspreads, where servants scrubbed and cleaned and
gardeners grew roses and jasmine.

Sarah had loved that perfect room and she had loved the
rigorous discipline of the dance. She practiced endlessly; the
dance became her diversion from her mother's torments.
Later it would occur to her that it was through dancing that
she had learned how to turn her pain into strength. After she

left ballet school, Sarah had worked summer shows and done some local television, unable to travel far because she never knew when Anna would have another attack. The debilitating, symbiotic mother-daughter liaison had continued until her mother's sudden and totally unexpected remarriage.

So Sarah found herself an innocent in Paris, a greenhorn in a sophisticated world, a former captive longing for the security of her prison, unequal to the demands of fast-paced cosmopolitan life. Above all, the huge gaps in her knowledge of people terrified her. She had studied and passed school exams with brilliance. She had become a stylish dancer, but she knew nothing of men and was mystified by the games people play in the name of love and power. Sarah believed what she was told and was ignorant of many of the facts of life, the complications of mind and body that she would encounter all the time in her new existence as a Paris showgirl.

Looking at her watch, Sarah hurried to pack her spare tights, pants, bra, and a clean blouse, plus ballet shoes and a pair of red tap shoes of which she was very proud. She was aware that the rehearsals would be long and arduous, with much to learn in a very short time. The show had already toured South America for eight months and was wildly profitable. Now the company was back in Paris, where new costumes were being made and a new star engaged to replace the previous one, who had married an Argentinian shipping magnate. Sarah and three other new girls had been taken on to replace two dancers and two showgirls whose contracts had not been renewed. They would be required to learn the entire show in three weeks, working from nine A.M. for twelve hours each day. Then, after the Paris opening at the Empire Theater, they would start the tour in the Spanish city of Seville. Sarah wondered about the other new girls. When a company had been on tour for some time, its members resented newcomers. Gaining acceptance by a group that had worked together for eight months would be difficult, if not impossible. Snapping her case shut, Sarah put on her gloves and a knitted hat and left the room, thinking grimly that she was well used to difficult times. After the years of childhood suffering, she could surely cope with a few hostile show-girls.

In the foyer of the hotel, Sarah handed in her key and collected her mail. There was only one letter, addressed in a neat hand in violet ink, the writing full of swooping loops. It said:

Dear Sarah,
I'm in room 15. My name is Holly Anne O'Malley. Like you, I'm here to replace one of the dancers in the show. Wait for me, will you, so we can go to rehearsals together. I'm scared and I'm sure I've grown two right legs since yesterday. If this continues, I shan't be able to dance at all. I'll be in the hall at 8:15 sharp. Please don't leave without me.

Sarah glanced at the clock and saw that it was eight-fourteen. Then the lift door opened and a tall girl with curly red hair, freckles, and huge blue eyes stepped out. She was dressed in a gray Donegal tweed overcoat with a pink angora hat and scarf. Her smile was enchanting, her accent a Dublin lilt that made even the most ordinary words sound fascinating.

"Hello there, you're Sarah Hallam. I'm Holly. Thanks for waiting for me. I've been up since four-thirty worrying myself sick."

"I haven't slept much, either."

"Let's walk to the theater. I love snow—and anyway, we'll never find a taxi."

The theater was cold and drafty, the proscenium arch

enormous. A group of people sat in the stalls, watching the ballet master as he began the class that would loosen muscles stiff from the cold. Among the group was the show's principal backer and the woman who had given her name to the troupe of girls who were legends all over Europe for their height, their beauty, and their unavailability. There were twenty dancers, all of them five feet eight or more, all beautiful and perfectly trained in classic and modern ballet, tap, and mime. There were sixteen showgirls, each one at least six feet tall, who would parade half nude in fabulous clothes. They could not dance, and some of them found thinking an unfamiliar exercise, but each one was original, a jewel chosen to enhance the spectacle of the year.

At a distance from the important watchers sat Madame Yvette, the veteran wardrobe mistress, with the group of men and women whose responsibility it would be to find shoes, hats, jewels, and clothes to fit the new girls. One of the watching showgirls remarked that the newies would be all right when they had been broken. Madame Yvette shook her head and looked hard at Sarah. She was thinking, *You'll get white hair before you break that one. The more you push her, the harder she'll grow.*

As the class began, all attention was focused on Sarah and Holly. Both girls were beautiful in very different ways. The Irish dancer was fawnlike, thin and luminous, with a style that was pure, perfectly trained and balletic. The English girl was in practice gray, an austere outfit with knitted leg warmers of striped black and white. Her style was elegant, with something unusual in the nuances of the gestures. She worked hard and concentrated on what was said to her, yet seemed to remain aloof from the proceedings.

The class lasted for an hour. Then the real work began as the two new dancers were taught the opening number of the show. The choreography was difficult, the moves intricate, and often Sarah and Holly exchanged glances of pure despair. Their situation was complicated by the discovery that they would be required to dance the opening and many of the numbers in three-and-a-half-inch heels. This had never been required in England, but Madame Rose expected newies to adapt immediately. The climax of their ordeal came when they were put on top of a thirty-foot-high white staircase, and told to descend regally without looking at their feet. Three hours later they had still not satisfied Madame Rose, and the torture continued until the tea break at four, when at last she pronounced them "satisfactory."

Sarah flopped down by the tea urn, her body a mass of pain. Her leotard was soaked with sweat, her hair plastered to her head, and she was furious that for five hours she had done nothing but tramp up and down a set of steep white steps. Glowering at the showgirls in the far corner, she took another currant bun and filled it with strawberry jam, closing her eyes in pleasure at the spicy cinnamon taste. She was about to reach for more tea, when she felt someone take the cup and fill it for her. Turning, she looked up into the suntanned face of one of the most beautiful girls she had ever seen. She was wearing a sugar-pink leotard with matching tights and five-inch heels. She was well over six feet tall and slim, though her breasts were heavy. Her hair was white-blonde and plaited in dozens of tiny knots ending in pink satin ribbons. Around her neck she wore a choker of tiny sparkling diamonds, and over her shoulders was a white cashmere shawl. As she introduced herself, her smile lit the room.

"I'm Mary-Ellen Tate. I'm one of the new showgirls. Drink your tea and I'll pour you some more. After that marathon you look as though you could drink the whole urn."

"I could, too. You're American, aren't you? I thought Madame Rose only took on English girls."

"The dancers are all English, but the showgirls come from all over. Hey, Arlette, come on over here and meet

Sarah. Sarah, this is the last of the newies, Arlette de Caze-nave. Arlette, Sarah Hallam.''

As they shook hands, Sarah assessed the tallest girl in the show. Arlette's jet-black hair was pulled back into a tight chignon stuck with bejeweled pins. Her eyes were dark blue, her neck long, her expression haughty, though her manner was friendly.

''Enchantée, Sarah. Mary-Ellen, the girls have put all our belongings outside the dressing room again. What are we to do? They refuse to make room for us.''

Sarah introduced Holly and the four sat together, discussing the tribulations of being new, unwelcome, and exhausted. Then they were called to start work again, the showgirls in the foyer, the dancers up on stage in the draft. The opening number was rehearsed and rehearsed until Madame decided to make a start on the cancan. Only eight of the dancers took part in this, and Sarah was called as the replacement for the missing eighth. Until nine at night she was put through a punishing routine of cartwheels, splits, and bloodcurdling whoops of ''joy.'' Aching from head to toe, she could not help wondering if being with the Tour of the Ballet Rose was a good idea after all. She had auditioned because she longed to travel, to be one of these celebrated dancers, but the reality was not what she had imagined and she longed to be far, far away.

There was a traffic jam at the Étoile, so, despite their fatigue, the four newies walked back to their hotel together. There was a cozy-looking bistro opposite, with checkered tablecloths lit by yellow lamps. Comforted by their newfound camaraderie, the girls entered and ordered goulash to be followed by bananas and cream.

Alarmed when Sarah ordered three helpings of the sweet and two cups of coffee loaded with sugar, Arlette could not resist a protest.

"I hope you don't mind my saying, but you will get fat someday, Sarah."

"Someday's the future."

"You never think of your looks?"

"I think of my work and trying to get to be secure in life, but I don't waste time on my looks. You can't stay gorgeous forever, so it's not a thing to waste time worrying about. Everyone loses her looks in the end."

"But you can stay beautiful longer if you take care of yourself."

"It's just not one of the concerns of my life, Arlette. Now, tell me about this problem of the dressing room. That really could be serious."

Arlette did her best to explain the situation.

"Each time we put our clothes and our makeup in the showgirls' dressing room, they put the cases and all our possessions outside in the corridor. They just don't want to share with new members."

Sarah turned to Holly.

"Is the same thing happening in our dressing room?"

"Yes. I could have choked that girl Liz this afternoon for the horrible things she said. She told me to my face that I didn't belong and never would and neither would you. She's malicious, Sarah. We'll have to watch her."

Mary-Ellen yawned, exhausted by the long hours and the hostility of the girls of the Ballet Rose.

"I'm beat. I need ten hours of sleep a night or I'm peaked. Let's go back to the hotel. I've a feeling tomorrow's going to be a pretty hard day. Someone told me they were breaking us in gently today."

They all groaned. Then, having pooled their resources, they paid the bill and left for the hotel. Outside, a neon light flashed and the night people of Paris were on the move: the men with hooded eyes who owned drinking clubs in the area, the pretty boys with insolent faces waiting for rich patrons to take them to dinner, the wide-eyed tourists gazing at the dazzling sight of the city after dark.

The girls were entering the hotel when they heard the sound of a flute being played in an adjacent attic. They hurried inside, said good-night to each other, and went to their separate rooms. Each felt empty and apprehensive of what the morning would bring.

Sarah opened her window and looked out over the rooftops of Paris. It was then she realized that the musician was playing "La Vie en Rose." . . . *quand tu me prend dans tes bras . . . when you take me in your arms.* . . . She sighed. Would any man ever take her in his arms and love her? And would she want him to? Or would she be like her mother, incapable of giving love to anyone? Closing the window, she lay down on the bed, waves of melancholy washing over her as they had so often ever since the days of childhood, when the mother she loved had rejected her.

Three weeks of physical strain and exhausting work produced incredible tensions in the company. Established members resented the newcomers for not learning the numbers fast enough. The newies resented the killing pace of learning fifteen numbers and the accompanying costume changes in twenty-one working days. They resented too the increasing intransigence of their companions, who continued to refuse them access to the dressing room. When they appealed to Madame Rose to sort out the problem, they were told with icy derision to grow up and sort it out themselves. It was Sarah who decided to do just that, on the evening of the all-important dress rehearsal.

She arrived an hour and a half ahead of curtain up, as was required. She found the dressing room full of chattering half-naked dancers. As she entered the room and looked for her place, Liz stepped forward, pushed Sarah's makeup tray into her hands, and told her to use the corridor. Sarah stayed where she was, conscious of Holly's protests from behind. By way of a reply, Liz handed Holly her things too and told her to get lost. Sarah intervened.

"Look, for three weeks you've been taking the piss out of the newies. Now it's dress rehearsal day and we *have* to have mirror space and a place to dress. So let's cut the comedy and settle down to work."

Liz's green eyes flashed and she returned to her place at the makeup bench.

"Get out, Hallam. You're not welcome here and neither is your bog-Irish friend."

Holly held her breath as Sarah moved forward and a sudden silence descended on the dressing room. Without warning, all hell erupted. First Sarah slapped Liz so hard that the redhead hit the floor with an anguished scream. Before anyone could intervene, Sarah had swept all the makeup from the table that ran the length of one side of the dressing room. Bottles and jars shattered; jewelry crashed to the floor. The air was drenched with scent of a dozen perfumes; shards from crystal flacons littered the floor. Without a word, Sarah picked up a broken bottle that had once contained several hundred dollars' worth of the world's most expensive perfume. Her face was calm as she looked around the room.

"Now," she said, as though nothing of consequence had happened, "which is my place and which is Holly's?"

No one moved. Then the dancers began to scream and shout at the same time. Accusing fingers were pointed and dressers called to clear the debris. Aggrieved faces stared from Sarah to the pile of broken bottles and jars on the floor. While one of the girls ran to the corridor to call two of their number who had fled in fright, the others moved over and tried to finish their makeup. One of the dancers burst into tears and swore when her false eyelashes fell off. All watched in astonishment as Sarah calmly undressed and began to make up. One or two of the girls noted that Holly's hands were trembling so much she could not apply her eyeliner. All of them remarked that Sarah's were rock steady. It was the end of the childish games in the dressing room.

The man was of medium height, wide shouldered and muscular, with a pale face and black piercing eyes. His chin was faintly blue from the heavy underlying beard that could never be completely removed. He wore a dark-gray suit, an immaculate white shirt, and a tie of sapphire-blue silk. Over his shoulders was an overcoat of the same material as the suit, on his wrist a Patek Philippe as slim as a wafer. In his hand he carried a cane with a chased-silver tip. With this, he pushed the dressing-room door open a fraction more, the better to see the incredible young woman whose outburst had drawn his attention. The dark eyes gleamed, the hawkish nose twitched, the cruel mouth with its sensuous lower lip broke into a smile. She was young, with a chiseled English profile and pale shoulders that were as broad as an athlete's. When Sarah turned, he saw her full face for the first time and caught his breath at the almond-shaped lilac eyes, the high cheekbones, the cascade of pale blonde hair. Her mouth was large, the lips full, her teeth small and square. Moving away from the door, the man made his way to the rear of the darkened auditorium and sat thinking of Sarah's response when she had been crossed by a group of silly schoolgirls. There were, he knew, only four new girls. He decided to invite them all to the party he would give after opening night. When the English girl saw his home she would be unable to resist him. No woman had ever been able to resist Umberto di Castelli when confronted with the full force of his personality, charm, wealth, power, and the magnificence of his mansion in the Bois de Boulogne.

Umberto rose and walked from the theater, images of the glacial blonde filling his mind. He told himself she was just another woman, to be used for pleasure and taught his ways. In his heart, however, he suspected that she was something different, a woman like no other he had known. He wondered what kind of life she had led to make her capable of such rage and what reserves of violence and sensuality were concealed beneath the seemingly calm exterior. He decided to play the benevolent brother figure, reassuring, all-powerful, friendly without being threatening. Then he wondered if she was a virgin and concluded it was more than likely. As he thought of Sarah's body, he forgot his plans to be brotherly, surprised to feel a breathless anticipation he had not experienced since the days of his youth in Sicily. Chiding himself for being a fool to attach importance to any female, Umberto entered his home and telephoned his wife at the clinic for alcoholics in Switzerland. Duty completed, he rang for his brother-in-law to come and bring in the reports of business transacted during the day.

The opening of the Ballet Rose was attended by the Duke and Duchess of Windsor, Maurice Chevalier, Bardot, Onassis, Françoise Sagan, and the Royal Family Monaco, as well as every notable from the world of show business lucky enough to be in Paris that night. There were snow scenes with real ice-skaters, a waterfall that cascaded into the stalls, and two dozen changes of costume that brought riotous applause. Half-naked showgirls paraded in pearls and *diamant*, priceless Arctic fox, and crinolines eight feet wide that hung from forty-pound web metal frames that bruised their hipbones. Some of the changes were so fast and so intricate that two stagehands were needed for each girl. At first the men developed erections at every touch, but within hours they learned to take for granted the sight of a naked body. It was easier to be indifferent to those who had to wear the ornate thirty-inch-high gilded wigs for the Roman orgy scene. Because it was necessary to secure the heavy wigs firmly, the girls' own hair fell out in handfuls from the friction and pins required to keep the piece in place. Those who had been with the show longest had the least hair of all.

As the spectacle continued, dancers masqueraded as clowns, butterflies, courtiers at Versailles, and cancan girls. The enraptured audience applauded wildly, unable to work out how it was all done, but loving every minute. Weeks of arduous rehearsal had resulted in near perfection. The only thing that marred a perfect evening was the overeager dresser who hooked Sarah's necklace into her skin instead of into its fastener. Blood trickled down her cleavage, only to be halted within seconds by Madame Rose herself, armed with a styptic pencil and a giant sticking plaster. Sarah thought wryly that even blood obeyed Madame Rose.

When the final curtain fell, everyone rushed back to the dressing room. Dancers and showgirls of the original cast were dining together at Valentine's, the newies having been excluded from the invitation. Sarah and her friends had said nothing of their own plans for the evening, but each one dressed with particular care. The house overlooking the Bois was surrounded by a walled garden of two acres. In Paris that meant money with a capital *M*. Out of curiosity, they had driven past the house, after having received the invitations hand-delivered by Umberto di Castelli's chauffeur. They had never met the gentleman, though they had all seen him on his visits to rehearsals and Madame Yvette had told them he was an entrepreneur and as rich as Gulbenkian. All four had talked of little else since. They had arranged to arrive at the Castelli house together and to return to the hotel in the same taxi, unless they were quite sure their host and his guests were legitimate. There had been a rash of articles in the newspapers about white-slave traffickers, and all four were terrified of waking up one morning and finding themselves in a Panamanian bordello.

Holly was wearing blue silk that matched her eyes, a

little-girl dress with one of her favorite white collars and buttons from neck to waist. Arlette was in a cream linen Chanel copy, with gilt chains at wrist and waist. Mary-Ellen looked a dream in a shocking-pink mini. Sarah wore a dress she had made in the dark evenings of an English winter. It was of fine white wool, hand stitched and austere. Umberto had sent orchid corsages for them all, but she put hers aside. She had always been repelled by orchids and had ordered instead a posy from the hotel florist. It was Victorian in style, circular and surrounded by white lace that matched the dress. The flowers were African violets and fragile pink-edged white daisies with one splendid English rose in the center. As she looked at the simple flowers, Sarah thought she would never develop a taste for orchids, just as she would never understand fashion as Arlette did. Lack of money had made her evolve her own style, and she was comfortable with her choice.

In the taxi, the girls talked excitedly. Mary-Ellen was certain she would find a millionaire lover that night.

"If I do, I'll ask him to buy us each a diamond necklace from Cartier."

Arlette described her own fantasy.

"I should like to meet a very rich French duke. It is my destiny to marry someone like that and to live in a grand chateau."

Mary-Ellen turned to Holly.

"What's your wish for the evening, Irish?"

Holly colored slightly as she thought of the day when she had first seen a naked statue of Christ on the Cross, red blood pouring from the wound in his side. At the tender age of ten, she had experienced a strange, sweet weakness of the inner core and had fainted clean away. Since then, she had become addicted to that elusive, enchanting moment of orgasm and in secret sought it out and with it the punishment she knew must accompany the sin. Longing for the desires of her body to be assuaged, Holly replied enigmatically.

"I should like to forget the real world, the show, and my aching feet and be transported for an hour or two to a magic island where all things are possible."

Mary-Ellen chortled delightedly.

"You're a real poet, Holly. I don't know what you're talking about, but it sounds pretty good."

Finally, Mary-Ellen turned to Sarah.

"And you, what do you want the fairy godmother to bring you?"

Sarah shrugged, uncertain how to reply. She had thought very little about men.

"I don't know what I want. I've never been to a big party like this before. I just hope I know which knife and fork to use during dinner and that I don't tread on anyone's toes when I dance."

"But what kind of man do you *want*, Sarah?"

"I know almost nothing of men, except that I don't like them with soup stains on their ties, strong perspiration, and no hair on their chests."

The other girls hooted with laughter.

"You want an ape for a lover? Is that what you're trying to tell me?" Mary-Ellen teased.

Sarah pretended to consider the question.

"I wouldn't say a real ape—maybe a man who looks like one."

"You're an idiot. What you need is a knight in shining armor and to hell with monkeys!"

From the outside, the house looked like a concrete bunker, a modern fortress of clumsy, square dimension, shrouded by century-old yews clipped in topiary spirals. The girls gasped as a manservant took their coats and led them to the hall, where a dozen couples were talking and drinking champagne. The air was full of the scent of scarlet

orchids massed in magnificent arrangements near the door.
There was a carved and gilded fireplace sixteen feet high,
full of logs as big as tree trunks that blazed merrily, casting
an amber glow on the room. The decor was Chinese in influence, with Ching vases, a Louis XVI table full of Cheng
Lung armorial porcelain, and two astonishing eighteenth-
century cypress-root chairs with twisted, knotted forma-
tions, the original growth transformed by a craftsman's
imagination into furniture like no other in the world. The
walls were hand painted in the mottled tones of faux bamboo. The paintings were French *singeries*, from the period
when monkeys were considered a fashionable novelty.

Mary-Ellen nudged Sarah.

"You want a monkey, you got plenty!"

Umberto looked across the room at the four girls and
thought how very different they were and how lovely. The
American was outstanding, if obvious in her sexuality.
The Irish girl was mysterious, veiled and full of surprises. The
French one held herself like a queen, but she was cold and
would be hard to get to know. The English girl was innocent, but ripe for picking. Umberto scanned Sarah's body,
with its perfect skin, rounded breasts, and fragile wrists. He
noted that she had disdained the orchids in favor of a posy of
violets that matched the color of her eyes. There was something enchanting in the idea of carrying a posy, an echo of
times past when "ladies" still existed. Fascinated by her
unworldly aura, Umberto walked toward the four girls and
introduced himself.

"I am Umberto di Castelli. This is my house and I am
happy you could come to the party. I think your show is
wonderful—*magnifique!* I almost cry when it end."

The girls shook hands, smiling at his curious turn of
phrase. Umberto continued as if he had not noticed.

"Soon we go into the dining room and I take the liberty of
arranging partners for each of you. Miss O'Malley, meet my

cousin Paulo, who visits Paris from his home in Palermo. Mademoiselle de Cazenave, may I introduce my friend Armand, Count d'Artois. Miss Tate, this is David Newman. He is American, but he speak French better than most. He comes to Paris to make a film and will be here for two months. Miss Hallam, you will have to make do with me as your dinner partner. Come, take my arm and I introduce you to some of my friends.''

Sarah looked into the startling black eyes and felt a shiver of uncertainty at the scratchy voice with its pronounced Sicilian accent. How sure he was of everything, how efficient at arranging all that had to be arranged. She looked again around the hall with its Chinese-warrior *torchères* and curved marble staircase. She knew that Umberto must be very rich and longed to ask what he did, how he had amassed such wealth, but her English reserve prevented such inquiries. Instead, she took his arm and walked with him to the corner, where a group of elderly Sicilians was arguing volubly about the form of horse in the next day's race. Umberto began to introduce her to his uncles and cousins.

"Sarah, this is my cousin Rocco, my nephew Beppe, and my brother-in-law, Mario Benedetti. He will be manager of the Tour of the Ballet Rose. Mario, may I present Miss Hallam.''

Sarah shook hands with a man of fifty, with gray hair and a deeply suntanned face. Struck by the cobralike quality of Benedetti's eyes, Sarah looked uncertainly to Umberto for guidance.

"I didn't know your family was in show business, Mr. di Castelli.''

"Call me Umberto. We are not really a show business family, though I own a film company and several theater and club venues in Paris. Mario will manage the tour because he understand the pitfalls of the touring spectacle and will enforce the rules with the managements in every city on behalf of our investors. If not, we all lose our money, because they try to cheat.''

Sarah looked again at the short, square-shouldered man with implacable eyes, surprised when he spoke gently.

''If you need something, Miss Hallam, you only have to ask. Think of me as a friend.''

When Sarah brushed accidentally by his elbow, Umberto felt the softness of her breast on his arm. He wanted to pick her up and carry her to the bedroom so he could love her till she was limp with exhaustion. He thought how quiet she was, docile yet dangerous in some indefinable feline way. He wondered what she was thinking, disturbed to find he had no idea of the way her mind worked. Then, smiling into the wide violet eyes, he felt his body hardening under her penetrating gaze.

''You are very beautiful, Sarah, but every man tell you that.''

''I don't go out, so no one tells me anything.''

''What do you want from your life?''

''I want to feel safe and to have money in the bank.''

''How much money?''

Sarah looked uncertain, suddenly afraid in case he thought she was asking for money. She did her best to sound flippant.

''Enough to keep me from worrying—and I'm a five-star worrier. But tell me about your beautiful house—who designed it?''

''I do it all myself.''

''You're a genius. Is that what you do for a living?''

The dark eyes flickered.

''No, I arrange things. I am entrepreneur. My main business is import and export of furniture and carpets from the Orient, but I back sometimes film and shows. Your show is one of mine, though not a very big investment.''

At that moment the dinner gong sounded and the guests moved to the dining room. The walls were of black velvet, the table of white marble, the chairs of matching leather. The meal was impressive, the service impeccable, and each of the girls felt as if she had been transported to an earlier bygone century, as white-gloved, liveried footmen served quails' eggs stuffed with imperial caviar, a mousse of crayfish tails, and whole roast lambs stuffed with truffles and foie gras. Finally, there were sorbets of champagne and passion fruit, cheeses from each *département* of France, and baskets of tropical exotica: papaya, tamarillo, loquat, and guava. Unobtainable even in Paris, the durian had been flown in from Burma, the rambutans from Malaysia on the same plane.

After dinner, two orchestras played. One was an elegant string ensemble with a soft, sensuous sound; the other was known as Oleg and His Russian Gypsies. The latter provoked Umberto to sentimental tears and a display of dancing that brought wild applause from his guests. Exhausted, he collapsed in a chair at Sarah's side, fanning his face with a copy of the *Financial Times*.

"I'm thirty-eight and getting too old for the dancing."

"You seem remarkably fit to me."

"Your friend Mary-Ellen has disappear with the movie director. Perhaps he will make her a star. Would you like to be a star?"

"Not if it means disappearing with David Newman," she said without thinking. Realizing that Newman might be her host's friend, she laughed and went on. "In any case, my ambitions lie in other directions. I want to own property. My grandfather always taught me that money was only safe in bricks and mortar."

"And what did your parents teach you?"

"My father died in a car crash when I was eight, and my

mother remarried recently. The most important thing she ever taught me is that hate's quite a useful emotion.''

Astonished by the remark, Umberto looked hard into the impassive violet eyes. His voice was very soft, very gentle, when he replied.

''Hate can move a mountain and fear can move the whole world.''

''I know it can, Mr. di Castelli.''

Sarah's eyes held his, and for a moment Umberto felt apprehensive. It was not going to be as easy as he had thought. The girl had a depth he had not anticipated and a hardness he found compelling. Obviously, she had suffered greatly. He was going to suggest a trip to see the rest of the house, when there was a commotion on the lawn outside as a private helicopter landed on the pad in the garden. Looking out, Umberto saw a beautiful woman in backless Dior black silk velvet with the pearl choker of the infamous nineteenth-century Countess of Castiglione. The world knew the pearls had been bought for her by the tall, slim, Venetian aristocrat who accompanied her. He was deeply suntanned, with dark blond hair and cloud-gray eyes. Umberto turned to Sarah to excuse himself and stopped, shocked by the expression on her face. Her lips were parted, the eyes full of awe and admiration as she gazed at the regal man in the white silk tuxedo. Furious at her reaction, Umberto charged from the room to greet the late arrivals.

''Princess, I was sure you let me down. Prince Aldobrandini, welcome to my house.''

Sarah gazed at the man in the white dinner jacket, her heart fluttering in her chest like a trapped butterfly. She had seen newspaper pictures of the Venetian Prince Vieri Aldobrandini dozens of times. He was often photographed in a yellow Ferrari—usually with a beauty at his side. But the pictures did not in any way convey his extraordinary presence. He was like a knight from a medieval love story.

There was something out of the ordinary in his every move—an elegant economy, a natural grace. She looked closely at the Prince's face with its long, straight nose, determined chin, and wavy hair worn swept back and long at the neck. Feeling the need for air, she rose and walked toward a door that led to the garden. Glancing at the woman as she passed by, Sarah saw perfection. The Princess's fuchsia nails were flawlessly polished, every hair was in place; the wonderful dress had clearly been made for her delicate frame. Suddenly Sarah felt shabby in her little homemade dress and as big as an elephant. Stepping outside, she leaned against the wall and let the cold wind revive her. *Someday,* she thought fiercely, *I shall have the most beautiful clothes and jewels and a helicopter to frighten the neighborhood dogs. I shall learn to make money, because only when you have money and lots of it can you choose what you really want in life.* She could not admit to herself that when you had money and position you could also attract men like Vieri Aldobrandini.

Stepping back into the room from the garden, Sarah tripped over one of the Prince's long legs as he sat, almost hidden, on a leather ottoman. A quick glance at the crowded floor told her that his fiancée was dancing with Umberto. Blushing furiously at her own thoughts, Sarah apologized.

"Forgive me, I'm as blind as a bat without my glasses."

"So why did you not wear them?"

"I wanted to look pretty, I suppose."

Vieri smiled at her honesty. Venetians never told the truth and he found the young woman's forthright manner amusing.

Sarah sat down suddenly, her knees vibrating like castanets in a gypsy's fingers. She glanced again at the man, at the beautiful hands and long, slim fingers. Then she gazed at the sensuous mouth, the determined expression. There was the faint glimmer of a smile in the gray eyes as he returned the scrutiny; Sarah was conscious of her cheeks reddening and an unfamiliar wayward feeling. It was the first time she had ever felt such a forceful emotion and she was overcome by its power. Vieri's next words filled her with pleasure and she tilted her head, enjoying his deep voice, with an accent that was faintly American yet wholly European.

"You did not succeed in looking pretty, but you look beautiful, so be satisfied. And I like the idea of the posy. I have not seen a posy like that since my aunt Annamaria decided twenty years ago that modern times were not for her and she was going to return to the styles of her youth. The rose is quite perfect."

"It's an English rose. They have wonderful perfume and very sharp spines."

Vieri looked at his hands and then at his fiancée, who was struggling to retain some semblance of her characteristic dignity, in the face of Umberto's antics on the floor.

At thirty-four, Vieri was in his prime, poised to marry one of the most elegant women in Europe, a woman he liked and understood. In Sarah's presence, he found himself uncertain. Her directness was puzzling and her obvious sensuality contrasted oddly with the innocence in her eyes. He looked at her hands, with their long narrow nails, and then again at the violet eyes and perfect cheekbones. As his gaze lingered, he saw the sudden onset of desire and the way she clasped her hands unconsciously, as if anxious to conceal or control it. He was about to ask the girl to dance, when he saw Umberto leading his fiancée back to join them. Vieri rose and introduced the two women, amused when Mariannina barely touched fingers with Sarah, before moving away with a disdainful but commanding look in his direction. He nodded good-bye.

"It was nice meeting you, Miss Hallam. I must come and see the show someday."

With that, he was gone, leaving Sarah staring after him as

Umberto pulled her toward the dance floor. She was wondering how the Prince knew she was in the show. It took less than a second to realize that her height would offer a clue to one far less observant than Prince Aldobrandini.

As Sarah looked around the crowded room, she saw at once how visible she was. It took her by surprise to realize that she was now the sort of woman that men fantasized about . . . and that other women disliked and feared. The four of them—the dancers—were as visible as daffodils in a snowbank. They glittered and beckoned—taller, lovelier, more desirable. In her own eyes, Sarah saw herself as a drab, terrified child or a gawky, dreamy adolescent. It was startling to find herself in this company, in this room, in Paris. She was now part of the Ballet Rose, not Anna's tormented daughter, not a trembling, aspiring ballerina. In that moment, Sarah realized both how far she had come and how far she had yet to go. She had dreamed of these things, but she had dreamed of them without ever believing that she would have them. That dream had been her escape; it had never occurred to her that she would have it as reality.

And her reality was now this Venetian prince . . . and these palatial houses . . . and the attention of men who wanted her: men with money, and power—men like Umberto di Castelli, who was now beside her.

"Come, I dance with you. I am the finest dancer in the city—at least the most enthusiastic!"

"Those two things don't always go together!"

"That woman is an iceberg. Just what Aldobrandini deserve. They will freeze each other to death in the bed and have marble statues instead of children."

"Why did you invite him? He doesn't seem to belong here."

"It's true, but I am one of those who give to the fund to save Venice. Aldobrandini would visit the devil for the sake of his city."

"When does he marry the Princess?"

"I don't know," he said, irritated by her interest. "In a few months, I think. He marry her for the family name. All those aristocrats marry to link the dynasties and not for love."

After they had danced for a few minutes, Umberto proposed a tour around the property.

"This house was built for me ten years ago and is quite remarkable in many ways. You want to see?"

"I'd like that very much. Where's your wife, by the way?"

"Lucia is sick. She takes the cure in Switzerland. My son is at school at Le Rosay. He's a very brilliant boy."

Umberto beamed with pleasure as Sarah took his arm. Perhaps he had been wrong about the girl. Persuading her to make love might be easier than he had thought. He led her upstairs, stopping to point out the subtly lit pre-Columbian statues that adorned the landing, then the black master bedroom, and on to a guest room decorated in English chintz. He was delighted by her surprised exclamation.

"This is just like a bedroom in England!"

"Will you accept if I invite you to stay the night?"

Sarah backed toward the door, suddenly afraid.

"I just met you tonight. How can you suggest such a thing?"

"Now you met me and it take only a minute to decide. I decide I want you the first time I see you at the Théâtre de l'Empire, when you give the beating to those bad girls."

Ignoring the fact that she was backing away from him, Umberto grasped her shoulders and kissed her—an eager, thrusting, passionate kiss. Then his hands moved to caress her breasts. When Sarah tried to push him away, he held her by the hair, a hand at either side of her head, so she could not avoid the savage kiss with his tongue thrusting deep into her throat. His voice trembled as he spoke.

"Let me love you. You want to, don't say you don't."

Sarah was dazed. She cared nothing for the man, yet she was not immune to the force of his desire. Her body was roused for the second time that evening. She had never thought of herself as wanton. . . . As Umberto began to unbutton her dress she knew she must leave the house at once. With a sudden burst of adrenaline, she pushed him away and ran for the door. She was shocked when he dragged her back and threw her down on the bed. Furious, Sarah rose, and as Umberto came at her, panting like an animal in heat, she hit him so hard and so suddenly that he fell to the ground. While he was picking himself up, she ran downstairs to rejoin the other guests. Mary-Ellen was nowhere to be seen, nor was Holly. Arlette was sitting alone, her lovely face relaxed and tranquil. When she saw Sarah's red cheeks and bright eyes, she hurried over to hand her a glass of champagne.

"Are you all right? What happened?"

"I'm leaving at once. Are you coming?"

"Of course. I'm tired and the Count had to go home. I'm invited to lunch with him and his family next week, though. Oh, Sarah, I just can't wait to visit his chateau," she enthused as they hurried off to get their coats. As they walked to the door, Arlette said, "Did that awful di Castelli try something?"

"He did. He's probably still spitting out teeth."

"You'd think after what you did in the dressing room, he'd have known better! But are you *really* all right, Sarah?" As her friend nodded, Arlette smiled. "Come along, we'll go back to the hotel and I'll tuck you up in bed with a glass of hot milk."

Vieri watched as the two women hurried to the door. The English girl was obviously agitated, but as she was about to leave, he saw her look around, scanning the room until her eyes settled on him. Vieri raised his champagne glass as

Sarah waved good-bye. Then she was gone. Minutes later, he saw di Castelli come downstairs, his face flushed with anger. One eye was discolored and swelling ominously at the outer edge. Vieri could barely control his laughter. Evidently Sarah Hallam had nerves of steel. Or perhaps she had no idea who the Sicilian was. Obviously she also had unusual strength and an admirable left hook. His thoughts were interrupted when Mariannina expressed her desire to return to the Italian Embassy, where she was staying. They left minutes later, delivered to their separate doors by Umberto's chauffeur.

In the early hours of the morning, as a blush-pink dawn filled the Paris sky, Sarah walked alone along the Champs Elysées, enjoying the silence and the shiver of the breeze in the chestnut trees. In her hand she carried the rose from her posy. The rose Vieri had called perfect. When she came to the avenue Foch, she turned and walked past the house Arlette had told her belonged to the Aldobrandini family. It was an impressive *hôtel particulier* originally built by one of the most expensive courtesans of the Belle Epoque. The stone exterior was colonnaded in the classic Italian style. Clematis climbed over a glass conservatory, and Vieri's much-photographed yellow Ferrari was parked outside the entrance. Sarah stood for a moment, then stepped into the drive and placed the rose under the Ferrari's windshield wiper. Then, smiling at her own thoughts, she walked back down the Champs Elysées toward the hotel she had left because she could no more sleep than fly like a bird. She was thinking of the elegance of Vieri's figure, the sensuous look in the worldly gray eyes. Compared with him, every man she had ever met seemed like a house cat competing with a panther.

As she thought of Vieri, she felt again the same trembling weakness that had troubled her in Umberto's house. To give herself a moment to recover, she entered a café and ordered coffee and a brioche. Alone with her thoughts, she gazed out the window. It seemed foolish to think of herself as being in love. She was not given to that sort of fancy; indeed, she had always mocked the very notion of love at first sight. And yet in her heart she knew that was what had happened to her. She shook her head despairingly. Of all the men to choose to fall in love with, Vieri Aldobrandini was the least available. Engaged to a Princess, due to be married in the fall, he could never be the man in her life. Tears began to course down her cheeks and Sarah wiped them away impatiently, telling herself she was tired from the stress of rehearsals and the shock of Umberto di Castelli's behavior. Vieri was out of her league, that was certain, and she was not a woman to wish for the moon.

Minutes later, Sarah saw a radiant Mary-Ellen step out of a taxi, a bouquet of red roses in her arms. Sarah was paying for the coffee and brioche, when she saw Holly walking alone toward the hotel. The Irish girl's expensive evening dress was in tatters; one sleeve had been torn from the shoulder. She looked dazed and exhausted. Dark circles ringed her eyes. Her right hand gently swung her satin evening purse by its chain. Unaware of the shocked gazes of passersby, Holly entered the hotel, leaving the door open behind her.

Sarah rose and hurried from the café, arriving in the reception area in time to see the elevator disappearing from view. A thousand unanswered questions filled her mind and she felt suddenly apprehensive. Until now, she had lived at home in England, working summer shows and doing a bit of television. Here in Paris, she had been plunged suddenly into the sophisticated world of men and women, where the games were very adult. The other three girls were older than she, and Sarah acknowledged the importance of that difference in age. She resolved to try not to show her ignorance of life, to watch and learn and grow up—as quickly as possible.

At that moment, she had never felt so lonely, so uncertain of herself, so in need of a shoulder to cry on.

At ten A.M., while the girls were rehearsing at the theater, Vieri emerged from his home on the avenue Foch. He saw the rose, removed it from the windshield wiper, and was about to throw it away, when he realized it was the same flower he had admired in the posy carried by the girl at the party. He smiled, looking about to see if Sarah was near. Then, having snapped off part of the stem, he put the flower in his buttonhole, stepped into the car, and drove away.

Sarah had been right: The rose had a sweet, lingering perfume, and the thorns were very sharp. Vieri thought of the violet eyes, the wide pink mouth, the pointed, foxlike chin. Then, turning into the forecourt of the Italian Embassy, he hurried inside to breakfast with his fiancée. He was half amused, half irritated, and totally puzzled to find that the image of Sarah Hallam remained with him, an elusive memory that lingered in the mind.

CHAPTER TWO

Holly, Seville, May 1967

Seville was a city of gardens, bullfighters, gypsies, and secret courtyards with wrought-iron gates where, long ago, duennas had watched over budding romances. The skyline was fascinating: ancient rooftops of faded pink, orange, and ocher tiles, pointed towers, triple-belled campaniles, and churches that betrayed the fact that they had once been used as mosques in the days of the city's Moorish occupation.

In this city of contrasts and contrariness, the Ballet Rose arrived like a tornado. The girls were met at the train by a group of dignitaries carrying carnations of red and yellow, the national colors of Spain. A long speech, which no one understood, followed. The artists were accompanied first to the theater and later to the hotel by a procession of loudly hooting cars, men on the white horses of Ecija, young boys on bicycles, and the gypsies of a traveling circus on elephants and llamas. This mayhem was accompanied by a gaudily painted truck with a barrel organ that played flamenco.

Opening night was a triumph that surpassed the one in Paris. Unused to theatrical spectacle, the city had done the company proud. Television cameras recorded the arrival of aristocrats, socialites, politicians, and the great names of Spanish show business. For days the newspapers had been

full of news of the Ballet Rose, and the public responded
with eagerness. Each of the dancers and all of the stars had
been profiled, so many of the local people felt they knew the
company personally and everyone wanted to give the artists
the warmest welcome possible on opening night.

Holly was at the dressing table, finishing her makeup and
saying a prayer that nothing would go wrong. Arlette was
staring into her mirror. She had a spot on her cheek and she
was furious with herself for having exposed her skin to the
burning Spanish sun. Even in May the air was like an oven.
She thought furiously that she would be very happy when
they arrived in Nice. The Riviera was civilized, even though
it was full of tourists, bag snatchers, and vacationing
Mafiosi. Mary-Ellen was sifting through a pile of letters
from men who had seen her photograph in the paper. She
wrote a reply to the only man who had written in English
and sent it by messenger to his office. She was thrilled to be
in Seville and had taken at once to the heat, the scent of
orange blossom, and the arrogance of the local men. At the
orphanage her original name, Maria-Elena, had been Amer-
icanized, and she had always wondered if her roots lay far
away in the wild emptiness of Castile or Andalusia. Now,
she felt certain, she would find the answers to all the questions that had plagued her for as long as she could remember. Was it imagination or a longing for her roots that made
her feel such an empathy with things Spanish?

Sarah was hurrying from the dressing room when Umberto stepped out of the shadows. She looked coolly into the
dark, searching eyes.

"What are you doing here?"

"I come to see you—what else?"

"I'm not interested in you, Umberto, so please don't
waste your time."

"I am a patient man."

"Don't be. There are lots of gorgeous girls in the show

and even more in Paris. You don't have to travel a thousand miles to see me. You're being contrary and wanting what you can't have.''

''I don't accept that I cannot have.''

Sarah moved past him on the narrow stairway, startled when he put an arm around her from behind and kissed her back. Turning, she looked into the face with its brooding, dark depths. The merry host she had encountered at the party was gone; a new Umberto had taken his place. This one was more menacing, mysterious, but in a strange way more touching, because instinct told her he was helpless where she was concerned. Sarah held out her hand.

''I'm sorry I was rude. The truth is I'm abroad for the first time and I'm scared. I keep feeling that I don't belong in this kind of world and that I'm ignorant of so many things I need to know. I know nothing about men and nothing about people. I'm a beginner in life, and since I arrived in Paris I've been uneasy every single day.'' She was somewhat surprised to have blurted all this out to a stranger.

''But what do you want in your life?'' he asked gently, still holding the hand she had offered.

''I need security. I don't want to hide from creditors like my mother did. I want to be someone, to do something, I don't know what. Dancing's not a career that lasts past the age of twenty-five, so I must find something else. Now please let me pass or I'll miss the opening.''

Umberto watched her go, his heart beating from excitement as she brushed against his body. He wondered if he should ask his people in Paris to check up on Sarah's background, but instead decided to ask Holly to dine with him. The four new girls were close and no doubt knew each other's secrets. He would begin with the Irish girl and elicit every scrap of information she possessed. Decision made, Umberto settled down to enjoy the show.

The cancan gave way to the Belle Epoque finale and the

parade of every member of the company. The showgirls were outfitted in massed osprey feathers, the dancers in tights of cloth of silver, the stars in *diamant* reproductions of peacocks' tails. As the last notes of the closing song died away, there was a moment of ominous silence. Then pandemonium broke out—wild applause erupted, and flowers were thrown, "Olé!" was shouted by the delighted spectators. Two hundred bouquets were placed onstage with gifts in specially woven baskets. Then, singing some of the best-known songs from the show, the Sevillanos made their way out of the theater.

Holly put on a tight-waisted ice-blue dress that tied on each shoulder, fixing the white camellias Umberto had sent her to the waist. She was standing back to assess her appearance when she heard Arlette call out.

"Where are you going and with whom?"

"I'm having dinner with Umberto di Castelli. He didn't say where."

"He will want to make love to you. You must be crazy to go out with him! He looks just like a gorilla!"

Mary-Ellen laughed. "Then he's just the man for Sarah. She's very keen on gorillas."

Holly put pearl studs in her ears and spoke defiantly.

"I find him attractive. He has a certain animal charm and it doesn't hurt to know he can snap his fingers and get anything he wants."

Mary-Ellen looked in puzzlement at her friend.

"You know, little Irish, you're a regular Jekyll and Hyde."

"And you, where are you going in your fancy pink satin?" Holly retorted.

"I'm dining with Don Luis Alarcon de Montevidal. He's a lawyer and related to the Duchess of Gijon. I'm going because I'm hungry, curious, and he wrote to me in English."

"What does he look like?"

"I don't know. I never met him. I just hope he's not sixty-five, bald, and afflicted with halitosis."

As always, they laughed at Mary-Ellen's humor. Then Arlette rose and moved to the door.

"I'm going to bed. This heat has made me so very tired. I'll start having wrinkles before I leave Seville."

Mary-Ellen called across the dressing room.

"Go get your beauty sleep. At your age you have to make a big effort to keep the wrinkles at bay. And don't let any night callers into your room or you'll leave Seville with more than wrinkles to worry about!"

When all the others had gone, Sarah walked to the window and looked out at a navy night sky. She did not really feel like going back to the hotel. On the other hand, she could not walk alone in this most Spanish of cities. She turned out the light, locked the dressing-room door, and handed in the key. Then she walked down the narrow, dark street in the direction of the hotel. Ahead, at a distance, she could see Mario Benedetti hurrying toward a busy square. For a moment she was tempted to run after him, to ask him to buy her a coffee at one of the sidewalk cafés. Instead, as a group of noisy revelers emerged from a tavern, she walked on alone, wondering why Sevillanos found it necessary to shout at each other while carrying on ordinary conversation.

Sarah had reached an intersection when she felt herself grasped around the throat from behind. As a voice whispered something incomprehensible in Spanish, she called one desperate plea to Benedetti: *"Help me, Mario!"* Then the man pulled her into a doorway, as a companion grasped her by the feet. They were about to carry her inside a deserted building, when Benedetti appeared and struck the first attacker so hard he fell to the ground. The other drew a knife. Benedetti pulled off his overcoat, wrapped it around his left arm, and moved forward, his face intent. As the attacker lunged at him, Benedetti hit him hard on the wrist, relieved to see Sarah picking up the knife as it clattered to the ground.

Sarah stood helplessly by, watching as the two men fought. Benedetti was getting the better of the struggle, despite the difference in ages, when another man appeared from the shadows behind him. Without hesitation, Sarah rushed forward with a cry of alarm, charging the newcomer and then turning and kicking him hard. She was aiming for his shins, but in the darkness she missed her mark. With a howl of pain, the man fell unconscious beside his companions.

Benedetti turned furiously to Sarah.

"Why didn't you run away? That's the first rule for any woman."

"I'm not given to running away."

He gave her a curious look, then picked up his hat. Taking her by the hand, he led her around the corner to the hotel.

"We need a drink, Sarah."

She noticed for the first time that his arm was bleeding, but said nothing, aware that Benedetti hated fuss. She walked with him through the reception area, where the night clerk was sound asleep.

"Come up to my room, Mario, and I'll tend to your arm."

She ordered cognac and mineral water, club sandwiches and passion-fruit sorbets. Then she turned to Benedetti with a smile.

"We'll have a midnight picnic after I bandage your arm."

"Where will you find a bandage at this hour of the night?"

"I'm a born pessimist! I always travel with a first-aid kit."

Benedetti watched as Sarah threw off her wrap and hurried to the bathroom, returning with a box embossed with a red cross. Her perfume smelled like honeysuckle and he could see the hardness of her nipples under the thin wool of her gray sweater. He closed his eyes, trying to still the pounding of his heart and the desire he knew could never be satisfied.

Sarah took off his jacket and shirt and bathed the wound, speaking all the while in a calm voice, as if Benedetti were a child. She put antiseptic on the wound and covered it with a gauze bandage, which she taped for good measure. Then she rang the reception desk and asked that a *practicante* be called to give an antitetanus injection.

Benedetti lay back on the sofa, thinking wryly that it had been worth the risk and the moment of pain to be alone with the girl. Then he remembered Umberto and hoped he would not be seen leaving Sarah's room. His brother-in-law was the jealous type and had talked of nothing but "that one" since their first meeting in Paris. Benedetti watched as Sarah poured him a brandy, shocked to see dark-blue bruises coming out on her neck where her attacker had gripped her. He raised his glass and looked at her, the cobra eyes impassive.

"To you, Sarah."

"Thank you for what you did, Mario."

"It was nothing."

"It was everything to me."

"Why didn't you run away?"

"I've told you already. I'm not given to running away."

"That fool will have swollen balls for a month."

"I was aiming for his shins."

Benedetti threw back his head and laughed.

"In my business it's not often that we get a chance to laugh."

"What is your business, Mario?"

"I work for Umberto," he said simply. "He relies on

me. The business is Umberto's life and his game, and he loves it.''

''What exactly does he do?''

''He owns many businesses, restaurants, clubs, holiday hotel chains, cinemas, import-export. I sometimes think it's his desire to own Paris!''

''He has wonderful taste. That house of his is a masterpiece. He told me he did it all himself.''

''He did nothing of the kind. He called in a famous English designer and spent a fortune on it. You're far too gullible, Sarah. You must learn that most people don't know how to tell the truth. Umberto's own taste runs to Sicilian brocade and wall-to-wall whores. Don't believe everything he tells you.''

Sarah blushed, but he could see she was pleased by the information. She poured him another brandy and put a blanket around his shoulders when the chill of the Spanish night and the shock of the wound made him shiver. By the time the nurse arrived to administer the injection, Benedetti was sound asleep.

The Hostería del Laurel in the Plaza de las Venerables was where Don Juan was said to have eaten before the evening's *paseo* along the Sierpes. Holly and Umberto adjourned to the restaurant to drink the rough red wine of Rioja that intoxicated with deadly speed. They ordered *chorizo al diablo*—spicy red sausage flambéed in alcohol—and *huevos a la gitanilla y zarzuela*—the stew of mussels, squid, prawns, and monkfish that is one of the legendary dishes of Spain. They were finishing the meal when a crowd came in from the Maestranza Bullring. *Espontáneos, picadores,* and members of the matador's *cuadrilla* took their place by the fire under a ceiling hung with *sobresada* sausages suspended from sycamore branches. The matador and his friends ordered black *palo* as an aperitif and gazed in open admiration at the beautiful girl in the ice-blue dress.

Holly's eyes flickered as they met those of the man who had triumphed that day in the corrida. She was thinking of the moment of orgasm, which some Spaniards likened to the moment of death. The seconds of the bull's dying had thrilled Holly, and she had remained in her seat long after the crowd had gone, reliving her feelings as the sword plunged into the thick black neck and the animal fell with startling suddenness. She had felt pity for the bull at the inevitability of its demise, admiration for the matador's courage, and something else—a wanton desire to lay herself bare, to be baited as he had baited the bull, and to achieve the little death that is the moment of total submission. Holly sighed, trying to work out when she had changed from a convent girl with pure thoughts to a sensuous creature whose body needed love as others' needed food and water. Knowing she could not control her desire, she sought to punish herself after each moment of satiation. The thought of punishment made her cheeks glow, and she closed her eyes so Umberto would not read the message in them.

Umberto watched the changing emotions flickering across Holly's face as she observed the new arrivals. He too had been at the bullfight and had found the entertainment geared to the taste of tourists who knew nothing of the real nuances of the corrida. He had left at interval, returning to his hotel to call Paris. But Holly had stayed to the end, fascinated by the ritual. He took her hand and turned all his attention to her. "Tell me about your life."

"I was born in Dublin and my family still lives there. My father's a judge on the Southern Circuit. My mother was a Tremayne before her marriage. Her family comes from County Clare, where they raise horses that race at the Curragh," she recited. Then she smiled. "We go to the farm in the summer and ride like dervishes all over the valleys."

"Tell me about your friends in the show."

"Mary-Ellen left the States after an unhappy love affair. She told me she came to Europe to find happiness. I don't know if she's found happiness, but she's certainly found admirers. Men gather around her like moths around a flame."

"Arlette, too, I suppose?"

"Arlette's a loner. She spends most of her time doing exercises to keep her figure. She wants to marry a duke and I'm sure she will. She and her mother planned her future when she was twelve, and I doubt if the end of the world would shake that purpose. Arlette knows the name of every French duke by heart and the name of his home and the size of his estate. She probably knows the size of his bank account, too!"

"Sarah seems rather dull," Umberto remarked with apparent casualness.

"She's harder to fathom."

"In what way?"

"She's just not like other women. She says she wants the peaceful life, yet she's capable of real violence. She says she's not interested in men, but I'm sure she is. She just doesn't want to think about such things. She trained as a dancer for ten years, but she doesn't really want to be a dancer. She's full of contradictions."

"What *does* she want?"

"She told Mary-Ellen she wanted to own property and to have a nightclub or restaurant. The main problem with Sarah is that she's led a very sheltered, reclusive life locked away in that house on the moors with her mother. She's clever, but she knows nothing about life. If you told her the moon was made of almond paste she'd probably believe you. She believes almost everything. But tell me about you. Why did you come all this way to Seville?"

"I wish to see Benedetti and to visit you. I was very impress that first time we met."

"But it was Sarah you tried to make love with."

"Did she say so?"

"No, Arlette told me. They went home together and Sarah was upset. She knows nothing at all about men and I think you scared her."

"I was provoke by her horrible coldness. I want to shake her out of the calm."

Holly laughed at his chagrin.

"Sarah's not cold or calm. Dear God, she *burns* with emotion! It's just that she had a very different upbringing from most of us. She doesn't talk about it, but I think she learned to hide her feelings from everyone."

"Why?"

"I don't know, Umberto. I only know that her mother threatened suicide all the time and rejected Sarah. That's why she got violent in the dressing room. She remembered all the other times in her life when she'd felt unwanted, and she just exploded. You threaten Sarah at your own peril, I think. Only the surface is cold."

Umberto watched as Holly continued to drink *carajillos,* tiny cups of strong black coffee laced with *anís dulce.* When it was time to leave, he led her to the car and they returned to the hotel together. She was surprised when he shook her hand and returned to his own room. Perhaps he would make love to Holly another night and find out more of what she knew. For the moment he was tense and in need of solitude. He wanted to indulge himself in thoughts of Sarah.

Holly sat in her room for half an hour. Then she called a cab and returned to the Hostería del Laurel. On arrival she walked directly to the table where the matadors were sitting and looked questioningly into the eyes of the man of her choice. She spoke no Spanish and he spoke only a few words of English, but he understood the look, because he had seen it so many times before. While Holly watched, he

rose, said good-bye to his companions, and led her to a
small hotel nearby. They went upstairs to a room furnished
with an ebony four-poster bed and an iron crucifix. The matador's suit of lights in peony pink was hung behind the door.
His sword and all the paraphernalia of the corrida were leaning against the wall or neatly laid out on the floor. Once inside the room, ignoring Holly completely, he went to the
bathroom, washed his hands, and then emerged, wiping
them on a thick white towel. His eyes were hard, his lips
cruel, and he gave the impression that he had only derision
for the women who pursued him.

Holly stood her ground, her eyes flickering momentarily
when the matador picked up the sword. She caught her
breath as he moved toward her and, assuming the position of
waiting for the bull to charge, aimed the sword at her shoulder. Aware of what he wanted, Holly moved slowly toward
him in an almost trancelike state. The knots on the shoulder
of the ice-blue dress fell, cut in half by a carefully aimed
blade. She turned, smiling faintly, the nipples of her small,
pointed breasts hard and dark against the translucent pale-
ness of her skin. As she moved to close on the man, whose
name she did not know, he cut the waistband of the skirt so it
fell around her ankles. Then, swiftly, he cut the blue satin
ribbons that fastened each side of the white lace panties.
When she was naked and trembling before him, he moved
the sword along her skin, drawing a line from navel to pubic
hair. Looking down, Holly saw a delicate red mark where
the razor-sharp blade had passed along the surface, breaking
a single layer of skin. Then, with a cry of ecstasy, she fell to
her knees before him.

"Love me, torment me, *hurt* me!"

Understanding nothing of her words, the matador undressed slowly as Holly kneeled before him, allowing her to
touch and to taste first the feet and then the knees and finally
the hard penis that throbbed titillatingly before her. As she

moaned from desire, he picked her up and threw her down on the old-fashioned bed. Then, putting away the sword, he moved toward her and penetrated her body like a machine devoid of affection or tenderness, bringing her swiftly to a climax. He withheld his own pleasure until Holly screamed for him to come inside her. Then, needing no words to understand the urgency of her longing, he held her down with iron hands and oscillated above her like a frenzied horseman galloping to his doom. Suddenly he cried out, one anguished, joyful lament as he came inside the moist, warm passage that tightened over him, milking him dry. Holly's back arched, and for the second time in her life she fainted from sheer ecstasy.

In the early hours of the morning, the matador dressed her in knee breeches of black velour and a frilly white shirt with sleeves that were far too long on her slim arms. Then he led her outside, called a taxi, and sent her on her way with a courteous kiss to the fingertips.

"Hasta mañana a las once y media."

Holly understood the first part of the good-bye and wrote down the second phonetically, so she could ask Benedetti what it meant. She was thinking of the moment when the matador had put the trousers on her. In those brief seconds, she had seen something enter his mind and knew that at their next meeting he would hurt her by treating her as a boy, who provided him with equal pleasure.

Umberto rose at ten and went to the theater to watch rehearsals. Then, having lunched with Benedetti, he called Holly and arranged to take coffee with her in his room. When she appeared, he saw that she looked tired. Scrutinizing the dark shadows under her eyes, he thought of the bullfighters in the tavern. He said nothing, however, and welcomed her with a deceptively engaging smile.

"You look beautiful, as always."

"I'm fine—a little tired from all the rehearsals. We do the two three-hour shows each night, and Madame called rehearsal four times this week for nine in the morning. Everyone's exhausted."

"She search for perfection. If she was in the army, they make her a general."

"Madame Rose would like that, and with her mustache she'd make a fine one."

"Drink some coffee and have a slice of this delicious cake. I ate four pieces and already I feel the energy coming on."

Holly smiled at his phrase. Unlike Mario Benedetti, who spoke all languages with ease, Umberto mangled everything but the Sicilian dialect he had spoken exclusively until the age of twenty, when he had been sent to Rome. She watched as he poured a potent herb liqueur for them to drink with the coffee.

"Isn't it a bit early for alcohol?"

"Not at all. Drink, Holly. It is *izarra,* a wonderful Spanish liqueur made from flowers and sunshine."

Their eyes met and he drew her to him and pushed her down, so she was sitting at his feet. Then he poured more of the liqueur into Holly's glass, watching closely as the alcohol lulled her into a state of sensuous comfort. Finally, he drew her to him and kissed her, the same aggressive, thrusting kiss he had given Sarah. Knowing instinctively that she wanted only to be used, he pushed her head down so her cheeks were rubbing against the hardness of his penis. Within seconds, he had unfastened his trousers and was letting Holly caress and taste the hardness of his desire. Then, with a cry, Umberto forced himself into her, closing his eyes as Holly writhed, assimilating every drop of the sperm that rushed into her mouth. Umberto was half amused, half shocked, when she turned, after a few seconds, and poured them more coffee, handing him a linen serviette and watching with dreamy eyes as he wiped himself and zipped his trousers. Then she cut herself another slice of cake, closing her eyes as she savored the rich scent of frangipane. Her voice was low and husky.

"I need the energy this will give me."

"What are you doing tonight, Holly?"

"I'm seeing a bullfighter."

"You have the manners of a great lady and the soul of a great whore."

"My soul is my business, not yours."

Umberto wanted to beat her, to catch her off guard, but it was obvious that the family who had bred this strange creature had instilled into her such perfect manners, such self-possession, that she was capable of retaining her dignity when walking up the street with a feather stuck up her backside. Suddenly impatient to be alone, he rose and went to the window.

"And how are your friends?"

"Mary-Ellen's found herself a Spanish grandee who wants to buy her a palazzo. Arlette's got sunstroke. Sarah's sightseeing."

"With whom?"

"Either alone or maybe with Mario Benedetti."

Umberto's face flushed with sudden anger.

"He is in love with her?"

"Oh, no, nothing like that. I have the impression that he's keeping her safe because someone told him to. Didn't you give him his instructions, Umberto?"

He fixed Holly with a stern look and lied. "I did not. Of course I did not. He has no right to follow the girl around."

"Are you jealous?"

"Of course not. I met Sarah once—how can I be jealous? She is not my type."

Holly looked at the flushed cheeks, at the eyes gleaming with rage, and smiled. Umberto might not be willing to ad-

mit it, but he was obviously much more concerned with
Sarah than he realized. She thought of her friend's cool attitude to men and wondered how the Sicilian was going to
overcome it and if he ever could.

Sarah loved the city and the houses bedecked with gerani-
ums. She found the *tapas* bars and their titillating snacks irresistible, though the corrida had distressed her and she had
left the ring at the interval and returned to her hotel in tears.
Recently, she had also discovered the Thursday market in
the Calle de la Feria and was learning to bargain for the
pieces she adored. She had bought a pen stand in chased
copper, an ancient ebony makeup mirror, a pair of hair-
curling tongs that had once belonged to an eighteenth-
century flirt, and a tiny box of papier-mâché inlaid with
silver. In the Barrio de Santa Cruz she had visited the square
where Murillo was buried and had enjoyed taking pictures
of the houses of what had once been the Jewish quarter. Best
of all, she loved Spanish food and had twice eaten in a famous tavern not far from the theater, the first time with Benedetti, the second time alone.

On the corner of a busy street, Sarah paused to watch a
policeman directing traffic from underneath a blue and
white striped sun umbrella. Life was good, she thought, but
it would be even better if she could stop thinking of Vieri Aldobrandini. He kept popping into her mind at the most inop-
portune moments. She longed to share with him the sights of
Seville, the moments of rare beauty she had seen nowhere
else: the scarlet sunset on the estuary, the little gypsy children of the Macarena district, the magnificent park with its
white iron-walled restaurant, where rich Sevillanos drank
their aperitifs before Sunday lunch. She told herself it was
all ridiculous but that did not prevent Vieri's image from in-
vading her thoughts. Often she found herself absentminded
and distracted. She thought wryly that love was worse than

asthma, taking over the mind and body completely. Sarah told herself she must work harder, attend every class given by the ballet master and then walk the city till she was exhausted. That would make her too tired to daydream of the man with the cloud-gray eyes and the profile of a Venetian doge. As she moved forward on the street, she was reliving the moment when Vieri had first spoken to her. It was a moment she would remember all her life because it was the one when she had fallen hopelessly, helplessly in love.

Umberto hurried into Benedetti's office and glowered down at his brother-in-law.

"I hear you follow Sarah around like a bloodhound."

"I'm not deaf; there's no need to shout."

"I want an answer! You do it or not?"

Benedetti pitied his friend's dilemma, but told himself to take care. After a lifetime of exploiting the women who pursued him, Umberto was in love and likely to blow the brains out of anyone who crossed him. Benedetti chose his words carefully, trying to conceal the pleasure he felt in knowing that Umberto would never possess even the smallest particle of Sarah's true self. Perhaps no man would ever do that, at least not unless Sarah herself willed it. Benedetti began a patient explanation.

"I was walking home from the theater the other night, when I heard Sarah screaming my name. She was being dragged into a doorway by a couple of Spaniards who didn't know better. I went to help and one of them pulled a knife on me. I'd knocked out one and disarmed the other, when a third man came up behind me. If it hadn't been for Sarah I might have ended up feeding the fishes in the Guadalquivir."

Umberto gazed in fascination at Benedetti.

"What did she do? Are you saying she join in the fight?"

"She called a warning to me and then charged the third

man. He stood back in surprise, and when he did she kicked him so hard in the balls he fell like a chopped tree.''

Umberto erupted into joyful laughter, wiping his eyes on a huge white silk handkerchief.

"You know, Mario, maybe she *enjoy* hurting him?"

"She told me she was aiming for his shins, but she can't see her hand in front of her at night and her foot landed in the wrong place."

"I don't believe her. She aim for the balls to ruin him for being bad. You did well to protect her, Mario, but since then why do you follow her?"

"I took her to lunch to thank her, and someone followed us back to the hotel. The next day he followed Sarah when she went for her afternoon walk. I figured I'd best keep an eye on her."

"Who is he?"

"His name is Petrakis and he's the Greek Consul to Madrid. He's in Seville for a holiday."

"How is he?"

"Handsome, charming, and mean. He has a reputation as the miser of the Diplomatic Corps."

"He can go to hell. Does she know he follows her?"

"She has no idea. Now she's accepted a dinner invitation from him."

"I forbid her to go. He will try something for sure. Greeks fuck everything, even grandmothers."

"I can't forbid her to go, you know that. Sarah doesn't belong to me or to you."

Umberto thought for a while. Then he poured them both a glass of wine.

"We follow her tonight and keep an eye on the Greek."

"She won't like it."

"You think I care? She is a woman and someday I teach her to do what she is told."

* * *

Sarah was in the dressing room, having her hair curled by Mary-Ellen, who was chattering excitedly.

"There, you look great. The Greek will fall madly in love. What changed your mind, anyway? You never go out."

"I'm trying to forget someone. Maybe if I go out with other men I won't think about him so much."

"Vieri's engaged to a princess. There's nothing for you there, though I'll admit he's a great-looking guy."

Sarah stared at Mary-Ellen as if she had sprouted wings. "How did you know? I've never spoken about him."

"I saw your face when Vieri arrived at Umberto's house. You're transparent, Sarah—at least to me."

"You know far too much. It makes me ill at ease."

"I won't talk and I give good advice. It's just my own life I muck up all the time, so trust me."

"There's nothing to tell, Mary-Ellen. I met Vieri at Umberto's house and never saw him again. He said he'd come to see the show someday and every night in Paris I hoped he would, but he never came. I just can't get him out of my mind. It's like being haunted by a ghost. I even wake in the night thinking about him."

"I was in love once, but he went off with a fifty-year-old heiress from Fort Worth. Bob was always more interested in money than anything else. Talking about money, I hear your date for the evening's the biggest tightwad in town."

"I hate mean people. I'd best cancel."

"Like hell you will. If he gets too obvious, teach the bastard a lesson."

"How?"

"You'll think of something. Women always do."

That night, in a restaurant in the Triana district, Sarah and the Consul dined on suckling pig stuffed with minced veal, herbs, and brandy. At first she had been amused to be brought to the area of small, whitewashed houses by the river, where daily life revolved around the maritime activities of the locals. Sarah was well aware that her companion had chosen the place because it was stylish but cheap. Her amusement passed when the Greek refused to give even a peseta to a pretty child who had danced a solo for the diners. Then, after a veritable feast of music in which a local troupe played the guitar and castanets, danced *taconeo,* and performed a breathtaking selection of *fandangos* from Huelva, *alegrías* from Cádiz, and the *medias granainas, serranas,* and *malagueñas* for which they were renowned, the Consul resolutely refused to put his hand in his pocket, the only person in the room not to show his appreciation.

Umberto watched the taut look in Sarah's face and knew that she was incensed. The violet eyes flashed and the slim fingers drummed on the table. He felt his heart quickening and beamed across the table at Benedetti.

"Now she kick him in the balls for the meanness!"

"Dear God, what does she think she's doing? Just look at *that,* Umberto!"

When presented with the bill, the Greek Consul took out a thick wad of notes, counted four off the top, and put them on the plate. He was about to replace the money in his pocket, when Sarah seemed to trip and fall against him. The wad of notes fell to the ground. While Sarah bent to pick it up, the Consul took out a cigar. Then, to his horror and Umberto's huge delight, Sarah rolled the notes into a taper and put one end of them to the candle on the table and calmly lighted his cigar with it. As shock made him choke on the smoke, she dropped the charred remains of the notes on the table and walked out alone into the cold night air.

Umberto leaped to his feet.

"What a woman! I tell you, Mario, she has the face of an angel and the mind of a monster. No wonder I am falling head over feet in love with her."

Benedetti was smiling that slow, calm smile the company had come to know so well. Later, he was to remember it as the moment when Umberto became totally infatuated with Sarah and when he found himself loving her like the daughter he had always longed to have. He rose and paid the bill and hurried after Umberto onto the dark pathway by the river. It was some minutes before they caught up with Sarah and fell into step at her side.

Umberto looked into the ethereal face with its halo of blonde hair that shone silver in the moonlight.

"You know something, I just see a woman light a cigar with a wad of money this thick. You need a drink after all that exertion. Benedetti and I take you to the Palacio for champagne cocktails."

"I'm going home to bed and I'm never going out again. Apparently I don't have the right nature for socializing."

"You come with us to drink champagne. It's Mario's birthday and you can't say no."

Sarah linked arms with the two men as they walked to the nearby square and stepped into a horse-drawn carriage decorated with yellow carnations. When they were settled side by side, she kissed Benedetti on each cheek.

"Happy birthday, Mario. Sorry I didn't realize it was your birthday or I'd have bought a card."

Benedetti sighed. It was not his birthday, just another of Umberto's tricks designed to help him have his way.

Umberto scowled as Sarah smiled into Benedetti's impassive face. Then, as she turned to him, he tried to give an impression of nonchalance, but the night breeze blew Sarah's skirt over her head, revealing the suntanned legs and wafting him with the subtle perfume that always lingered in the room after her departure, a scent of rose and hyacinth, amber and the green leaves of summer. As he caught her gaze, Umberto saw a gleam of amusement in the violet eyes. He closed his own, so Sarah would not realize the effort it was costing him not to leap on her and make love to her in the middle of Seville in an open, horse-drawn carriage.

CHAPTER THREE

Arlette, Nice, July 1967

They had imagined Nice to be a picturesque town of ornate villas, swaying palms, and expensive women. Reality was cement high-rise buildings, pizza parlors, and traffic jams. The film-star houses of the twenties and thirties had, for the most part, been demolished; those that remained in the suburbs were fast being encircled by tower blocks built for the new rich, who preferred modern-day facilities to old-world charm. Despite the despoilation wrought by the developers, Nice managed to retain its ambience. The Place Massena still looked like an old Italian city square, its buildings painted terracotta, the shutters faded green. The stylish Hotel Negresco still beckoned those who could afford to be pampered, its doormen in eighteenth-century coachmen's outfits with cockaded hats, its wedding-cake towers pushing upward into the azure sky of the Bay of Angels.

The Tour of the Ballet Rose was scheduled to open at the Opera House in the rue St. Francois de Paule, and the daily rehearsals were long and arduous. Madame Rose, well aware that Nice would not be a walkover like Seville, was ruthless. The Spaniards had never before seen anything like the touring spectacular, but the international set who lived for part of each year on the Riviera were the cream of European society and used to the best. Nothing was left to chance. Every scene was rehearsed again and again, the orchestra augmented, new costumes brought in for the opening to replace less-than-perfect ones from the previous months of the tour. Finally, with only twenty-four hours to go to opening, Madame pronounced herself satisfied and gave everyone the day off.

Having bought a white silk parasol to shield her face from the sun, Arlette walked the labyrinthine streets of the old town of Nice, looking up at laundry strung high above, from one balcony to the next. As she passed the old houses, she remembered Naples, where she had been raised. Her father had been a star of the Opera House there, and she had lived like a princess until the age of twelve, when he died suddenly of a throat hemorrhage. From that moment on, the good life had ended and economy had become the order of the day. Gradually, she and Mama had seen the old house fade and crumble, the shutters break, so they creaked incessantly on shattered hinges. When Arlette was sixteen, they had been evicted and the house sold to pay their debts. She and her mother had gone to live in one room in the former servants' quarters of her grandmother's property near Paris, and there they remained to the present day.

Arlette emerged from the dark streets of the old town, into the Cours Saleya, where the Flower Market was in progress. The sudden burst of color, coupled with the heady scent of lilies, mimosa, and lilac, made her happy, and she thought defiantly that she must never allow herself to be diverted from her ambition. In order not to be poor again and to help Mama live to the end of her days in style, she must find a rich husband and learn to be a good wife.

Entering a café, Arlette ordered a *pastis* and read the morning paper. The second-page headline of local news showed a photograph of Charles Leclerq, Duc de Chantilly, who was in Nice to launch a new champagne from his family firm. The deluxe offering would be known as Cham-

pagne Grand Cru Bal Rosé. Arlette thought for a while, then
paid for her *pastis* and made her way to the Hotel Negresco.
With the Ballet Rose about to open in one of the finest shows
ever seen in Europe and the owner of one of the great cham-
pagnes of France about to launch a new brand called Bal
Rosé, surely a publicity linkup was possible?

On arrival at the hotel, Arlette went to the powder room
and checked every detail of her appearance, from her shoes
to the collar of the simple white linen sheath. Then she went
to the reception desk and asked for the Duc de Chantilly.

He was very tall, very thin, and forty years old, a man
bored by life and spoiled by an indulgent mother. He had
been raised by the Jesuits and had not discovered the pleasure of women until the age of thirty, when his innocence
had been challenged, toppled, and exploited by a voracious
widow of forty-five. His hair was sandy-beige, his face
suntanned, the eyes pale blue with long fair lashes. He wore
an English Prince of Wales check suit and was carrying a
copy of *The Wall Street Journal*. On seeing Arlette, he
paused to weigh the short black hair, newly cut in a perfect
square fringe, the dark-blue eyes, the slim, elegant body and
perfect legs. The dress was costly and understated, the pale-
beige crocodile purse well chosen. She was certainly not a
whore, but there was about her a certain glamour, an indefinable aura that made her different from the women of his
own milieu. He walked up and shook Arlette's hand.

"I'm Charles Leclerq. I understand you asked to see
me."

"Arlette de Cazenave. I'm due to open with the Tournée
du Ballet Rose at the Opéra de Nice."

"What can I do for you, Mademoiselle? May I first invite
you to coffee in the lounge?"

Arlette walked like a queen past a curious concièrge and
two American tourists arguing about currency exchange
rates. In the Louis XIV salon of the hotel she arranged her-

self on a brocade sofa of a color that matched her eyes and
began to explain her idea.

"You're here to launch the new champagne Bal Rosé.
The show I'm with is the most expensive spectacle ever sent
on tour in Europe. I thought there might be a publicity angle
in the similarity of the names and the image of perfection,
prestige, and luxury."

"Are you the publicity director for the show?"

"No. I'm a showgirl. I was in the Flower Market this
morning when I saw an article on the new champagne, and I
came on impulse to tell you about my idea. I won't stay
more than a few minutes."

"Nonsense. I've walked up and down the Promenade des
Anglais this morning trying to think of something new for
the media. Of course, the ad men have been at work for
months and they've done a good job, but for France I'd like
a local linkup. Your idea has possibilities."

They drank coffee and talked about the Champagne region, where Charles lived. Impressed by her seemingly en-
cyclopedic knowledge of the area, Charles was unaware that
Arlette had studied him and others like him for years, in the
way that some study the stock market or the form before a
horse race. As the clocks struck twelve, he looked at his
watch and motioned for her to follow.

"Let's drink an aperitif in the bar and then lunch on the
terrace. You'll eat gourmandise de foie gras and charlotte de
Saint Pierre, which is a fantasy of fish and cream. I have it
every day. I'm not a man who likes change."

Arlette nodded politely, forgetting her rule never to eat
lunch and listening intently as he continued.

"I'll come and see your Monsieur Benedetti this afternoon and arrange a presentation of Bal Rosé after the opening night with full press coverage. You're a very clever
young lady and I'm delighted you came."

Arlette blushed with pleasure. It was the first time in her

life she had had an idea like this and she was overcome by
the success of her venture. When the Duke rose, she followed him into the bar, impressed when the celebrity-
hardened staff hurried to serve his favorite before-lunch
drink. As she sipped her own kir royale, she was asking herself if this was the moment she had longed for all her life.
Was this the man who would marry her and make her mistress of a chateau, just as she and Mama had dreamed? She
glanced surreptitiously at her reflection in the mirror,
terrified in case she saw something less than perfection.

After lunch, the Duke invited Arlette to take coffee and
liqueurs in his suite. She demurred.

"I couldn't come to your suite. I barely know you."

"We've lunched together—and anyway, this is nineteen
sixty-seven and not nineteen *thirty*-seven, you know."

"I'm sorry, Charles. I have to leave for the theater in any
case. I have an appointment at three."

The Duke looked into the dark-blue eyes, with their
mocking expression. At twenty-five she surely could not be
a virgin? The thought was titillating, but he showed nothing
of his true feelings and simply made a small nod in Arlette's
direction as he shook hands.

"Thank you for your company. I shall see you again after
the opening of the show, I hope."

"I shall look forward to it."

Arlette walked along the busy seafront, past the Jardin
Albert I to the avenue des Phoceens and the street in which
the Opéra was situated. She was thinking of the Duke's perfect manners and the sudden gleam of anger—or had it been
curiosity?—in his eyes when she had refused to visit his
suite. The deference with which the staff had treated him
and the lack of curiosity he had shown when signing the
lunch bill had thrilled her. The rich *were* different.

Pausing outside a postcard shop, Arlette examined the
tourist view cards, the pastel nudes, the sepia-toned render-

ings of the Riviera in times long past, and a selection of
beautiful photographs featuring ancient stone houses surrounded by lavender fields, closeups of the scarlet poppies
of Provence, and the one that she eventually bought, which
showed a pair of white fan-tailed doves in a cream stone
courtyard covered in blue tendrils of plumbago. On the card,
she wrote a message.

Dear Charles,
Thank you for the perfect lunch and your most amusing
company. Today was a lovely surprise.

Arlette

She put this in an envelope and sent it to the Negresco by
messenger. Then she hurried to the theater, afraid that she
would be late for her rendezvous with Sarah.

On the dressing-room door she found a note in Sarah's in-
imitable hand, telling her to come to the beach at the Rond
Point. Eager to have her friend's opinion on the happenings
of the morning, Arlette hurried to the hotel, changed into a
sundress, and made her way to the promenade. She could
see Sarah plowing through the sea like a bronzed mermaid,
watched by Umberto di Castelli, who was shouting instructions from the safety of the shore. Arlette could not help
laughing at his consternation.

"Come back at once! There is a shelf under the sea and
you will fall down into the depths. Watch what you are
doing, Sarah, do you hear. Come back! I order you to come
back! Soon I need a telescope to see you."

Umberto mopped his forehead and turned to Benedetti.

"She do this on purpose because she know I never go in
the water. It is her game to torment me."

"She's a wonderful swimmer. Calm down."

"And what about the sharks? Tell me that, Mario! You
don't kick sharks in the balls."

"Let's go and drink a cappuccino in the bar across the road."

"I don't *want* a cappuccino. I want for Sarah to do what she is told."

"Umberto, how long have we been friends?"

"Twenty years, maybe more."

"Since you were sixteen and I was twenty-eight. Now, will you please listen to a word of advice? This girl can't be given orders. She'll do anything for you, but only if and when she wants to."

"But she wants nothing at all from me."

"Make her, tempt her—it's the only way. You'll never get anywhere by shouting orders."

Arlette watched as the two moved away from the edge of the water and toward her as she stood by Sarah's belongings. She was momentarily caught off balance when Umberto invited her to dinner. She looked at him with distaste.

"I'm afraid I can't dine with you tonight or any other night, Mr. di Castelli."

"Why not?"

"Because your real interest is Sarah and you only want to take me out for the same reason you wanted to invite Holly. Perhaps next you'll invite Mary-Ellen. You want to know all you can find out about the person who really interests you."

"You drink too much with the lunch," Umberto said as he turned and walked away.

Sarah was gleeful when told about Arlette's visit to the Duke of Chantilly. Determined to do all in her power to help her friend, she proposed a trip to the local reference library, where they could research the Duke's hobbies and interests in life. She was shocked when Arlette recited in parrot fashion his entry from the *International Who's Who*.

"He likes skiing and mountain climbing, and he is an expert on trees and flowering shrubs. Charles Leclerq is one of

Mama's favorite dukes. She was always reading about him. His house near Chantilly is fabulous, with gardens laid out by Le Nôtre, who did Versailles. The chateau has forty-eight bedrooms and a hall of mirrors one hundred and eighty feet long.''

"Do you ski, Arlette?''

"I detest snow.''

"Do you like flowers and shrubs?''

"Yes, very much.''

"We'll go and buy a book on flowering shrubs. You must learn a few names and the pictures that go with them so you can talk on one of his subjects when he invites you to dinner.''

"Are you sure all this is necessary, Sarah?''

"Of course, it's part of the game. If you win you marry your duke. If you lose you've learned something new.''

"Umberto said you liked playing games and I think he may be right.''

"It's true, but where he's concerned I just can't resist the frustrated way he screeches when I don't do what I'm told.''

Arlette looked hard at Sarah to see if she was joking.

"He's a very powerful man, Sarah. And he's used to having his way. Don't play with him. Inside that amiable exterior there's a heart of solid lead, if there's a heart at all. At this moment, you're too young and you've been too sheltered in your life. You don't understand people like Umberto. You think everyone's as pure and truthful as you are, and it isn't true.''

"The ones with no heart are the most interesting, Arlette. They're the biggest challenge you can find in life.''

Arlette wondered if she had been wrong about Sarah. Thrown by her obvious innocence where men were concerned, she tended to think of her friend as a child. Now she recognized the natural manipulator with a desire to have power over someone or something. Arlette sighed apprehen-

sively, wondering how to tell Sarah that she had surely
chosen the wrong playmate in Umberto di Castelli.

Before the afternoon was over, Arlette had learned about
Japanese cherries of the varieties Amanoggwa, Manzan,
Tai-Haku, and Shirotae. Sarah was a fearsome taskmaster,
and at five Arlette was obliged to take some aspirin for a ferocious headache. Then, her mind still buzzing from facts,
she joined Sarah for a trip to the cinema with Mary-Ellen,
who was dying to see the new Jeanne Moreau movie, because the leading actors were rumored to have made love for
real during the shooting of the sex scenes.

The girls were drinking coffee after the movie when the
Duke of Chantilly entered and shook hands with Arlette.

"Everything has been arranged, my dear, and there will
be a presentation of champagne after opening night. Are you
still free for lunch on Sunday? We could go to Monaco and
eat at the Hotel de Paris."

"I'd like that very much."

"So would I. Until Sunday, then. I'll send my car to your
hotel. We'll have a drink at Beaulieu on the way."

Mary-Ellen leaned over to Arlette, her eyes wide.

"Who on earth is *that?*"

"He's the Duc de Chantilly. I've only met him
once. . . ."

Mary-Ellen looked to Sarah.

"She finally found her duke! When's the wedding, Arlette, or haven't you proposed yet?"

Arlette spoke frostily, but the girls saw the blush of pleasure in her cheeks.

"I have no intention of proposing to any man." Her face
was soft. "I do hope, though . . ."

In her room later, as the clock struck midnight, Arlette
examined herself closely in the mirror. Satisfied that the
harsh light revealed few flaws, she walked to the window
and stood in the darkness looking down on the narrow street

below with its bars, restaurants, *hôtels de passe,* and twilight girls. Her mind turned to the film she had seen that
evening and the panting, eager coupling the actors had simu-
lated. Mary-Ellen had found it all highly amusing. Sarah
had sat tense and still, watching in seeming detachment. Arlette had felt a wayward longing for the thing she enjoyed
most, the only release that provided her with real satisfaction.

In one of the hotels opposite, a light went on, revealing a
room crudely decorated with cabbage-rose-patterned paper.
Arlette watched in fascination as a street girl and her client
entered and locked the door. The silent pantomime was all
the more intriguing for the fact that the onlooker was obliged
to imagine the conversation as money was exchanged and
the man undressed. Then, as the girl unzipped her dress and
stood naked before her client, Arlette's hand wandered to
her own rigid nipples and began to caress them. The girl in
the room opposite looked patiently on as the client lay like a
corpse waiting in passive expectation for a miracle. Arlette's fingers began to tug her nipples as the girl moved
astride the man and slid slowly down on his penis. Then, as
the street girl vibrated back and forth with ever increasing
speed, Arlette moved to the bed and lay on top of the covers,
her hand moving from her nipples to part the pubic hair and
reach the center of feeling. The finger moved slowly, deliberately, back and forth. Toes curled, she raised her knees,
and as the client in the room opposite cried out in the moment of orgasm, Arlette closed her eyes and let the finger
quicken until suddenly she felt as if she were falling from a
great height. The cramping, numbing moment of release
was hers alone and all the more satisfactory because she had
needed no one's help to achieve it. No man had ever made
love to her, and she knew instinctively that no man would be
able to give her the intense pleasure she could give herself.

By the time Arlette rose and looked again out the window,

the room in the *hôtel de passe* was in darkness. The client had gone his way and the girl in the black zipped dress was waiting patiently in a nearby doorway for the next night-walker.

Sarah could not sleep. Images of the film kept intruding into her mind and she was appalled to find herself full of longing. As always when desire entered her mind, she thought of Vieri and tried to imagine how it would be to be loved by him. She turned on the light, picked up the evening paper, and read again the article about his visit to a charity ball in nearby Monaco. He had arrived by helicopter, landing in the palace grounds and staying only for an hour before returning to Venice for a cousin's wedding. Sarah sighed. Wealth, breeding, and power made everything possible. She looked at the photograph of Vieri, dreamily tracing the lines of his face with her finger. Then, impatient with herself for her unabated desire, she threw the paper down, dressed, put on her coat, and went out to walk along the beachfront. It was one A.M. and the only sounds were those of waves against the beach, traffic moving toward the sharp curve of the headland, and the distant music of a discotheque. Sarah walked slowly along the promenade and sat down on a bench, her eyes fixed on the dark horizon. She was thinking the same romantic thoughts of Vieri that had filled her mind ever since their first meeting, of a perfect future, a future that could never be.

Umberto had been gambling at the casino in Cannes and was on his way back to the hotel, when he saw Sarah sitting on a bench by the seawall, her hair lit by the mellow tones of an ancient lamp. Tapping for his chauffeur to stop the car, he stepped out, lit a cigar, and walked over to her.

"What are you doing here all alone? It is almost two o'clock."

"I'm thinking."

"What about?"

"My life and my future."

Umberto moved and sat at Sarah's side, glancing at her face and trying to assess the strangely hopeless look in her eyes. He puffed the cigar for a few minutes, then held out his hand, surprised when she grasped it in her own. She was cold and he hurried to take off his overcoat and put it around her shoulders.

"Come, I take you back to the hotel."

"I don't want to go back to the hotel. I don't want to be alone. Let's walk on the beach."

They walked in silence, pausing on the esplanade to gaze down at the empty sand and the smooth, silver sea. Umberto looked again at Sarah, her sadness so profound it hit him like a blow to the gut. Impulsively he kissed the tips of her fingers.

"What's wrong? You tell me and I fix. I do *anything* for you, Sarah."

She shrugged, unable for the moment to put her confusion into words. The fact was that the film had unsettled her, making her long for the one man she could not have. When she replied, Umberto remained silent, assessing every word.

"I went with my friends to the cinema to see a sexy film last night, and afterward I wanted to be loved—really loved, not just had—by a man. I realized that no one had ever really loved me in my life." Sarah paused for a second, startled that she was again revealing herself to Umberto, but she plunged on. "My mother's mad and incapable of loving anyone. I think she hates me for having been born, though that was her fault and hardly mine."

Sarah stopped to collect her thoughts.

"I wanted to be loved by someone special and I felt lonely deep inside my soul, lonelier than I ever felt before. I shouldn't talk about such things with a stranger, but you asked. . . ."

"I'm not a stranger. You and I are friends, even though you don't accept it. I do all I can for you, Sarah, now and always. You want something, I get it. If I don't have myself, I arrange. You just ask and I fix. Remember, because it's important. In your life you meet men who only give and men who only take and most of them want only to take. I give and I take only what you offer, when you offer."

Sarah looked into the dark eyes, sensing his tension. She had rejected Umberto as a lover, but for the moment he was at her side and doing all he could to help, support, and encourage her in the lonely hours of night, the hours she had always feared. She leaned forward and put her head on his shoulder.

"Sometimes I wonder who I am. Other times I wish I could be anybody else."

"Why? You are a special person at the start of your life."

"I grew up under the constant threat of being given away by a suicidal mother. At ten I was her jailer, because she wouldn't see a psychiatrist, so I gave her her pills and locked her in her room and kept charts for the family doctor. I could never quite rid myself of the idea that she was ill because of me, that somehow I had destroyed her. I still think that, and sometimes I find it hard to like myself and to believe anyone else can like me."

Umberto put his arms around her, caught off guard when Sarah looked up into his eyes, inviting him to kiss her. For a moment he hesitated. Then he bent his head and touched her lips with his own. Her body moved closer to his, and as his tongue entered her mouth he felt a shiver of anticipation run through her, followed at once by the same resistance she had shown at that first meeting. This time he did not fight her, but let her draw away from him. She pulled back only for a moment, then of her own volition kissed him again.

Somewhere in the distance a clock chimed two. Sarah stared disbelievingly at Umberto. Was she as mad as her mother? Was she pretending this was Vieri? But she knew she was not mad and that a contrary desire had made her want to be kissed and desired with urgency by a real man. She began to walk in the direction of the hotel, Umberto followed a few paces behind her. She was halfway across the road when he spoke.

"You want to sleep or to have a surprise?"

"A surprise at two in the morning?"

"Come, I show you."

He ordered the chauffeur to drive them to the airport, where he made a phone call that evidently pleased him. Minutes later, they were taxiing along the runway in a private jet.

Sarah watched Nice disappearing and was alarmed.

"You know I have to be back by two in the afternoon for the first show of opening night?"

"You'll be back, I promise. When Umberto promise it happen."

They landed at Naples airport, took a private helicopter to Capri, and in the early hours of the morning ate breakfast together on the terrace of a magnificent villa perched on the edge of a cliff. The coffee was rich and scented, the rolls warm and crisp, the selection of jams exotic, with passion fruit and wild rose, violet petal and amber. Sarah watched tiny emerald lizards darting back and forth between the stone walls of the house and enjoyed the shimmering dawn light on the pellucid blue sea. For the moment, she had forgotten her heartache about Vieri and her sadness of the previous night. It had been wonderful to be flown in a private jet summoned at a minute's notice and amazing to arrive and find a house perfectly arranged and full of staff waiting to do their bidding. She realized for the first time the extent of Umberto's power and longed to know more about him.

"Is this your house?"

"One of them. I own it, but my sister Valeria live here. She is in New York with the family."

"Where else do you own houses?"

"The main house is in Sicily, near the village of Montelepre. It is very large, very dark, and very grand. My house in Paris you saw. I have also an apartment in Rome. Have more coffee and more of the bread. It was bake by the best cook on the island. Do you like your surprise, Sarah?"

"I like it very much, but why did you bring me here?"

"I want to make you happy. Also to impress you."

"You impressed me, all right."

"You swim? The water is very warm."

"I haven't got a bathing suit."

"I arrange it, don't worry. What you want, we arrange."

Sarah chose a white satin swimsuit appliqéd with tendrils of lilac that matched her eyes. Then, when Umberto urged her to take a silk dress and underwear because she could not travel back in the clothes of the previous day, she chose a set in pale pink silk, so luxurious and costly it took her breath away. She was wondering if he would take her inside the house and try to make love to her, now that he had bought her a gift and given her a costly surprise, but Umberto was looking at his watch.

"We leave in half an hour. Go and swim and then change into your new clothes."

Umberto was following Benedetti's advice: *Do the unexpected. Don't push her, don't try to own her. When she thinks you're here, be far away. When she's sad, make her happy.* Sarah would surely be expecting him to make demands after the trip to Capri and the new clothes. He called out to her as she swam up and down the pool.

"In five minutes you come out. After we arrive in Nice I take you to lunch and then deliver you to the theater. Then I go back at once to Paris."

"How long will you be away?"

"I don't know. Maybe I come back before the end of the run. It depend on work."

In the plane, conscious of the warmth of Sarah's thigh against his own, Umberto was pleased to see uncertainty in the beautiful face. Benedetti had been right. Sarah did what she wanted to do, when she wanted to do it, and was puzzled when men did not react predictably. He closed his eyes, inhaling the perfume of her body and wondering why she affected him so. From the first moment he had been struck down by the gravest of maladies, burning desire. At first he had thought it was a simple mania to possess her body. Now he was appalled by the realization that he might be in love. He shook his head in disgust at the idea. Love was for men with long hair who wrote poems or gained a meager living painting pictures. It was not for men of power, who manipulated events and dominated great organizations. In any case, women were perfidious. Every man in Sicily was taught that a woman's place was in the home or in the confessional that kept her faithful. Umberto closed his eyes, unable to control his longing for the woman at his side. Once he had loved Sarah, if she could ever be persuaded to surrender, the malady might diminish. On the other hand, he might suddenly become her slave, dominated by and obedient to her every whim. The thought of making love to her gave him an erection, and he thought angrily that he had best get back to Paris and try to put his life and his obsession in perspective.

Sarah entered the hotel at one-thirty, in time to collect her ballet shoes and all she would need for the class before opening night. Mary-Ellen was waiting for her in the upstairs lounge.

"Where the hell were you? I thought you'd been murdered. Seriously, Sarah, you mustn't ever do that again. I had no idea where you were or if you'd had an accident, and Arlette was ready to call the gendarmerie."

"I went out walking on the beach last night and met Umberto. He came with me for a while."

"Till one-thirty the following afternoon? Come on, what happened?"

"He flew me to Capri for breakfast. Then we came back, ate lunch at La Casita because I felt the urge for Spanish food, and here I am. Speaking of food, did someone burn the lunch?"

"God knows—there's been a weird smell for a while. Probably the new chef sabotaged the *poulet au pot.*"

They were in Sarah's room, getting her things together and laughing at Arlette's preparations for the evening, when they noticed smoke filtering through the space under the door. Sarah ran and looked out into the corridor, shocked to find it full of choking black fumes.

"Dear God, this place is on fire! Open the window, Mary-Ellen. We'll have to try to get out that way."

"There's a drop like Everest out there. We'll break our necks!"

The air quality was rapidly worsening, and Sarah's breathing was affected. She looked anxiously to her friend.

"I have to get out, Mary-Ellen, and you'd best come with me. These furnishings will go up like rockets and the fumes are deadlier than flames."

"You'll have to hold my hand. I suffer from vertigo and— Holy Jesus! I just realized I'll lose all my possessions—and I just bought a new cabin trunk to house my spares!"

"That's the least of your problems. That door won't hold much longer, and once it's gone the fire'll be in here."

They were both close to tears, and certain they were going to die, when the door opened and Umberto and Benedetti ran in. They were wearing oxygen masks and handed one to each of the girls as they lifted them in from the ledge. Then, motioning for them to follow, they made their way down the corridor in the opposite direction from the main elevator shaft. Using the ancient service stairs overlooking the rear courtyard, Umberto led them through an area that was comparatively fire free, albeit heavy with smoke, making signs all the while for them to hurry. They thought they were out of danger when, from somewhere in the heart of the building, they heard a sickening, creaking sound, followed by what seemed like an earthquake hitting the hotel as the center section caved in. Masonry fell and plaster covered their bodies as pillars began to lean at alarming angles. They ran on, conscious that time was short and they had seconds to clear the building.

Umberto hurried the girls into the daylight and took off his mask. His face was ashen, his hands bleeding, and Benedetti's back was cut on the shoulder bone. Sarah could not help but smile at Umberto's childish pride in his own courage.

"Another five minutes and you would have been roast. Benedetti and I organize everything, even the masks."

"What about the others?"

"We locate everyone except two of the showgirls. Janine and Mireille we cannot find."

Mary-Ellen sat down on the wall, gazing at Umberto and Benedetti as firemen arrived and began to train hoses on the burning building. Her eyes were wide with shock, her voice shrill.

"Why'd you take a risk like that? You could both have been killed."

Umberto shrugged, glancing at Sarah.

"I could be kill crossing the road. You all right, Sarah? Why you cough so?"

Mary-Ellen put her arm around her friend, who was vomiting from one of the attacks of coughing that racked her frame. She turned and explained to Umberto.

"Sarah has weak lungs. Just leave her be for a while. She'll be better when the fresh air gets into her."

"Leave her be! To hell with the leave her be. We call a doctor. Her face is gray and she needs more than fresh air."

At the theater, the class was delayed and then postponed until an hour before opening. There were more urgent things to attend to than dancers loosening their muscles with pliés. The company had lost all its possessions, except those the girls had carried to rehearsal. Two showgirls were still missing, and as time passed it became obvious that both had been in the building when it caught fire.

At four-thirty, an hour and a half before the opening of the first show, two bodies were found in one of the hotel bathrooms on the second floor. Burned beyond recognition, they were identified by rings found on the charred fingers as Mireille and Janine. The company gathered onstage, many of them in tears, all of them profoundly shocked. Sarah was still suffering the effects of the smoke, and Mary-Ellen had fallen into a reverie from which nothing seemed to rouse her. The disaster had taken its toll and suddenly she felt bereft. The carefully constructed illusion of security she had created for herself had been taken away without warning, and death had come uncomfortably close. In addition, the precious trunks of clothes, shoes, scent, and presents from men, which to her were synonymous with safety, were all gone. She was back where she had started at the beginning of the tour, empty-handed and afraid.

Arlette carried tea to Sarah and Mary-Ellen. Holly hurried to find out where the nearest pharmacy was and then delivered Sarah's prescription with a smile.

"I'll get you a glass of water and you can take the first tablets now. You'll feel better almost at once—that's what the doctor said."

"I hope so. I can't see my lungs taking me through six hours of exertion in their present state."

Holly stroked Sarah's hand.

"I'll do the cancan in your place tonight. I know the steps and your costume'll fit me fine."

"Thanks, Holly, you're a real friend."

At that moment, Madame Rose appeared in a white evening gown and diamonds, to inform everyone that the show would go on. An announcement would be made before the curtain went up, explaining the events of the day and the deaths of the two girls, but the Ballet Rose would open as scheduled.

The audience sat in hushed expectation as the overture was played. Polite applause greeted the maestro's bow and curiosity the entrance of Madame Rose. The face was old and tired, the face of a matriarch and a virago, with its halo of white hair and piercing gray eyes. The voice was low and melodic.

"Ladies and gentlemen, welcome to the opening of the Grande Tournée du Ballet Rose. This afternoon, the hotel in which the members of our company were staying was burned down. We have lost not only all our personal possessions, but also two of our showgirls, Mireille Raquin and Janine Voulon. We grieve their tragic deaths and pay tribute to them by opening as planned. The company begs your indulgence for any small hesitations on the part of its members. We are shocked, but we shall do our best to please you and hope you have a most enjoyable evening. Ladies and gentlemen, the members of the company of the Ballet Rose."

As Madame left the stage, the orchestra struck up the deafening fanfare that heralded the opening number and the red plush curtains rose on a scene of breathtaking beauty, a tableau of dancers, showgirls, and stars stood tall on the staircase that rose high above the stage. For a moment there was silence. Then, in its own tribute to the courage of the company, the sophisticated audience rose to its feet and applauded.

In the still of night, after the bouquets had been presented and the speeches made, the members of the Ballet Rose made their way to the hotel found for them by Benedetti. All of them were tired, physically and emotionally drained by the events of the afternoon.

Sarah emerged from the theater alone and walked slowly, thoughtfully, in the direction of the hotel. Holly had gone out alone, seeking relief in the old quarter of the city, where the bizarre was normal and the normal was a bore. Arlette was having dinner with her duke, and Mary-Ellen had disappeared with the son of an Arab sheik. Sarah began to cough, her lungs still aching from the afternoon's trauma. She was wiping her eyes on a handkerchief when she felt Umberto take her arm.

"Come, I buy you something to eat."

"I'm not hungry. My stomach's still full of smoke."

"You eat anyway. We go to Villefranche and have lobsters in one of the restaurants on the harbor. I love to see the yachts."

"But not the water?"

"I like to *see* the water, I just don't like to touch. On water I am like Samson without the hair."

"Where's Mario?"

"He has much to do. The insurance company send men down on the night plane."

"When do you leave for Paris?"

"I should have gone today, but I go in the morning at eight instead. I want to stay to check you are well again."

Sarah closed her eyes and listened to the soft purring of the car engine. Umberto was wearing a new suit and silk shirt that had cost a fortune. He had ruined the ensemble's perfection by inserting a carnation of glaring vermilion in the buttonhole. It was a color Sarah detested, but she smiled wearily, fatigue, shock, and fear of being alone and ill robbing her of her usual wary resistance. For the moment, she was content to let Umberto take care of everything. What was it he had said? *You want something, I get it. If I don't have myself, I arrange.* Sarah felt his hand on hers and did not resist as he kissed each of her fingers. Then she slept, waking only when they stopped outside a lantern-lit restaurant overlooking the water. Umberto was watching her with a curiously intent gaze. Sarah sighed, conscious that in letting him invite her to dinner she was making it more and more difficult to stay free from his advances. Was that what she really wanted? Or was Umberto a substitute for the man she really desired? She shook her head, cross with her own confusion. The only thing she knew from childhood was to depend on no one. But Umberto was tempting her to trust him and the feeling was not unpleasant.

CHAPTER FOUR

Mary-Ellen, Rome, September 1967

It was four A.M. and Mary-Ellen was walking home after a date with Umberto. It had not escaped her notice that he had spent most of the evening pumping her for information about Sarah, and she had told him what she knew of her friend's childhood and early life. She smiled wistfully at the thought of the girl she liked and admired. The previous day, she had found Sarah having a long conversation with a house painter in the Via Margutta. Inquiring what on earth she wanted with the painter, Mary-Ellen had received the reply that the colors of the walls of Rome would come in useful someday. The city buildings that glowed amber, ocher, and terracotta in the sunlight seemed to fascinate Sarah. Mary-Ellen now realized that her friend's seemingly detached exterior hid a cauldron of intensity.

She sighed, wishing she could be a cauldron of intensity instead of a deep freeze hidden behind a sensuous, painted mask. The previous evening Umberto had made love to her like a machine, pumping his lust into her body as if it were his last moment on earth. As usual, she had acted emotions she could no longer feel, but he had not been deceived and she knew he would never invite her again. Mary-Ellen shivered despite the warmth of the night as she thought of Umberto, whose smile concealed a man as ruthless as any she

had ever met. There was little he did not know about the
hopes, secret thoughts, and ambitions of those who interested him and little he could not find out by some mysterious
alchemy she did not understand.

Mary-Ellen sat on a green-painted bench in the Borghese
Park, watching the sun rise slowly over the horizon and
reliving the moments in bed with Umberto. There had been
no love; that she did not expect. But what was so wrong with
her body that it could not respond? Once it had responded,
but that had been a long time ago. A tear fell down her cheek
as she remembered the day of her thirteenth birthday, when
she had been adopted and taken away from the orphanage.
Proud to have been chosen, she could still call to mind the
relief she had felt that at last she would be part of a real family. Then, two years after the adoption, her new father, Joe,
had come to her room, undressed her with trembling hands
before the fire, fondled her till she was mad with longing,
and then fucked her until the small hours of the morning. He
had come back night after night for weeks, obsessed by her
beauty and her desire. She had known it was wrong, but as
he taught her to please him, her body had lived as it had
never lived before, nor ever would again. Then, one night,
his wife had appeared brandishing the carving knife. Mary-
Ellen had been too shocked to react. The struggle had been
short, and she had been given a sedative by the doctor called
to tend Joe's cut thigh. The following day she had been sent
back to the orphanage, and nine months later a daughter had
been born and named Cathy. The baby had died within
hours, despite valiant efforts by the orphanage doctors.
Since then, Mary-Ellen's body had refused to allow her the
pleasure she had once taken for granted. Men had become a
stepladder to security, their gifts hoarded against the inevitable rainy day.

Willing herself not to think of the past, Mary-Ellen wondered what would happen when Umberto finally trapped

Sarah, as he surely would. That would be a remarkable duel, the sting of a Sicilian scorpion against the poisonous thorns of an English rose. She thought how he had invited each of Sarah's friends to dinner to elicit information about her, failing only because Arlette refused to be seen with him in a public place. Mary-Ellen's own reaction had been a certain annoyance that he had invited her only to talk about her friend, and she had tantalized him with a brief comment, thrown away as innocuously as she could: *I often wonder if Sarah's in love. If she is, she keeps it to herself and she's a big one for secrets.* Umberto had listened in silence, but she had been conscious of the brain ticking like a time bomb as he assessed the statement.

Mary-Ellen walked on through the streets of Rome, deserted but for the cats that were an ever-present feature of city life. The *portiera* of the apartment block over Otello's restaurant was sound asleep. As she climbed the stairs, Mary-Ellen hoped that Sarah would be awake so they could talk. She was afraid of being alone and sick of going over and over the same thoughts and finding no solution to her problems.

Sarah and Mary-Ellen were drinking their breakfast coffee when Holly emerged from the bathroom, her hair stiff with a waxlike coating of coconut oil. Having poured herself a cup of coffee, she picked up the morning paper and scanned the ads for massage parlors, smiling impishly across the table at Sarah.

"You know how much they pay an old whore in Rome?"

"I've no idea."

"Twelve dollars short time. Young ones can ask two hundred if they're pretty. I'm telling you this because you always ask how much everything is and write it down in that little black book!"

Outside, the hum of traffic had risen to a roar and expletives called by exasperated motorists filled the air. *Stronzo!*

was the Eternal City's favorite insult. *Becco!*—cuckold—
was a word offensive to the Roman male proud of his *bella
figura* and certain that every woman in the city was unfaith-
ful with the exception of his own wife.

Sarah sipped a cup of milky coffee on the terrace overlooking the street, with its busy market selling fruit and veg-
etables. She was relaxed and at home in the city. In their
street the most renowned delicatessens were situated, and it
was more peaceful since being turned into a pedestrian
walkway. Only in the nearby Piazza di Spagna did the daily
comedy of the traffic jam escalate until early evening. At the
moment they walked to the theater, it achieved a bedlamlike
intensity. But Sarah loved her Roman home. She stared
down at the busy street, wondering again about her mother.
She had written home each week since the start of the tour,
but had not received a single reply. She wondered if this was
her mother's way of worrying her or if something was
wrong. She was pacing up and down the kitchen when the
telephone rang and she heard Benedetti's voice.

"A flower arrived for you with a note."

"One flower?"

"One flower, Sarah."

"He's stingy, whoever he is, and I can't stand that. Why
did you call me?"

"You'll be interested in this flower, and I think you
should come and collect it. Then I'll take you to lunch at
Otello's. Hurry, it's only a five-minute walk."

Puzzled, Sarah left the apartment and made her way to the
theater, where she found Benedetti waiting in his office. He
handed her a single pink rose wrapped in the distinctive
white and green paper of her favorite London florist.

"*Voilà,* the rose."

On the accompanying card was a message written in sepia
ink in an unusual upright hand of great force and original-

ity. . . . *This is a real English rose.* Sarah's heart missed a
beat and she sat very still, staring at Benedetti.

"Do you know who sent this?"

"Of course. Aldobrandini's chauffeur delivered it. I
knew he was in the city with his brother and assumed he'd
come to see the show. He'll be in the house for the second
show tonight."

Sarah said nothing for some time. Then she licked her
lips, conscious that her throat felt as dry as ground seaweed.
"I only met him once."

"I know you did."

"You know too much. You're like Mary-Ellen—you
even know my thoughts!"

"Don't be angry, Sarah. Take your rose, keep it in the
apartment, and I'll buy you lunch at Otello's."

"Why must I take the rose away?"

"Umberto is a very jealous man. He wants you to belong
to him. You want other things, but what you want is impossible. I've know Umberto since he was a child. In fact,
we're distantly related. After I married his sister, he came
every day from school for his meals and I taught him everything he knows. The only thing I never could teach him was
that certain things are impossible, that he can't have everything he wants. He wants you, Sarah, and he'll have you."

Suddenly Sarah's eyes filled with tears and she stared at
the rose as if it could give her the answer to all the questions
that had haunted her since that first fateful meeting with
Vieri. Was she like Umberto? Was she chasing moonbeams
that for her could never exist? She was startled when Benedetti spoke.

"Are you in love with Aldobrandini? I'm your friend and
that gives me the right to ask."

"You're Umberto's friend, too. Anyway, I'm not in
love. I only met him once and I hardly spoke with him."

Benedetti took her firmly by the arm.

"Come on, I'll buy you lunch and we'll talk of something else."

They walked past fountains shaped like goddesses and galleons and into the Piazza di Spagna, with its ever-moving crowd of tourists and hooting traffic. Sarah started when a yellow Ferrari passed by. Was it Vieri? Where was he going? Had he seen her? She felt foolish even contemplating the questions. She followed Benedetti into the courtyard of Otello's, striving to control the thoughts of Vieri that kept rushing through her mind like a silent movie.

Observing how tense she was, Benedetti spoke gently.

"May I give you a word of advice, Sarah?"

"Of course you can."

"This man, he's not for you. Don't let him use you."

"Vieri never contacted me in the three weeks we were in Paris, so he's not very eager to use me."

"His fiancée was in Paris and she's known to be very jealous. Now she's in Switzerland and he'll feel free to pursue you. I am sure he'll invite you to dinner. Just try to remember that to a man like Vieri Aldobrandini, a dancer is someone to be used and enjoyed and then discarded. Don't let him do that to you."

"Are you saying all this for Umberto's sake?"

"I'm saying it for yours. Men like Aldobrandini don't understand the real world and real women. His marriage to Mariannina was probably arranged when they were children."

"I won't do anything foolish, Mario."

"And I won't say anything of the rose or this conversation to Umberto."

Sarah and Mary-Ellen arrived at the theater at five-thirty. Holly would come later, after she had helped Arlette move her possessions back from the room where she had been obliged to stay for a few days until the collapsed ceiling of her bedroom in the apartment had been repaired. The keeper of the stage door handed Sarah her own letters and some for Holly when she arrived. She promptly read her own to Mary-Ellen, as was her custom. "This is from my Aunt Letty:

"Dearest Sarah, Your mother is well and seems happy. I am sorry she hasn't replied to your letters, but she's become bone idle since she married. He even does the washing and floor polishing. The garden is a treat at the moment, with the best roses we've had in years. The dog died of old age yesterday. Reggie has the croup, but apart from that everything's fine.

                              "Your aunt, Letty"

The other letter was on heavy cream vellum with deckled edges. It was brief and to the point. Under the coat of arms of the Aldobrandini family, Vieri had written, *My brother and I will be at the show tonight. If you're free, I invite you to have dinner with me afterward. My chauffeur will come to the theater for you at 11:15. Vieri.*

Mary-Ellen was shocked by the unconcealed joy in Sarah's face and the consternation that superseded it as she called out, "I have nothing to wear! I'll have to wash my hair and do my toenails, and I won't have time by eleven-fifteen."

"Keep him waiting, idiot."

"I can't bear tardiness and I'm sure he can't, either."

"Wear something plain and expensive."

"Like the black Saint Laurent I bought in the sales?"

"No, that's his fiancée's kind of thing, not yours. Wear that white dress you showed me, the Grecian one that looks like something out of *Ben Hur.*"

When the show ended at eleven, Sarah rushed to the dressing room, tearing off her clothes as she went. The friends ran after her, eager to fulfill their prearranged roles.

While Sarah took a shower, Holly checked and rechecked the dress, the slip, the shoes, the contents of the evening purse. Arlette took cotton wool to put between Sarah's toes while she polished the nails, and Mary-Ellen waited with brush and heated rollers. They all laughed joyfully as Sarah sat before them and redid her eyes and lips, screeching when Mary-Ellen accidentally pulled her hair.

"Watch it, will you! I don't want to arrive bald. Are you nearly done with the toes, Arlette?"

"They need only one more minute to dry."

"Did the flowers arrive, Holly?"

"They just came. The florist was stuck in a traffic jam."

Sarah fixed a headband of fern and tiny pink rosebuds in her hair. Then, twirling before the mirror, she acknowledged the applause of her friends. She was surprised when Liz, her former enemy, offered her the loan of a fine gold chain for her neck.

"This will bring you luck, Sarah."

Holly stared from Liz to Sarah, her face incredulous. Liz had never spoken to any of them since the day of the row. Was it possible that the "newies" had been accepted? She was amused when Mary-Ellen spoke to Liz in her usual flying-tackle style.

"What got into you? Did you go get blessed by the Pope or something?"

"It's time we were all friends."

Sarah ruffled Liz's short red curls.

"That's the nicest thing I've heard in ages."

Sarah walked downstairs, turning back halfway to wave to Mary-Ellen, who was hanging over the balustrade of the stairs. Her voice was unsteady, her face tense.

"I'm scared to death. Does it show?"

"Of course not. You look like a dream, Sarah. You just have fun and don't worry about a thing. Tonight *you* are the princess in his life."

At the stage door, Sarah was surprised to find Vieri himself waiting for her. He was dressed in a suit of dark-gray silk and looked more handsome than ever. He stepped forward, ignoring the men waiting for the girls they had chosen, and took her by the hand.

"I am so pleased to see you again, Sarah. I thought the show was marvelous and so did my brother."

"Where is he?"

"Elio went on to my club. We'll have a drink with him and then go to the country to eat."

"Aren't you afraid of being photographed by the paparazzi?"

"I'm not afraid of anything."

Sarah gazed into the big gray eyes with their dark surrounding lashes, at the wavy dark-blond hair lit by the lamp above the stage door. To her, he looked like a Greek god in a Savile Row suit. Dazed by her reactions, she followed him to the Ferrari. As they drove off toward his club, Sarah was furious to feel her heart beating like a trapped animal in her chest, her palms damp with sweat, her brain short-circuited by her nerves. Vieri did not seem to have noticed and continued to talk easily, glancing at her now and then with a scrutiny that seemed amused, curious, and affectionate. Once, he held out his hand and squeezed hers.

"Your hands are frozen and you look as if you're about to visit the dentist. Where are your glasses, by the way?"

"I left them at home."

"You wanted to look pretty, I suppose?"

Sarah smiled at the echo of their first conversation and nodded shyly, thrilled when Vieri spoke.

"You are beautiful and I'm sure you're always lovely, even at six in the morning with your hair in curlers."

"I don't put my hair in curlers and at six in the morning I'm usually drinking coffee on the terrace."

"So am I. My family all love the dawn. I don't think Father has slept more than two hours a night in his life."

The Circolo della Caccia was housed in a piano nobile, seventeenth-century palazzo in the Largo Fontanella Borghese. On entering, Sarah was stunned to see sixty-foot-high ceilings encrusted with gold and the massive coats of arms of Cardinal Camillo Borghese, later Pope Paul V. Three-tiered chandeliers lit this magnificent relic of the past, and liveried footmen in dark-blue tailcoats and breeches trod the rare Persian carpets, ushering in female guests with elaborate ceremony.

On the terrace, overlooking a garden full of statues, Vieri introduced his younger brother.

"Elio, may I present Sarah Hallam, from England. Sarah, this is my brother Elio, who works at the Salk Institute in La Jolla, California. He's the clever one of the family."

Elio shook hands and smiled into the beautiful upturned face.

"Delighted to meet you, Sarah. I loved the show, especially the scene where you danced the butterfly solo. Where do you get the energy to do two three-hour shows a night?"

"I swim and I eat a lot, that's all."

Vieri smiled into his brother's wide blue eyes, thinking wryly that Elio looked more American every day with his sporty clothes and his curly blond hair.

"I told you Sarah was given to direct answers."

Then, turning to Sarah, Vieri asked what she wanted to drink, and was surprised by her reply.

"I'd like a glass of English Pilton white wine. If they don't have that, I'll have a Bellini."

"At the Circolo della Caccia they have everything, or so they say. We shall now put them to the test."

Elio turned to Sarah while his brother left to make a phone call, and she was amused by the difference in the two men.

Vieri was totally European, enigmatic and like an iceberg, with two-thirds of his true personality hidden. Elio had learned a more direct approach in America and had a healthy and obvious curiosity about people.

"How long will you stay in Rome, Sarah?"

"Another four weeks. Then we do Palermo for three weeks and Vienna for the same period. After that, we go back to Paris."

"What are your plans when the show closes?"

"I haven't any. I'd like to work in Paris if I can find another job, but I don't know how difficult it will be."

"Someone who sees the show is sure to engage you for the butterfly solo."

"I've learned never to take things like that for granted."

"You sound disillusioned."

"Realistic. I realized very young that I mustn't trust anyone but my reflection in the mirror."

After Vieri's return the three of them talked for an hour, the two men obviously amused by Sarah's forthright views on life. Then, while she went to the powder room to put some drops of water on the rosebuds in her hair, Vieri took leave of his brother. His eyes were twinkling merrily as he spoke to Sarah on her return.

"The director sends his regrets about the wine. I have a feeling he won't sleep tonight for thinking how the club failed in its duty to a client. Next time you come he'll have every Pilton wine that's made."

"Next time I come I'll ask for Irish Poteen to keep him on his toes."

They traveled on a major highway for two miles, then turned off onto an unlit country lane. Sarah watched the strong hands on the wheel and admired the classic Venetian profile. She was wondering how the Aldobrandinis had managed to instill such poise and confidence and quality.

Vieri seemed to her to be a man who had never had a doubt in his life. She decided to venture a question.

"Tell me about your life, whatever you think I'll enjoy. Did you live in Rome as a child?"

"No, I came here at Christmastime for the family reunion and a visit to the Pope. I lived in Venice until the age of fifteen and had tutors for my lessons. Then Father was told I wasn't working hard, so I was sent away to Paris to do an intensive three-year course in languages. There I found out that I was far from being the cleverest fellow in the world, so I became one of the most stubborn and passed all my examinations despite the professor's pessimism. After that, I returned to Italy and learned about my heritage. Administering the land and property of the Aldobrandinis takes most of my time these days."

"I didn't realize you were in business."

"We're one of the biggest quality wine producers in Italy. Elio and I also own the Club Paradiso resorts, and my mother owns the publishing house of Longueville in Paris. But tell me about yourself and your childhood."

Vieri did not miss her hasty intake of breath and the sudden reluctance that shadowed her eyes. He concentrated all his attention on her as she began to speak.

"I lived in the South of England when I was small. Then, when Daddy died, we went to live in a cottage on the moorland in the Northwest. It was like something out of *Wuthering Heights.*"

"What did your father do?"

"He was in the Army. My mother had periods of deep depression, and I grew up in an atmosphere of total insecurity. I've been running ever since."

"After your father died, what did your mother do?"

"She had a pension from the Army and a very small income from her own family. We were poor, but we got by."

"Did she work?"

"Oh, no, Mother never worked. She's far too lazy for that. *Work* isn't a word in her vocabulary. She likes to sleep most of the day and all of the night. That way she never has to think. Her bathroom has more sleeping pills than a chemist's shop."

"Does she have any good points?"

Sarah thought of the earliest days of her childhood, before her mother's mind had clouded and hate replaced love in her actions.

"She taught me about poetry and bought me lots of books. I was a Tennyson fan from the age of four and started on Shakespeare at nine. I think the most important thing she instilled in me apart from that was the belief that nothing is impossible."

"Except for her to stay awake all day!"

They drove into what looked like a farmyard, but was in reality a very original restaurant with real hay and antique implements. Despite the rustic surroundings, the prices were outrageous, and as she chose what she wanted from the menu, Sarah saw that her fellow diners were movie stars, politicians, and socialites with a genuine penchant for privacy.

Armed guards in battle gray patrolled the periphery of the grounds, and some of the gypsies in the orchestra looked as if they knew more about pugilism than Puccini.

They ate a soup of chestnuts and watercress, then *panzarotti* filled with ricotta. The main course was pigeons glazed in honey, cooked in sage and butter and served with a Brunello di Montalcino. While they ate, the gypsies played romantic music near the blazing fire on the outskirts of the enclosure.

Vieri smiled across the table at Sarah.

"Elio and I once ran away with some gypsies. When I was eight and he was five. Papa found us before we reached the outskirts of the property. We were saved from a thrashing by our English nanny, Miss Perkins, who told my father it was all his fault for having taken us to see *Carmen.*''

Adoring the story of the two little boys, Sarah remembered an incident from her own early days.

''I once ran away, too. I was six and I only got as far as the field next to the house, when I fell down a cesspit that had just been emptied. Mother scrubbed me for hours, but I smelled like a sewer for a very long time.''

Vieri laughed delightedly.

''Only you could get away with such a story at table, Sarah. And how is your friend di Castelli?''

''He isn't my personal property.''

''He wants to be.''

Sarah glanced into the seemingly impassive face, wondering where Vieri had got his information. Her voice was wistful when she spoke.

''Wishing and getting are two different things. There are lots of things I wish I could have, but I haven't a hope and neither has Umberto.''

Their eyes met. Yet again, Vieri was surprised by her directness and puzzled by her statement. What did Sarah want that she could never have? He had the sudden and contrary urge to go out and buy it for her. Then he controlled himself and the distant gaze returned, infuriating and intriguing her. He proposed a visit to the Piazza Navona to eat the famous bitter-chocolate ice cream at Trescallini's. Then, if she was not too tired, they would make an expedition at dawn to the flea market of the Porta Portese to look at antique embroideries, Russian amber, and all the other items dear to Sarah's heart.

As they left the restaurant and drove into the city, Sarah was wondering how Vieri had found out about her tastes and habits. She decided to ask him directly.

''How did you know I liked antique markets?''

"Umberto isn't the only person in the world who asks questions about you."

"I wasn't aware he'd been making inquiries."

"He has made a great many."

"How do *you* know?"

"I have friends who work with companies that deal with him. In my position you get to know a great many people. The difference is that Umberto inhabits a milieu I avoid and he can't enter mine. They don't admit Sicilian savages to the Circolo della Caccia. Well, here we are. This is my favorite square in the city, the Piazza Navona. In ancient times it was a racecourse. Every time I come here I imagine it full of buglers and horsemen in wonderful outfits and flirtatious ladies with their knights errant."

Sarah's expression was intent, but Vieri knew she had heard nothing of his comment on the square. She was thinking of Umberto di Castelli and the questions he had asked about her. With a sigh, Vieri parked the car, nodding a curt greeting to a passing carabiniere and ignoring the protests of pedestrians obliged to step into the road to avoid the Ferrari. Holding out his hand, he led Sarah to a table at Trescallini's and ordered bitter-chocolate ice cream, to be followed by cappuccino and thin glasses of Strega. When she remained silent, he spoke gently.

"Don't worry about di Castelli. I only told you so you'd be aware of the extent of his interest. It wouldn't surprise me if he has even made inquiries in England. He is arming himself with information, because that is his way both in his business and in his private life. He wants you and he is not used to being rejected. Quite the contrary, he is used to having his way in all things."

"'I wish I knew how to have *my* way in all things."

"Then learn from him, watch him, take from him—but be on your guard. He's a very dangerous man and he seems obsessed by you."

"May I ask you again how you know all this?"

Vieri looked across the square at the fountains gushing water and the picturesque buildings of pale amber stone that had stood for centuries. He loved this square when it was full of people and when it was emptying, as now, of all but the most persistent nightbirds. His reply left Sarah longing to ask more questions.

"My friends are not all listed in the *Almanac de Gotha;* I have some who know di Castelli personally." She understood at once that he would say no more.

At four A.M. waiters stood patiently by, watching as Vieri and Sarah talked. There were only two other clients in the café and a few tired night workers walking slowly home across the square. Dawn was breaking, streaking the dark night sky with amber and pink, and somewhere in the distance music drifted on the still air like an old, haunting love song. Gradually, as the sky lightened, the music grew louder, the tinkling notes an invitation to romance.

Looking across the square, Vieri saw three young men in medieval dress. They were students earning extra money by playing outside cafés. One carried a balalaika, one a mandolin, and the third a violin. All looked tired and were obviously on their way home after a none-too-successful evening on the Via Veneto. Vieri handed some cash to one of the waiters, who hurried across the piazza and spoke to the musicians. Then he watched as they took their places by the fountain and played the music generations of lovers had adored: ancient, long-forgotten melodies from Naples and the last waltz from *Floralie*. Vieri held out his arms to Sarah.

"Shall we dance?"

Surprised, she looked around the deserted square, at the old roadsweeper clearing up the debris of a thousand tourists and the waiters in their impeccable black and white. From a high window a young girl was watching the scene, and to

the east the sky was pure gold as the sun came up over the
horizon. Sarah moved into Vieri's arms, and as the music
swelled they danced together around the square. Closing her
eyes, she tried to remember every precious detail of the
scene—every sparrow picking at crumbs under the tables,
every flicker of lamplight on the fountains. Vieri smelled of
cigar smoke and lemons, and as his body drew closer to
hers, Sarah longed to do all the things she had only read
about until now. Instead, as the music of the balalaika trembled in the air, she let him draw her into a darkened doorway
and kiss her goodnight. She felt Vieri's hands cupping her
face and shivered as she saw the expression in his eyes.
Then his lips touched hers and she began to move instinctively against the hardness of his body. The kiss was slow at
first, his lips closing on hers, the tongue darting like a tiny
probe into her throat. Sarah wound her arms around his
neck, and as Vieri began to thrust more aggressively, she
opened her mouth to admit him, closing tightly around the
ever-searching tongue. Images of what he was really wanting to do flashed through her mind and she let him push her
back against the wall and kiss her throat and her shoulders.
Forceful emotions filled her mind and tears began to fall
down her cheeks, wetting Vieri's face. Then, suddenly, the
spell broke and he stepped back and stroked her hair, obviously shocked by the force of her emotion and the power of
his own.

"Why are you crying?"

"I don't know. Perhaps no one ever made me feel like
that before. Or perhaps I never wanted to."

The regal mask slipped and Vieri grasped her again in his
arms, so her head was on his chest near the pounding of his
heart. He was thinking of the directness of her words and the
feelings she had provoked in him, feelings he too was unused to experiencing. For a moment the image of his fiancée
flashed before his eyes and he frowned at the thought of

Mariannina's perfection. Then Sarah raised her face to his and he bent his head and kissed her on the cheeks, the lips, the shoulders, pulling back only when he knew he was in danger of losing control.

From the darkness of the ancient porch, Vieri led Sarah across the square to the car. As they drove away, the music of the troubadors faded until they could hear it no more. Vieri felt a pang of regret and a moment of intense sadness. He was wondering if it had all been an illusion, an enchanted moment never to be experienced again. He told himself that he was the head of one of the great families of Europe and soon to be married into another family of similar background, but the thought was hollow. He tried to remind himself of the responsibilities instilled since childhood and told himself he must avoid Sarah. She was temptation with a capital *T,* all the more potent because of her innocence and lack of guile. But she could never be more to him than a mistress, a plaything to be installed in a deluxe apartment to sit by the telephone waiting for his calls. Vieri sighed wearily, unwilling to contemplate such a situation for her or anyone.

At the gate of the street market, they left the car and walked hand in hand around the stalls. Conscious that Vieri's mood had changed and that he was already preparing for the moment of parting, Sarah tried hard not to show her disappointment and to take an interest in the merchandise that ranged from majolica tiles to secondhand radios, from copies of Michelangelo's best-known works to antique lace and slabs of Carrara marble. Finally, she watched as Vieri purchased an Edwardian chain of gossamer-thin gold, the locket studded with amethysts. He put this around her neck, looking into her eyes with the searching, questioning gaze she had come to know and love.

"I give you this as a souvenir of a beautiful evening. I so enjoyed being with you. Now I must drive you back to the apartment. I promised to take Elio to the airport at eight."

Unable to park the car in the street where Sarah lived, Vieri left it in the Piazza di Spagna, bought all the white daisies from the flower vendor, and put them in her arms. His face was soft as he walked with her across the square.

"You told me daisies were your favorite flowers. Think of me when you see them."

"I think of you far too much."

Sarah walked in silence to the entrance of the apartment, biting her lips so as not to cry. When she had opened the outer door with a big iron key, she held out her hand to Vieri, but he ignored it and stepped inside the dark inner courtyard, pausing only when he reached the stairway that led to the apartment.

"Thanks again for a lovely evening, Sarah. It was quite an experience to hear you talking about the postal system in China in the days of Kublai Khan, the Czar of Russia's affair with Catherine Dolgoruky, and the price of shares on the London Stock Exchange."

Sarah shrugged wryly.

"I'm a mine of useless information."

As she spoke, a solitary tear fell down her cheek and she looked suddenly like a child at the end of a birthday treat. Despite his better judgment, Vieri took the flowers from her, put them on the ground, and held her in his arms.

"You're not to be sad. You have your whole life before you and I'm sure it will be a wonderful one."

"Kiss me again, Vieri. Kiss me to last a *long, long,* time."

Their lips met and again Sarah's body seemed to soar. The scent of his skin filled her with longing, and for a moment time was suspended as she struggled to get as close to Vieri as possible, her mouth on his, her heart against his, their hands entwined. She wanted to sob out loud for all the heartbreak she was feeling, when he stepped back and finally took his leave.

"I return to Venice in the morning, so we shan't meet again in Rome."

"I'll look forward to the next time."

Vieri hesitated. Then he strode to the massive outer door and disappeared from view. Sarah took one of the rosebuds from her hair and ran after him, slipping it into his inner pocket.

"Souvenir of a beautiful evening."

"Look after yourself, Sarah. Perhaps we'll meet again in Paris."

Sarah walked upstairs to the apartment, threw herself on the bed, and gazed at the ceiling. She was going over every word Vieri had said during the evening, when Mary-Ellen hurried into the room.

"Umberto's been looking for you. He called eleven times during the night and he's *screaming!*"

"To hell with Umberto. I'm in love."

"Oh, Sarah, don't be. Vieri's not for you, and you know it. Now, why don't you change your clothes and we'll go eat breakfast at the Café Greco. It's only a couple of hundred yards from here. If Umberto comes around, he'll think we went out early to the flea market. Holly told him you'd taken a sleeping pill and couldn't be disturbed, but he didn't believe a word of it."

In the café where Stendhal, Shelley, Bizet, and Corot once gathered, Sarah and Mary-Ellen sat together eating croissants with raspberry jam and drinking cups of milky coffee. Mary-Ellen was worried. Sarah had insisted on wearing the necklace Vieri had bought her and was obviously head over heels in love. Used to disillusion and the hurt it brings, the older girl sighed.

"Look, Sarah, you're heading for trouble. Vieri's engaged and he won't ever break it off. It just isn't done in his world."

"I can't help what I feel. What can I do?"

"You can be realistic. It's nineteen sixty-seven and these are hard times. You're not Cinderella and you just can't wave a magic wand and have that man."

"Let me dream a little. I never let myself dream before. I always lived my life like the robot Mother trained to do her bidding."

"I just don't want you to get hurt. Here, have some more coffee and tell me everything."

Umberto drove from the Excelsior Hotel to the square near Sarah's apartment. As he walked toward the entrance, his heart was pounding with anger and there was something in his face that struck fear in the hearts of the early-morning stall holders of the Via della Croce. He was thinking of Benedetti's description of the night before. . . . *I've no idea where Sarah went. She was dressed in white with rosebuds in her hair, and she looked like a princess.* Umberto swallowed hard. When he got his hands on Holly he would beat her to a pulp for her lies of the previous night. He ran upstairs and hammered on the door of the apartment until Arlette appeared, her face covered with a white paste mask.

"Really, Mr. di Castelli, it's seven-ten and you knock loud enough to wake the whole building."

"Where is Sarah?"

"She and Mary-Ellen went to the Café Greco for breakfast."

"And Holly?"

"She's gone to buy figs for lunch."

"And where was Sarah all the night?"

Arlette glowered down at Umberto.

"I have no idea where she was. I went to the Hosteria del Orso and came home at two-thirty. You telephoned every fifteen minutes until six, and none of us has been able to sleep. Now, *please* go away. As Sarah never goes out at night, I suppose she was in her room, but I really don't know and I don't care.''

''She was out—don't tell lies.''

Arlette fixed Umberto with a baleful gaze.

''Sarah is twenty years old and unattached, and you have no right whatever to behave like this. You are married, and if you make more of these telephone calls that ruin my beauty sleep *I* shall make a phone call or two to your wife. Now please go away. I am not in the mood for unnecessary dramatic confrontations.''

''I remember what you say today, Arlette. You remember always that Umberto di Castelli has a very long memory.''

''Remember your own situation and leave the girl alone,'' Arlette retorted coldly and slammed the door.

Sarah and Mary-Ellen were on their third cup of coffee when Umberto appeared like a black cloud hovering over their table. His face was paler than usual and there was a look in his eyes that gave Sarah a momentary feeling of apprehension. She concealed this, however, and called for a waiter to bring more coffee as she motioned for Umberto to sit at her side.

''What are you doing here?''

''Where were you last night?''

''I went out to dinner with a friend. I ate ice cream in the Piazza Navona and danced with him to the music of a balalaika. Then we went to the market at the Porta Portese and finally home. I changed my clothes, took a shower, and Mary-Ellen invited me here for breakfast. Now you have a full account of my movements. Why are you looking so angry?''

''Who is he? I demand to know who he is!''

Sarah stared disbelievingly at the question.

''That is none of your business, Umberto.''

He roared his fury at her, ignoring the startled glances of waiters and breakfast clients.

"Who is he? You tell me or I—"

Before he could stop her, Sarah rose and walked briskly from the café.

Mary-Ellen put a restraining hand on Umberto's arm.

"Cool it, friend. You're angry but she's angrier. You can't own Sarah; no one can."

"She make love with a man and stay with him all the night."

"Don't be ridiculous. Sarah never made love in her life."

"Why did she stay out all the night?"

"She probably enjoyed his company."

"Who is he?"

"I don't know. She would probably have told me if you hadn't arrived."

"But you *know*. You are the one who know everything about Sarah."

"Drink your coffee. It'll make you feel better."

"Don't treat me like a child."

"Then quit acting like one. Sarah's not for you. She'll never love you and she's not the kind of woman you can teach to obey like your pet poodle."

"I kill him when I find who he is."

"That would be stupid. If you kill him he becomes a martyr in Sarah's eyes. Now, I'd best get back to the apartment. We have a rehearsal at ten and we need all the rest we can get before we leave for the theater. Your calls didn't make for a settled night."

Umberto had his hand on the door of his car when he saw the Aldobrandini chauffeur delivering something to the *portiera* of Sarah's building. When the chauffeur had gone, he went to speak with the woman and then returned to his car. The package had been square and wrapped in the cream and gold paper of a famous city bookshop. It had been addressed to Sarah Hallam. Rage blinded Umberto's judgment and he sat for a time in the car, wild thoughts rushing through his head like trains through a tunnel. He told himself he must obtain proof that his suspicions were correct. Then he would do what had to be done. He wanted Sarah, and nothing and no one in the world would stop him. He looked at his watch, verifying the time with a clock nearby. Then he drove away, furious, because all the clocks in the city gave different times, despite the gun fired at noon each day to tell the inhabitants of the Eternal City the hour. For Umberto, Rome had been an experience to forget as quickly as possible.

In the apartment, Sarah unwrapped a book with a gilded leather cover. It was a collector's piece entitled *Love Letters*. Inside, Vieri had written a note. *People said things in such a beautiful way in times past, didn't they? I particularly like the letter on page 110.*

Turning to the page, Sarah saw that it was a letter from Byron to his lover. *You are the sun and the moon to me. I deny myself sleep, the better to spend all my waking hours thinking of you.*

Chapter Five

Sarah, Palermo, October 1967

Palermo was beautiful, secret and full of strange contrasts. The sky was cobalt-blue, the buildings cream stone, in style a mixture of Arabic Phoenician and Italian baroque. The weather was perfect and everything went well until three days after opening night, when Sarah arrived for the eleven A.M. rehearsal and glanced at Liz's copy of *Le Matin*. There, on the front page, was a picture of Vieri and Mariannina at their engagement party held the previous evening at Maxim's and the Chateau of Vaux-le-Vicomte. Sarah read every line of the account, then burst into tears and sobbed her heart out. She was being foolish and she knew it, because Vieri had always been engaged and had made no promises to her about the future. Yet in her heart she had hoped he was fond of her, that he might delay or even cancel the wedding. She had told herself a thousand times that he did not love Mariannina and, more important, that he was drawn to her. Was it true? Or was it a feeling engendered by her own longing for it to be true? A thousand thoughts tore through her mind, the predominating one being that she wanted to die. Tears gushed down her cheeks like a fountain and even Mary-Ellen could do nothing to reassure her. At last, ashamed of her outburst, Sarah ran to the dressing room, colliding with Benedetti because she was blinded by tears. Behind her, the rehearsal began. Before her, Benedetti was holding out his arms.

"Whatever has upset you? Tell me what it is."

"I just want to be alone."

Sarah ran from him and sat gazing at her face in the dressing-room mirror. As she looked at the red, swollen eyes she thought resignedly that she must not make a fool of herself over Vieri, but the tears began to fall again. Soon she was lying on the daybed in the corner, crying out the anguish that was tearing at her heart. She had been an idiot, imagining that because she had fallen in love with Vieri he had fallen in love with her. It was not true and she knew it. His world was not hers, his training and conditioning in life had probably precluded his ever feeling deep passion. Sarah sobbed for herself and for the man she loved, certain she would never get over what had happened and unwilling to try.

Umberto arrived in Palermo after four weeks in Paris, rushed to the theater, and sat back contentedly to watch the rehearsal. Then, realizing that Sarah was absent, he hurried to Benedetti's office to find out where she was. He was in an excellent humor, because Vieri's engagement party had been the talk of the city before his departure and at last he was feeling more secure in his chances with Sarah. After he had embraced his brother-in-law, he spoke of Sarah.

"What happen to her? Why is she not onstage with the others?"

"Sarah's upset. I ordered coffee for her from the Café Romanella with some of their fig tart. She can't resist fig tart, and if she won't eat that I'll know it's serious."

"Serious! What happen? Does she say why she is upset?"

"She's sobbing so hard she can't put two words together."

"I go ask her what is wrong."

"Leave her be, Umberto. She's heartbroken."

"She is in love?"

"In my opinion, yes."

"You know who he is?"

Benedetti shrugged, unwilling to condemn Vieri to a life of purgatory for no good reason. He was shocked when Umberto smiled the dark saturnine smile that to some was worse than a death sentence.

"I know who he is. It is Vieri Aldobrandini. I check when I was in Paris."

"How did you check?"

"I ask him. You know what he say? 'Ah, yes, Sarah Hallam, a most charming young lady. I took her out to dinner when I was in Rome and she talked about the most fascinating things.' Ha! I wonder what she tell him. I see a look in his eyes that tell me Mariannina is going to have competition."

Just then a waiter appeared with coffee, cake, and a silver dish of sugared almonds. Umberto took the tray and walked upstairs to the dancers' dressing room, alarmed to find Sarah on the daybed, her body convulsed by sobs. A copy of the Paris issue of *Le Matin* was on the floor, the photograph of Vieri on the front page. Umberto put the coffee tray down on the makeup bench and threw the newspaper in the wastebasket.

"You take two lumps or three?"

"No sugar."

"Mario order fig tart for you."

"I don't want it."

"You eat anyway. Sit up and I help you drink the coffee. Now tell me why you cry."

"I can't discuss it."

"You are too English."

"I can't change and I don't want to."

Umberto shrugged helplessly and kissed her hand.

"For you, Sarah, I change and learn to be an English gentleman."

She smiled despite herself at the very idea. Sensing his small gain, Umberto handed her a cup of coffee and sat at her side while she drank. He continued talking to distract her.

"I shall stay in Palermo for two weeks and I take care of you. When you stop crying I show you my family home."

Sarah let him hold her hand, touched when he spoke from the heart.

"You cry because of that man and you must not. Men like him are born different from people like us. They understand nothing but the heritage, the responsibility of their great position and the need to continue the family. They don't care about feelings and passion. Maybe they don't *have* feelings. Even when they do they don't take no notice of them, because the whole life is planned when they are born."

"I don't want to talk about him."

"You want only to cry?"

"I haven't cried like this since I was eleven."

"Well, the crying is over, because *I* am here. First you drink the coffee. Then we go see my house. Then I bring you back for the performance. Tomorrow is Sunday and there will be no show, so we spend it together. You are not allow to say no. From today I decide what is good for you. I told you before, I am the man for you. I teach you all you want to learn. I make you a very important person. With me, there is nothing you cannot do or be. You dream of having a business, I arrange. You want to own clubs, you can. You become rich and powerful if you stay with Umberto."

Sarah thought wryly that one thing he could never give her was Vieri. She shook her head then, as if trying to rid herself of the very thought of him, accepting that she must put ideas of love behind her for the moment. Vieri had said she was just starting out on life and it was true. She had her

whole future before her and must not spoil it for a man who
could never be hers. Still, tears filled her eyes whenever she
dwelled on the magic moment in Rome, when they had
danced together in the Piazza Navona. She would never forget that, and she knew that if she lived another fifty years
nothing would ever equal it for sheer enchantment.

At Umberto's insistence, Sarah ate the tart and drank another cup of coffee. Then she followed him to the big black
car with its funereal windows and was driven out of the city
on to the road to Monreale.

The landscape was sepia, every blade of grass and fur-
rowed field bleached by the sun's torrid heat. There were
few trees and the tough vegetation was full of unexpected
barbs, like the inhabitants of the area. Esparto grass with
knife-sharp blades vied with thistles and corn stubble to hurt
the unwary. The air was still, the only sounds the howl of
the sirocco and the rattle of cicadas in a thorn tree. The
countryside was flat, with a narrow road winding like a
white ribbon upward to the palazzo on the hill. In the deep-
blue sky, black-winged ravens wheeled over the only sign of
life, a shepherd walking with a flock of ragged brown goats
over the stony track that led at a distance to Palermo.

Umberto relaxed visibly as they drew nearer the property,
because this was the real Sicily, the place where his roots
were and his heart would always be. He remembered the
days of childhood and enjoyed the scene as they passed
through a hamlet, where women were sitting outside their
houses drying figs, pounding tomato paste, bathing babies,
and sorting through piles of grass to be stuffed into mat-
tresses for their beds. Hens, goats, cats, and dogs ran everywhere. Then, as they passed the last of the houses, the
silence returned and only the lament of the wind and the
swirling white clouds of dust revealed that this was not a
painting, but a real place of passion, drama, deception, and
the legendary laws of *omerta*.

The Palazzo di Castelli was one of the finest remaining examples of Sicilian baroque on the island. In the seventeenth and eighteenth centuries there had been many like it, but gradually the style had fallen out of favor. Built to the plans of Filippo Juvara in 1714, the apricot-tinted complex rose above a palm-shaded courtyard. Inside, majolica floors painted with the labors of Hercules echoed the Capri blue of a multifaceted cupola. The rooms were cool and dark, full of ebony furniture and richly textured velvets in claret and aubergine. Faded tapestries covered the entrances to secret passages used by the lawless as hideouts in times past. And in the salon, where Umberto led Sarah at the end of the tour of the ground floor, statues by Marabitti vied for the visitors' attention with olive moiré walls and magnificent tortoiseshell cabinets.

He turned to Sarah, eager to have her reaction.

"Well, what do you think of my home?"

"It's magnificent, not at all what I expected! I thought it would be white, very low and light, with a fig tree outside. This is a palace."

Umberto rang for wine to be brought and smiled expansively.

"Next, I show you the grounds, but first we drink to you and to friendship."

Sarah looked from the Murano-glass chandeliers into his intent eyes, then to a deferential servant pouring Marsala into gilded glasses and watching her with hawklike interest. She raised her glass.

"To friendship, Umberto."

He leaned forward to clink glasses with her, aware that for the first time he had the advantage, thanks to Vieri Aldobrandini. He knew he must tread warily, however, and not shock Sarah. That tension made his body feel alive; he was an animal ready to pounce. He poured them more wine and held out his hand.

"Now I show you something very interesting. In the Palazzo Castelli I give you your first lesson in power."

Sarah took the outstretched hand, and together they passed from the house through the garden to the fields beyond. Thistles scratched her legs, making them bleed, but she did not hesitate, curious to know what Umberto was going to show her as they moved together toward a well that had fallen into disuse. She picked an ear of corn. Its pale-gold length was covered with tiny white snails, and Sarah plucked them off one by one with gentle fingers. Then, tilting her head, she listened to the barking of wild dogs on a distant hillside.

Umberto squeezed her hand.

"The dogs are far away and I will not let them harm you. Now watch closely, Sarah, and remember what you see."

Lifting a white limestone boulder, he took from underneath it a lizard, its body long and light-brown, like a miniature crocodile. Gently he placed it on the ground, a small distance from Sarah's feet. Then he whispered to her.

"See how he looks into my eyes. He is still sleepy, because we wake him in the heat of the day."

Sarah watched as Umberto fashioned a running noose from a long piece of esparto grass, his hands moving slowly but with infinite skill and care. All the while, his big black eyes were fixed on the lizard, which watched him, its basilic gaze unblinking. Breathless with excitement, Sarah watched as Umberto slipped the noose over the lizard's head, his gaze never wavering from the reptile's face. His voice made her shiver.

"*Eccolo!* He is looking into my eyes and has forgotten to watch what my hands are doing. It is a mistake and he pays for it with his life."

With one rapid, snapping movement, the noose was tightened and the lizard fluttered at the end of the grass blade like a stranded fish, swinging back and forth between Sarah and the man who wanted to teach her his way of life. For a moment, the silence was infinite. Then he spoke in his low, husky voice.

"Never forget the lizard, Sarah. When you are face to face with an enemy, make him watch the eyes; distract him so he forgets to watch your hands. Then you have him where you want him and he is powerless to see the danger."

Umberto weighed the flush in Sarah's cheeks, the languor in her body, and held out his hand.

"I am thirsty. We return to the house and drink a pitcher of orange juice and then I show you the rest of the property."

There were bedrooms with six-posters hung with priceless Turkish brocade. Others had beds carved from ancient olive trunks and hung with white embroidered panels made by women from a nearby village. The last bedroom was all in white, with gauze curtains that fluttered in the breeze. As she stood at the window, looking out at the sun-dappled landscape, Sarah felt Umberto kissing her neck. This time she did not pull away. She was thinking of the moment when he had tightened the noose on the lizard. It had looked so easy, but had probably taken years to learn, as she must learn so many things. She had understood the meaning of the lesson: Distract the adversary, so he lowers his guard, the Sicilian method of shaking hands while a *compadre* puts the knife in the back. She forgot everything when she felt the hardness of Umberto's body pressing against hers, his breath on her back, his hands moving to caress her breasts. Then he handed her a glass of champagne from an ice bucket that had appeared magically on the bedside table. Sarah drank because she was thirsty and then held out her glass to be refilled, because she wanted to forget the agony of Vieri. Mary-Ellen had told her once that a great lover made you forget everything, and Sarah trusted her friend's opinion on such things. Closing her eyes for a moment, she felt Umberto turning her about to face him, so he could kiss her full on the mouth. She gazed at him, shivering as he spoke.

"I want to love you, Sarah."

He watched the thought passing through her mind and waited, trying to hide the longing and the anxiety he was feeling. Her reply made him want to cry out with elation.

"I'm not running away."

He gripped Sarah by the shoulders and drew her to him, thrusting into her mouth with a kiss that took her breath away. Then he threw back the covers of the bed, locked the door, and returned to where she was standing, drowsy from the champagne and uncertain of herself. He knew he must take her quickly, before she panicked or changed her mind. He wondered if she had ever been loved before, or if he would be the first man and the one to make her his own for always. He unbuttoned the white blouse and threw it onto the chaise longue. Then, as Sarah stood quite still and unresisting, he unhooked the bra with its satin shoulder straps and pattern of English roses. Her breasts were fuller than he had expected, and as he cupped them, the nipples hardened like ripe fruit. He untied the skirt and slipped down the panties. Then he picked her up and carried her to the bed, savoring the glazed look in her eyes, the violent trembling of her limbs.

"You made love before, Sarah?"

She shook her head, her eyes suddenly showing the fear in her heart. Umberto spoke reassuringly.

"Maybe it hurt for a moment, but I try hard to be very gentle."

He placed her arms above her head, triumphant at the lack of resistance. She was his to do with as he wanted and the very thought inflamed him. Throwing off his clothes, he lay at her side, caressing her, tasting the sensitive nipples and then moving with gentle hands from her stomach to the mound of fair hair and the honeyed secretions of the place he wanted to possess.

As his fingers began to titillate, Sarah clutched the barley-twirled bedposts, her breath coming fast through her lungs. Umberto's fingers quickened on her clitoris, hardening the pressure until she cried out as the first orgasm took away fear and replaced it with ecstasy. Moving her legs apart, she felt him put a pillow under her bottom, raising her most secret parts to his gaze. She wondered if she was going to faint or if lovemaking was always an intoxicating route to amnesia.

Holding Sarah down with powerful hands, Umberto entered her body, exultant to feel the resistance of the hymen and to hear her cry of pain and pleasure as it broke. He plunged on, thrusting like a piston until he brought her again to orgasm. Then, suddenly, the passive creature of moments previously vanished and Sarah clutched him around the neck, her mouth seeking his. Excited beyond recall, Umberto's body quickened, until, oscillating before her, he cried out, one loud, joyful exclamation of pleasure as he poured love into her in the moment of giving.

Touched to find tears in Sarah's eyes, he took her in his arms and kissed her gently, rocking her back and forth in the age-old Sicilian way.

"You are the perfect lover for me." She stroked his hands with fingers still trembling from the confusing emotions that had assailed her with such force. At the moment of ecstasy she had soared like a bird on the wing. Then, as sadness replaced elation, she thought how she had dreamed of living that moment with Vieri. Determined not to dwell on the agony of unrequited love, Sarah wiped the tears from her eyes. Mary-Ellen had been right. She must not waste herself on a dream. Yet again, though, images of the Piazza Navona came into her mind and the lilting of the balalaika and the mandolin made her smile. Though that would be her only memory of Vieri, nothing would ever dim its radiance.

Umberto clutched Sarah to his heart, closing his eyes and savoring the magic moment when he had made her his own. It had been one of the great moments of his life and he knew he would never forget it. He wanted to rush out and buy her half of Palermo. Instead, he lay very still, enjoying the scent of her skin and the feel of her fingers stroking his back.

Within minutes Sarah began to stir at the memory of what had happened between them. She felt Umberto's hands again on her breasts, this time not as gentle as before. She gasped as he pulled the nipples close together so he could bite them both at the same time. Then, as he pushed her down on his rigid penis, she began to devour him as she knew he wanted to be devoured—eagerly, longingly, and with genuine hunger. Seconds later, to her intense excitement, Umberto lifted her over him and pulled her slowly down on his penis, like a tight-fitting glove. Within seconds he was deep inside her, satisfying the emptiness she had known for most of her life. Sarah began to writhe, to vibrate, to push back and forth, back and forth, withdrawing for a moment and then sliding again to the place that made him happy. Finally, unable to continue for the force of the feelings the movement provoked, she tightened over the penis and brought them both to orgasm, slipping like a butterfly on the bed, her arms outstretched, her fingers clutching the linen sheet, her eyes closed as wave after wave of intense feeling took her strength away.

While Sarah went to shower, Umberto lit a cigar and went to stand at the window, gazing out at the countryside he loved. After a while, he returned and looked down at the bloodstained sheet. Exultation, joy, shock, and something he had never felt before, pride in a woman, filled his heart. He thought only that he would fight to the death to keep this rare creature, who knew nothing of her own power and who was ignorant of the sensuality that would plague her for the rest of her life.

The following evening, Mary-Ellen was made up, ready for the opening, and impatient, as always, to hear the call for overture and beginners. She was gazing thoughtfully at Sarah, conscious of a subtle change in her friend, when a messenger brought her a note, which she read out to the others, interrupting the message with endless hoots of laughter.

"Listen to this! It's from that Spanish lawyer who took me out all the time in Seville. He's a worse speller than I am."

Holly called from across the room, "*He*'s spelling in a foreign language. *You*'ve no excuse for your perfectly horrible mistakes."

"Shut up, Holly, and listen.

"My dear Maria-Elena,

"I decided yestirday to fly to see you and hope you will dine with me. I am staing at the Palacio and will be in the city for one week. Please send your reppy back with the mesenjer. If you agree, I shall meet you after the last show. My complimints to you and my afecionate wishes. I will wait at the stage door.

"Luis Alarcon de Montevidal"

Sarah put on her headdress and secured it with pins. "Who is he?"

"He was always at the theater in Seville. He's very tall, thin, and black haired and he's related to the Duchess of Gijon. He has a lovely house with a patio near the river."

"Married? How old?"

"He's not married and he's thirty-eight. He took me out to dinner lots of times and we went to a private gambling club that's against the law. I won four thousand pesetas, but he lost his shirt. He must be very rich to lose like that and not flicker an eyelash.''

Sarah turned to Arlette, who had been in a black mood for days.

''Anything we can do to cheer you up?''

''I shall cheer up when I leave this island.''

''How's Charles?''

''He has the gout, but he sent me a most beautiful gift of a crucifix studded with seed pearls, so I shall excuse him for talking constantly of his health.''

Holly looked at the clock she kept on the makeup table.

''We're late opening—I wonder why. Madame's usually so strict about starting on time.''

Five minutes went by; then the call came for overture and beginners. Sarah hurried down at Holly's side.

''How's that mafioso who collected you from the theater the other night?''

Holly beamed conspiratorially.

''He's delicious. He offered to steal me a Ferrari and ship it to Paris to await my arrival. Imagine such a thing from a good, God-fearing father of ten!''

Sarah wondered if the Ferrari could be Vieri's. Had he come to Palermo to see her? She leaned forward and whispered to Holly, ''What color was the Ferrari?''

''Red. Don't worry, Sarah, it wasn't Vieri's. He's in the States with his fiancée. I read in the paper yesterday that they're guests of the Car Club of New York, which has borrowed the Aldobrandini collection of vintage Bugattis for an exhibition.''

Sarah sighed wearily. So, Vieri was still with Mariannina and still living the jet-set life they were both born to. What a fool she had been ever to think he might do otherwise. As the curtain rose, she stood tall, smiling as she had been trained to smile, furious to feel a tear trickling down her cheek. She told herself she must get back to reality and put her heart into her work. Then, as the audience applauded the opening tableau, she forgot Vieri in the enervating movements of the dance.

Umberto was in one of the boxes, training his opera glasses on Sarah. When he saw tears falling down her cheeks, he sighed. Was she still crying for Vieri? Had she seen his photograph again in the local paper? Rage filled his heart and with it pride as he saw her wipe the tears away and produce one of her wonderful mischievous smiles. After the show he had decided to drive Sarah to a restaurant on the beach and then, if she was willing, to the palazzo. There he would make her forget Aldobrandini or die in the attempt. If she was unwilling to stay with him overnight, they would leave Palermo early the following morning instead and stay together from breakfast time till dinner. The thought filled him with warm excitement and he wanted to rush down to the wings, grab Sarah, and take her away at once to the house on the hill. Instead, he began to make plans.

No one had yet been told that fifteen minutes before curtain up, Madame Rose had died suddenly in Benedetti's office. For complicated legal reasons, Umberto knew he would now have to return to Paris to discuss arrangements with the investors. In any case, only Vienna remained on the itinerary. After that, the company would return to Paris to be paid off. Umberto realized that if he wanted to keep Sarah he must move quickly and arrange new work for her in the capital. After that, he would study her closely and make himself indispensable in her life. He knew that she was attracted by the idea of power, though she was, as yet, barely aware of the extent of her ambition. He smiled, wondering if she had any idea what doors he could open, what dreams he could make come true when he had transformed her from the innocent young dancer to the woman of influence she could someday be.

* * *

Sarah sat in the moonlight, listening to the lapping of water on the beach and enjoying the wholesome smells of peasant cooking. They had eaten tuna with *fagioli* and a salad of local oranges with salt and oil. Then the owner had produced beef cooked with olives and the rough red wine of the region. Bearing in mind Mary-Ellen's advice not to let Umberto dictate his wishes to her all the time, Sarah had refused to spend the night at the palazzo. She had agreed, however, to be ready to leave at seven in the morning so they could breakfast there together. For the moment, she was content to listen as he explained his plans.

"Now the tour is getting to the end, you will need new work. I telephone a friend this evening and arrange a new contract for you for six months at the Lido. You do the butterfly solo and learn one new number. You will replace the principal dancer, who will work only one month more because she is pregnant."

"That's wonderful. It's definite? Even though they haven't seen me work?"

"They take my word for it."

"I'm very grateful, Umberto."

"Don't be grateful. I arrange also double the money you get now."

Sarah leaned over the table and kissed his cheeks, startled when he held her in a viselike grip and kissed her resoundingly on the mouth.

"You are everything to me, Sarah."

"No, I'm not, Umberto. You have a wife and family."

"They have what they need, but my wife does not get pregnant, no matter what I do. When she returns from the clinic in Switzerland, I will ask her if she take the pill. If she say yes, I think I kill her."

They walked together in the moonlight, his jacket around Sarah's shoulders in case "the lungs get disobedient." Now and then Umberto threw a stone in the water, pausing as he had as a boy to enjoy the plopping sound as it fell to the depths. At thirty-eight he felt fifteen years old again, as if he had regained his youth, his innocence, and the ability to enjoy life. He put his arm around Sarah, wishing he could change her mind about spending the night with him, but not daring to spoil the moment with an attempt at persuasion.

Sarah was trying to remember when she had last felt at peace with the world. In the earliest days of childhood, running in the poppy field behind the house, there had been moments of calm. Then everything had changed and she had never had a real explanation of what had occurred. Had the man who had visited that day so long ago been her mother's lover? Had he said good-bye, leaving Anna alone, broken, bitter? Sarah remembered the first time her mother had run away, leaving Sarah locked "for safety" in her room. Five hours later, she had been set free in a hysterical condition by a neighbor. Her mother had been found two days later in a disoriented state at a railway station fifty miles from her home. It had been the first of many such occasions, alternating with suicide attempts real and threatened.

Sarah felt Umberto's hand turning her face to his.

"You look sad. Tell me what is wrong?"

"I was thinking about my childhood and it made me unhappy. I try never to think about the past, but sometimes it surfaces."

"To hell with the childhood! To hell with the crazy mother. I make you happy. You want to change your mind and come to the palazzo tonight? You decide; I don't try to force you."

"I'll come, but I didn't bring my case."

"I send someone for it."

Sarah stood alone, looking out at the moonlit water while Umberto hurried inside to the telephone. In the bay she could see fishermen with lantern-lit boats, and in the distance she could hear the chug of a *tonnara* going out. The sea was so calm, it looked like black satin shot with silver. Sarah closed her eyes, willing herself to accept the fact that despite the loss of Vieri she was not alone. She was with a man who wanted and needed her, who could teach her all she needed to know. She was protected, cossetted, and adored. If Umberto was second best to Vieri, he was the most powerful and seductive second best she would ever find.

At dawn Sarah was at the window of the bedroom where she and her lover had slept. In the field nearby, a modern combine stood by the side of a donkey and a goat munching yellow flowers. The landscape was faded gold, the machine orange, the donkey and the goat brown. Yet again, Sarah thought how the scene looked like a painting and not reality. She asked herself if her relationship with Umberto was also unreal, a substitute for what she really wanted in life, a vivid make-believe embarked upon to bring comfort to a mind in torment.

Opening his eyes, Umberto savored the sight of Sarah's naked back, long legs, rounded buttocks, and powerful shoulders. His body began to stir and his penis to harden. He rose and moved behind Sarah, cupping her breasts in hands eager to excite.

She turned to face him, her eyes uncertain.

"What now? You want breakfast or. . . ?"

"I want to love you right here in front of the window."

"Someone's sure to see you."

"You are everything I adore, an angel and a villain and above all a puzzle I cannot understand. You will never bore me."

Sarah brushed his shoulder with her lips and then kneeled and caressed his penis, kissing it playfully and tasting it so he moaned from the effort of controlling the sexuality that burned in him like a furnace. Before she could provoke him further, he had pushed her down on the wolf-fur rug that covered the icy marble floor. Then, parting her legs, he ran his finger along the length of the clitoris, enjoying the spasmodic raising of her knees and the cry of pleasure he provoked. As he entered her, he felt again the sheer joy of possession. Then, looking at the unfathomable expression in Sarah's eyes, he whispered, "What are you thinking?"

"I'm still surprised to be here with you."

"I get the addiction, I think. Maybe I do it so much I *die* loving you."

Sarah wound her arms around his neck, rocking back and forth so that they changed positions and she, not he, was master of the game. Their movements became increasingly frenzied and soon she felt the approach of orgasm and then the violent sunburst when her body exploded like a firework. Below her, Umberto was panting, his hands caressing her body, his mouth uttering words she could not understand, words of love and desire in the only language with which he was really at ease.

They ate breakfast in bed, then dressed and walked from the palazzo through the olive groves, orchards, and bamboo thickets of the estate to the beach, where a fisherman was selling fresh-caught sardines. Having bought some for lunch, they returned through the sharp esparto grass to the outskirts of the Castelli land. Umberto pointed out the animals and reptiles of the area, many as dangerous as the razor-sharp vegetation.

"That is a gecko. He eat flies and mind his business. That one is a hornet. When you see one, you kill him, like that."

The hornet fell like a missile as Umberto's hand shot through the air with a swift chopping movement. Then they walked on in silence, passing a staff cottage on the land, its pastel-blue walls hung with bunches of myrtle to bring good fortune to the occupants. From a high point above the palazzo, they could see distant Palermo, the city Umberto loved. He motioned for Sarah to sit at his side and then put his arms around her.

"I leave for Paris on Friday. Say you are disappointed I go."

"I am. You said you'd stay two weeks."

"Because Madame Rose die, I have many things to arrange, but we shall be together when you arrive in Paris."

Sarah was silent for a moment, apprehensive because she realized that she had already started to need Umberto. Her mood changed when he continued. "Today I invite Mario to lunch. He will guard you in my absence."

Sarah looked alarmed for the first time since her arrival at the palazzo.

"I don't need a guard, Umberto. I'm not a prisoner."

"You need protection and Mario will do it. I don't want the *lupara* coming to the stage door to give you the temptation."

Sarah was first amazed, then amused, and then angry. She controlled her feelings, however, and spoke calmly.

"I let you make love to me, Umberto, and I like it when you do, but you're a married man and I'm just twenty and free. You don't own me and I told you from the beginning you never will."

Struggling against rising fury, panic, and rage, Umberto replied with equal calm, conscious that he was on dangerous ground.

"If I don't care for you, I leave you alone and ignore when the wild dogs attack you. But I *care*. So I ask Mario to protect you. You are free, but I am responsible and I want to be. Now we go back. Your legs are scratched. I will put cream on them for you."

Sarah showered in the white marble bathroom, closing her eyes in pleasure at the forceful jets of lukewarm water that cooled her burning body. The scratches on her legs were hurting and she winced as she stepped out of the shower and began to dry herself. Then she saw Umberto entering with ointment and a roll of gauze. His voice was soft and she was tempted to forgive him for being too possessive.

"Come, Sarah, lie on the bed and I spread a towel under the legs."

He began to massage cream into her ankles, feet, and calves, kissing her knees and thighs as desire tantalized. When he had put gauze over the worst of the scratches and secured it with tape, he bent forward and kissed her stomach, breathless with anticipation when she motioned him to her side.

"Is this all part of the treatment for scratched legs? Are you going to lick the cream off next?"

"I love you and someday you love me, too."

Umberto saw the frown, but cared nothing for Sarah's resistance. Instead, he bent his head and kissed her full on the mouth, exploring the warmth with his tongue, as he would soon explore the wetness of the place he had possessed. Before she could stop him, he had pushed her legs apart and was thrusting with a hard, inquisitive tongue inside her, trembling with excitement when she writhed at the sensuous feelings he provoked. His fingers found her clitoris and moved with rhythmic strokes, forever searching until she cried out in abandon, her body arching as he brought her to orgasm.

They were lying together after love, when they heard the sound of a car making its way up the hill to the palazzo. Umberto rose and began to dress.

"That will be Mario. When you are ready, you join us. Wear the white dress with daisies that I like best of all."

Having bent to kiss her shoulder, he disappeared. Only a faint tremor in the hands betrayed the force of emotion he had just experienced.

Sarah lay still for a while, letting her body grow calm. Making love was addictive, as Umberto had said. Once you started doing it, you wanted to continue and to keep on until your body was too tired to move. She rose and went to the bathroom to shower. Then, as she dressed, she went over what Umberto had said about Mario guarding her during his absence. Increasingly uneasy and disquieted, she knew only too well that Umberto had the Sicilian mentality, that he believed because he had possessed her body he owned her forever. He must be taught that it was not so, but how?

They ate prawns in *aioli,* then sea strawberries, tiny squid served with saffron rice and a red sauce. The servants wore white gloves, each one moving silently, skillfully, always there when required with whatever each person needed. The atmosphere was relaxed until Umberto started to talk about his departure for Paris.

"Promise me you watch the local men, Mario. That one Rosario Valente has already got the eye for Sarah. He always want what I have—his cousin Vincenzo, too. You make sure he understand that she is mine."

Sarah stared openmouthed at this. Then she spoke in a soft voice that belied the expression in her eyes.

"I belong to myself, Umberto."

"You belong to *me!* You don't know it yet, but you do and you always will."

He recoiled in shock when Sarah roared across the table at him.

"Take that back, you unmitigated bastard! Don't ever think you own me because we made love. I'm a free bird and I want to stay that way. I'll do what I want with my body now and in the future!"

Umberto struck her a sharp blow to the cheek, stunned when Sarah dragged the lace cloth from the table, shattering priceless glasses, plates, and everything in sight, as she had once before in the dressing room in Paris. Then she ran from the room and out onto the terrace. Umberto ran after her, catching up as she rushed down the drive toward the road.

"Come back! You want to get hurt?"

"Go to hell, Umberto!"

He rushed back to the terrace, got into his car, and drove at speed after Sarah, screeching to a halt at her side.

"Get in, please, and we talk."

Enraged, she kicked the car, making a small dent in the side. Then she walked on, her face scarlet with anger.

Umberto shouted furiously, "Get into the car! You crazy or something?"

By way of a reply, Sarah struck him a glancing blow to the side of the head, but he was too fast for her. Yanking her by the arm, he pulled her headfirst into the car and drove back to the palazzo.

Umberto dragged Sarah into the dining room and pushed her down on the chair she had recently vacated. He was about to roar at her when he saw the warning look on Benedetti's face and closed his mouth. Instead, he rang for coffee and *strega*, sitting with as much dignity as he could muster at the head of the table, while the staff served liqueurs amid splintered glass, broken pottery, and piles of antique linen red-stained with wine. After what seemed like an age, he spoke.

"I am sorry I hit you, Sarah. Please forgive me."

"I don't forgive you, you bastard."

"You want to be bad all the time like your mother?"

"I want to be *me*. You won't ever change that."

Benedetti watched in fascination as the two faced each other across the table like a pair of fighting bulls. He was about to say a conciliatory word when Sarah snatched the keys from the sideboard, dashed out of the house, and drove away in Umberto's big black car.

Left alone to watch her departure, Umberto roared his frustration from the terrace. Men came running, orders were given, and two brothers were dispatched to bring her back. Then Umberto returned to the dining room and flopped down at the head of the table, surveying the debris with despairing eyes.

"She is a savage. Somehow, I have to break her."

Benedetti spoke patiently.

"Don't be a fool. You've made enough errors for one day."

"What am I to do, Mario?"

"You start all over again. Send her flowers. Go on your knees and apologize."

"Never! I kill her first."

"Then you'll lose the game. You don't seem to realize that you need and want Sarah more than she needs or wants you. Someday, if you're very clever, you'll reverse the situation, but for the moment, she's the one who dictates what she wants."

Umberto walked to the terrace and stood looking out at the silent landscape. The black car was a dot on the horizon, but it had stopped moving. Puzzled, he called for Benedetti to get out the other car. Minutes later, they found his own vehicle deliberately smashed into the rock face of a hillside ten kilometers from the palazzo. While Benedetti did his best to be comforting, Umberto stood gazing in silent fascination at the crumpled metal frame.

"Sarah do that deliberate, you know. She is a fiend."

"Then leave her alone."

"I cannot. I love her and you know it."

"You never loved anyone in your life."

"It's true, but now I am sick with the love. She smash my car and next time she smash my head. She is capable of anything. She is magnificent and terrible. Send more men out to find her, and when you find her bring her to the palazzo. She cannot have gone far. She was wearing only her thin shoes and the thorns will cut her feet. Madonna, I need a brandy. My head ache like I drank a river."

Bereft of comfort, suffering as he had never suffered because of a woman, Umberto took from his pocket a letter from his son. He tried to calm his nerves by reading again the affectionate lines . . . Dearest Papa, I am top of my class and I am so happy because you will be proud of me for beating the Count of Luxembourg's son into second place. Yesterday I fell off my horse, but I am uninjured. I will send you a copy of the class photograph soon. In the meantime, I send you my love and respect. Your son, Pietro.

Umberto wiped a tear from his eye, his emotions in a turmoil. The letter was wonderful and he loved his son dearly, but Pietro's words could not assuage the shock and the hurt Sarah had inflicted and he turned with a despairing shrug to Benedetti.

While Umberto and Mario were consoling one another, Sarah was sitting on a cart loaded with bamboo en route to Palermo with six children and the farmer's wife. There was a faint smile on her face and laughter in her heart as she thought of what Umberto would do when he found his precious car crumpled like a broken toy.

Chapter Six

Vienna–Paris, November 1967

Everyone loved Vienna, with its scarlet streetcars, carnation-bedecked carriages, and old-world charm. There was, therefore, a melancholy atmosphere as the company gathered onstage to drink champagne after the last performance of the Ballet Rose. In the morning, they would take the train for Paris and assemble on arrival at the Théâtre de l'Empire to be paid. That would be the end. Dancers who had once been hostile to the newies linked hands and sang "Auld Lang Syne." Liz astonished everyone by kissing Sarah resoundingly on the cheek and pronouncing her a good kid with the makings of a real bastard, the highest compliment she could construct.

Arlette raised her glass to the others.

"To friendship and luck for us all in the future."

Mary-Ellen clinked her glass against Arlette's.

"To you, froggie. I hope the Duke proposes tonight so we can all come to the wedding before we leave Paris."

Sarah turned to Mary-Ellen with a smile.

"And what about you and Luis? I saw him in the box again."

"He couldn't get a seat for the last night, so Benedetti let him use the directors' box. Umberto would be furious if he knew. He's so possessive about things he thinks are his."

"Are you thinking of marrying Luis?"

"God knows. The thought of marriage scares the hell out of me, but I love Spain and feel at home there and he's been so very kind."

Sarah spoke reassuringly, despite her doubts.

"Don't do anything rash—that's my only advice. You don't know anything at all about Luis. Make a few inquiries of your own before you accept any proposal of marriage."

"You're getting more like Umberto every day. Make inquiries indeed!"

Holly was fastening a dress of emerald silk shot with Tuscan blue that matched her eyes. She was going to dinner with a producer who had already tested her for a small role in a film to be shot in Egypt. As she brushed her hair one last time, she looked across the room at Sarah.

"What are you going to do tonight?"

"I'll go to bed early, so I can wake you three in the morning. We don't want to miss the train back to Paris."

Sarah took a horse-drawn fiacre from the theater, ordering the driver to take her home via the boulevards in the center of the city. In a crowded square she heard the melancholy chant of the lavender wives of Vienna, who had been selling sachets and blooms to scent linen cupboards for over two centuries. The driver paused in the traffic of late evening near Kugler's, once the imperial delicatessen, its windows full of sausages and cheese of a dozen nations. Outside Demel's, theatergoers were eating ice cream with champagne and whiskey, and in cafés on every street, merry-faced Viennese were drinking the new season's wine, a deceptively fragrant white renowned for raising the spirits.

Sarah thought wryly that on this last night in the city she could do with something to raise her spirits. She detested change, and the thought of arriving in Paris with nowhere to live was disturbing. It was also unsettling to lose the routine of living established over many months with the show. At least, thanks to Umberto, she had a job and a good salary for the next few months. She told herself she must stop worrying and start thinking in an optimistic way, but optimism was not in her nature and change made her afraid of everything. She thought how Umberto had not contacted her since their row in Palermo and wondered if he would have had the new contract nullified. Would she arrive in Paris and find there was no work, no security? For a fleeting moment Sarah thought of telephoning Umberto, but she knew she must not. He was the eager one and he always would be the one full of promises and declarations of love. She must simply control her anxiety and let him prove that he was a real friend. If he was not, he could go to hell with all the other people who had let her down.

The carriage stopped outside a block of apartments with geranium-bedecked balconies, where Sarah and her friends had been staying. She paid the driver, wished him good-night, and was about to enter the building when she saw a yellow Ferrari parked farther down the street. Walking toward it, Sarah peered inside and saw that it was empty. She was debating what to do, when she heard Vieri's voice behind her.

"Are you thinking of putting a pink rose under my windscreen?"

She turned to him, her face radiant with pleasure.

"I haven't a rose to give you tonight."

He opened the car door, motioning for her to get in.

"Let's go to Grinzing and have dinner and a bottle or two of the *heuriger*. Do you like the new wine of the season?"

"I never had it. Shall I change my clothes first?"

Vieri looked at the neat gray dress with its cutout neckline and starched white collar.

"You look perfect as you are."

Sarah sat at his side in the car, thrilled to the depths of her soul. Vieri had come to Vienna and was taking her out to dinner. She looked at him out of the corner of her eye, suddenly fearful in case he knew about Umberto. His voice interrupted her thoughts.

"You've changed. You're much more sophisticated than before."

"Is it a change for the better or the worse?"

"For the better, of course. Are you worried about something, Sarah?"

She shook her head, closing her eyes as he touched her hand. The sensation the touch provoked made her shiver, and she felt very alone and very uncertain of herself. Then she noticed that Vieri's face had hardened since getting into the car. Wondering if he was angry about something, Sarah could not control the urge to ask what he was thinking.

"What's wrong? Are you annoyed?"

"I'm a little angry that we are being followed. I don't know who he is, but he has been behind me ever since I arrived from Venice earlier in the day."

Sarah was shocked to think that the press had discovered something of her friendship with Vieri. What would Umberto say if he saw a photograph of them together? More important, what would happen to Vieri? She spoke uncertainly.

"Are you absolutely sure?"

"Of course. Well, I had best lose this imbecile before he ruins our evening. Make sure your seatbelt is fastened, Sarah."

Vieri put his foot down and the Ferrari shot forward as the traffic lights changed to red. Then, to Sarah's astonishment, he turned the car in the opposite direction, by pulling hard on the hand brake. The other driver did the same, and the two cars raced along a boulevard on the outskirts of the city. Turning a sharp bend, Vieri pulled into the darkened entrance of an underground parking lot and drove slowly out onto the next street that ran parallel. Within minutes they were driving over a bridge on a road that wound through a pine forest. There was no sign of the car that had been following, and for the first time Sarah was able to relax. She rested her head on the back of the seat and closed her eyes.

"Why did you come to Vienna? It's a long way from your house in Venice. Have you a business meeting here?"

"No, I came to take you out to dinner."

"When are you getting married?"

"In three and a half weeks' time in Paris. What are your own plans?"

"The company returns to Paris tomorrow morning on the train and I have a six-month contract at the Lido. I'm going to do the butterfly solo and one other number and rehearsals start in two days' time."

"Did Umberto get you the job?"

"Yes. They took me on his recommendation."

"Take care, Sarah. Don't ever let yourself become dependent on that man."

She shrugged, uncertain how to reply.

"Right now I'm not even sure I'll be seeing Umberto again. We had a terrible row in Palermo and he's not been to Vienna in the three weeks we've been playing here."

"He'll be back, and when you return to Paris he'll be determined to impress you. Paris is Umberto's city. There isn't much he doesn't know about it and not many things he can't arrange there."

The restaurant Vieri had chosen was a cream-painted cottage with a green stripe down the lower half of the wall and jade-colored window frames. Outside, strings of red peppers had been hung to dry in the sun. Inside, the smell of food was delicious; in the garden a group of musicians was playing Strauss. They ate sour-cherry soup and beef with green apples and drank the new season's wine. As Vieri spoke of his travels, Sarah tried to remember every detail of the moment, as she had in the Piazza Navona, entranced to hear him talk of his businesses and his life.

"Tell me about America."

"I've made two trips there recently. The first time I loaned some cars for an exhibition in New York. The second time I had meetings with the corporate lawyer who handles our business in Nassau and the Caymans."

For an hour Vieri talked about tax shelters, shelf companies, dummy directors, and the Swiss banking laws, which kept most of the Aldobrandini fortune secret. He was intrigued by Sarah's interest and fascinated by her questions.

"Is all this illegal, Vieri?"

"Not at all. We pay the finest brains in Europe and America to find ways to minimize family tax liability, that's all. I don't engage in fraud or anything that's against the law."

"And what's a shelf company?"

"It's a company controlled from Switzerland but based in Panama, for example. Thousands of them are created each month and sold to foreigners for tax avoidance or the avoidance of the disclosure of directors' names."

"How exactly does it work?"

"Usually there are three members of the board—or *junta directiva*, as they call it in Panama—all locals. They give power of attorney to a Swiss-based lawyer and control of the company effectively passes to Switzerland. No one knows who owns the company or what its real business is."

"It all sounds very odd to me."

"It's normal business practice. Don't forget, Sarah, that our adviser in New York earns on average one and a quarter million dollars a year for finding ways to do what his clients need. But enough of business."

"No, one more thing. Can *I* have a shelf company formed? How much would it cost? I want to do it."

"But you have no reason to do it."

"I want to have a company for when there *is* a reason to

do it and I'd rather form it now, when there's no reason for anyone to check up on me."

Vieri looked hard into her eyes, smiling at the determination of her manner.

"What are you planning, Sarah?"

"I want to own some property in Paris, a club or something like that. When I find a place, someday, I want to buy it, but I want no one to know who owns it or any subsequent property I buy. I don't want Umberto, for instance, to be able to check up on my finances or my life."

"I'll make you a present of a shelf company. Dear God, imagine, a woman owning a company but no business to go with it. That I never did hear of before! You are unique, Miss Hallam, unique!"

"Thank you, sir, but I don't like it when you talk to me as if I were a child."

"I don't take children out to dinner, Sarah, and I really will make you a present of the company."

"Why did you come to Vienna?" she asked again.

Vieri lit a cigar and smoked it for a while, trying to find an honest answer to the question he too had asked himself.

"The truth is I wanted to see you, or perhaps I needed to see you."

"Why are you marrying Mariannina? Are you really in love with her?"

"I admire her immensely and have known her since I was five and she was in her cradle. In family unions like ours, passion is not the priority."

"You didn't answer the question. Why did you come to Vienna?"

"I just wanted to be with you, Sarah. There is no other explanation."

She drank her coffee and after it a thin glass of schnapps that took her breath away. Then she let Vieri lead her to the garden and take her in his arms under a bower of scented mock-orange blossom. As he kissed her, Sarah felt her body becoming tense and vibrant with desire.

"Make love to me, Vieri."

He entered her mouth, the kiss so passionate and urgent it was hard to reconcile his cool exterior with this tornado of desire. Pulling down the loose-fitting top of the dress, he kissed her shoulders and her breasts, lingering over the nipples and enjoying the writhing movements of her body. Then, as he pushed Sarah back against the wall of flowers, Vieri felt for the first time in his life the madness of a longing he could barely control. Sarah was almost incoherent with desire, and he knew he must stop or be unable to avoid the inevitable. He stepped back, wiping his brow with a silk handkerchief.

"I told myself a thousand times I must not come to Vienna, but I did. I don't want to use you, Sarah. I'm going to marry Mariannina and if we make love you *will* feel used, I assure you. I'll take you home. I don't want to, but I must."

"Please don't leave me yet."

Vieri took her hand and led her to the car, offering her a sprig of scented mock orange, which Sarah put in her purse, thinking resignedly that she would keep it forever, because it would be her only tangible proof of his presence in Vienna. She held her breath as Vieri turned and looked at her, his face still full of desire.

"You are the most beautiful woman I have ever met and the most desirable. I wanted so very much to see you again and to take you out. Forgive me if I made you sad."

"Don't let's go home yet, Vieri. Let's go to the Prater and ride on the big wheel or to a palace to walk in the grounds and look at the fountains."

"I'll take you to one of my favorite places."

Vieri drove to a hill high above the city, so they could watch the sun rise over the Danube. In the moment before dawn came, lighting the dark water with a golden glow, everything had seemed still and empty. Then, as the sun appeared over the misty banks of the river, they saw people cycling to work, fishermen baiting hooks, children running home with loaves from the bakery, and a hundred other tiny details of everyday life that at this moment of awakening were special. A dawn chorus of birds filled the air and in the distance a cuckoo called. Sarah turned and looked up at Vieri.

"In England we wish when we hear the first cuckoo call."

"What do you wish for?"

"When I was little I wanted a toy car, a kitten, and a pink velvet dress. Now I wish for things I can never have, impossible things, and all the time I tell myself nothing's impossible. It's in my nature to fight for what I want. I never learned to accept that there are things I can't have."

Sarah looked defiantly into the cloud-gray eyes. Then she cupped his face in her hands and kissed him, slowly, languorously, with warm wet lips, thrusting her tongue into Vieri's mouth with tiny, penetrating movements. Her body began to tremble violently from desire and the knowledge that in a few seconds they would leave this magic vantage point on the city of Strauss and return to the real world. After that, they might never meet again.

They drove to the Hotel Sacher to breakfast on fragrant coffee, croissants, and wild-strawberry jam. Sarah stole the menu and put it in her purse as a souvenir of a special moment, amused when Vieri spoke in his usual laconic style.

"Are you thinking of stealing the coffeepot as well?"

"You're the only thing I want to steal and you know it. But sometimes I think you're a very infuriating man. You don't seem to feel things with the violence that I do."

"Mama used to say the same thing when I was a child. I think I was born with a fatalistic streak. I accept my fate and know that what will be, will be. I believe in predestination and not free will, that my life will be how it's destined to be and not how I make it. I accept my fate, whereas you fight yours.''

"Umberto says in life we fight for everything and the end justifies the means.''

"And what do you think?''

"I agree with him. I never question whether I control my existence or if it's controlled for me. I try to plan what I do, where I'm aiming to go, but perhaps you're right and everything's decided for us. The only thing I know is that we have to fight for what we want. Otherwise life would be a boring, routine nothingness.''

"What do you really want from life, Sarah?''

"I want the man I love and a measure of security, and I don't think I shall ever get either.''

"Has di Castelli promised you everything?''

"He's promised to teach me all I'll need to know to get into the business world.''

Vieri's slim fingers drummed the table and for a moment he looked angry. Then, controlling his emotions, he spoke firmly.

"Never become dependent on that man for finance. Never ever let his accountants, his lawyers, or his organization handle your business and your books—but you already know to avoid that, I think. Always have your own people to advise you. I'll give you the names of reliable men in every field, if you wish, and you can always contact me at this address.''

Vieri handed her a gilded card with a Paris box number. Then he continued, trying not to intimidate Sarah with his comments.

"Di Castelli's people like bright youngsters who start businesses with money borrowed from them, and they like it even more when they can take over those businesses once they prosper. You can't fight them because to do that would be dangerous.''

"Are you saying they'd kill me?"

"There are worse things than being killed. There are situations none of us can live with. Just remember what I've told you. Everything you are, everything you buy in the future must be yours, and the details of your business life must be yours as well.''

"Do you hate Umberto?"

"Of course not. In the jungle we admire a tiger or a crocodile for its aura of menace, its swiftness and expertise in disposing of its enemies. We don't hate them because they're dangerous. We just keep our distance, because we know what harm they can do. Umberto is a crocodile who swallows his victims whole.''

"And what am I?"

"You, my dear Sarah, are a tigress."

"And how would you describe yourself?"

"I don't belong in the same planet as Umberto.'' He smiled and continued. "I am an old-fashioned knight on a white horse; I understand very little of the world and nothing of the jungle.''

Nearby, a clock chimed seven. Startled, Sarah gathered her belongings.

"My train leaves at seven forty-five. I'll have to go back to the apartment to collect my cases.''

"I'll drive you there and then to the station afterward.''

Sarah's friends were together in a taxi, excitedly discussing the fact that the Duke had at last proposed to Arlette and they were to be married in just over three weeks' time in Paris. Luis had proposed to Mary-Ellen, but had been turned down, though with Spanish persistence he had invited her for a holiday to Seville in the hopes of trying a second time and getting accepted. Holly had lost her film contract, but had hopes of another. Sarah was not to be found, and all of them were debating where she had gone and if it was possible that Vieri Aldobrandini had appeared at the last moment to take her out to dinner.

All too soon, they saw the somber outlines of the station and in front of it Vieri's yellow Ferrari, a pink English rose pushed under the windshield wiper. As the three hurried to group with the rest of the company on platform three, they passed Sarah and Vieri standing under the clock, hand in hand, oblivious to everything and everyone. They also noted that Mario Benedetti looked uneasy, his face tense as his glance passed from Sarah to an observer in the first-floor café of the station, a young man in a dark suit with black, searching eyes. Mary-Ellen spoke all their thoughts out loud.

"I wonder if Vieri's deliberately trying to get seen by the press. I can't believe he'd do such a thing, but he's certainly a man who takes risks. Sarah always said he wasn't in love with that fiancée of his and I'm beginning to think she was right."

Vieri stood on the platform, waving as the Paris train pulled out. He remained there until Sarah's fair hair and scarlet kerchief were spots in the far distance. Then, with a sigh, he returned to his car, noting out of the corner of his eye that a young man rose from a seat in the café on the first floor and followed him. For a moment, he sat in the Ferrari, looking at the rose Sarah had managed to find. He was thinking of her face as she had placed it there and the expression of sadness mixed with determination he had come to know so well. He thought wryly that there were times when he glimpsed in her a grimness he could not understand, a hardness and deep-down sadness bred of deprivation and suffering endured from an early age. They were emotions he had never felt and could not even imagine. Suffering he had always avoided, because it put courage and the very soul of a man to the test. Vieri watched as the watcher took his place in a white sports car and sat waiting for Vieri to move off. Then, tired of being followed, Vieri drove away in the direction of the Sacher Hotel, putting the Ferrari in the garage and retiring at once to his suite. He could not stop thinking of the tears in Sarah's eyes at the moment when she had stepped onto the Paris train. How beautiful she had looked, how filled with conflicting emotions, and how her words had affected him. Sometimes Vieri imagined she could reach down into his soul, and the feeling was both disturbing and curiously comforting.

Alone in his suite, Vieri scanned the morning papers, assimilating nothing of what he was reading, because he was trying to find reasons for his intense reaction to Sarah. Normally, he would have loved and left such a woman. With Sarah, he could not countenance using her. Under normal circumstances, he would not have been seen out with a girl as beautiful as she after the announcement of his engagement to Mariannina, yet he had risked being photographed by paparazzi in Rome and seen by the ever-watchful press of Vienna. He felt a compulsion to take such risks and debated if he could have fallen in love. He rejected the idea at once. The Aldobrandinis were a family to whom passion was a stranger and he was surely no exception. Uneasy at his own inability to stop thinking of Sarah's every word, recalling her every action, Vieri decided to return home at once to Venice, instead of staying until the morning. Having rung the garage and asked for the Ferrari to be brought to the main entrance, he called for a valet to pack his case.

Minutes later, an explosion shook the building. In the subterranean garage all that remained of the yellow Ferrari was a shattered shell. The attendant lay, gravely injured, on the ground. The pink rose, miraculously blown clear, was almost intact. As he looked down at the flower, Vieri wondered which of his enemies had planted the bomb. For years the Aldobrandinis had lived with kidnap threats and the demands of political groups and professional extortionists. Was he on the Red Brigade's list? Or had a fanatic suddenly taken exception to him for no reason at all, like the time Elio had been shot by a madman at the station in Turin? Vieri returned to his suite to await the arrival of the police, having instructed the management to put a complete news blackout on the incident.

The train drew into the Gare de Lyon and porters rushed to pile the company's luggage onto trolleys. The girls stepped down and began to drift along the platform in twos and threes, chattering happily, because it was a beautiful fall day, full of the magic of Paris. The last to leave the train, Sarah and Mary-Ellen were walking together toward the gate when they saw Umberto waiting on the other side. He was stern faced and dressed in an unusually restrained fashion. Mary-Ellen turned to Sarah, her eyes wide with apprehension.

"I'd best leave you alone with him. Try to be nice, Sarah. He's swallowed his Sicilian pride and come to meet you and he looks as tense as hell."

For a moment Sarah stood gazing into the piercing black eyes. Then she walked slowly toward Umberto, her face showing nothing of the apprehension she was feeling. Her voice was casual as she motioned for the porter to put her luggage in his car. Then she turned to him.

"I didn't expect to see you here."

"What do you think I do, wait for you to come to my office? If I do that, I wait forever."

"I'm hungry and I'm tired. I hope you're not going to start a row."

"I never start a row. You are always the one who get into a fury. Come, I take you to Maxim's for lunch to celebrate your return to Paris."

He took her by the arm, turning her to face him.

"Kiss me, Sarah. I arrive hours early at the station and I am *so* happy to see you."

"You can kiss me in the car."

"Kiss me now, damn you!"

As their lips met, Sarah felt the contrary longing he always inspired and, closing her eyes, let him do all he had been longing to do for weeks. Then she walked at Umberto's side to the car, amused to find he had bought the latest model of the same car she had smashed in Palermo. Like her, he was a creature of habit, disliking change and preferring to keep to the car he knew, the women he knew, the *compadres* who had proven themselves over twenty years. When the chauffeur opened the rear door, Sarah saw a huge bouquet of violets and her favorite pink-edged daisies on the seat. She turned to Umberto with a smile.

"Thank you for remembering the flowers I like."

He gazed into the mysterious face, whose expression he could never fathom, and felt waves of longing lashing over him like an angry sea. Then, sliding his hand across the back seat, he clutched hers.

"You wreck my car pretty good, so I buy a new one."

"I'll try not to get tempted to wreck this as well."

"I ask myself a dozen times a day why I want you, but there's no answer."

"Where are we going?"

"First to the apartment I find for you and then to eat."

"Thank you for all you've done for me, Umberto."

Sarah looked at his hands, the knuckles white as he gripped hers. In her mind's eye she was comparing their wide, forceful shape with Vieri's long, aristocratic fingers. When Umberto gripped her thigh, squeezing it till she winced, Sarah asked herself what she was doing with him, why she had ever let him love her, why she had allowed herself to become enmeshed in the violence of his life and his emotions. The truth was she needed him and the security he gave. There was something reassuring in the knowledge that what she wanted he would give her, when she was down he would help her, and when she needed to feel loved he would love her with all the passion in his intense Sicilian soul. She was surprised when the chauffeur drove them into the underground parking area of a block of expensive apartments in the elegant sixteenth arrondissement.

"Is this where I'm going to live? Are you sure I can afford it, Umberto?"

"*I* afford it. What do you think I am, a man who make love and do not take his responsibilities serious?"

"I don't want you to pay my rent. That makes me a kept woman, which is not something I want to be."

"What you want, that I give the Lido management more money to pay you a bigger salary and pretend I don't help you? You want the lies and deceptions? I don't agree. I pay and you let me. Between us it must always be direct."

Sarah entered an apartment that was small but luxurious, one room for entertaining, one bedroom, bathroom, and dressing room. The furnishings were a mixture of ancient and modern, colorful Arrailos rugs from Portugal with a design of her favorite daisies, white-painted Dutch wicker furniture in the kitchen with its cupboard full of blue-patterned pottery. The bedroom had curtains of Indian silk and a Cartier clock studded with diamonds in the style of the thirties. The bed, of carved bleached walnut, was shaped like an upturned shell, the cover hand embroidered in the same silk as the curtains.

Sarah sat on the sofa in the living room, her fingers running over the kelim rug that covered it. She was delighted to see a pair of snowy owls under a Victorian glass cover on the table, the same ones she had admired in an antique shop in the boulevard Haussman months previously. Touched that on Umberto's instructions the decorators had incorporated all her favorite colors, pieces, and styles, she walked over to him.

"You're a miracle. You even remembered that I wanted a blue and yellow kitchen like Monet's at Giverny."

"I remember everything you like, Sarah, and I always will."

Sarah gasped when he picked her up, carried her to the bedroom, and threw her down on the white silk spread. She could not resist a smile when he began to undress as if there were no tomorrow.

"I have to love you. It's been three weeks and two days since I last see you and I am full of the nerves."

Umberto took off the last of his things and turned to her, his eyes full of desire, his body hard and thrusting. When Sarah continued to gaze at him, her face full of uncertainty, he tore off the white cotton blouse, then the skirt, becoming more excited by the minute as she remained like a statue, seemingly unaffected by his urgency. When he had torn off the bra, he pushed her down on the bed and stripped her of everything but the silk stockings and frilly garter belt. As desire came to her, he saw her face change and wanted to shout out loud how much he loved her. Instead, he kissed her and stroked her hair, his voice husky with emotion.

"Tell me you want me, Sarah. These weeks of our separation have been the most horrible of my life."

"You talk too much. Why don't you just show me how much you miss me?"

He gripped her shoulders and kissed her again, moving his hands over her breasts and caressing the nipples that became hard at once under his touch. Then parting her legs, he pushed his penis deep inside her, crying out because she was all he longed for and he was mad to be locked in the prison of her body, to feel the strength of her thighs milking him dry. As their movements quickened against each other, Umberto felt the iron control of which he had always been so proud slipping away and knew he could wait no longer to reach the peak of ecstasy. He whispered frantically to Sarah.

"Come *now*, I want to give you everything."

She closed her eyes, forgetting Vieri and the problems of love and life as her body flared into a powerful explosion and then subsided as satiation lulled the senses. She could not resist a smile when Umberto fell to her side, shaking his head.

"Now I am too weak to eat the lunch! Oh, Sarah, it is so good that we are together again. I don't want that we are separated again. I have the temptation to imprison you forever."

At Maxim's, they were led to a table in the section favored by habitués and known to everyone as "the omnibus." Waiters hovered attentively as the maître d' took their order and the sommelier appeared and beamed a greeting. As always, Umberto insisted on eating the food with which he was familiar, disdaining haute cuisine in favor of *tuna e fagioli* with wild mushrooms and meatballs.

Sarah was debating what to order when she saw Vieri entering the restaurant with his fiancée. As they were led to a table nearby, she handed the menu back to the maître d' and ordered a smoked-salmon soufflé. Then she turned attentively to Umberto.

"What are your plans for the afternoon?"

"I take you back to the apartment and make love till the knees tremble."

Seeing Sarah's intent gaze wavering, he followed her eyes and looked into the mocking face of Vieri Aldobrandini. For a moment Umberto remained inscrutable. Then, with a smile, he rose and walked over to kiss Mariannina's hand with elaborate ceremony.

"How are you, Princess? Is everything ready for the wedding?"

Mariannina spoke perfect French in a high, brittle voice

and Sarah noticed that every detail of her appearance was perfect, as before. She also saw that Mariannina was very, very happy. She frowned at the reply.

"I'm exhausted, but almost triumphant. Some of the arrangements have been left a little late, but we'll be married in three weeks' time and that's certain."

Umberto turned to Vieri and gripped his hand.

"And how are you feeling at the prospect of losing your liberty?"

Vieri's cool glance moved from Sarah to Umberto, whom he regarded with ill-concealed impatience.

"Losing my liberty has always been something I dreaded. I believe I suffer from claustrophobia of the soul."

Umberto shook hands again and then returned to his table, gazing moodily at Sarah as he sat down.

"He get the claustrophobia when Mariannina lock him in the house to stop him from wandering, that's for sure!"

"You think she'll employ guards to keep him chained to the wall?"

Umberto took in the teasing glance and fought to keep his anger under control.

"I think she need to—but what do *you* think, Sarah?"

"I think his sense of duty is so strong he'll probably make a very good husband."

"Is he also a very good lover?"

Sarah saw the blush of anger and knew that Umberto's jealousy was in danger of boiling over. She spoke softly, as if to a child.

"I don't know. I've only made love with you and that's the truth."

He took her hand and kissed each of the fingers, longing to believe what she had said. "You know, my Sarah," he said, "I think I fall in love with you the first day I saw you and I stay in love forever."

"Don't say that. No one can ever be sure of feeling something forever."

"I can. When the sky turn green and my blood turn to water, that is the day when I stop loving you. Remember it always."

"I don't want you to love me. I never asked you to."

"Ask, not ask—what does it matter? You got my love, so take care of it. I never give it to anyone before."

Chapter Seven

Paris-Rheims, December 1967

The Chateau de Brouillard stood in five hundred acres of poplar and chestnut trees, an imposing building, its entrance decorated with grisailles, its rotunda clad in Carrara marble and crowned by a cupola of translucent caissons. The family motto—*Quo non ascendum*, "How far shall I not rise"— had been carved and gilded on the lintels of every door and worked in prostrate juniper on the parterre. For this special occasion, the wedding of Charles and Arlette, the servants had been dressed in the style of the nineteenth century, with frilly white aprons and full skirts of royal-blue. The footmen were in powdered wigs and velvet jackets with gilded epaulets. Every room had flowers in the same family colors, and the great hall was full of scented orchids in exotic arrangements created by a Parisian designer.

Arlette gazed at her reflection in the mirror and tried to grasp the fact that she was about to be married. She was pleased that her three best friends had been able to come, but she had had very little time to spend with them. Her mother had not stopped sobbing since her arrival from Naples, and Arlette's nerves were taut. Her hands kept twitching from spasms of tension of which she seemed unaware.

Sarah looked at the magnificent St. Laurent wedding dress with its tulip line and regal train appliquéd in vine leaves. She also took in Arlette's rigid stance and ashen face, worried by the fear that was evident in every movement. Then her mind turned to thoughts of Umberto, who had sulked because he had not received an invitation to the wedding. Instead, he had sent his chauffeur, Enzo, to drive them all to Chantilly, and Sarah was well aware that the young man had his instructions to follow her like a bloodhound and to make a note of the name of every man who spoke to her.

In a chapel decorated with massed roses, orchids, and tapestries showing what had once been the royal hunting grounds of the area, Sarah and her friends watched as Arlette was married. When the priest linked her hands with Charles's and the rings were exchanged, tears began to fall down Arlette's cheeks and her mother's sobbing grew louder. The Duke raised an eyebrow in obvious irritation, catching the besotted gaze of one of his groom's daughters as she sat in her best Sunday straw hat decorated with cornflowers.

Mary-Ellen nudged Sarah and whispered, "What's the betting Charles'll claim his rights from that little *poule* before she's much older?"

"You're disgusting, but you could be right. Say nothing to Arlette, though. She's a great believer in marital fidelity and none too certain of herself at the moment."

"She's scared she'll let him down in the bedroom. She bought three sex manuals last week and all that happened was that she took herself off to bed for two hours and came out red faced and exhausted. If I read our friend right, her big interest in life is herself."

"Now you're being malicious!"

"But I'm right."

The reception was held in the ballroom of the chateau, with its famous inlaid floor and walls of raspberry watered silk. Two hundred guests drank vintage champagne and

toyed with food from a buffet heavy laden with boned
smoked duck and stuffed turkeys. Several deer had been
roasted on a spit and arranged with antlers in a miniature
woodland scene at one end of the room. Sarah, Holly, and
Mary-Ellen were aware that Arlette was nervous, but wedding guests noted that Arlette had already learned the correct
nuances of attitude required when speaking to servants, re-
tainers, and estate workers. She was also able to protect
herself from unwelcome curiosity. When an overeager jour-
nalist asked her for her measurements, she replied that her
body was for the pleasure of her husband and not the readers
of *Le Matin*. Her real test came, however, when she found
herself face to face with Charles's mistress of many years.
Aware of the liaison and none too pleased by the appearance
of the elegant but aging Minouche, Arlette welcomed the
lady with a deceptively radiant smile.

"How kind of you to drive all this way for the wedding,
madame."

Seeing the hostility behind the friendly words, Minouche
replied with equal sweetness.

"I haven't missed one of Charles's receptions for ten
years and I wouldn't have dreamed of missing this one."

"Well, now you'll be able to have a well-earned rest. I
hope the check he sent you was satisfactory."

"Of course, he's such a generous man—but I'm sure you
already know that."

Arlette took a deep breath and raised her chin an extra
inch.

"Charles never had any reason to send *me* a check madame. He married me instead."

"Well, I hope you'll be very happy. If you need any advice do call me. I've known Charles so long he's almost like
a . . ."

"Son to you? I know, but I have to learn to be his wife
and that is something you can't teach me."

Arlette went upstairs and sat on the bed, looking at the bouquet of rosebuds and stephanotis that had been put in water and placed on an inlaid Sheraton table. The wedding had been perfect, the guests charming, and Charles had told her she was the most beautiful bride he had ever seen. She rose and walked back and forth, nervous, uneasy, and uncertain precisely why. She had expected to feel ecstatic once the duke of her dreams proposed. Instead, she had fallen into a deep depression. She was wondering if she could throw off the black clouds gathering over her head, when Holly entered the room.

"You feel sad and empty. Right?"

"Absolutely. But how did you know?"

"All your life you've worked for this moment and now that you've satisfied your ambitions, the purpose is gone. If you don't want the rest of your days to seem like an anticlimax, you have to find a new purpose. Perhaps you'll have a family or become one of the best-dressed women in France. If those ideas don't appeal, you could learn the champagne business and become a tycoon."

"Never! I leave ambition like that to Sarah. She has all the makings of a female Umberto."

"Well, you have to think of something or you'll be wandering around with the miseries forever. Now, come down and say good-bye to the girls. Sarah has to get back to Paris, and Luis is waiting for Mary-Ellen at the hotel. I think they're going off to Seville together. I just hope she won't do anything impulsive."

"Talk with her," Arlette said urgently. "Or get Sarah to do it. She's the only person whose advice Mary-Ellen respects."

"She's the only person whose advice we all respect, but who gives Sarah advice?"

"No one. That's why she's so involved with that awful man."

Holly tossed her curls. "Umberto's very attractive, but he's bad to his bones, it's true."

"He's a gorilla and everything I most detest. I just don't understand—"

"I know," said Holly. "Now let's get downstairs."

The four friends stood together by the long pond of the chateau, looking out at the woodland and the magnificent house that was now Arlette's home. After months of living and working together, they all felt apprehensive at saying good-bye.

Sarah kissed Arlette's cheeks. "You just listen to me now. You've married your duke, you have your chateau, and you'll never have to worry about money like the rest of us. Stop thinking about the past. Get your mother a little apartment and see she stays there till she can stop crying. Charles obviously doesn't like tears."

Sarah turned to the others. "We once talked of having a reunion after the show ended, remember?"

They nodded. "I propose that we make a rendezvous for lunch on the first of May ten years from now. We may meet all the time in between. On the other hand, it's possible that we'll never see each other again."

Mary-Ellen spoke excitedly.

"May first, nineteen seventy-seven, is the date for lunch at one at the Ritz! No excuses for not being there."

The girls hugged each other and kissed again. Then, when Holly and Mary-Ellen had got in the car, Sarah turned to Arlette. "I know you're terrified of making love, Arlette, but it's not an ordeal, it's one of the pleasures of life."

"I'm not like you, Sarah. I'm not like other women. If I were, I would have made love long ago. I've never been interested in trying."

"You're stunningly beautiful," Sarah said as she kissed

Arlette's cheek again. "And Charles wants you. That's all you need to remember."

"I'll do everything I can to make him happy, Sarah, you know that. I will be the wife he needs and wants. If I don't enjoy our lovemaking, I'll give an Academy Award-winning performance. I promise!"

Sarah and Mary-Ellen dropped Holly off at the airport, accompanying her to the gate and kissing her good-bye as she passed through to the departure lounge for her flight to Dublin. She too was afraid of the future and troubled to think she might never see her friends again. It would be hard to be alone.

Mary-Ellen held Sarah's hand in the car as it sped to the city center. For a long time neither spoke; then she turned and looked questioningly into the violet eyes.

"What now, Sarah?"

"God knows. I'm going to be at the Lido for some time and you're going to Seville. Are you in love with Luis?" she asked bluntly.

Mary-Ellen looked at her hands, uncertain how to reply. "I could be. I've been fighting the idea of marriage, though, because there are still so many things I'd like to do. But his life is very appealing to me. I might just do it."

"Don't do anything stupid, Mary-Ellen. Make sure you know enough about him and what his life is really like before you make a decision." She stopped abruptly and laughed. "Well, I'm certainly acting as though I were the world's mother, aren't I?" She squeezed Mary-Ellen's hand.

"Try not to lose touch. I've given you my Paris address and my aunt's address in England; those should be sufficient."

On parting, they hugged each other one last time. Then Sarah ran back to the car, turning to wave before disappearing behind the anonymous black windows.

Mary-Ellen stood very still, tears falling down her

cheeks. She had fled America after an unhappy love affair
and had found friends and peace of mind in the uproarious
days of the tour. Now she was alone again. The word
echoed in her mind like a nightmare and she was hard
pressed not to sob. She was about to enter the hotel when
Luis appeared and kissed her hand.

"You are sad, *reina*. I knew you would be and I took the
liberty of arranging for us to leave immediately for Seville.
If you stay in Paris your head will be full of unwelcome
memories."

Mary-Ellen rushed upstairs without a word of protest, relieved that she had something to do, somewhere to go,
something to look forward to. In this moment of parting
from her friends, Luis offered concern and strength and she
was grateful. She thought of Seville and the reassuring
warmth of the Andalusian sun. It would be good to go back
there, good to forget everything she longed to avoid, like
planning the future and looking at bank statements. She
would leave all that until another day and with luck the other
day would never come.

Sarah gazed out at the passing scene. On the corner of the
rue Brey, by a restaurant with scarlet-poppy art nouveau
windows, a waiter in horseshoe waistcoat and spotless shirt
was running at high speed along the pavement, swaying to
avoid passersby and balancing a loaded tray on one hand.
Sarah watched wide-eyed as he snaked through the early-
evening rush hour, obviously practicing for the race that
would soon take place between the most experienced waiters in the city; the prize was enough money to make the first
payment on the bar each of them longed to own.

Sarah realized with something of a shock that she loved
Paris dearly and felt more at home in the city than she had ever
felt in London. She tapped on the window and asked Enzo to
wait while she bought an evening paper. Then, like a real

Parisienne, she sat back and read the news . . . prices up three percent on the same period last year, another kidnapping by the gang known as *les perroquets*—"the parrots"—so called because their ransom instructions to distraught relatives were repeated over and over again from tiny machines found abandoned in telephone booths all over the city. Sarah studied the face of the latest victim, the nineteen-year-old daughter of a multimillionaire French banker. The girl, who had disappeared from her Paris home after her birthday party, was beautiful, though her face showed something of her father's hardness. Sarah thought it was a good sign. In order to survive the rigors of a kidnapping there had to be steel in the soul. Then she turned to the fashion page and set to studying a drawing of Mariannina's wedding dress, previewed for the eager readers in great detail. By Dior, the dress was a dream of iridescent silk, hand embroidered with paillettes in the crests of her own family and Vieri's. With it, the article said, Mariannina would wear the legendary Aldobrandini diamond choker and tiara originally made for Empress Catherine of Russia.

Sarah thought how cunning Umberto was, how possessive, even in this moment of triumph. The Aldobrandini wedding had been chosen as one of six major social events of the season to be televised in a series designed to let French viewers know how the other half lived. She had planned to watch it during the afternoon from her apartment, but Umberto had insisted she spend the night in his house in the Bois de Boulogne. Benefiting from his wife's absence, he was obviously making sure he did not lose Sarah at the last minute to Vieri.

She put the paper aside and watched the road ahead as they entered the Bois de Boulogne. In less than twenty-four hours Vieri would leave Paris with his new wife. It was time to forget him, but she could not. It was time to control the urge to let her mind keep wandering back to thoughts of Vienna and sunrise over the Danube and waltzing to the tune of a balalaika in the Piazza Navona. A dozen times a day, Sarah picked up her pen and wrote to Vieri, tearing up the letters and cards or throwing them away instead of sending them. Once, she had tried to obtain the telephone number of his private house in the avenue Foch, but the number was unlisted. These exercises always made Sarah furious with herself for being unrealistic and refusing to grow up. She thought again that she must work like a demon to get to be rich, as rich as Vieri and as powerful as Umberto. Once she was rich, once she had power, no one would ever deny her what she wanted. With all the innocence of her years, Sarah identified wealth and power as the means to have her way. Then, as tears began to fall, she told herself that a new chapter of her life had begun and she must do her best to make a success of it. What was past was past. What was impossible must be accepted.

Over dinner that night, Umberto was in a rare good humor, regaling her with stories of his uncle Fabrizzio, whose penis was the biggest in Palermo and whose appetite for food, women, and defying the law were equally grandiose.

"One time, he got put in the prison. He had been hiding out on the island, but he was caught when the police followed the village whore who came to relieve his tensions."

"And did he escape from prison?"

"Of course. One day he was visit by the governor and a team of journalists from Rome. One of them was a widow of fifty. She look from Fabrizzio to his physique and get the burning desire. Two days later she pay some friends to get him out. He spend two months with her on Capri and then give himself up to the *guardi*. He say he rather go back to prison than die of exhaustion in her bed."

The following day, Sarah sat in a darkened room, a late lunch on a tray on her knee, her newly polished glasses on the low table at her side. The wedding of Vieri and Mariannina would start in five minutes. In the meantime, the news program droned on with financial reports. Sarah put the tray aside, conscious that in the past few days she had lost her appetite. She longed to be far away from Paris at this moment, yet she was unable to resist watching the ceremony that would bring tears.

The scene changed and the cameras moved to the exterior of the Madeleine Church, where Vieri and Mariannina were to be married. Leading society figures of France, Italy, and America were arriving. A politician of the French opposition followed ex-kings living in exile, show business personalities, and members of the two families. When Mariannina arrived and stepped from the limousine, she was helped into the church by a dozen tiny bridesmaids, each one taking a section of the shimmering train.

Sarah gazed in awe at the bride. As always, not a hair was out of place, not a crease wrinkled the shiny silk of the dress. Mariannina was perfectly poised and in full control of her emotions. Sarah thought wryly that if she was about to marry Vieri she would be singing arias from *Pagliacci,* unable to conceal the joy she was feeling, as she was unable to conceal all the other emotions in life. She realized at last that Vieri's existence was a very different one from her own and that Mariannina was part of it, conditioned from childhood to be the wife of someone like him. As the cameras moved inside the church, Sarah saw the man she loved standing with his brother at the altar. Tears began to fall down her cheeks and she blew her nose loudly, struggling not to give in to the grief that had filled her heart for weeks. Until this moment, she had hoped that Vieri might call the wedding off, but finally hope died and with it the child that had been Sarah Hallam. In a moment of anguish, she grew up and accepted that what she had taught herself was wrong. Some things in life *were* impossible.

Sarah watched as Mariannina walked up the aisle to the rousing tones of the wedding march. On reaching the spot where Vieri and his brother were standing, she barely acknowledged her bridegroom as he turned and smiled at her. She was obviously determined to guard the perfection of her carriage, her outfit, and the aura of calm for which she had always been known. Sarah's gaze wandered from the couple to Vieri's father, sitting in the front pew with his daughters. A tall man of sixty, he was the perfect Venetian aristocrat and the man Vieri would resemble when he was the same age.

Sarah leaned forward, the better to see Vieri's face as the rings were exchanged, but he betrayed nothing of his feelings as he and Mariannina became man and wife. Sarah was still regarding him intently, when, like millions of television viewers in France, she was startled to hear a staccato voice with an Oriental accent calling for everyone to lie down on the floor. From the rear of the church, tiny black-clad figures rushed forward, stabbing at the disobedient with rifle butts and smashing a young man on the head when he tried to shield his mother. Sarah stared entranced as Vieri turned to face the intruders, who grasped his arms and began to drag him up the aisle. Suddenly, she saw that Mariannina's icy calm had broken and she was struggling with one of the intruders, pulling off the head mask and revealing an inscrutable Japanese face and clipped dark head. For her pains, Mariannina received a blow that smashed her front teeth and left her unconscious and bleeding on the ground.

As she collapsed, pandemonium broke loose. Vieri's father rushed to his son's assistance and was shot through the chest by a member of the gang hidden in the roof of the church. Security men hired by the Aldobrandini family had been overcome before the Japanese entered, and the only one left was shot by the leader of the group. The fairy-tale marriage of the season had become a nightmare.

Sarah sat frozen in horror as Vieri was dragged from the church. From there, the gang obviously intended to take him via the sewers of Paris to a secret destination to be ransomed or murdered or both. She rose like a sleepwalker, barely conscious of the volatile tones of the commentators. Her nerves were shattered as she ran from the lounge to Umberto's bedroom and then to his office on the second floor. Not finding him as she had expected, she hurried from the ground floor down the steep stone steps to the two subterranean floors of the house. She was about to open the first of the doors, leading to the service rooms and wine cellar, when she heard a loud, agonized, animal scream of a dying man or one in excrutiating pain.

Terrified, Sarah stopped and listened, panic-stricken for the first time in her life. When she had recovered, she moved as silently as she could along the dark corridor, looking into rooms on either side through portholes in the solid oak facades. The kitchen store was empty. The gardeners' equipment room and fountain engine alcove likewise. Sarah moved toward the wine cellar and, opening the door a fraction, almost fainted at the sight of two of Umberto's *compadres* dragging an unconscious man across the floor. His face was beaten and bleeding and it was obvious that he had been tortured. Sarah thought of Vieri's face as he had been dragged past the television camera, blood pouring from his mouth and nose. Then, closing the door silently on the gruesome scene, she stumbled along the corridor and upstairs to her room.

Locking the door behind her, Sarah tried to still the questions coursing through her mind about the man in the cellar, about Vieri, and most of all about Umberto di Castelli. What did it all mean? Did Umberto even know the man was there—and, if he did, what had been the reason for the beating? Sarah wet a washcloth and bathed her burning forehead, telling herself to stay calm, to avoid doing anything foolish. She knew she had to escape before Umberto found out what she had seen, but despite her resolve her legs re-

mained leaden and it was all she could do to stagger to her
bed.

Sarah was gazing at the ceiling when she heard the sound
of Umberto's car in the drive. Suddenly, her shocked leth-
argy vanished and she moved with desperate swiftness
pulling her purse, shoes, and wrap from the drawer. Then
she ran down the servants' stairway and into the drive, as
Umberto entered the house by the front door. He had left his
keys in the car while he ran in to call her to come out to dinner with him. Sarah locked the car door, backed out of the
drive, and steered into the winter streets of Paris. At this
moment of trauma, the sight of the bare trees black against a
snow-pink sky frightened her and she drove faster and
faster, heading instinctively for the hotel where Benedetti
lived. She parked the car on a double line in a strictly forbidden zone, to make sure it was towed away by the police.
Then she ran into the hotel.

Seconds later, Benedetti appeared and guided her to the
bar.

"A brandy for mademoiselle and a Calvados for me. I
never saw you like this, Sarah. When can you tell me what
happened?"

"I have to get out of Paris immediately without Umberto
knowing."

"What about your contract at the Lido?"

"I'm leaving, that's all."

"Tell me what's happened, Sarah."

"Vieri's been kidnapped. I saw it all on television and it
was terrible. His father was shot and Vieri was beaten on the
face and dragged out to God only knows where. I can't say
what else happened today, but I can't stay in Umberto's
house. For God's sake, help me, Mario!"

"Have you your passport? I suppose you want to go to
England?"

"I hope to and I always carry my passport in my purse,

but I've no money. Will you lend me enough for an air ticket?''

She saw the decision in his eyes. "Take the train to Brussels and get a flight there. Umberto's people will be watching the French ports, stations, and airports. And go on the métro to the Gare de Nord. I can't take you there in my car. It would be more than my life was worth. Here, take this and don't ever tell anyone I gave it to you.''

Benedetti handed Sarah a wad of notes, touched to see tears falling down her cheeks. As he walked with her to the foyer of the hotel, he gave her a final word of advice. "Take the first train you can find to get out of France, anywhere out of France. And write me a note to tell me you arrived safely.''

"Thanks, Mario. I won't forget what you've done.''

"You will, but it doesn't matter.''

Sarah ran to the nearest underground station, took a train to the Gare de Nord, and found an express to Brussels. It was leaving in four minutes and she had to dash from the ticket office to the platform to get aboard as the whistle blew. Once inside, she knew she was safe until she reached the border. But what then? Was it possible Umberto had men watching the borders? She told herself she would face the situation if it arose and tried to settle in the corner of the compartment, but she remained terrified every time someone paused outside the window or moved too often along the corridor.

It was five in the evening when Sarah arrived in Brussels and took a bus to the airport. On entering the plane, she closed her eyes and tried to formulate a plan. Surely she was safe now. Even Umberto's power did not extend across the Channel. But she had lost all her belongings and would arrive in London with no clothes except those she was wearing. She had the equivalent of fifteen pounds in cash, all that was left of what Benedetti had given her. Sarah leafed through her address book and found the number of Holly's sister in London. She knew she could ask for help when she arrived. Like Holly, Eira was sympathetic, and Sarah had met her a number of times in Rome when the O'Malley family had had a get-together. Decision made, Sarah wrapped herself in a blanket and slept for an hour, unaware of a young man who watched her with intense curiosity from across the aisle.

Umberto's rage was terrifying and the house in the Bois looked as if a tornado had hit it. Finally alone with Benedetti, he paced the marble floor of his office, trying to put the confusion in his head into words.

"I don't understand Sarah and I never understand her. What does she want of me?"

"I told you a long time ago to take care how you handled her."

"I take care. I am a lamb when I am with her."

"Aldobrandini was kidnapped today and it distressed Sarah. I think she'd almost accepted that he was marrying someone else, but now she has to face the fact that he might never be seen alive again. She loves him, Umberto. She only came to you because she couldn't have him."

"And now what will she do?"

"She'll run like a wounded animal and wait for news of him. If he's dead he'll be a martyr in her eyes. If he's alive she'll go after him. She's as single-minded as you are. When she wants something she can't let go."

"And he, what of the great Prince Aldobrandini?"

"I don't know him, so I can't say. Where is he, Umberto?"

Their eyes met and Umberto shrugged.

"How do I know? I know nothing of the kidnapping."

"Don't try to bullshit me after all these years."

The phone rang and Umberto listened intently, looking from time to time at Benedetti with an expression of incomprehension, his face paling until it was the color of tallow. When he replaced the receiver, he turned with icy calm to his friend.

"She came to you, Mario, and you say nothing. If you were not my friend I would kill you. *Why* did you say nothing?"

"Sarah asked me to drive her out of Paris and I refused. She knows your ways, Umberto; I didn't have to help her. She knew she must avoid the French ports and airports."

"I will never trust you again."

"That's for you to decide. I'm going to have dinner at Gregory's. Come with me—you always liked it there."

"And Sarah?"

"Forget her. She's not for you. You've lost your judgment since you fell in love with her—and for what? She'll never belong to you."

"Someday she love me, then she belong. When a man like me love a woman, really love her, he can do things and give things and promise things others cannot. Sarah will love me in the end—you see, Mario."

"She'll never love you; accept the fact."

"You think you know everything, but time will show that I am right."

They left for the restaurant and drove from Umberto's office past Vieri's house to the Left Bank. The iron lamps of a bygone age glowed mellow gold, casting romantic reflections on the water, and Umberto remembered how Sarah had loved those lamps and how she had once stood on the bridge in the middle of the night, gazing at the beauty of the scene. Wiping a trickle of sweat from his brow, he thought of Benedetti's deception. For the moment he would say nothing, because he still needed Benedetti's subtle instincts to know how to deal with Sarah, but someday he would show the man he had trusted that Umberto di Castelli *never* forgave a Judas. He asked himself then where Sarah would go without clothes or money or a place to stay, closing his eyes as he thought of the softness of her body and the effect it had on his own. Someday, she would come back and he would be ready. When that moment came, he would show her how much he really loved her and she would stay at his side forever.

Part II

MARRIAGES ARE MADE IN HEAVEN

There are certain temperaments that
marriage makes more complex.
They retain their egotism and add to
it many more egos. They are forced
to have more than one life. . . .
—Oscar Wilde
The Picture of Dorian Grey

Chapter Eight

Vieri, Marseilles, January 1968

Vieri felt the needle entering his body and soon a warm, tender feeling of lassitude overcame his resistance. He knew nothing more until he awoke alone in a small attic room devoid of furniture. The windows were broken and a sharp breeze was blowing in through the jagged panes of glass. His first thought was of escape, but he was trussed in a way that made each movement agony. His mind, emerging from weeks of drugged sleep, struggled to assess where he was. Then, closing his eyes, he listened to the sounds of the area. The traffic noise was deafening and there were seagulls and the sound of ships' sirens in the mist. There seemed to be little activity in the immediate vicinity, and Vieri assumed correctly that he was in a deserted building. His nostrils picked up the scent of pine and jasmine and he thought he must be in Marseilles or Toulon or even Nice. He also knew that escape was highly unlikely. Even if he could get out of the house, there would be guards watching from buildings nearby, men who owed allegiance to the organization that had taken him.

Vieri was sweating and trying with every ounce of his strength to release his hands, when a girl entered the room. She was a very young Oriental. Her tiny figure was clad in a shapeless gray tunic and baggy black cotton trousers. Her feet were small, her hands perfect, her voice harsh. When she looked down at him, Vieri saw that her deep-set eyes were cold, her face devoid of expression.

"You are in Marseilles. Since you were taken prisoner at the church, you have been sedated and transported from Paris to this house, via Switzerland, Italy, and the Midi. You have lost twenty pounds in weight and I warn you that your bodily functions and your mental capacity are already severely diminished. Do not try to escape. Do not try to attack me or any of the people you see here. We are angels compared with what you will find when you are moved in three days to another location."

"I need to go to the lavatory."

"I cannot release you. What you wish to do, you do where you sit."

Vieri stared at the impassive face, ignored the reply, and spoke with all the authority he could muster. "Get the guards to take me to the lavatory."

"I cannot; it would be against my orders."

"Where am I going when I leave here?"

"I do not know. Eat or you will grow even weaker."

"How much are you asking for me?"

"Five million dollars, but we will accept three."

"Have you been in contact with my family?"

"No. Our way is to leave the families to rot like oranges in the sun. Then, when they are soft, we squeeze them of their juice and throw them away."

"With whom will you negotiate?"

"Your father died two days ago and your brother, Elio, is now head of the family. He will no doubt wish to engage an expert negotiator to act on his behalf."

Vieri sighed, panic seeping into his soul. Hope of getting the girl to help him died when she turned and addressed him from the door of the room.

"I will return later. Do not try to escape or waste your en-

ergy shouting. The building is heavily guarded and the quarter is deserted. No one will come here but our men.''

"I want to go to the lavatory.''

She spoke patiently, as if to a backward child, her
robotlike voice infuriating Vieri.

"What you wish to do, you do where you are. I cannot
release you.''

"I can't do that; it's inhuman.''

She smiled, weighing the handsome face, the gray eyes
that were the color of clouds in a storm.

"They tell me you are a prince and that you have lived all
your life in luxury, with servants to tend your needs. Now
you are going to live like a pig. You will stink like a pig, and
before we are through with you, you will think like one. For
you, Mr. Aldobrandini, life in captivity will be very difficult. You will lose the dignity you value so highly. Your
great family will go on their knees and beg for your release
and you will grovel like an animal for food, even for refuse.''

"That day will never come.''

Their eyes met and for the first time she looked happy.
"They all say that, but they grovel and they shit in their
Savile Row suits, and they plead for a bullet through the
brain and sometimes we give it to them. I will return later
with your lunch.''

As she left the room, Vieri closed his eyes, his bladder at
bursting point, his bowels likewise. His wrists were bleeding from struggling with the ties that bound him. Panic was
rising and falling in his gullet. He tried to think of the legendary courage of the Aldobrandini men, but kept asking
himself if any of them had ever been subjected to a torture
more painful than sword thrusts and bullets. Had anyone
ever attacked the mind of an Aldobrandini? Suddenly, as nature had its way with his body, Vieri felt tears falling down
his cheeks. He thought of Mariannina and the disgust she
would manifest if she was here in this cold room filled with

the stench of excrement. She would never understand or forgive, because for her control was everything. Then his mind
turned to thoughts of Sarah and he tried to imagine *her* reaction. The only thing he knew was that in a strange way she
was unshockable. With that enigmatic smile of hers, she
would wash him like a baby, put him to bed, and join him
there, lavishing her love and her body on him to make him
forget the hours of trauma. Vieri wondered if she was still
with di Castelli and wished he had told her all the facts about
the Sicilian. Then, closing his eyes, he imagined how it
would be to love her. In his mind's eye, he saw her in the
white dress with rosebuds in her hair, waltzing in the Piazza
Navona. She was a dream, a curious mixture of old-
fashioned romanticism, modern sexuality, and independent
thinking. He was certain she would be sensational when she
made love. In the squalid room that was his prison, Vieri
imagined he could smell her perfume, the sensuous odors of
iris and rose, hyacinth and freesia that followed her everywhere. Then, opening his eyes, he saw the reality of his situation: broken windows, a chilling wind from seaward, and a
man at the start of the long slide into degradation.

In the afternoon the girl returned and cut off all Vieri's
hair, putting it into a paper bag and smiling delightedly at
his chagrin. It was obvious that the task had given her curious satisfaction and Vieri did his best not to react to her
taunting words.

"Now you really look like a prisoner! You will be pleased
to hear that I have received instructions that you are to be
moved tomorrow instead of Friday. You will travel by ship
to your destination, which is Messina. You will be held
there until the ransom is paid."

Vieri's mind raced to assess the statement.

"Sicily is Mafia territory. You and your so-called associates are members of the Japanese Red Army faction at present hiding in Paris. What is the connection?"

"We do not hide."

"You hide from the police and from each other because your organization is riddled with traitors."

With no change of expression on her face, she struck him hard across the cheek. Then, as if embarrassed to have shown any emotion, she began to pace the room. "We do not hide. We *wait*," she said emphatically.

"And your connection with the Mafia?"

"We have none. We do service for others when required. In return they supply us with what we need."

"Arms and information, I suppose."

"Of course. We need nothing else."

When she had gone, Vieri surveyed the room with weary eyes. It was already dark outside and he thought it was about seven in the evening. He began to shiver uncontrollably, shock, hunger, and cold conspiring to undermine him. He tried to do the exercises Elio had taught him long ago, the isometric pressing and pushing that would keep his legs strong, but after a while he lost interest. Instead, exhausted, humiliated, anguished, Vieri leaned his head against the crumbling plaster of the wall and tried to sleep. Yet again, images of Sarah came into his mind and he thought of her life and how she had been conditioned to suffering. For the first time, he wished he understood the things she knew from instinct: the swift, defensive reaction to threat, the hardness under fire, the ability to become harder and more resilient as suffering came her way.

At five o'clock the following morning, Vieri was put into a car and driven to a deserted beach five miles west of the city. In the bay, a fishing boat was anchored, waiting to transport him to his final destination. He looked at the girl and the men who had guarded him, all of them dressed in the same formless black and gray, and wondered who had made them into obedient robots. He also wondered if he too would become one under the punishing treatment of his captors.

Then he scrutinized the Sicilians rowing ashore from the fishing boat and saw two big, brawny men calling to each other over the noise of the waves. Vieri caught the girl's eyes as she issued instructions to the men at her side, surprised when she turned to face him.

"You will go with the men to the fishing boat and you will never see us again, though you might wish you could. The people who will take over have no love for men like you. They may feed you or they may not. They may treat you well, or they may make your life hell. The only thing of which you can be certain is that you will never escape."

Vieri eyed the little boat and the men walking toward him over the shingle. The woman was right. Once he reached Messina there would be no escape. His chance and his only chance was now, before he was put aboard. He decided to take the risk and gamble that he could convince his captors that he had drowned. His face was calm as he was led away from the group on the beach. This, he recognized, was the moment when he would have to prove his courage for the first time in his life.

The men had rowed halfway from the shore to the fishing boat when Vieri hurled himself overboard. One of the Sicilians leaped up, the other hauled in the oars, and both peered over the edge of the boat, searching the water for signs of life. When none appeared, the younger of the two undressed and dived into the sea. Within minutes he was swimming back to his partner.

"He's there, but I can't take him alone. Hurry, Falco, or all we'll take back is a corpse."

Vieri saw them coming and lashed out with all his strength. His lungs were almost bursting, but he fought like a madman for his freedom, until the moment when the men separated. Then one came up behind him and struck a stunning blow to the back of the head. He remembered nothing more until he heard the chugging of the fishing boat's engine

and realized that he had lost the gamble that could have
ended in freedom. Opening his eyes, he saw through an
unfocused blur a dark-haired girl holding out a mug of
steaming coffee. When he spoke, she did not answer, but sat
regarding him with eyes full of sadness. Vieri drank the coffee, smiling to reassure her, but her gaze was empty and she
manifested only a tragic acceptance of a life not worth living. He wondered desperately if he could make her his ally,
or if she was too far beyond the limits of despair to find herself again.

Chapter Nine

Sarah, London, November 1968

Sitting alone in the tiny apartment she had rented, Sarah was taking stock of the events since her return to England. It was her birthday and she felt the need to assess her life. For the first three weeks after her arrival, she had stayed with Holly's sister, Eira, glad of her help in the black days of depression that had come after the delayed reaction to the shocking events in Paris. There had been no news of Vieri, which frightened Sarah, and none of Umberto, which gave her hope that he knew nothing of where she was and what she was doing. She had found work without difficulty, first in a musical show and then as a hostess of a television quiz program. She remained demoralized, however, shocked and empty, her mind perpetually full of questions about Vieri. Sleep had become an elusive luxury and she wondered often if she was descending into a breakdown.

Sarah rose and walked to the stove to make sure she had turned it off. It was the third time she had done the same thing within the hour, her anxiety manifesting itself in such small curious ways. Often she found herself buying three newspapers—the morning, afternoon, and evening editions—to scan the headlines and foreign news for some mention of Vieri's fate. Frequently she accepted invitations from people she barely knew, because she could not bear to be alone.

She had perversely chosen to be alone on her birthday and she was unhappy. All the while, her mind kept returning to the hours spent with Vieri in the magic dawn moments in the Piazza Navona. She had taken to writing cards to send to him when he was found, but he had disappeared with an ominous finality. Press and police opinion seemed divided on whether he had been flown out of France to a hideout in either Algeria or Corsica, to be held until the ransom was paid. Only one demand had been made, for five million dollars. Since that time, the Aldobrandini family had heard nothing, and despite extensive searches by the police of nine countries and assistance from psychic researchers and private detectives, no trace had been found. Vieri had simply vanished.

Sarah put on a heavy coat, scarf, and knitted hat with violet pom-pom that matched her eyes. Then, having locked the door of the apartment, she ran downstairs into the street. The wind was icy, the sky leaden, the atmosphere depressing, but at least she did not feel so alone. For a while she gazed longingly into the shop windows of Bond Street, telling herself she must not be tempted to buy, that she must save every pound she could muster for the future. Vieri might be dead. On the other hand, there was still hope and she clung to that hope with increasing desperation.

Pausing outside the Irish Tourist Board's shop, Sarah admired Waterford crystal in emerald velour boxes and Arran sweaters that looked as if they would keep even the bone-freezing wind from the Thames from the body. Sarah was about to move away when she saw a familiar figure reflected in the window. The man was fair, tall, very thin, and wearing a tweed overcoat, a deer-stalker with the flaps pulled down, and a cheerful expression in his pale-blue eyes. Sarah smiled happily as he addressed her. "How are you, young lady? It's been such a long time since we met."

"How lovely to see you, Nolan. It's years since I visited
Thistleton."

"I heard you were in Paris."

"I was, but I came back at the end of the Ballet Rose tour
and I've been in London ever since. I'm feeling cold and
miserable." She adjusted her muffler as she spoke.

"I have just the solution for a young woman in distress.
I'll buy you tea at the Ritz. Then we'll go and see the first
house of Juliette Greco's one-woman show. I'm *so* glad to
see you. I've often wondered what happened to you since
your mother remarried."

They walked together to the Ritz and settled on a green
silk sofa to order Earl Grey with crumpets, Madeira cake,
and strawberry jam. Sarah felt renewed. Nolan James had always been one of her favorite people, a tower of strength in
the unhappy days of childhood in Sussex, a pen friend after
she and her mother moved north, a wise and wonderful figure always eager to help, support, and amuse. She smiled
into his lazy eyes, weighing the sandy side-whiskers and elegantly clipped beard. Nolan looked like a painter of the late
nineteenth century, a man out of his time, old-fashioned but
reassuring. Noted as a friend and confidant of some of Britain's most beautiful women, he was one of the most eligible
bachelors in the country—rich, cultivated, and known for
his perfect taste. Sarah began to ask him about his work.

"What's happening in the high stakes of literary life?"

"I'm almost through a novel set in seventeenth-century
Russia and I'm doing a TV adaptation of *Bleak Island*, but I
want to hear about your life. I saw your mother the other day
and she was charming till I asked about you and then she
wasn't charming at all."

"She was furious when I left for France, and now she's
furious I'm back. I think she's afraid I'll ask to go home and
disturb her nuptial peace."

"Not much danger of that."

"I'd rather die than go home."

Touched by her words, Nolan longed to comfort her, to soothe the small unhappy child she still was in so many ways.

"You'd even rather spend your birthday alone?"

"What about you?" She parried. "Why are you still one of Britain's most eligible bachelors?"

"I've been feeling a bit sad and reclusive myself," he said soberly. "Mother went to stay with her sister, who has pneumonia, and Teddy died very suddenly of cancer in September. He was thirty-eight and he'd been my agent for fifteen years. I've been walking around like a zombie ever since."

"I'm so sorry, Nolan. And it's a shame your mother's away now. But she's always traveled a great deal hasn't she? In all the time that I've known you and all those times that I visited you at Thistleton, I don't think I ever met her. Or maybe I just don't remember . . . It was such a long time ago." She stopped for a minute, remembering some of the happiest moments of her childhood. "Have you taken on someone else to handle your business?"

"I'm handled by A.C.A. now, but it's not the same. They know how to get the money, but there's no creative feedback from them."

Sarah poured them both more tea, suddenly glad to be in England, glad to be drinking Earl Grey and eating crumpets at the Ritz. Above all, she was glad to be speaking English with a trusted friend. She wondered if Paris had been a dream, suddenly admitting to herself that she had only wanted to stay on there to be near Vieri. Even now, she found it impossible not to think of him night and day, morning and evening, every time the wind whispered and the sun rose over the horizon. Love was a malady worse than malaria, that was certain. Afraid of her own emotions, Sarah thought wryly that even when she was interested in some-

thing she found a small part of her mind revolving indepen-
dently on Vieri. Sweat broke out on her forehead and she
apologized to Nolan, who was watching her closely.

"I was daydreaming. I'm sorry, Nolan."

"It looked more like a nightmare! Come down to
Thistleton for the weekend. You're obviously tired, Sarah,
and in need of a rest and a bit of spoiling. You haven't been
to Thistleton since you were fourteen and I was a mere lad of
thirty-two. Do say you'll come."

Built in the seventeenth century of gray and amber stone,
Thistleton House was magnificent. In summer, its leaded
windows reflected the surrounding countryside dotted with
meadowsweet and the clover-flowering musk thistles after
which the property was named. Wild clematis and bramble
filled the drive, and topiaried yews graced the lawn outside
the east wing. In winter, everything was white with snow,
the only color the scarlet of holly berries and spirals of pale
gray smoke rising from the tall chimneys. The place had
about it an air of old England, a haunting beauty irresistible
to someone longing for peace of mind.

As they drove up the drive, Sarah felt suddenly very tired
and very happy. Since her return from Paris, she realized,
she had continued to be both shocked and exhausted. Her
mind was slow, her only real desire to have definite news of
Vieri and some peace of mind. She was almost grateful
when Nolan patted her hand.

"These surroundings suit you, my dear. You're not a
very present-day person, you know. Oh, by the way, I met
the man who lives in the next house along the lane. He's the
new head of Special Branch in London and I asked him
about the Aldobrandini kidnapping. He said the French police are making no effort at all to find him. I suppose they're
convinced he's dead."

Sarah sighed, wondering if it was true, if the man really

knew about Vieri or if he was trying to show off his position to Nolan. In her debilitated state, she could not assess the situation and was relieved to enter the old house and to feel its peace around her. At Thistleton, it was easy to forget Vieri and all the other problems in life. For the moment, Sarah knew she wanted to do just that. As she gazed at the painting on the wall of Nolan's prize bull, nicknamed Buttercup, she remembered the days of childhood, when this house had been her refuge. Then her eyes wandered to the portrait of Charles II looking lustful and another ancestor, Lady Fanny Shirley, volume of Wesley in hand, trying to convince herself and generations to come that she was a paragon of virtue and not the lascivious mistress of the Earl of Chesterfield. At Thistleton everything had been in place for centuries and the effect was infinitely reassuring.

In Sarah's bedroom, the carving over the marble fireplace said "Where welcome ever smiles." The four-poster was hung with curtains bright with the rainbow colors of Florentine stitch. The floorboards were glossy with wax polish, the oriel windows overgrown with yellow winter jasmine. Sarah threw herself down on the bed and was sound asleep within seconds.

Lunch was watercress soup, potted crab, pigeon pie, and lemon posset. Sarah felt ravenously hungry, though since her arrival in England she had found it almost impossible to eat and had lost weight. She turned to Nolan and smiled across the table at him.

"I'm so glad I came to Thistleton. It makes me realize how much I love England."

"Do stay till you have to go back to the studio on Thursday. The old house is a real home again when you're here."

In the next few days, Nolan showed Sarah the beechwoods, the newly discovered barrel-vaulted ceiling of the Long Gallery, a collection of lacy Madagascan coral kept in his bathroom, and another of exotic shells of the world

bought at auction from the Duke of Westminster's house at
Eaton Hall. Time passed quickly, each day a pleasure for
them both. Then on Thursday, as the ancient grandfather
clocks struck six and Sarah packed her bags, Nolan appeared with breakfast for two on a tray.

"We have kedgeree, bacon and eggs, hot rolls, and your
favorite bitter-orange marmalade."

"I don't want to leave. I feel as if I've taken root."

"Then stay. You could come every weekend till the
series ends. I want to be with you, Sarah. I've been so happy
just doing the simple things together. Don't disappear for
months on end again."

When Sarah reached the apartment in London, she found
a note in Nolan's ornate hand and violet ink. *Dearest Sarah,
Please hurry back. Just realized that I've been more than a
little in love with you since you were fourteen. What are you
going to do about it? Yours, Nolan.*

Opening the morning paper that had been delivered during her absence, Sarah stared at the front-page headlines and
the article that followed. Police in Palermo had found the
bodies of two men burned beyond recognition near the village of Castellamare. Jewelry found on the bodies would be
used to identify one of the men as the missing head of the
Aldobrandini family. Sarah felt suddenly hot and breathless.
Was it true that Vieri was dead at thirty-five? What had he
been doing in Sicily? Had his kidnapping been one of the
new-style liaisons between the Mafia and the political ter-
rorist groups that were growing all over Europe?

Sarah ran to the newsstand on the corner and bought each
of the leading dailies to read in the car on the way to the studio. She was reentering the apartment when she heard the
phone ringing and, picking it up, found Nolan on the line.
His voice was solemn and his words made her flinch.

"Sarah, I just had a call from that friend in the Special

Branch. He says Aldobrandini's dead, no doubt of it. I wanted to tell you so you wouldn't read it in the papers.''

Sarah stood quite still, thinking how Nolan had advised her to forget Vieri, to get on with her life and not dream of phantoms she could never in any case have. Was he telling the truth? Or was he using the latest news to sever her link with Vieri? She replied guardedly.

"Nolan, I want the *truth*. Are you saying this to relieve me of my stress about Vieri, because if you are I can tell you it's *agony*, no other word for it.''

"Of course not. Why would I do that?''

"You said I should forget him and stop thinking about whether he was alive or dead.''

"You've seen the papers, haven't you? My friend has privileged information, Sarah dear. The family has imposed a news blackout. I just wanted to save you a shock.''

Sarah managed to choke out a good-bye as she put the phone down. The receiver missed the cradle, but she let it fall to the floor. She began to sob, great body-shaking sobs. Every dream she had hidden in the recesses of her mind died in the moment of acceptance of Nolan's words. At last she knew and the truth was everything she had feared. She struggled to find a solution to her own dilemma, her obsessive desire for peace and security. Had Vieri been part of that? Had he been more than a symbol of love? Had part of the attraction been that he was the head of a family established over many centuries in their Venetian domain? Sarah thought back on her own life and sighed. From childhood, trauma had superseded trauma. There had been moments of peace, but they had been rare. Now, at twenty-two, after the events in Umberto's house in Paris and the suspense of waiting for news of Vieri's liberation, she was faced with the catastrophe of his death. Reality slipped momentarily and she knew that she was in danger. For so long she had taken the

stresses of life bravely. Now she knew she could take no
more.

Sarah rose unsteadily and let in the studio driver, watching in puzzlement as he replaced the receiver, then called the
studio and explained that she was in a distressed condition
and would need the attention of the company doctor. She
felt herself being led to the car, covered with a blanket, and
given a stiff brandy from the chauffeur's hip flask. Closing
her eyes, she curled into a ball on the back seat of the car and
let sleep claim her.

When she finished work on the second day in the studio,
Sarah returned to her dressing room and found Nolan waiting for her. For a moment, he held her tight against the old
tweed jacket that smelled of cigar smoke, grass, and
Thistleton, all the while whispering words of reassurance.

"Everything's all right, Sarah. I'm here and I'll look after
you."

She closed her eyes, wanting more than anything in the
world to be in the old house again, secure in her bedroom
with its fireplace of blazing logs and touching motto,
"Where welcome ever smiles." Gazing into Nolan's
thoughtful face, she asked herself how she could ever have
let Umberto love her and how she could have dreamed of
marrying Vieri. For a few months she had traveled far from
her roots and had let herself drift on the powerful currents of
the tide of life. Now that she was home in England, it was
time to return to reality. Was reality Nolan James and
Thistleton House? Sarah followed him to his car and sat
barely listening when he spoke.

"We'll be home in time for dinner if I put my foot
down."

"I can't wait to be at Thistleton again."

Sarah closed her eyes as he drove away. Soon they would
see the flint and stone cottages of the Sussex downs and the
villages with curious names, Cocking and Midhurst, Good-

wood and Lavant. She looked at the fields flooded with melting snow, the mistletoe cascading in round balls of green and white from the trunks of ancient elms. Everything was gray in the pale, cold winter light. Then, suddenly, she found her mind wandering to the day in Palermo, to the golden sunlight on the sepia landscape around the palazzo. She thought of Umberto's strong, square hands as he trapped the lizard. There had been a brute force in the action that had thrilled and reassured her, as she had always found his willfulness reassuring. Umberto had been an earthquake in her life, eradicating all opposition and making her forget both scruples and reason. Sarah sighed. When they had been together, she had been so sure nothing in the world could hurt her, no one could oppose her will, her ambition, her desire. It had been a good feeling and one she had longed for all her life. Nolan's voice broke into her thoughts.

"Sometimes I have the impression you're very far away."

"I was thinking of Umberto's house in Sicily."

"He's in Paris and we're here and you'll never see him again, so relax."

After dinner, they drank homemade blackberry liqueur with their coffee in the library. Lined with a fascinating collection of books, a big fire glowing in the hearth and casting coral lights on the Indian yellow and lapis lazuli of the carpet, this was one of Sarah's favorite rooms. Nolan stood looking down at her as she sat in a winged velvet chair and tried to put into words all he was feeling.

"I want to marry you, Sarah. I know it's sudden and a little mad, but I love you and there's no better reason for marriage than that. Also, I really believe I can offer you something no other man ever has, namely peace and security. It's something that has eluded you all your life."

Sarah wondered what to do. Her mind was still lethargic from the shock and anguish of Vieri's death. If she could not

have the man she really loved, was it wise to opt for security
in the form of Nolan, who adored her, and Thistleton, where
she was at peace? For the moment, ambition was forgotten
and peace of mind became the order of the day. She stared
from Nolan to the cat purring in front of the fire and thought
how peaceful it was in the house. Then she replied to the
proposal, bringing Nolan to his feet and rushing to ring for
champagne.

"I accept and I'd like to get married by special license."

"Done! We'll be married before you return to London on
Thursday. Dear God, Sarah, I feel as if I could walk on
water!"

On a chill November morning, Sarah put on a dress of
cream cashmere and walked with Nolan to the church at the
end of the drive. With them was the cook, Mrs. Peel, and
her daughter, Felicity, the only witnesses to the linking of
Nolan Winchester James and Sarah Elizabeth Hallam.

Half an hour later, Nolan was stretched out on the settee
in the living room with a cold compress on his head. Sarah
was drinking champagne at his side, while in the kitchen the
staff were singing bawdy songs, most of them still stunned
by the suddenness of the union. No one was more stunned
than Sarah, who felt as if she had just wakened from a long
and painful nightmare only to find herself with a husband.
She looked around the room with its Chippendale chairs
made in 1754 and its painting by Stubbs of the Melbourne
family in a leafy glade. On one wall, a Flemish tapestry of
the sixteenth century had faded from its original indigo to lilac, and Sarah thought to herself that everything in the house
was centuries old and intensely satisfying because it had
lasted throughout the tribulations of history. Then she
sighed, wondering through a haze of champagne and shock
if she had married Nolan or Thistleton House.

The wedding night was something to remember. First
Nolan bathed. Then he went for a walk in the garden and did

not return for two hours. When he finally appeared, it was obvious that he had come to bed by way of the library, where he had tested the merits of a new delivery of tawny port. Looking down at Sarah, he spoke in obvious embarrassment.

"Well, here I am at last and nervous as a twelve-year-old."

Sarah smiled at the flannel pajamas with his monogram on the pocket. Everything about Nolan was positively archaic and she liked that, because it gave her a feeling of security. She rose naked from the bed, enjoying the sharp intake of his breath and the look of uncertainty in his eyes. Perhaps women were something Nolan knew little about. After all, his mother had lived in the house until recently, only moving to the Dower House in the garden in the weeks before her recent departure. Sarah unbuttoned the pajama jacket and kissed the bony chest. Then she untied the trousers and slipped them down. Nolan's penis, like the rest of his body, was long and thin like a stiletto. She decided to take him quickly, this first time, in view of the nervous condition he was in. Sliding onto his erection, she vibrated back and forth until he came inside her. Then she lay at his side, shocked when tears began to course down his cheeks. Nolan made no move to take her in his arms, so she took him in hers, watching his face as he began to suckle her nipples like a baby. Then, closing her eyes, Sarah let the teeth and tongue provoke. Finally, aroused by the sounds of his enjoyment, she began to moan from desire unfulfilled. As he bent over her, she whispered, "Put your prick inside me when you do that, Nolan."

He raised her knees and spread them, putting a pillow under her bottom. Then he pushed inside her, still concentrating his energies on the breasts that were his obsession. As she tightened over his penis, his cries pierced the silence of the night, cries of abandon and anguish, pleasure and pain.

Within seconds they had both reached the climax of feeling. Then, to Sarah's astonishment, Nolan jumped out of bed, put on his dressing gown, and walked to the door. She called after him.

"Where are you going?"

"I'll sleep in the Blue Room and come to you for breakfast at seven."

Shocked to the bone by this unexpected defection, Sarah sat bolt upright.

"Nolan, what on earth are you talking about?"

He looked down at her, his face uncomprehending.

"I've never slept with anyone and I'm too old to change my ways. Please don't be upset, Sarah. It's just that I can't relax if there's someone there."

When he had gone, Sarah lay staring at the ceiling and wondering what it all meant. Why had Nolan done that? Could he not even sleep with her on their wedding night? Tears of confusion began to fall down her cheeks and she turned off the light, needing the comfort of darkness and the warmth of the bed for solace. For an hour she tossed and turned, her mind in a state of turbulence, the state it had fallen into on hearing the news of Vieri's death. She tried to think logically, as was her habit, but images of Nolan's voracious mouth on her breasts mixed with memories of Vieri's eyes watching the sunrise over the Danube. In her shocked state, tears began to fall faster and faster, until finally Sarah could stand it no longer. Putting on a wrap, she hurried along the corridor to the Blue Room. She had her hand on the door handle when she heard the sound of her husband sobbing. She retreated, pausing for a moment in the darkened corridor, her head tilted as she listened to the outpouring of Nolan's grief. Then, without further hesitation, she hurried back to her room and leaped under the bedclothes. What did it all mean? Questions drummed at her bewildered brain, exhausting her, questions that had no answers. Finally, as the clocks struck three, she slept and dreamed of being chased by men with no faces.

Sarah was eating her breakfast when Nolan entered the room with his own tray loaded with food. His voice was full of admiration as he parted the kimono and exposed her breasts.

"I love to see your body. You must expose it all the time when we're alone, even when you're dressed. That really is exciting."

Sarah watched as he rose and locked the door. Then he delved into a trunk under the bed and produced a pile of pornographic magazines, most of them featuring women in astonishing outfits designed to expose their breasts. He seemed quite unembarrassed by his obsession.

"I've always been like this. Mother breast-fed me till I was two and that's probably the cause."

Sarah realized suddenly that she knew nothing of the man she had married, nothing but facts any newspaper reader could discover and the little things she had known about him since childhood. She leaned forward as Nolan whispered to her, feeling a certain wayward excitement as he removed her kimono.

"Lie back, Sarah. Now, all you have to do is relax. For the moment your body is all mine to do with as I want."

Memories of Umberto's attitude entered Sarah's mind, making her scowl, but she said nothing because Nolan was running his hands over the mound of pubic hair, his fingers rotating the clitoris until she cried out as a harsh orgasm took her breath away. Then, as if his duty to her body was fulfilled, he returned to her breasts, his fingers plucking the nipples that grew hard under his touch. Again Sarah found herself thinking of Umberto, who had been so urgent in his desire to enter her body and whose penis had filled her with satisfaction. Nolan seemed unwilling to enter her, until the moment when he had no alternative but to do so. She began to urge him on.

"Make love to me—*please!* I need you inside me."

Ignoring her, Nolan sucked her nipples so hard that Sarah's breasts began to feel full to overflowing, her core hungry from longing for the relief only a penis could bring. But he remained at the breast, digging his fingers into the soft flesh and provoking the nipples to a new zenith of feeling by tugging and biting and sucking. Finally, he entered her body, his fingers still caressing the nipples that obsessed him, until, without warning, he came inside her.

Six weeks after the marriage, Nolan began to behave strangely. When Sarah inquired what was wrong, he began to pace the living room.

"Mother's coming home today. I'll be meeting her from the two o'clock train and there'll be hell to pay when she finds you here."

Crestfallen at the remark, Sarah asked for an explanation.

"Your mother surely wouldn't expect your wife to live somewhere else, would she?"

"Oh, she has no idea I've married. If I'd told the old girl she'd have forbidden it absolutely."

Sarah leaped to her feet, alarm bells jangling in her mind.

"Are you telling me you never told your mother we married? I can't believe it!"

"Mother lives in the Dower House. She's very happy there, and if she loves me as much as she's always saying she does, she'll want me to be happy. The trouble is, she's always been so possessive."

Sarah spent the day organizing the servants in frenzied polishing sessions. Then she arranged meadowsweet, scarlet poppies, and tendrils of honeysuckle and put them in the hall, dining room, and salon. A special menu that included everything Nolan's mother liked best was worked out with the cook, and they would dine splendidly on parsnip soup, eel and sage pie, lamb with mint sauce, and amber pudding.

By one o'clock Sarah was feeling apprehensive. By one-thirty she had gone to her room and changed her clothes yet again, finally settling on a lilac silk with white coin spots. At two, she was in the hall, waiting for her mother-in-law's arrival and willing her hands not to tremble. Then she heard the sound of a car in the drive and the crunch of footsteps on the gravel.

Nolan appeared with a tiny birdlike woman of seventy-five, her white hair worn in a halo of corkscrew curls, her dark beady eyes taking in every detail of Sarah's appearance. As Nolan moved to introduce them, the tiny figure veered suddenly toward the salon, completely ignoring Sarah's out-stretched hand. It was a moment of rejection unequaled in her life, but she stood firm, picking up the newspaper Nolan's mother had thrown down on the linen chest and going to her bedroom to read it. If Mrs. James wanted a war, she could have one. Still, the insult had stung and in Sarah's depleted condition she was hard pressed to deal with it. Longing only to be at peace, she locked the door of her room and threw herself down on the bed. It was then she saw a photograph of Vieri on the front page of the paper and read a report saying that the body found in Palermo had been proven not to be his. The Aldobrandini family had heard again from the kidnappers and negotiations were taking place. Shocked to the core, Sarah dropped the paper and stared into space. For weeks she had believed Vieri dead. Now she knew he was alive, but instead of being free to rush to his side if he needed help, she was married to a man she liked but did not love, and certainly did not understand. She sat quite still, listening to the howling of the wind outside her window and trying to still the desolate thoughts careen-ing through her mind. She remained frozen into immobility until her husband came to call her to dinner.

"Do come and eat, Sarah. Mother's ready to meet you now. I've got her in a better humor at last."

"To hell with your mother!"

"Don't be like that. She's old and it's my fault she's so angry. Please, I beg you to come and meet her."

Sarah entered the drawing room and was introduced to Mrs. James, who remained seated, barely touching Sarah's hand and addressing her by her maiden name.

"Miss Hallam, I won't pretend I'm pleased to meet you, because I'm not, and I believe in telling the truth at all times."

Sarah steeled herself to reply.

"If you believe in the truth you'll address me as Mrs. James, since that is my name. Playing silly games won't change it back to Miss Hallam."

The old lady looked away and Nolan hurried to the piano and began to play. Sarah barely heard the music, though she knew he was playing her favorite tunes. She was thinking of Vieri and wondering how he was and where he was and just how damaging the kidnapping experience had been. Above all, she was regretting the hasty marriage contracted because she had thought him dead. Nolan was kind, but it was obvious his mother wanted trouble. Sarah closed her eyes and thought of the golden hairs on Vieri's hands, the intense look in the cloud-gray eyes. Tears began to fall as she thought of the mental and physical torture he had endured and the endless weeks he would have to spend in a clinic fighting for a return to normality. No one would really understand his anguish, because few had ever suffered such agony of the soul. In that moment of thinking deeply about Vieri's life and future, Sarah came to her senses, conscious that for months she had been in a less than normal state and that now she was herself again it was too late.

Chapter Ten

Arlette, Chantilly, December 1968

Arlette entered the clinic and went at once to her room, nervous and angry because her husband had left her at the entrance, saying he would return later. Looking out from the window over the fields of wood sorrel and valerian, she could see the chateau in the distance and the pointed spire of the nearby church. She shuddered, remembering the last time she had been in the clinic, to undergo minor surgical intervention for the removal of the hymen Charles had been unable to penetrate. Since then, he had made love with her on every possible occasion, even in the presbytery of the family chapel during the interment of one of the staff. His lack of sensitivity and his pleasure in provoking pain had appalled Arlette, but she had striven to please, to act emotions she could not feel, to accede to demands she found frightening. Sometimes, alone in her room in the still of night, tears came and she longed for affection, a gentle kiss on the cheek, a hand linked in hers. Instead, she had a husband whose sexual tastes leaned toward the sadistic, whose sole desire was to dominate every hour of her waking day. Taught from the earliest days of childhood that women must please their husbands, Arlette had done everything Charles asked, but nothing pleased him and she had begun to wonder if the price of living in a chateau and having a luxurious life was too high. At the moment of disillusion, she had discovered she was pregnant. At first she had panicked. Then she had settled to the idea and now, in labor, was praying for a boy.

As the pains increased, Arlette thought of the car accident that had killed her mother earlier in the year. When Mama had been alive they had talked on the phone for hours each day and Arlette had found it easy to accept that no one's life was perfect, but that her own in the chateau was better than in one room in Naples. With her mother dead, there was no relief, no escape from the despair that daily engulfed her, no light at the end of the tunnel.

Opening the window, Arlette listened to the song of a thrush in the sallow tree nearby. In the long-unused cemetery on the other side of the road, feral pigeons with gray bodies were massed on granite tombs overgrown with yellow moss. Arlette thought resignedly that if there were no complications she would have a baby in her arms by morning, a tiny child to love and look after for the rest of its life. If not, she would be with the pigeons in the cemetery. Her vision blurred momentarily as pain engulfed her. She returned to bed and lay looking resignedly at the mound of her belly and wondering how the child was going to come out. A nurse entered and examined her, followed by the doctor. Arlette felt sweat dripping from her brow and closed her eyes, willing herself to conquer the pain. Then, to her intense relief, she felt herself lifted onto a gurney and wheeled to the creaking elevator at the end of the corridor. She was thinking that once she had produced a fine child, life with Charles would be easier. She would show her husband she was not only one of the most beautiful duchesses in France, but also the very best mother. Someday, she thought grimly, her husband would forget his infantile desire to fuck every woman he met and appreciate the woman he had. As pain engulfed her body, Arlette bit her lips, determined to face the ordeal of giving birth in a manner that would make her husband proud.

At seven in the evening, Arlette was wheeled back to her room under sedation. The child she had already begun to love and on whom she was depending to relieve the stresses in her marriage, had been stillborn. Despite the tact and gentleness of the staff, Arlette had become hysterical. On being faced with her husband, she had broken down completely. The two nurses who resettled her in her bed, checking her pulse and blood pressure, exchanged anxious glances. They were young and still shocked by the Duke's open disgust. On being told that the baby had been born dead, Charles had looked down at his wife with angry eyes and said only, *You're a loser, Arlette. You can't do anything right.* No one in the clinic had ever heard such derision in like circumstances, and though they knew the rich had their own rules of life they found the Duke's attitude shocking and unacceptable. The consultant had protested, but Charles had turned on his heel and left the clinic.

Arlette woke at midday and stared at the ceiling, her eyes full of despair as she remembered the horrors of the previous night. Tears fell down her cheeks and her nose ran, but she could not find the strength to wipe it. Suddenly, the rigid control she had exercised all her life snapped and she wanted only to remain in bed, gazing into space, relieved of all responsibility and sheltered from her husband's fast-diminishing respect. Arlette thought of all that had happened since the marriage and knew that Charles was not only disappointed in her sexually, but also changed irrevocably in his own nature. What had caused the change, she did not know, though she suspected that it was his relationship with Ernestine. She thought of the times she had done her best to please her husband, conscious all the while that he needed white-hot sexuality, not a perfectly dressed body and gentle caresses. There had been savage rows when he had forced her to submit to oral and anal intercourse, but even that she had done to try to salvage something of a marriage fast hastening toward the point of rupture. Nowadays, she revealed her inner thoughts only to her diary. Sleep had become elusive and she had lost all confidence in herself as a woman. Her self-esteem had sunk to its nadir with the realization that Charles had made the upstairs maid his mistress. The staff knew about it, and probably the whole of Chantilly, and her life as the Duchess had become something of a mockery.

Closing her eyes, Arlette tried to continue thinking of her marital problems, instead of the image of her dead child, but in her mind's eye she saw the baby, so tiny and pale and wrinkled, its hands clenched as if battling against some outside force for the breath of life that had been denied it. Without warning, Arlette felt the panic of the previous night returning and thoughts rushing through her head disjointedly. Frantic for reassurance, she pressed the bell to summon the nurse, but before anyone appeared, Charles arrived with his chauffeur, Gaston. Arlette looked uncertainly into her husband's face and saw impatience, annoyance, and something she now recognized as dislike. The tone of his voice was patient, but his words cut her to the bone.

"Are you ready to leave, my dear? I'm so very busy at the moment. I haven't much time."

"Of course, Charles, if the doctors say it's all right."

"To hell with doctors. After yesterday I'll never trust one again. I'm sorry for what I said, Arlette; I was very distressed. Get dressed and I'll take you home."

"Is there any reason for this urgency?"

"I'm leaving for Martinique in the morning and I need you to be at the chateau in my absence to help keep an eye on things."

"Of course I will, Charles."

Arlette wondered, but did not ask, what her husband was

doing going on holiday to Martinique when he had only just returned from a holiday in Switzerland. He had no property in the Antilles and had never shown any interest in the area. She rose unsteadily and began to dress, her head whirling because she remained weak and shocked. Unwilling to let Charles see the extent of her hurt and anguish, Arlette followed him from the room to the car. He said nothing on the way back to the chateau, but on arrival left her with the footman who would carry her cases to her suite.

Arlette closed the door on the world and sat for a moment on the edge of her bed, thinking. Then she rose and walked to the window, watching as her husband put his cases into the Bentley and drove away. Charles had not even bothered to come upstairs to say good-bye. Minutes later, she watched Ernestine following in the taxi of Monsieur Florent, the local driver. He had lied in saying he was leaving the following morning. He had brought her from the clinic because he was anxious to leave immediately for a holiday with the peasant who had taken her place, the teenager who was going to be her humiliation and penance for the years to come.

Arlette sat again on the edge of the bed, wondering resignedly why she could not feel angry. Usually she was quick to anger, but at this moment she felt only a strange, distant thunder in the head. Then, without warning, she heard a high-pitched scream coming from somewhere in the interior of the house. She did not realize that she was screaming and that the terrible sound came from the anguished core of her being. She was unaware when the doctor came and gave her a sedative injection. She saw only the ancient yews in the drive and a man with a gentle smile, who held her hand and tried to reassure her.

"Everything's going to be all right, my dear. I shall call morning and evening and look after you until you've recovered from the shock. Try not to think too much of the baby or of your husband. Charles will recover in his own time and in his own way.''

Arlette wondered wearily if Charles's own way would be with Ernestine. Would he want a divorce? Would he ask her to leave? What did the future hold—or was there no future for her?

Chapter Eleven

Vieri, Sicily, March 1969

Vieri sat in a corner of the cave, naked but for a blanket around his shoulders. He had been in the cave for many weeks, chained at first and then, after pneumonia and a scorpion bite weakened him, released, but obliged to live without clothes and shoeless, whatever the weather. He had lost thirty pounds and, having been locked for days at a time in a darkened cell hewn out of the rock, had become disoriented, lost in time and trapped in anguish. Thoughts rushed through his head with alarming rapidity, of his home, his brother, his businesses, his wife, Sarah, but gradually, as suffering purged him of all the preconceived standards by which he had lived his life, he thought less and less of Mariannina, whose very perfection seemed daunting. Her rigid adherence to the rules of society bored him and he wondered in confusion why he had married her. Vieri, who had lived his entire life in the rigid manner of his class, now found the standards of his upbringing meaningless. All that mattered was to find food to soothe the pangs of hunger, water to drink, and tenderness to heal the pain in his body. Here, in the caves of Calcelrama, the rules of the jungle prevailed and at last he was learning the art of survival.

Vieri gazed down at the festering sores on his body, the lacerations on his legs, the marks and bruises that came from

the harsh treatment meted out by his captors. He had made a
point of avoiding speaking to the men who guarded because
the very sound of his voice seemed to inflame their tempers.
His only contact had been with the girl with the tragic face,
Flavia, but though he had spoken to her many times, she had
never once replied.

On this cold March morning, it was evident that something was about to happen. Flavia's eyes were wide with
fear, and Vieri did all in his power to extract some information from her.

"You look sad. Tell me, what is frightening you?"

She stared at him, inclining her head in the direction of
Falco, the chief, who was sharpening a long knife used by
the men to cut up hares hunted in the surrounding countryside. Puzzled, Vieri looked again at the girl.

"Is he going to kill me?"

She moved her head imperceptibly from side to side.

"To move me?"

She repeated the action.

"What, then? In God's name tell me *something!*"

A solitary tear fell down her cheek and she turned on her
heel and ran from him.

Vieri looked across at Falco, who was testing his knife on
a newly killed rabbit. At his side, Rizzo was honing a sisal
spine, its long black spike as hard as ebony and as sharp as a
needle. Outside the cave, the sirocco was blowing, the landscape obscured by swirling clouds of chalk-white dust. Wild
dogs howled near the summit of the Monte d'Oro and the air
was full of taut anticipation that made Vieri prone to terrifying imaginings. He was trying to work out what was going
to happen when he saw one of the younger men returning to
the cave, his face wreathed in smiles.

Falco called to the newcomer.

"What happened with the widow?"

"I took all her jewels like you said."

"Did she put up a fight?"

"Not that I noticed. When I'd packed the stuff and given it to Salvatore to deliver, I went back and told her I thought she was beautiful."

"Beautiful! She has the face of a parrot."

"And the mind of a whore. I've been there since three this morning and only just managed to get out with my skin. If I know her type, she'll buy herself some new jewels so I can rob her again."

Falco went into a huddle with the men. Then, when they had drunk a bottle of *grappa* and eaten some of the rabbits cooking over the fire, they approached Vieri. Falco motioned for Salvatore and Rizzo to hold his arms and the young jewel thief to take his hand and place it carefully on the table made from a rough-hewn tree trunk. Then, without a word of warning, he raised the heavy knife and with one swift blow cut off the index finger.

Vieri felt the blood draining from his face and the contraction of every muscle in his body. Despite the agony, he did not cry out, determined not to give Falco a grain of satisfaction. Instead, he gritted his teeth to hold back the screams of anguish and pain, unable to control the tears that streamed down his face, despite his determination. While Falco made a parcel of the grisly object and hurried to deliver it to an address in Montelepre, Vieri found himself alone with his torment. After a while, he began to vomit, soiling the blanket that covered him. There was blood everywhere and in his head a thousand voices screaming like banshees. For months, he had kept his emotions under rigid control, as he had been taught to do throughout his life. Now all the fear turned in on him and he could think of nothing with clarity. Family, friends, hope were all forgotten as he sat gazing at the mutilated hand and listening to the scornful voices of his captors in the adjacent section of the cave. Each time the waves of pain overwhelmed him, he vomited, though his stomach was empty and nothing came but foul-smelling bile.

Flavia waited until nightfall, then crept to Vieri's cell with bandages and antiseptic for the hand. She was gentle, but his face was expressionless as his brain struggled through clouds of shock and despair. Gazing into the hollow eyes, black ringed from pain and lack of sleep, Flavia wondered what the prisoner was thinking and if he could feel her affection. She longed to comfort him with the age-old motherly, wifely words that every Sicilian woman learned from childhood, but Falco had forbidden all communication between them and she feared him too much to disobey. Still, Vieri's condition distressed her and Flavia felt she must do something to show that he had one friend in the world. Leaning forward, she kissed his cheeks. Then, having secured the bandage, she kissed his hand and rose to leave the cell that was his prison for the hours of night. She was raising the lamp to light the way when she came face to face with Falco, his eyes livid, his mouth contorted by rage.

"You bitch! You think I brought you here to fall in love with him? I brought you here to cook for us and to service the men. Instead, you get hot for that stuck-up imitation of a man!"

As Falco struck her a powerful blow to the cheek, Flavia fell, hitting her head on a rock on the floor of the cave as she landed. With a furious cry, Falco ran to her, cursing because he knew before he reached her that she was dead. He called out to Rizzo.

"Come here, for Christ's sake! Flavia's dead. I hit her because she was playing around with that bastard and she caught her head. What is La Mamma going to say?"

"Now we'll have to cook for ourselves!"

"Is that all you can think of? She was our sister, even if she was a whore. Keep a civil tongue in your head."

While Rizzo and Falco carried the body into the main section of the cave, Vieri sat in the light of a solitary candle, staring into space. He had seen and heard everything of the exchange between brother and sister and the terrible dull thud of the blow Flavia had taken. He remembered her gentle hands bandaging his wound and the kisses she had planted on his cheeks. Most of all, he remembered the look in Falco's eyes when he entered the cell and saw her. Vieri tried to still the voices wailing like banshees in his head, the wild thoughts careening through the confusion, and the panic he could no longer control. He wondered yet again if it would be possible to escape, but the thought was no longer real, because he had not enough strength to move more than a few yards from his hiding place. He was trying, unsuccessfully, to concentrate his thoughts, when Falco entered the cell and began to beat him. Vieri fell to the ground under a glancing blow to the head. He never felt the kicks that left his entire body a bloody travesty of what it had once been.

A month after Flavia's death, the captors received instructions to move Vieri one last time. The guards had been changed, because Falco was considered incapable of controlling his loathing for the prisoner, who was worth millions to the organization. The injuries he had inflicted on Vieri had been grave: four broken ribs, a fractured jaw, a damaged testicle, and a shattered kneecap. He had been moved to a clinic on the outskirts of Taormina, to be treated by the finest surgeons money could buy. Then he had been returned to the caves of Calcelrama, the guerrillas' paradise from which few ever emerged.

Vieri sat alone, naked and filthy, the overpowering stench of his body no longer of any concern to him. He saw nothing of his surroundings, focusing his eyes as best he was able on a dark spot on the wall. Perhaps it was a scorpion, perhaps not. He struggled to identify the object, but within seconds lost his concentration and forgot about it. For a moment he

recalled an incident long buried in childhood memory, when
his mother had found a scorpion sleeping peacefully in one
of her satin evening shoes. Vieri's face twitched from the effort of trying to recall where they had been living at the time,
but everything was blurred and out of focus. He heard the
men calling his name then and thought he should reply, but
since the night of Flavia's death he had not spoken and was
unsure if he would ever want to speak again. All he really
wanted was to sleep, to float, to forget. He barely noticed
when he was dressed in a pair of old blue denims, a clean
white shirt, and pullover of darned gray wool. Instinctively,
he reached out for the flea-ridden blanket that had been with
him ever since his arrival in the cave and with fumbling hands
wrapped it around his shoulders. Then, as he was led outside
into the light, his eyes began to stream as the sun assailed
them. He stumbled and fell, his body so weak he could not
walk without assistance. He showed no interest when he
was driven into Messina, put into a private plane, and flown
across the gulf to Milan. From there, he was taken at high
speed to a spot twenty kilometers from his home in Venice
and pushed out of the car on the empty road. He felt a pang
of regret when he saw the men driving away and an un-
speakable loneliness as he tried to stumble along the highway. Sweat poured from him and he wondered desperately
if he was dying. His heart was pounding like a gong in his
ears and he kept thinking of the dark cell in the cave with
something close to longing, because there, at least, no witnesses had seen his decline. In the caves of Calcelrama it
had been easy to stop fighting and let decay take its course.

Vieri paused and looked into the window of a deserted
cottage. The face reflected in the pane of glass made him
frown in puzzlement. Then he looked again, more closely,
at the man he had become. Gone were the legendary good
looks, the golden hair, the mocking eyes. The face was
skeletally thin, making the nose seem prominent. The eyes

were sunken, the hair snowy-white. The expression was furtive, haunted and full of fear. He stepped back, stumbling as his knees gave way. Then, somewhere behind him, he was conscious of a voice. As he fell to his knees he realized that it was a child crying to its mother.

"Mama, the man's hurt."

The young woman hurried to Vieri's side, peered into his face, and touched his hand.

"What's wrong? Can I help you? Where did you come from? No one ever comes here."

Vieri struggled to find his voice, but no words came and he fell at the woman's feet, his face upturned as the clouds opened and the rains came.

The paramedics put Vieri on a stretcher, and he watched with resigned eyes as Elio ran forward and grasped the mutilated hand, kissing it and weeping unashamedly. One of the *guardi campestri* could not resist a smirk of satisfaction. The great Vieri Aldobrandini was great no longer. The rich had no balls, that was certain.

Doctors called in by the family accompanied Vieri to the hospital, where his physical and mental condition would be assessed. And as they drove through the flat, empty countryside of the Veneto, Elio did his best to reassure his brother.

"Try to understand, Vieri, you're safe now. It's over and you're on your way to the hospital. I'll stay with you for as long as it takes. I've been given leave of absence by the Institute."

Vieri listened to the sounds and the reassuring tones of his brother's voice and watched as doctors monitored his blood pressure. Then he closed his eyes. If only he could be at peace. If only silence absolute and eternal could take him in its arms and make the world go away.

Chapter Twelve

Sarah, England, Summer 1969

Sarah was in the cornfield at the back of the house, hidden from view among the tall, golden crops of summer. She was reading a letter from Elio Aldobrandini, sent in reply to her letter about Vieri's health. The words blurred as tears came, and she thought resignedly that since her marriage she had done very little but cry. The knowledge that her unhappiness was all of her own making made it doubly hard to bear. She had fled the anguish of Vieri's death and chosen Thistleton, the house she had always loved, without a thought for the real implications of marriage, or a real knowledge of her husband's character. She now had to confront a nightmare of her own creation.

Sarah looked again at the letter, wondering desperately what could be done to help Vieri. Elio's words seemed ominous and without hope.

My dear Sarah,

I was so happy to hear from you.

Congratulations on your marriage and my best wishes for the birth of the baby. My brother remains in the Clinic of the Holy Family outside Rome. He has not spoken since being returned to us and is not responding to treatment. Though his physical condition has improved, his

mental state is giving rise to alarm. The doctors have tried
everything, but Vieri doesn't want to return to the world.
They say he intends to stay locked in the prison of his own
mind. I'm sorry to burden you with all this at a time when
you must be tired, but you asked for the fullest details.
The fact is, Vieri as you knew him doesn't exist anymore.
I send you my affectionate regards. Do write again soon.

Elio

Sarah looked at her swollen stomach and felt trapped. She
wanted to rush to Rome to be with Vieri, certain that with
love she could lead him out of his black tunnel of despair.
She wanted to lie at his side, kissing his back and stroking
the smooth skin of his shoulders, the fine gold hairs on his
hands. As she thought of him, despair came like an angry
sea, washing over her mind and body.

Then she looked again at the most haunting line in the letter: *The fact is, Vieri as you knew him doesn't exist anymore.* Was it true? Had the months of captivity in the caves
of Calcelrama destroyed him?

Sarah rose and walked to the riverbank, picking a bouquet
of wild lupine as she moved through the long grass. She was
thinking about her mother-in-law and wondering what she
could do about her situation. Mrs. James's jealousy was
both tragic and ludicrous. Though she had returned to the
Dower House, she arrived each morning at Thistleton to
open all the mail, including Sarah's. When asked not to
open those letters, she had retorted that as the letters were
addressed to her name she had a perfect right to open them.
Sarah had responded by asking her correspondents to write
to her in her maiden name. The letters continued to be
opened, the daily rows increasing to fever pitch. Sometimes
Sarah received no letters at all for a week and knew that her
mother-in-law had decided to destroy them.

Sarah closed her eyes and listened to the buzzing of bees

in clover flowers. Thistleton was England at its most beautiful and peaceful, yet there was nothing but turmoil in her
heart. Nolan was kind, but no match for a mother who held
the purse strings, paying off his overdraft every three
months. When he bought her a gift, his mother removed it to
the Dower House and kept it. When he responded by buying
two, one for his wife and the other for his mother, Mrs.
James forbade the extravagance. Sarah shook her head wearily, unable to believe that her life was being ruled by an
aged virago' of unstable temperament, whose only desire
was to drive her away.

Sarah was walking back to the house when Nolan came
running toward her.

"Friend of mother's just arrived and invited her to go to
Australia. God, I hope she accepts!"

"I'll tell her I don't want her to go—that's the surest way
to put her on the next plane!"

There was China tea and Darjeeling and a table full of
English specialties, cinnamon spicy buns and sandwiches of
anchovy paste. The family friend was a lady of stalwart physique and gin-pink cheeks, who viewed Sarah with ill-
concealed hostility, conditioned by the remarks of Nolan's
mother on her daughter-in-law.

Mrs. James sat tensely watching Sarah, thinking furiously
that the girl had no morals at all. Even now, late in her preg-
nancy, she had insisted on sunbathing half naked in the garden and had shocked the village postman to the bone. The
old lady sighed. She had always wanted a daughter-in-law
of whom she could be proud. Instead, Nolan had chosen a
blonde desired by every man for miles around, a woman
with a past that was certainly reprehensible. Mrs. James
thought of the letter from Italy and wondered who Vieri Aldobrandini was and how she could find out more about him.
She had told Nolan about the man, but he seemed not to care
about past lovers and simply said Vieri was terribly unwell.

Finally, ignoring Sarah completely, Mrs. James turned to her son.

"I'm thinking of visiting Australia with Cordelia. What do you think of the idea?"

"I think you should do what you want to do, Mama."

Sarah poured herself more tea and passed the sandwiches around, remaining silent, because she knew she must show no curiosity at all. When she ignored her mother-in-law, the old lady found it impossible not to provoke some kind of contentious discussion. She waited patiently, until Mrs. James at last rose to the bait.

"Sarah, have you nothing to say? I am thinking of going to Australia."

Sarah took a deep breath and spoke in a casual manner.

"It's a dream place and I'm sure you'd enjoy it, but you're far too old for such a journey and you'd be unable to get insurance in view of the fainting fits you keep having."

Mrs. James opened her mouth and closed it again suddenly. Hoist with her own petard in pretending to faint every time she was refused her own way, she was uncertain what to say. She remained defiant, however, and spoke with a confidence she did not feel.

"After tea I shall go and ask the doctor for a certificate stating I'm in good health."

Sarah shrugged, as if resigned to the fact that the idea was hopeless.

"He won't give you one, and if he does, Australia really is too great a risk for a woman of seventy-six. What if you died out there? The cost of bringing back the body would be enormous."

Mrs. James turned to her son.

"I need you to run me to the village, dear. I must catch Hamish Bell before his surgery begins."

"What if he refuses you a certificate, Mama?"

"I shall give him a check for the charity box, and we all know what he does with that."

On a mellow autumn morning, Sarah stood at the window of Thistleton, a basket of blackberries over her arm. Outside, the leaves were falling and the beech trees had turned gold, the maples a vivid scarlet. For three weeks, since her mother-in-law's departure, there had been peace in the house. She and Nolan had walked together in the woods, appreciating the crunch of dry leaves underfoot and the breathtaking beauty of a countryside turning sepia and bronze under the mellow Indian-summer sun. When his mother was absent, it was possible for Sarah to enjoy Nolan's company again.

Sarah left the room and delivered the basket of blackberries to Mrs. Peel in the kitchen. Suddenly, she was feeling very tired and unwell. "Have you a cup of tea for me, Ellis?"

"Of course, my dear, and some jam tarts, too."

Sarah closed her eyes as the room began to tilt at an alarming angle. When she rose, she was obliged to sit down again abruptly. She turned to the cook with a wan smile. "I think you'd best ring the doctor. I'm in labor—at least, I think I am. Then go and find Nolan."

"He's disappeared. He's terrified of being here when the baby comes." The older woman shook her head in a way that indicated disapproval.

At this special moment in her life, Sarah had a sudden ferocious and contrary desire to telephone Umberto. Nolan was absent or hiding and none of the staff had been able to find him since the morning. Her body was a mass of pain, her mind in need of constant reassurance. In a rational way, she remembered that Umberto's possessiveness had driven her mad, but he had always helped her when she needed it. She kept hearing Umberto's words and tried not to think how much she needed to hear them right now. . . . *What you want I give and if I don't have I arrange.* There was nothing he would not do for her, nothing he could not arrange, except to have the child for her. If he were present, Sarah knew Umberto would not have hidden; he would have been at her side, holding her hand, making wonderful promises and roaring orders at everyone in sight. She looked to the door, but there was still no sign of her husband and that abandonment filled her with despair. Nolan was a child; he needed a mother, not a wife.

The following morning Sarah recovered consciousness in a room full of flowers. She saw Mrs. Peel sitting by the bed, eating grapes. A tall, pale doctor was looking down at her from behind round wire-rimmed glasses.

"Everything's over, my dear, and you have a very beautiful blonde daughter. We delivered her by caesarean and you're in the recovery unit."

"Where's my husband?"

"They haven't found Nolan yet. It hits fathers like that sometimes, I'm afraid. Last week I had a fellow lock himself in the lavatory overnight."

Sarah began to sob. In her debilitated state, anger, disappointment and hurt magnified her unhappy emotions. She longed to be taken into Nolan's arms, to be reassured that he wanted the child, that he would protect her, but she knew he would not, could not, because he was incapable of assuming any responsibility. There was no point in hoping that would change. She would have to take the full burden for her daughter's upbringing now and in the future.

Sarah was trying to control her grief when a nurse appeared with the infant and handed her into Sarah's arms. As she gazed at the tiny creature, with her heart-shaped face and downy blonde hair, Sarah was entranced. The hands were elegant, the fingers long, the mouth a miniature of her own. For Sarah it was a moment of indescribable joy in

which she forgot about her husband, his mother, and everything else. The child smelled of baby powder and a sweet,
subtle odor unique to the newborn. Enchanted by the baby's
beauty, Sarah closed her eyes and slept.

Five days later, Sarah returned to Thistleton with her
child. The Indian summer was over and the trees were dark
and leafless. The staff had laid log fires in the hall, sitting
room, and bedrooms. Mrs. Peel's daughter, Felicity, had
been engaged to look after the child when required. Of
Nolan there was still no sign and the cook was insisting they
call the police.

The following morning, there was a storm, with violent
lightning and thunder claps so forceful the ancient windows
shook. Sarah stood looking out at the drive and thinking that
the weather matched her mood. She was about to move
away from the window when a taxi entered the main gates.
At the front door, Mrs. James stepped out, followed by
Nolan and a tall, slim, blond young man dressed in a dark-
blue velvet jacket. Sarah weighed her husband's solicitous
attitude to his mother and felt anger rising inside her. Then,
her face tense, her hands clenched, she walked to the stairs
and waited there till the three entered the house. In her
mother-in-law's face she saw triumph, and in Nolan's, fear.
In the handsome young man's there was curiosity and a con-
spiratorial friendliness that puzzled her. Sarah descended to
a point halfway to the hall and looked directly at her husband.

"What happened?"

"Sarah, this is my friend Fritz von Haffen. I've been
staying at his place in London."

"Why didn't you call me? Mrs. Peel wanted to contact
the police and so did Hamish Bell."

"I was under the weather. It all got too much for me.

Please try to understand. Not everyone has the strength of the devil like you.''

"I want to know *why* you ran away like that.''

Mrs. James interrupted in her usual grande-dame drawl.

"Don't be tiresome, Sarah. Nolan was feeling off-color. He's often like that when things are tense.''

Sarah roared like a virago.

"Out! I don't want you in this house at the same time as me and my child!''

Before anyone could protest, she had bundled the old lady through the front door and thrown her suitcase after her. Then she rang for Mrs. Peel and ordered all the entrances to the house to be secured and Mrs. James to be refused admittance. She noticed with a certain grim satisfaction that Nolan's hands were shaking like aspens as she ordered him to follow her.

"This way. I suppose you *do* want to see your child?''

"Please don't shout, Sarah. I have such a headache.''

Yanking Nolan's arm, she propelled him into the nursery, watching as he stood gazing down at the baby. Her mind was full of the anguish of total rejection when he made no effort to touch the child. It was the moment when Sarah knew irrevocably that she could not remain married to Nolan and she could not remain at Thistleton House. Her voice trembled as she looked into the anxious face.

"Have you nothing to say to me, Nolan, no words of explanation for your behavior?''

He led her to the bedroom and sat for a long time looking at his hands. When he spoke, Sarah was shocked to the core.

"Until I made love with you, Sarah, I'd never made love with a woman. Teddy and I were lovers from a few days after his arrival at Eton until the week before his death last year. There were others from time to time, but Teddy was the only person I ever really loved. I do care for you a great deal and since you came here I've been happy enough, but sometimes I need . . .''

"A man?"

"I've resisted until now, but when I saw you with a swollen body and a child about to be born I couldn't stand it any longer."

Sarah gazed out the window, uncertain what to say. She longed for him to ask for a divorce, so she could be free again, but she sensed that Nolan wished to stay married. She spoke gently, not wishing to frighten him.

"I think it's best if we get a divorce, Nolan."

"No, I won't ever divorce you. I want you and the baby to stay here. I want you to be happy and to help me to be normal."

Sarah shook her head. "It's much too complicated. I can't police you. I'm not your nurse or your mother, and you have to remember that. Now you'd best introduce me to your friend."

Fritz was charm itself, an attentive, elegant man of thirty-nine, educated at Heidelberg and Eton and working as a researcher at the Tavistock Clinic. Intuitive, half amused, and greatly impressed by Sarah's presence, he followed her from room to room, finally asking the question that had been on his mind ever since the moment she had hurled her mother-in-law out of the house.

"What are you going to do when she knocks on the door at dinnertime?"

"She can knock till her knuckles bleed. I shan't let her in."

"Are you really so hard, Sarah?"

"I just have to be. I have no intention of letting that woman rule my life any longer."

Sarah was at the head of the table, watching as the maid served watercress soup from a Coleport tureen, when Mrs. James hammered at the front door. Sarah showed no sign that she had heard and motioned for the maid to continue serving the meal. The knocking increased in intensity, accompanied by cries of outrage.

Nolan turned appealingly to Sarah.

"I've *got* to let her in. She's seventy-six and frail."

"She's as strong as an ox. If she comes in, I leave with the child."

Suddenly, the knocking ceased and the door reverberated with a loud thump. Nolan leaped to his feet, his face ashen.

"Mother's fainted! If I can't let her in, at least I must go and help her."

Sarah locked the door behind her husband, furious when he called out, "I shall have to bring Mother inside; she's cut her head."

Sarah handed the first-aid kit outside and relocked the door. Then she returned to the dining room and ate her soup, trying not to show the tumult in her heart. For a long time there was no sound at all. Then Mrs. Peel appeared.

"Your husband wants his dinner sent to the Dower House with his mother's. He wants his bed made up there, too."

Sarah barely hesitated, though she was disappointed that yet again her husband had taken his mother's side.

"Send Nolan's clothes, too, and the papers from his desk. Make sure nothing's lost."

After a while, Fritz spoke and Sarah realized that however unlikely it seemed, he was trying to be her friend.

"I know you're furious, Sarah, but try to remember that Nolan loves you dearly."

"He has a funny way of showing it."

"There are different degrees of love, you know. Some men love with pride and are horribly jealous, because they fear their pride will be hurt. Other men love with admiration, like Nolan—from afar, if you like. They can't really imagine making love with the object of their adoration, and when they do, they become obsessed with her. Women are

the same. To some, love means possession, and Mrs. James
is one of those. I must tell you, Sarah, that she's trying to
persuade Nolan to divorce you and apply for custody of the
child."

"There's nothing I'd like better than a divorce, but I
won't *ever* let anyone take my child."

"I think you'd better find yourself a good lawyer. Mrs.
James is very rich and she's determined to have her way."

After dinner, Sarah thought of what Fritz had said. She
needed a very special lawyer and had no idea how to find
one. The English courts were snobbish and a man of less-
than-honest reputation would be suspect, but she did not
want a by-the-book thinker. She needed an old-school-tie
lawyer, with a fancy accent, friends in high places, and a
mind like Umberto di Castelli's. On impulse, Sarah picked
up the phone and rang Mario Benedetti's number in Paris.
Fifteen minutes later, she rang back, as he had instructed,
and took the name of a man who would be ideal for her purpose. Talking to Benedetti had given her more confidence
than she had felt in months. She told herself that if Nolan
and his mother tried to take her child, she would show them
a few games learned while observing her former lover. Till
then, she would never let her daughter out of her sight.

Sarah stepped off the train holding the baby, her heart
light, her spirits renewed by the lawyer's reassurances. It
was raining, and on reaching Thistleton she ran inside the
porch and fumbled with her keys, afraid her child might
catch cold. The key turned in the lock, but the door did not
open, because it had been bolted on the inside. Then she saw
an envelope addressed to her and taped to the paneling. She
read the message in her mother-in-law's hand, making sure
to show no reaction at all in case the lady was watching from
some vantage point in the house. *Your belongings have been*

moved to the Dower House. From today I intend to reside
with my son in Thistleton, which belongs to me. Ada James.

Sarah drove to the Dower House and opened the front
door. There was no fire and her belongings were piled in a
chaotic array of boxes in the hall. She was close to tears
when she heard Fritz's voice behind her. Turning, she saw
that he was carrying the cradle filled with diapers, under-
shirts, receiving blankets, and every conceivable necessity
for the child.

"Nolan forgot these. Sarah, do sit down—you're looking
very pale. I'd best light the fire for you or you'll both catch
cold; it's terribly damp in here. How did the meeting with
the lawyer go?"

"Better than I expected."

"What are you going to call the baby?"

"Alexis. I decided on the train."

"Has Nolan been consulted?"

"Not yet. His mother wants her to have a nice old-
fashioned name like Lettuce, Turnip, or Violet."

"Oh, Sarah, Nolan was right when he said there was no
one quite like you. Now, you just stay where you are and I'll
make you a nice cup of tea."

In the moments before sunset, when the black beech
branches were outlined against a vermilion horizon, Sarah
sat alone, holding her child in her arms and gazing out at the
somber beauty of the scene. Fritz had gone to the house for
dinner, having promised to return later with the rest of the
baby's things. Of Nolan there was no sign. Sarah knew he
was ashamed and would stay with his mother until he convinced himself he had been right in allowing the old lady her
way. Sarah closed the window as a stiff breeze rose, making
the trees lean to the east. She felt very lonely, uncertain, and
tempted to run away. Thistleton, which had once been her
dream house, was now a prison, albeit a beautiful prison.
This was England as it had always been and would be for

only a few more years, before encroaching housing made
mallow and lavender things of the past. Sarah shook her
head wearily, conscious that there was nowhere to run, no
safe port in this storm. Her mother might let her stay for a
week, but it was more than likely that after two days she
would become belligerent and ask when Sarah was leaving.
She could not work and leave such a young baby with a
stranger. She was trapped and it was a feeling she could not
abide.

For a long time, Sarah remained in the rocking chair,
thinking about her life. Her reflections were interrupted
when she heard the sound of voices raised in anger coming
from the direction of the house. Having put the child in its
cradle, she ran to the kitchen door in time to hear Nolan and
his mother screaming at each other.

"I won't have it! Do you hear me, Mother? You've
caused nothing but trouble since the day you came home. To
do that would be the limit!"

"And what do *you* plan to do, let her have her way as
usual? Do you want your child christened with some ridiculous name?"

"She can call it whatever she wants and that's final."

Sarah was about to close the door when she heard the
sound of glass shattering, followed by a horrified scream.
Then Fritz came rushing across the lawn toward her, his
face pale with anguish.

"For God's sake, come and help me, Sarah! Bring Alexis
with you."

"What happened?"

"You heard the row, I suppose. Well, Nolan's put his
arm through the window and cut himself appallingly. He's
bleeding all over the carpet, and she really *has* fainted. Mrs.
Peel's calling the doctor."

When Sarah arrived, Nolan was staring at the blood
spurting from his arm, as though unable to comprehend how

it got there. He was also talking in a strange, flat voice and pronouncing every other word incorrectly. Frowning in puzzlement, Sarah applied a tourniquet to stanch the bleeding. She then gave him some sweet tea and settled in to waiting for the doctor to arrive.

When Bell had bandaged and taped the injury Sarah took him aside.

"What's wrong with Nolan? Why is he saying his words wrong?"

"I don't know exactly, but he seems to have lost track of reality for the moment. In the morning I'll bring Paul Cannon here to assess him. Cannon's the director of psychiatry at the new Brighton Clinic and one of the leading men in the field."

"What caused it, Hamish?"

"Stress, I suppose. He's been trying to be someone he's not. Try not to worry too much, Sarah. I'll be able to tell you more in the morning."

In the still of night, as she sat alone in her bed, Sarah took a writing pad and pen and wrote from the heart. . . . *Dearest Vieri, How are you? I thought you might like to hear from an old friend.*

Chapter Thirteen

Holly, Damascus, Autumn 1969

From a courtyard scented with lemon and jasmine, Holly passed through the gate to the street. It was six-thirty and she had just returned from the last day of the film location. This was the time when she always went to the Hotel Aya, drank a cocktail with other visiting foreigners, ate dinner, and then went out in search of adventure.

Passing from the Saahat el Chouhadaa to the Kojrjiyeh Haddad, Holly looked straight ahead, ignoring the curious glances of men still unaccustomed to European women. Damascus was a city of secrets and watchful eyes, its ancient walls covered with blue plumbago and feathery tendrils of jasmine. Alien smells of leather, cheese, paraffin, and new-baked bread were everywhere. The senses were constantly assailed by sights rarely encountered in the West: a man with a pushcart selling fresh-shelled almonds, sightless beggars importuning, their bony hands outstretched in supplication, and bazaars where traders still offered everything from trembling filagree brooches to chick-peas, cardamom seeds to brass kettles. The sounds of the city fascinated Holly: the monotonous tapping of a copper beater's hammer, the neighing of a donkey with a too-heavy load, the cry of the muezzin in his pink marble minaret, and the crunching of camels chewing thistles.

Turning into the hotel, Holly went to the bar to order a whiskey sour. She was drinking more and making love more than she had ever done before, but nothing seemed to calm her, to assuage the sense of uncertainty and disquietude in her soul. As the mad whirlwind of her life speeded up to unsettling proportions, she felt more and more isolated from her roots and sought solace in the unknown more and more frequently. It was a vicious circle, and often she thought of the advice Sarah had given her on the day of Arlette's marriage. *Someday you must go back to Ireland and sort yourself out. You're running from something and perhaps what you're running from is better than what you have.*

The hotel was crowded, the bar smoky, the babble of foreign voices deafening. Holly was on her third drink when she felt someone watching her. She looked from table to table, trying to decide who it could be. At the moment when she was beginning to think she had imagined the feeling, she saw a young man standing with his back to the fireplace, looking at her with an intensity that made her shiver. As their eyes met, he raised his glass and smiled. Holly raised her own, assessing the man as South American or Cuban, rich, spoiled, and with a gleam in his eyes that heralded danger. Her heart began to pound from excitement as he approached, his hand outstretched.

"I am Carlos Hamid."

"Holly O'Malley."

"May I invite you to dinner, Miss O'Malley? There's a very interesting restaurant on the outskirts of the city, and afterward you might like to visit the Temple of the Sun."

"I've never heard of it." She smiled. "What is it?"

"A very special place and one a woman like you will enjoy."

Carlos watched as she assimilated the information, her blue eyes gleaming with anticipation. He was conscious that every man in the room was envying his contact with the elegant, willowy creature in the violet silk dress, whose decadence was already something of a legend in the city. He had come far to meet Holly, certain she would be invaluable to him in his work. In the arms business, an intelligent woman who could distract a saint was worth cultivating. As he watched her nostrils flaring, Carlos knew that his journey had not been in vain.

They ate in a private club open only to foreigners, a delicious meal of *felafel* and pigeons cooked with grapes and *arak*. They talked of their lives, though Carlos said little of himself, other than that he was born in Cuba and had lived for much of his adult life in Paris. Intrigued when he said that the things he loved best in life were women and literature, Holly had no hesitation in following when he led her to the vintage Citroën and drove her into the desert. Instinct told her that this man was different—important and perhaps deadly—but she could not resist the stimulation that came with great risk.

The moon shone silver on the stone pillars of the Temple of the Sun and from the interior came the sound of low, rhythmic chanting that filled Holly with perverse desire. She began to tremble with excitement, instinct telling her that tonight her desire for sensual pleasure would be fully satisfied.

Carlos explained what was happening inside the temple.

"Once a year, the men of the Sun Cult meet here in the temple built for their worship centuries ago. They chant until daybreak to summon the Goddess of the Sun to be worshiped in the time-honored way. You must never talk of what happens tonight, but I promise you it will be an experience you will never forget." His eyes gleamed as he spoke.

Holly followed as if in a trance, passing through the pillared entrance into a stone chamber so high she could not see the ceiling. The temple was lit by massive candles that gave off the scent of incense. Fifty naked men with oiled bodies stood motionless on either side of the room, their eyes half closed in a trancelike state of near ecstasy.

Carlos led Holly through the ranks to an altar at the far end of the temple, remaining at her side as a Priest of the Sun removed their garments. He was pleased to see her body trembling, her eyes wide, her hands fluttering uncertainly from her face to her side. Then, raising his arms to signal silence, Carlos spoke.

"I promised she would come and she is here to be worshiped. Gentlemen, the Goddess of the Sun."

Before Holly realized what was happening, she had been lifted onto the altar, her wrists secured and her feet placed between stirrups on either side of the altar. She felt the advent of orgasm as a cymbal clashed and the men formed a line and began to chant the anthem to the Goddess of the Sun.

Carlos was the first to enter her body and Holly screamed in abandon at his touch. This scene was the culmination of every erotic dream she had ever had. She was here with the men of the Sun Cult, and each and every one of them would dissipate his lust inside her before the night was over. She began to move back and forth in a frenzy of desire, as man after man penetrated her body till she was barely conscious, because the force of their sexuality had provoked her beyond sensibility. After a while, she knew nothing of time or place, only the entry and withdrawal of the iron-hard penis of a new man and then another and another until she thought she would die from ecstasy.

After what seemed like an age, a gong sounded and Holly found herself alone with Carlos. The disappearance of the men was so sudden that she wondered momentarily if it had all been a hallucination, but her vagina was swollen and every muscle in her body ached. She looked on uncertainly as Carlos unfastened her wrists and feet.

"Tell me why you brought me here, Carlos."

"I knew you would enjoy it. You need a man like me and we shall stay together from now on. In this Temple of the Sun I marry you—in my fashion—Holly O'Malley."

"What do you want with me?"

"You are a woman who needs to be punished, because you live a life of dissipation and it is not really in your true nature. I am a man who likes to punish, so we shall do well together."

Holly watched in fascination as he took a thin leather-stranded whip from the wall. Unable to resist when he began to trail it gently over her skin, she fell back onto the altar. Then, suddenly, she felt it sting the clitoris, making her cry out.

Closing her eyes, she stretched out her arms as the whip cracked over her stomach, her breasts, her thighs, and back again to the inner core that had been used by the worshipers of the sun. When her screams rose in the silence of the night, Carlos threw down the whip and entered her, forcing the hardness of his penis into the wetness of her vagina and smiling in satisfaction.

"You are mine now, Holly. When I travel you come with me. When I tell you to do something you do it. You will be a wonderful distraction for my clients."

Holly sat up, suddenly alarmed. "I'll not be used! I decide—"

"You decide nothing. You will do what I say. If you do not, I shall beat you till there is no skin left on your body. When you obey, I shall make you happier than you have ever been before."

On arrival at the house, Holly ran inside, exhausted by the events of the night. Carlos had said that in his way he had married her, and she felt a curious relief that the years of restless searching for excitement were over. From this day on, he would be her excitement. She wondered if he would be gone like a nightmare with the dawn or if he really intended to stay. Then, as she looked into the suntanned face with its dark, slumberous eyes, she knew he was the man she had sought for so long, the punishment for her sins.

Chapter Fourteen

Vieri, Rome, February 1970

For months the doctors had done what could be done, shaking their heads in despair when none of the conventional treatments had any result. It was now clear that the patient had no desire to return to normality. For weeks after Vieri's arrival, Elio had remained at his side, trying to break the seemingly impenetrable barrier between his brother and the outside world. Finally, he had contacted Sarah and asked her to write to Vieri. Her letters had been read to him, but Vieri had shown no sign of understanding what was said. It was noted, however, that he showed distress when the letters were removed from the room, and in a moment of inspiration Elio had left them in the drawer of the bedside cabinet. Nurses had reported that Vieri made his first conscious effort by stretching out to touch them. Elio thought sadly of the doctors' description of the treatment Vieri had received from his captors: the regular and vicious beatings, the weeks of starvation, the blackness of the cell, the scorpions, the bout of pneumonia that had robbed him of his physical reserves. Elio shook his head wearily. The doctors had now intimated that Vieri might never come out of the labyrinth of shock and despair. That was why he had clutched at the straw of Sarah's suggestion. It seemed ludicrous, but conventional methods had done nothing, so what had he to

lose? It had taken weeks to arrange everything Sarah
wanted, weeks of expensive searching, locating, transport-
ing to Rome the characters who would recreate the scene she
wished to enact. To Elio it seemed like something out of a
romantic woman's dream, but desperation made him comply. If it worked, he would have a brother again.

Vieri stretched out his hand and touched the letters that he
liked to keep in view day and night. This morning, as a light
snowfall surprised the Eternal City and carillons rang out
from churches in ancient piazzas, his mind struggled to
emerge from the black cavern where it had taken refuge.
Taking the top letter from the pile, Vieri read it, going back
over each sentence when concentration failed.

Dearest Vieri,

Lexy and I are going shopping in London today. The
weather's icy and every morning the trees are silver with
hoar frost. It's very beautiful but sad, because the only
thing I want is to be with you. I've come to the conclusion
that life is a series of mountains and valleys with more de-
pressions than moments of elation and happiness. I think
of you all the time and tell myself I mustn't. Why don't
you come and live with me, at least in your imagination.
We'll have breakfast together and walk in the woods and
watch squirrels rushing up trees. In the evenings we'll make
love and in the night, when the owls hoot in the chimneys,
I'll give you a thousand kisses and tell you the things I always wanted to tell you, but never did, that I want you and
admire you and love you. I'm not free and neither are you,
but I'll love you till my body turns to dust.

Write me one word and I'll be happy.

Sarah

Mariannina entered the room and saw Vieri lying on his
back, staring at the ceiling with his usual vacant expression.

He was clutching a letter in his left hand and there was a tear falling down his cheek. Astonished that after all these months he was doing something, if only holding a letter and producing a tear, she tried to take the page from him.

"What is it, Vieri? Where did you get it?"

He stared at her with what seemed to be loathing and Mariannina felt a pang of alarm. Again she demanded to see the letter, her brittle voice rising in anger when Elio appeared and looked from her to his brother.

"What's happening? Vieri looks upset."

"I have no idea; I'm only his wife," she said with cold sarcasm. "When I arrived, he was holding a letter and there was a tear on his cheek. It's progress, Elio—you realize that. I asked to see it, but Vieri looked at me as if I were an insect he wanted to squash. There are more of those letters on the table over there. I wonder who they're from."

She stretched out her arm, but Elio stepped between her and the cabinet. His face was gentle, but his voice was firm.

"Leave them, Mariannina. They've been put there for a very specific reason by Vieri's doctors."

"I demand to know who sent them."

"Please don't, at least not in front of Vieri."

"Elio, for months my husband's been lying here, full of self-pity and refusing to try to get well. I'm a patient woman, but either Vieri's going to come out of his state and return home or he isn't, and I'm getting very unnerved with the waiting. If he can react to a letter, why can't he react to me? I love him, I always have, and I'm his *wife.*"

Mariannina made a sudden snatch for the letter in Vieri's hand and was rewarded by a primal scream that echoed in the corridors of the clinic. Doctors and orderlies rushed to the patient's side as the tormented cry went on and on. Vieri's face was contorted in what seemed to be agony combined with rage, frustration, and hate.

Elio hurried Mariannina from the room.

"I want you to go home. You're not to come back to the clinic until you have the doctor's permission. This is the third time you've upset Vieri and it must be the last."

"I won't wait forever, you know! He has no courage; that's the fact of the matter."

Even in rage, Mariannina was perfectly composed. That composure now infuriated Elio.

"Vieri always had courage. If I know my brother he took the beatings without a murmur and the amputation of his finger without a cry. He probably starved and suffered in silence during all the months when he had no idea which day was going to be his last. Try to imagine the stress and the destruction of his nervous system. Now he's fighting for his sanity and trying to come back, but he's locked in some kind of battle with himself. Perhaps he's scared to come back, because he knows that the Vieri who emerges isn't going to be the one who left us all in the church in Paris."

"What *do* you mean?"

"He'll have changed, Mariannina. He may not love you anymore. He may not love himself or the family. He may decide to travel the world alone, to enter a monastery, to become something different from what he was. You must prepare yourself for the worst."

"Dear God, I'm losing him without his even saying a word!"

Vieri woke from a deep sleep to find his room full of pink English roses. He closed his eyes and then opened them again, clutching one of Sarah's letters in his left hand, his eyes turning to the pile on the bedside table. Nothing had been moved. He was safe and surrounded by the scent of flowers. He closed his eyes, trying with all his strength and will to concentrate. Instinct told him Sarah was near and he wanted with all his heart to see her, but his mind slipped constantly and he found even his most precious thoughts

fragmented. He was shocked when Elio appeared in a dinner
jacket and white silk shirt. Then nurses came and dressed
Vieri in a similar fashion. He was put in a wheelchair and
led to the elevator and out of the building. Vieri wanted to
scream, to be taken back, to hide, but he saw the family
chauffeur, Tassilio, bowing to him and knew he must try to
preserve what was left of his dignity.

Vieri remembered nothing of the journey from the clinic
to the city center, only opening his eyes and trying to work
out what was happening when he saw policemen removing
traffic barriers from the entrance to the Piazza Navona. He
gazed out at the square he had always loved, at the old-
world lamps that cast gold reflections on the sidewalk, at the
waiters in black and white standing deferentially at attention. There were no cars in the square, every entrance having been sealed by the police. There were no clients in the
cafés, and the only sounds were the distant roar of traffic
and the tinkle of water in the fountains.

Vieri was wheeled into Trescallini's and seated facing the
old buildings he loved. His favorite champagne was brought
and with it the twirled sugar biscuits he adored. No attempt
was made to feed him or to help him drink, and the glass remained untouched on the table as he took in the scene. He
was on the point of retreating from reality when he heard the
sound of music and saw three young men in medieval dress
entering the square. One was playing a balalaika, one a
mandolin, and the other a violin. They were smiling as they
took their places under the bare-branched trees and began to
play the love songs dear to all Italians. Vieri gazed at the
musicians and then at the doorway where he had kissed
Sarah, his heart pounding when she appeared in the same
white dress and the same headband of rosebuds worn on that
magic night long ago. Vieri saw that there was a smile on
her face and stars in her eyes as she neared his table. He

never knew where he found the strength to rise to his feet and embrace her, closing his eyes in ecstasy as she spoke.

"Hallo, Vieri, I'm so happy to see you again."

He opened his mouth, determined to reply, sweat pouring in rivulets down his face.

"Sarah, my dearest Sarah . . ."

The music tinkled and she sat at his side as Vieri stumbled and fell back into the chair. His eyes were closed, his hands were on hers, and there was a smile on his face. Sarah said nothing at all but simply sat sipping her champagne and stroking his wrists for what seemed like a very long time. Then she did what the doctors had ordered her to do and, having kissed Vieri's cheeks, rose to say good-bye.

"Next time we meet in the Piazza Navona we'll dance together like we did that first time, so hurry and get well. Promise you'll get well for *me.*"

Opening his eyes, Vieri watched as she walked away from him across the square. When she reached the spot where the musicians were playing, she turned and blew him a kiss. Then she disappeared into the darkened doorway where he had kissed her with all-consuming passion in the days before his mind lost its way. The musicians also rose and began to move away, still playing the waltz from *Floralie.* Within seconds, Vieri could hear nothing but an echo, a haunting melody of an enchanted dream.

It was five o'clock on a cold winter morning. Vieri's hand was on Sarah's last letter. The others were on the bedside table and the circlet of rosebuds she had worn on her head was in a crystal bowl nearby. He reached out and touched it. Then he closed his eyes, struggling to keep from returning to the black hole in the caves of Calcelrama. It was very tempting to lie in the darkness, relinquishing all responsibility, but he knew now that he must make an effort to get well. Somehow, he must find the strength to force his mind to obey, his body to become strong again. But how long would it take? And for what purpose? After all, Sarah was married and had a child. But she had said that they would dance together in the Piazza Navona on their next meeting and she had asked him to get well for her.

Vieri's eyes closed and he slept at last. This time, instead of dreaming of the knife that had mutilated his hand, he dreamed of running through cornfields that stretched as far as the eye could see, and of meeting Sarah, her arms open, her smile drawing him like a magnet.

He did not see the nurse, sent by Mariannina, who came into the room, read each of Sarah's letters, and disappeared like a phantom into the night.

Chapter Fifteen

Sarah, Summer–Autumn, 1970

Sarah arrived home from the hospital, clutching her daughter and sweating from the pain of a broken jaw. The weather was the hottest in forty-five years and Thistleton had never looked so beautiful. There were peaches on the tree outside her window and apricots espaliered against the south wall. In the field beyond the wicket gate, a cuckoo called and the garden was full of old-fashioned flowers, their scents a Victorian posy of heliotrope and verbena, heartsease and musk.

Sarah put Lexy in her playpen and made herself a pot of tea. Her jaw ached and she was still profoundly shocked that Nolan had attacked her, inflicting such an injury. It had been obvious for months that he was descending into a complete mental breakdown, but even now Sarah could not believe the horrific things that had taken place. Tears began to fall as she thought of the sudden and brutal change in her husband. Nolan, who had always been so clean, now refused to wash at all. Nolan, who had always written such beautiful prose, now sat at his desk, staring at the pad of thick white paper without touching it. Above all, Nolan refused adamantly to see the psychiatrist and denied emphatically that he had ever been violent in his life.

The attack that had put her in the hospital had finally made up Sarah's mind and she had returned to Thistleton only to collect some clothes and a few precious books. These she packed and put in the car. Then, having settled Alexis in the car seat, she drove slowly from the Dower House past Thistleton, pausing to let the doctor's car pass. When Nolan saw the suitcases in the rear of her vehicle, he had a sudden and blinding attack of rage. He yanked Sarah out of the car and threw her like a rag doll down the steps of the Italian garden adjacent. She felt a sharp pain at the base of her spine and then nothing at all.

She woke in a hospital room painted pale green. She was lying in a white bed and Lexy was in a crib at her side. She tried her fingers and toes, relieved that they worked, but the lower half of her body was numb. When she tried to move she could only turn her head and raise her arms. As the baby began to cry, Sarah pressed a button for attention, looking appealingly into Hamish Bell's homely face as he arrived at her side.

"What's wrong with me? I feel paralyzed."

"The fall Nolan provoked injured your coccyx and the surgeons have removed it. You're going to be fine and you'll walk and dance again. In view of the violence of your husband's actions of late, I've had him admitted for psychiatric evaluation to the York Clinic of Guy's Hospital. He's going to be there for a long time, Sarah."

"If his mother's in the house alone I'll never get my post. She burns my letters unless there's someone there to stop her."

"I'll get Mrs. Peel to do her best to deliver them to you."

"I want a divorce, Hamish, but I can't get one without Nolan's consent."

"Try not to despair, Sarah. They're going to change the law very soon."

Days of pain and anxiety followed, Sarah's condition not helped by the lack of news from Italy. Mrs. Peel had delivered what letters she had found, but there was nothing from the Aldobrandinis. Sarah sent two telegrams, but still there was no response. In despair, she finally told herself for the second time that she must forget Vieri. She had done all she could, but still the newspapers spoke of him in the past tense, as if he were already dead. The fact was that Vieri either could not or would not break through the wall of silence. She had written to Elio four times since her return from Rome, but he had not replied. Tears began to fall down Sarah's cheeks and she wiped them impatiently, telling herself she had cried enough because of the Aldobrandinis. It was time to make plans for the future and to forget the love that had blighted her existence. She held out her hand and touched her child's fingers through the bars of the crib. Then she wrote to her lawyer in London and told him to try to start proceedings for divorce. Whether Nolan granted it or not, she knew now she would never live in the same house with him again.

That night, Sarah lay in bed, thinking over Hamish Bell's suggestion that she apply for a job as a live-in housekeeper. In that way she would have a roof over her head, pleasant surroundings in which to live, and children for Lexy to play with when she was older. She could not resist a wry smile at the ambitions she would now be obliged to forget. The only thing that was certain was that she could either keep her child and take domestic work, or she could abandon Alexis and go looking for the big time. As the baby gurgled, Sarah smiled, all her love going out to the tiny blonde child in the white cotton nightdress. Then, closing her eyes, she tried to sleep, but her back was a mass of pain and she was obliged to ring for the nurse to give her a sedative.

It was midsummer when Sarah returned to the Dower House to finish packing her things. Mrs. James watched, a smile of satisfaction on her face. Sarah was leaving at last and would never return. It was a pity about the baby, but better to lose contact now than later, when they had come to know and love the child. Mrs. James rang for the cook, but there was no reply. Then, looking out, she saw Mrs. Peel helping Sarah carry out her things. Nolan's mother frowned, deciding to give Mrs. Peel notice the moment Sarah was off the grounds.

Nolan was in bed brooding. The clinic was comfortable, the doctors friendly, the examinations none too trying. He spent most of the day walking from ward to ward gossiping with newfound friends or writing sensuous letters to Sarah. The letters were enormously long and after he had signed them he invariably tore them up. Today, however, he had received a fourth letter from her, informing him that she wanted a divorce. Nolan leaned over to talk with one of his favorite patients, unaware that his psychiatrist was listening.

"My wife is still refusing to divorce me."

"Where is she at the moment, Nolan?"

"She just arrived in London. I suppose she came to see her publishers."

The psychiatrist approached and sat at Nolan's side.

"You're reversing things again. You know it's Sarah who wants the divorce and you're the one who won't consent. And you're the author. Your wife never wrote a line in her life and doesn't want to."

"It's not true."

"Why did you hurt Sarah?"

"I didn't hurt her. I damn near killed my mother, though, and I wish I'd succeeded."

The psychiatrist sighed imperceptibly, but his voice was calm, his expression bland.

"Your wife wants a divorce and I think you should give her one. You don't love her and you probably never did. Turn around, Nolan—I won't have you facing the wall every time I ask you something difficult."

"I won't divorce her. Write and tell her it's a waste of time asking."

"She's coming tomorrow; you can tell her yourself."

The clock struck midnight. The clinic was silent. On Nolan's floor a solitary night nurse sat at his desk making notes and completing the records for the day.

Umberto walked briskly up the stairs, looking neither to right nor left. On reaching Nolan's room, he stepped inside and stood gazing at the man on the bed, his face a mask of derision. When Nolan's eyes flickered open, he spoke.

"You don't know me and you don't need to. I am here only to tell you to give your wife a divorce or I shall see you go for a very long swim."

Nolan sat bolt upright, his blue eyes taking in every detail of the perfect suit, the menacing face, the black eyes lit by an almost supernatural loathing. The man was handsome, but Nolan had no doubt he was in the presence of evil. Nolan recoiled, his arm reaching for the bell that would summon help. The stranger's voice rasped an order.

"If you ring the bell, I will cut off your hand."

"Who are you?"

"I am Sarah's friend."

"But who *are* you?"

"You don't need to know my name. All you need to know is that I am a man of my word."

"I shall tell my doctors in the morning and they'll call the police."

"What will you tell?"

Nolan hesitated, conscious of the black eyes on his, the powerful body moving menacingly nearer. When the stranger smiled, Nolan felt his body trembling from sheer terror. The man's voice was scratchy, his hands broad and strong like the hands of a strangler.

"In the morning, look from the window and you see my men watching you. They wait only for my order to destroy you. You are an insect and insects are born to be destroyed.''

"I won't sign the papers, ever.''

"There you make the mistake, Mr. James. You will *beg* to sign them.''

Umberto walked to the door and left the room without a backward glance. He was relaxed as he moved along the corridor and down the stairs and through the front door. Outside, his driver was waiting. As he stepped inside the car, Umberto motioned for the driver to take the turn for central London. Within seconds he had disappeared into the darkness of night.

Nolan rang for the nurse, his body still shaking from fear. When the young man appeared, he blurted out the story.

"A man just visited me and threatened that if I didn't sign the divorce papers I'd be sent for a long swim. I want you to call the police. I'm certain he was a member of the Mafia.''

The nurse telephoned Nolan's doctor, took instructions, and returned to the room with additional medication.

"Everything's been taken care of, Mr. James. Now, let's give you something to make you sleep.''

"I don't *want* to sleep.''

"Take it, please. You trust the police to look after you, don't you?''

"I'll never forget that man's eyes, never ever. I'll have nightmares about them for the rest of my life.''

Nolan woke the following morning and went at once to look out the window. There, sure enough, parked directly below his room, was a car with black windows. In a fever of apprehension, he gazed down at it, trying to see who was inside. Then, soaking with sweat, he rang for the nurse.

"That man who came and threatened me last night is waiting to kill me. He's in a black car with dark glass windows. Get the police officer who's been sent to protect me. I want to speak with him.''

"I don't know about any police officer, Mr. James. And there's no black car outside."

Nolan leaped up and looked disbelievingly out the window.

"It was there a minute ago, I swear it was, but you don't believe me, I suppose."

The psychiatrist entered and looked down at Nolan with patient eyes.

"The night nurse reported you were saying a member of the Mafia had visited you at three o'clock in the morning to make threats against you."

"He *was* here."

"Did he remind you of anyone?"

"Yes, the devil. His men are here now, or they were a minute ago. Why isn't someone doing something?"

"Your wife's here to see you, Nolan. We'll talk about all this later."

Nolan watched as Sarah entered the room in a white silk sailor suit. Her face was beautiful, but without mercy, and he thought how she had changed. In the early days of the marriage, she had still been a child, full of wild enthusiasms and ideas that would never work. Now she was formidable in a way he found hard to define. He flinched when she greeted him.

"I hear you've been telling tall stories again."

"They weren't tall stories. It was true. A man came here and I think it was Umberto di Castelli."

Sarah looked hard at her husband, knowing instinctively that he was telling the truth as he saw it, but Nolan had always had difficulty in differentiating fact from fiction. She took the papers from her purse and handed him a pen.

"Sign these, please."

"I won't sign, Sarah."

"I don't want to be married to you anymore, Nolan. I

know now that I only ever accepted your proposal because I thought Vieri was dead.''

"That's why I told you he was dead. I realized at once that you loved him and that I wouldn't have a chance otherwise.''

Sarah was so shocked and outraged she could say nothing at all, but simply sat looking into Nolan's spoiled face as if seeing him for the first time. Then she pushed the pen toward him, but he shook his head.

"I won't sign and that's final.''

Sarah rose and walked from the room without a word. In the corridor, she paused for a moment, close to tears. Then she reminded herself that the crying years were over. She had a child who was dependent on her and she must get on with her life.

Returning to the apartment, Sarah took a phone call from the bank manager, informing her that her weekly allowance had been stopped. She was still trying to work out what to do, when there was another call, but when she picked up the phone there was no response. Sarah wondered if her husband was playing games, but no longer cared. All that mattered was that she get her divorce and start all over again. For a moment she thought of Vieri and longed as she longed every day to contact him, but she had still had no response to the endless letters sent to Elio and to the clinic. In any case, Vieri was married and belonged to Mariannina. Perhaps *she* had been the one to put her foot down and stop the correspondence.

Sarah spent the evening going through the files she had kept on her job applications in the last three months. She had written one hundred and forty letters and had received only six replies, all of them negative. With millions unemployed in the country, no one wanted a young woman with a babe in arms. In the coming week, Sarah knew she must step up her efforts. She would post the new job application letters, make

phone calls, and visit all the agencies again, but the reply
was always the same: *We take live-in domestic staff with
young children, but not with babies.* She had found a nursery in which youngsters could be left while their mothers
worked, but the establishment would not take children under
eighteen months and neither would any other nursery in
London. In desperation, she had even rung her mother and
asked outright for help, but the reply had been as expected:
*Come for Christmas, dear, when all these boring troubles
are over.* She had tried to return to television work, but her
Equity card was out of date and she did not have enough
money to renew it.

In the middle of the night, Sarah rose and went to look at
her child, her eyes filling with tears as she thought of the advice Charles Elford, her lawyer, had given her that afternoon: *Either go back to Thistleton and eat humble pie with
your mother-in-law or find work fast, any kind of work.
You're in grave danger of losing custody of your baby. At
the moment, you've no money and no visible means of support and you're almost out of cash. Your mother won't take
you in and though the courts in Britain are lenient, under
the present circumstances they'd certainly rule that until
your life's more settled custody of Alexis should pass to the
grandmother. It's not my personal opinion, and I'll loan you
money as a friend. I'm simply telling you what the courts
will say.*

Panic rose in Sarah, as it rose a dozen times a day, and she
turned on all the lights and stood at the window, looking out
into the darkness of night, as if willing it to give her the answer to the conundrum of her dilemma. Her mind clouded as
she thought of her husband's financial situation. Nolan had
earned a fortune, but spent it all like water. Now he was unable to work and the doctors had implied that he would remain so in the foreseeable future. Sarah wondered how he
would pay alimony, assuming the court awarded it to her.

The only thing of which she was sure was that Mrs. James would never loan him the cash to keep the daughter-in-law she hated.

Sarah was making hot milk when the telephone rang again. It was four A.M. and winter was in the air. Shivering, she picked up the receiver and spoke wearily.

"Five-eight-four, seven-five-one-eight."

"What are you doing?"

She looked into the receiver, stunned by the sound of the familiar voice.

"Umberto! Where are you?"

"In my house in Paris. What are you doing?"

"I can't sleep and I'm making hot milk. How did you know the number? I've only been here two weeks."

"I find out what I need to know, like always, and what I learn is that you are in trouble. You want I arrange things?"

The words shocked and thrilled Sarah's weary mind and she found herself unable to speak. She was trying to accept that after all the months of distress and the weeks of looking unsuccessfully for work, Umberto had come to her rescue. She listened in wonder as he continued.

"In the morning, you go to Cook's in Berkeley Square. A ticket to Paris is waiting for you. The plane depart Heathrow Airport at two in the afternoon. Are you listening, Sarah?"

"I won't leave my child behind."

"Your child is call Alexis and you say always Lexy. You have a husband who is crazy and he won't sign the divorce papers. His mother is horrible. Your mother is horrible, and if you are not careful you lose custody of the baby. I know about the marriage and how you try all these months to find work. Now *I* take over and you come back to Paris. When you are feeling better, you work for me in my new club in the avenue George Cinq. You learn the business and soon I help you find a little club of your own. You live in the apartment with Lexy and I take on a nurse to look after her when you work. The nurse is Swedish with big muscles and she stand the nonsense from no one, not even Umberto di Castelli.''

"Why are you doing all this?"

Sarah heard him sigh and smiled in spite of herself at the patience in his voice.

"I told you once, what you want I get, if I don't have I arrange."

"I remember, but that was all a long time ago."

"You remember too that I say I never let you go and I never stop loving you, not till my blood turn to water? You remember that, Sarah?"

She felt the tears running down her cheeks as Umberto continued, his voice gentle.

"Come back to Paris and to me."

She thought of her situation, of the child she loved and of Vieri, who had vanished from her life for the second time. It took only seconds to make the decision.

"I'll collect the ticket in the morning."

"Your husband sign the divorce papers in the morning, I promise. You make an error in marrying that man, Sarah, but it is over and you must forget the past. In Paris you become the woman you tell me once you want to be, independent and full of ideas for opening clubs and making fortunes. Tomorrow, I come to the airport to meet you and I order sunshine for your arrival. You hear me, Sarah?"

"I hear you, Umberto."

With that, he was gone, leaving Sarah sitting with the phone in her hand and a bemused expression on her face. Profoundly shocked, touched, and thrilled, she asked no questions about the wisdom of the move. In Paris she would have work, a place to live, security for her child and herself. In Paris she would be outside the jurisdiction of the British courts, so Nolan would be unable to take the child. It no longer mattered a damn what Umberto might have done in

the past. All that mattered was that he was a man who loved
her and kept his promises. He would look after her, teach
her a new profession, and worship her till his blood turned to
water. Sarah thought of Vieri, lying locked in anguish in the
clinic near Rome, and longing for him welled within her, as
inevitable as the surging tide. But she accepted that there
was nothing more to be done where he was concerned. She
had written endless letters. She had arranged with Elio to
replay the events of the night in the Piazza Navona, all to no
avail. Since her visit to Rome her letters remained unanswered. Was it possible that the experiment had hindered
Vieri's recovery and that the Aldobrandini family members
were unforgiving?

Umberto stood on the roof of the airport, a cigar in his
hand, a look of intense excitement in his eyes. It was a fine
autumn day, crisp and clear with a smoke-blue sky and a
gentle breeze. Scents of resin and fallen leaves, bonfires and
ripe fruit wafted from nearby farms as harvests were gathered in, and he thought of Sicily and the days Sarah had
spent with him there at the palazzo. After the plane landed,
he watched the passengers descending, his heart leaping
when Sarah came into view. Hurrying to his car, he was
driven directly onto the tarmac, where he stood, like a rock
waiting for her to come to him. He was touched that she had
chosen to wear the white dress with daisies at the hem that
had always been his favorite. It still fitted her perfectly and
looked as new as on the day he had first seen it. But it was
not suitable for a chilly autumn morning and she was shivering. He took off his coat and put it around her shoulders as
she kissed him on both cheeks like a stranger.

"Hello, Umberto."

"It's been a long time. Now we make up for the years we
lose."

"This is Alexis."

He glanced at the baby and then back to Sarah.

"She is very pretty, but not yet a temptress like her mother. Come, it is time to take you home."

In the car, Umberto rested his hand on Sarah's, closing his eyes and enjoying the scent that he remembered so well. Powerful emotions filled his mind and he wanted to sob like a child because she was back in his life. Instead, he vowed grimly never to lose her. He had made one error, but he would never make another. This time he would make sure Sarah stayed, not only because she needed what he could give, but because she wanted him.

On entering the apartment, Sarah gazed around her in wonder. Everything was exactly how she had left it on the day of her departure from Paris, except that there were fresh flowers in vases in each of the rooms. Tears filled her eyes and she turned to Umberto, grasping his hand.

"I can't believe you changed nothing at all. I just can't believe it. Why did you keep this place on? It must have cost a fortune."

"I want for you to come back and I don't pay rent. I buy the building instead."

Sarah laughed for the first time in months.

"You're unique, Umberto. I'm so glad to be home."

"Come and meet the nurse. Her name is Mitzi and she occupy the next apartment."

Sarah followed Umberto into the other apartment. She chatted briefly with Mitzi, sensing immediately that the woman was warm and affectionate as well as competent. She left Lexy with her, feeling relaxed and comfortable.

In the hallway, Sarah stepped close to Umberto, looking questioningly into his luminous black eyes, relieved that he had not changed, except that the hairs at his temples were showing signs of gray. She was touched to see that he was trembling from emotion when he spoke.

"This is a great day for me, a very great day. This afternoon I take you shopping and we buy new clothes and shoes and fur coats for the winter. You will be working at night and it is very damp here in Paris. We have to take care the lungs don't get ill.''

Sarah kissed his cheeks. Then, winding her arms around his neck, she kissed him on the mouth, taken aback, as always, by the force of his desire.

As he looked into her face, Umberto saw desire and something new, a smoldering, hard quality that made him burn. He tried to sound flippant, but he could barely control the desire that tantalized every nerve in his body.

"Maybe we buy the new clothes tomorrow."

She replied in a whisper, direct as always.

"Make love to me, Umberto. Make me forget everything except that I'm here and a new life is about to begin."

He picked her up as if she weighed nothing at all and carried her through to the bedroom, locking the door behind them. Then, as the sun set like a vermilion phantom over the city, the lovers renewed old acquaintance. For Umberto, it was a moment of triumph. For Sarah it was the dawning of hope and relief. She was on familiar territory and no longer alone. She vowed silently not to waste a single moment of the chance that had been given her.

Chapter Sixteen

Mary-Ellen, Seville, Spring 1972

It was the period of the Easter *feria* and Mary-Ellen was looking forward to the excitement of the spectacle and festivities. Her twin sons had been born six months previously and she knew that Luis was very proud of them and would give a party in their honor. He had even promised to give up gambling, but had started again after a week. Mary-Ellen had resigned herself to the fact that even the birth of twin sons did not warrant such a sacrifice. She sighed; her husband's obsession with gambling and his jealousy were the principal clouds on her horizon. In the stylish hacienda, with its walled courtyard and fountains, it was easy to relax and feel secure, but was she secure? Doubt gnawed continually at Mary-Ellen's mind, because she had no idea of her husband's financial position and no way of finding out if he was actually in debt or if she was worrying needlessly. When she asked Luis about money, he told her that no Spaniard discussed such matters with his wife. On the one occasion when she insisted, Luis left the house in a fury and did not return for forty-eight hours.

For the moment, however, things seemed better. Luis was working hard preparing a case to be presented before the tribunal in Madrid. After the *feria* he would travel there with Mary-Ellen, his brother Ignacio, and a distant cousin, and they would return one month later. Mary-Ellen hurried to check the guest bedrooms. Then she returned to the library. Earlier in the morning she had checked her wardrobe and found to her dismay that she had nothing at all to wear in the demanding atmosphere of Madrid. She had had no new clothes since her marriage, and Luis had never offered to buy her any. Mary-Ellen gazed resignedly at the courtyard, thinking about the dresses that were fast becoming threadbare. The shoes would also have to be replaced. She decided to talk with her husband at once. She sprayed herself with his favorite perfume and put on a confident smile, then hurried to Luis's office, where he was working. First she poured them both a glass of sherry. She liked it when he worked at home. He seemed to be in a good humor, and she was ready to make allowance for almost anything except total rejection.

"Luis, I need some new clothes and shoes. I've had none since the end of the Tour of the Ballet Rose and that's a long time ago. I have to throw out a lot of the stuff that's too worn to wear and I'd like to replace the things in Madrid. Will you please give me some money?"

He smiled expansively, kissing her cheeks.

"Of course I will. Here, take ten thousand pesetas and I will give you more next week before we leave for Madrid."

Mary-Ellen's eyes widened in alarm. Did he realize that ten thousand pesetas was equivalent to about one hundred and twenty dollars, scarely the price of two pairs of decent shoes? She spoke calmly, however, allowing none of her uncertainty to show on her face.

"I'll need a lot more than that to buy dresses and shoes and to replace my basic underwear. I can buy a small wardrobe for around one hundred thousand pesetas. Can you give me that much, Luis?"

"Your clothes are beautiful; why do you wish to throw them out?"

"I don't want to throw them out, but a lot of the garments are coming apart at the seams and wearing thin. The shoes are broken and the underwear is worn through. I've been using my own savings to replace some of the things, but I don't have any cash left. You're my husband and you like it very much when people admire my clothes, but it costs money, you know, and this is the first time I've ever asked for any."

"I cannot give you one hundred thousand pesetas. I don't have it."

"Then give me what you can."

"I can give you ten thousand pesetas now and another ten thousand in Madrid and that is all."

Mary-Ellen leaped to her feet, enraged by his attitude. "Then sell a painting, like you did when you owed Don José a fortune in gambling debts!"

"Reina! Please don't be angry. I am not a rich man; try to understand how it is."

"You're not a poor man, Luis, and I need the new clothes. Call the bank and tell them to let me have some cash, and do it now."

Luis looked into the big blue eyes that seemed suddenly icy. He wondered how to divert Mary-Ellen's attention, how to keep from her the fact that there was no money in the account, that in fact there was an overdraft he had no hope of covering. There was no cash anywhere, except his monthly salary, and that was automatically debited with the costs of running the house and paying the bills for food and drink. Luis thought of his gambling debts and sighed. Then he turned to Mary-Ellen and spoke gently.

"Now is a bad time for money, my darling. Soon, though, I will give you what you need for the clothes. Please trust me. It will not be long."

Mary-Ellen spoke quietly.

"I won't be put off with promises. I'm not being unreasonable in asking for clothes. We've been married for nearly four years, and before that we were together for almost a year after the tour ended. Since you won't let me work, it's your responsibility to feed and clothe me. Now, I want the clothes and I want them today.''

''But I have no money.''

''Then find some. I don't intend to walk around Madrid like some bare-assed poor relation.''

With that, Mary-Ellen strode out of the room and out of the house, well aware that Luis hated her to go out alone. Since their marriage she had been a virtual prisoner, albeit a well-treated one. At first she had been flattered and reassured by her husband's attitude, equating possessiveness with love, jealousy with desire. Now, though, both traits grated on her nerves because she recognized that they were merely symptoms of Luis's vanity. She walked on, still enraged, and found herself in the most exclusive shopping area of Seville. Pausing outside Loewe, she saw a window full of leather clothes. A jacket in pine-green suede collared and lined with fox dyed to match caught her eye, and with it a shoulder purse of the same velvet-soft dimension. Mary-Ellen entered the shop, tried on the jacket, bought it, and ordered it to be delivered to the house. Then she went to La Hacienda, an exclusive lingerie shop, and tried on cobwebby camisoles in silk and lawn, negligees trimmed with lace, and a selection of petticoats in every color of the rainbow, each layer of the voluminous skirts edged with satin. She bought only what she needed, some sets of underwear in rose and pistachio and a couple of lacy slips that she knew Luis would adore. At the establishment of Berhanyer, she purchased two silk dresses, one rose and one violet, and a black suit of light wool, its collar appliquéd with velvet, and a white blouse with an artist's bow that matched the tiny hat to complete the ensemble.

It was seven in the evening when Mary-Ellen returned to

the house and found her husband pacing the courtyard frantically, his face as pale as tallow. He shouted at her as she stepped through the gate.

"I demand to know where you have been!"

"I went shopping."

"Where? How did you buy? You said you had no money."

"Your name's good, Luis. They don't think grandees of Spain default on payment."

"And where are your purchases?"

"They'll be delivered in the morning. Now, stop shouting and pour us both a sherry."

Two of Luis's friends came through the gate as husband and wife were facing each other like fighting bulls across the courtyard. Unable to control his rage, Luis poured sherry for himself and his friends, ignoring Mary-Ellen completely. She was debating whether to return to her room and give him the same treatment, when she heard her husband explaining his dilemma to the two men, one of whom had pursued her with great tenacity ever since the marriage.

"My wife has been shopping and ordered new clothes to be delivered here to the house. You know my finances at this time. What am I to do? What would *you* do in this situation?"

Don Antonio smiled at Mary-Ellen.

"You are an American and cannot be expected to know our ways, but in Spain our women do not buy without permission."

Mary-Ellen rose to her full six foot three, towering over everyone in sight.

"I've bought nothing since I left the show in Paris; that's almost five years. When I asked permission, Luis said he had no money. Now I'm going to my room. If my husband wants to discuss his private affairs with you he can, but I don't want to and I *won't.*"

With that, Mary-Ellen marched across the courtyard and slammed the door on the handsome landowner, Antonio Duarte, his brother, and Luis. She was furious with her husband for discussing his private affairs with friends, but satisfied that she had at least represented her own side of the affair. Throwing off her clothes, she hurried to the bathroom and stood under the shower, closing her eyes and trying not to panic at the thought of what would happen when the clothes arrived the next day. Would Luis send them all back? Would he become violent? And how would he pay for everything? Mary-Ellen dried her body and looked at herself in the mirror, knowing in her heart that she had done wrong. Only morning would tell whether her attitude justified the consequences of Luis's anger.

By eleven A.M. the patio was full of boxes and parcels delivered from the most expensive shops in the city. In the salon Luis was raging at Mary-Ellen, and in the patio his friends were drinking sherry and trying to pretend that nothing untoward was happening. Finally, they decided that the row had gone on long enough and Don Antonio strolled through to the room where Luis was roaring at his wife. Don Antonio's voice was soothing.

"Luis, my friend, come and join us. What are you worrying about, after all? The clothes cost nothing."

"They cost one hundred and sixty thousand pesetas and I don't have it! Try to understand my feelings."

"I will lend it to you. Mary-Ellen, do bring your sons to see us and we'll all drink a sherry together. Luis, I am your friend for twenty years and I am happy to take this worry from your shoulders. Now that Mary-Ellen has her new clothes she will be happy, and you can pay me back when you have had a good night at the tables."

After midnight, Luis lay in his bed watching Mary-Ellen trying on her new outfits. His dark eyes glowed as he admired the curves of her body, the sensuous tilt of her hips.

Then he frowned, his mind returning to the moment when
Antonio Duarte, his friend for twenty years, had decided to
loan him money for the new clothes. Why had he done that?
Luis looked again at Mary-Ellen and thought how Ameri-
cans were different. To them everything was simple and life
traveled in a straight line. What they wanted they got, somehow, in a pragmatic manner that mystified him. He resolved
to watch Mary-Ellen closely in the coming weeks. If she
gave even the tiniest hint of flirting with Duarte, he would
send her away for a year to one of his family's houses in the
north. In the meantime, he would simply observe her every
move.

Six months after the affair of the new clothes, Mary-Ellen
discovered she was pregnant again. She was emerging from
the doctor's surgery and feeling groggy, when Antonio
Duarte stopped his car and motioned for her to get in.

"Why are you so pale? Is something wrong, Mary-
Ellen?"

"I just found out I'm pregnant again. God knows what
Luis is going to say. He keeps worrying himself sick about
money, and this will be just one more financial drain on his
pocket."

"He will be delighted. All Spanish men love children.
Come, I shall take you home. You must rest and try to get
strong again. For many weeks you have been losing weight.
Is something wrong?"

"I've been upset."

"Tell me about it."

She was tempted to unburden herself, but decided it was
prudent to remain silent. Since Duarte had bought her the
new clothes, Luis had watched Mary-Ellen like a hawk and
she knew exactly what he was thinking. She knew too that
she was playing into his hands by letting Duarte drive her
home, but she felt so unsteady and in need of care that she
no longer wanted to concern herself with her husband's un-

reasonable jealousy. Duarte had made no advances since the purchase of the new clothes and she felt certain he had long since resigned himself to the fact of her unavailability. She thought defiantly that Luis could rage as he liked. All she wanted was to be home and in bed.

Luis watched as Duarte handed Mary-Ellen out of the car and followed her into the house. She went at once to her room and he heard her door closing. Both anger and fear of humiliation filled his heart but his face was calm as he went downstairs to the library, where Duarte was pouring himself a glass of sherry.

"We should drink champagne, my dear Luis. Your wife tells me she is to have another child. I saw her leaving Dr. Alvarez's residence, and as she was very pale I brought her home to you."

"And she told you she was pregnant?"

"Of course. Don't look so shocked. Mary-Ellen is very direct; it's time you got used to the fact that she is not like our women. And, after all, I have been a friend of the family for two decades."

Luis swallowed the sherry and looked uncomprehendingly into Duarte's eyes. Then, without warning, and to Duarte's astonishment, he hurried outside, got in his car, and drove away. Obviously, Duarte was Mary-Ellen's lover and the child could be his. Luis had hardly made love with his wife since the affair of the new clothes, because Mary-Ellen had been resentful and bitchy. Now she was pregnant and he would never know if the child was his or Duarte's. He drove wildly for an hour. Then he returned to the house and shouted to his wife.

"Come down here, I have some questions for you. And where is your lover? Did he run away? He informs me that you are pregnant again, and I *demand* to know who is the father!"

Mary-Ellen rose from her bed and sat for a few moments

controlling her rage. Then she walked resignedly downstairs to the library. She felt beaten, tired and empty of the sparkle that had once been an integral part of her character. She heard Luis shouting again and wondered how to reason with him and if there was any point in doing so. He would never believe her and she was unsure whether she cared or not. She cared only for her sons and for keeping them safe and well in the future. The rest was hollow and empty, a future without love in a house full of resentment and anger.

Part III

HALLAM INTERNATIONAL

It is the feet of clay that make the gold image precious. Her feet are very pretty, but they are not feet of clay. They have been through the fire and what fire does not destroy it hardens. She has had experiences. . . .

—Oscar Wilde
The Picture of Dorian Grey

Chapter Seventeen

Paris, Spring 1973

In the two and a half years of her training by Madame Zezette, Sarah had been taught all the lady had learned in nearly thirty-five years of managing nightclubs. She had learned the all-important art of remembering clients' names and faces, of enforcing bills without seeming to insist, how to cope with staff who banded together at holidays and parties to demand more money. Madame's maxim was *Dismiss the bastards and take on new. There's no room for a Judas in this business.* Sarah had her own ideas, but knew she must keep them until she had a club of her own. She was convinced that participation in ownership was essential in the modern age. Better to have one hundred percent of each worker's energy and desire to succeed than one hundred percent of a scanty profit margin. Sarah's biggest success in the period since her arrival in Paris had been the introduction of a stylish champagne breakfast from two to three A.M. The idea had appealed, and the receipts had increased by ten percent as clients from other clubs began to arrive each night in time to eat English venison sausages, oak-smoked ham, and coddled eggs with the finest champagne.

Sarah had made a point of visiting fellow club owners in the area during the late afternoon, always taking Lexy with her and drinking a glass of wine with even the crustiest competitor. Some had laughed when she invited the club's biggest rival, Madame Nicoletti, to Malmaison for a picnic. No one had found it amusing when the monstrous lady had insisted from that day on that Sarah was one of her "acceptables." Some had been trying for twenty years to become one of Madame Nicoletti's acceptables and found it hard to believe that the newcomer had done the magic trick with a simple visit to the country. They were unaware that Sarah had hired a Rolls-Royce for the occasion and sent to Fortnum and Mason, the prestigious London store, for one of their Edwardian-style picnic hampers. Madame had been impressed and the unlikely friendship had been founded.

Madame was forty-four and had been in the business all her life. She knew every club owner in Paris, every business that came up for sale, and the disadvantages and advantages of each. She was also prone, after a few glasses of champagne, to some uproarious indiscretions, her frizzy red hair and bulbous blue eyes coming alive as she described her rivals. Sarah had also learned, though nothing direct was said, that Madame detested Umberto di Castelli for reasons that lay in the dim and distant past.

Late one morning, Sarah was drinking coffee at the counter of a bar near her apartment, when she saw Liz, her onetime enemy from the Tour of the Ballet Rose. She hurried over and extended her hand.

"Have you forgotten me? I'm Sarah Hallam and this is my daughter, Lexy."

"Sarah! What a lovely surprise. I read you're managing a club for Umberto di Castelli. How is he?"

"He's fine. What are you doing in Paris?"

Liz's eyes filled with tears.

"I married Daniel Lind a few months after the tour ended and I've been living here ever since."

A shadow crossed Sarah's face as she thought of the brilliant young violinist, whose future had seemed so golden, but who had been struck down by multiple sclerosis. As she saw the tears falling down Liz's cheeks, she asked herself how she could ever have thought this vulnerable creature the toughest girl in Paris. Sarah listened as Liz explained her situation.

"Dan won't ever work again, so I'll have to find a job. I've been looking for weeks, but I've no qualifications and no one's interested in an ex-dancer of twenty-eight who doesn't want to work at night."

"If I hear of anything I'll call you. What about modeling? You used to do a lot of that."

"I'm too old, Sarah. Nowadays you're too old at twenty."

Sarah walked back to the apartment, chattering to her daughter as they hurried on their way.

"That lady used to work with me when I was a dancer."

"She's pretty, but not as pretty as you, Mummy. Are we going to our club now?"

"Of course. You can have a grenadine and soda while I work for a while. Then I'll take you home for supper."

"Will you steal my sausages, like yesterday?"

"I might if you don't eat them all."

"And can I eat some of those green cocktail cherries when we get to our club?"

"We'll take a bottle home with us and you can eat them with your yogurt for dessert."

"Bruin likes cocktail cherries."

"Bruin's going to be the fattest teddy bear in Paris if he doesn't watch it."

Sarah walked on, thinking of Liz's gaunt face and the catastrophe that had hit her life. For the hundredth time, she realized how lucky she had been to be given the job by Umberto and the apartment with it. She was profoundly grateful to him for all he had done.

In the early evening, Sarah was returning to the club when

she saw in a store window the reflection of Umberto's cousin Rocco following her. She tried to tell herself it was a small price to pay for the security she craved, but she had never grown accustomed to surveillance and the sight riled her. She had been certain Umberto would come to trust her in time, but as his passion increased, the watchdogs grew in number.

At midnight Nino Ortolani appeared. Another former member of the company of the Ballet Rose, he was looking very prosperous.

"I saw Liz this afternoon and she told me you want a club of your own, Sarah. I know of one not far from me in the rue Fontaine."

"I want a place I can upmarket."

"This may be it, why don't you at least come and look. The owner's got six months to live and he's been married to a woman who's driven him crazy for thirty-five years. It's his dearest wish to sell fast and blow the profits at the casino in Monte Carlo. He's absolutely determined not to leave her a shilling. I left my car outside. If you can spare half an hour I'll show you the place."

The street was narrow, the atmosphere alive with neon club signs flashing scarlet, orange, and gold. *Hôtels de passe* abounded, and many of the streetwalkers had been there for so long the locals joked they were ready for retirement pensions.

Sarah looked uncertainly about her, wondering if the rich people of Paris could be persuaded to come to such an area. She noted that there was no room to park, no security, no quality, only a frenetic gaiety.

Tucked away between a cabaret and a horsemeat butcher's shop, there was a small green-painted door. Over it, a shabby sign hung precariously off one hinge, its faded letters indicating that this was George's Bar. From the entrance, a dark passage led to a large, gray-painted room presided over by a man with the jowls of a bloodhound. Once, it was obvious, he had been a big, solid fellow, but illness and approaching death had bleached the color from his skin and taken the weight from his bones, so the flesh hung in slack folds, giving him a mournful expression. He greeted Nino with a handshake.

"How are you, my friend? Have you opened the hotel yet?"

"Friday's the big day, George."

"We'll drink to your success. What will the young lady have?"

Sarah was reading the lines written on the wall behind the bar.

In England, everything is allowed, except what is forbidden.

In Germany, everything is forbidden, except what is allowed.

In Russia, everything is forbidden, even what is allowed.

In France, everything is allowed, even what is forbidden.

She smiled at the truth of the words, unaware that the owner was watching her. Then Nino nudged her and asked what she wanted to drink.

"I'll have a glass of white wine, please."

George weighed the long blonde hair, the heart-shaped face, and wondered what a woman like that was doing working for Umberto di Castelli. He spoke respectfully, however, touched by her obvious interest in her surroundings.

"What are you doing in Paris, mademoiselle?"

"I manage Le Train Bleu, as Nino told you, and I hope to continue living here for as long as it takes to establish myself."

"Nino said you're looking for a place of your own. When you've drunk your wine I'll show you around."

Sarah followed the two men to the back room used to store crates and bottles and then to a kitchen left over from the days when home-cooked lunches had been served. Above, there was an apartment consisting of two tiny rooms, in addition to a minuscule kitchen and bathroom. Everything was in the worst possible state of repair, though the roof had been renewed and the structure was sound. The lease was for three years only and would never be renewed. George was asking twenty thousand for the goodwill and stated defiantly that he would rather die than sell to a developer, a rival, or one of the newfangled self-service restaurants. Realizing how he clung for security to the ideas of the past, Sarah stated her own position.

"I've no money, so I'll have to raise it from scratch, but I'm interested in buying. Can you give me a month to arrange things?"

"In my condition a month's a long time."

"I'll need it. I'd have to have twenty thousand sterling for the purchase, plus at least fifteen percent on top of that for legal fees and taxes, and then twenty thousand more to do up the place. It's a lot of money."

George scratched his head. The doctors had given him six months to live, but they were all liars and six months might mean six weeks. Still, he had always been a gambler and he could not change his ways. He looked at Sarah and shook her hand.

"Go home and think about it. If you haven't changed your mind during the night, come back and see me."

In the small hours, Sarah lay in bed wondering how she could raise such a large sum of money. She had a job, an apartment, and charge accounts that Umberto settled monthly, but she had no cash of her own and her future was entirely dependent on Umberto. For the first time she realized

that her precious security was not real security at all. She
was living in paradise, but it was a fool's paradise. All her
eggs were in the basket of Umberto di Castelli and without
him she was nothing. She remembered Vieri's emphatic
warning: *Never become dependent on that man for finance. . . . Always have your own people to advise you.*
Sarah thought fiercely that she must correct the situation,
but she did not know how. The easiest way would be to open
her own place, raising the money to buy without Umberto's
help. That would prove to both of them that she was not totally in his power. She would arrange to have the property
put under the title of the company Vieri had given her before
his kidnapping. As she remembered the day he had sent her
the details about the company, she thought of the little note
he had written and tears filled her eyes. The company's
name was Meteor, and Vieri had joked that it was a very apt
name for her.

At five A.M. Sarah rose and made a pot of tea, watching
the street below as dawn broke and a newspaper delivery-
man arrived with the early-morning editions. Already the
scent of new-baked bread was drifting up from the shop on
the corner, and on the Seine rowers in scarlet shirts were
practicing in two-man racing sculls under the shadow of the
Pont de Neuilly. Sarah ran downstairs to buy a paper. Upon
her return, she settled on the sofa with a brioche and a second cup of tea to look at the headlines. Her eyes widened at
an old photograph of Vieri, showing him as he had looked
on the day of their first meeting—handsome, unforgettable,
the perfect man of her dreams. Next to the old photograph
was one taken after his ordeal, revealing a broken creature
with vacant eyes and a skeletal body. The headline was simple: WHERE IS THIS MAN?

Sarah read on, relieved to learn that Vieri had not vanished again but had simply not been seen for over a year.
Speculation as to whether he was locked away in an asylum

was increasing, and the article stated that the head of the Aldobrandini family had last been seen in an expensive private
clinic near Venice. Another purported sighting had been in
Australia, at a spa used by alcoholics. Sarah sighed, looking
at the telephone and debating whether to ring the Aldobrandini house in Venice. She had frequently considered telephoning Elio or Vieri, but she was well aware that if either
brother had wanted to contact her he could have done so.
She rose and paced the room in agitation, her longing for
Vieri so forceful it could not be denied. She tried to tell herself it was over, that he would never contact her again, but
her mind would not accept the idea and constantly sought
reasons for the sudden and inexplicable loss of communication between herself and the Aldobrandinis.

Sarah was standing next to the telephone, her hand on the
receiver, when she had an idea that took even Vieri out of
her mind. Minutes later, she had phoned in an advertisement
for the evening edition of the Paris paper. The ad read, *Lots
of little people would like to own a business, but haven't got
the money to do so. English entrepreneur seeks partners to
invest in a new and stylish drinking club. Minimum investment ten thousand new francs. Interested parties contact
Sarah Hallam.* Her telephone number followed her name.

When Umberto arrived at the apartment the following
evening, he was surprised and disappointed to find Sarah absent. Puzzled, because she was always there at six o'clock,
he knocked on the nurse's door and asked where she was.

"She's gone out to interview the investors, sir. Madame
found a club she wants to buy and she's looking for people
to help her raise money."

"Where is she?"

"She asked every one to meet her at the Hôtel Napoléon,
sir."

Sarah was sitting on a velvet sofa in the hotel off the
Champs Elysées where she had stayed on her first arrival in

Paris. With her were a dozen people who had answered the advertisement and listened patiently as she described the club as it was and as it would be. Of the twelve, two had withdrawn because they felt the risk of the club's location in the Pigalle area was too great. The remaining ten ranged from a housewife who normally played the stock market but was now seeking something more personal, to a retired actor, two hairdressers, and a middle-aged florist from the rue de Berri. The youngest of the potential investors was twenty-eight, a mechanic working at the Renault factory at Boulogne Billancourt. The oldest was sixty-two and investing because he liked the idea of drinking his daily bottle in a place he partly owned.

Sarah watched the door, hoping the advertisement would bring in more applicants, but none came and those who arrived were not enough. She had ten thousand pounds, half the purchase price, but nothing for the restoration, taxes, and preparations for opening. She decided to run the ad for one more day and made a phone call from the lobby giving instructions to the paper's classified department. Then she went back to the lounge and spoke to her potential partners.

"I've put the ad in for another night. If that doesn't bring in more investors we'll have to think again. I've given you my address and phone number, and we'll meet again on Saturday at the club when we see the premises. Do try to talk to your friends about the idea. Maybe some of them will want to take a gamble with us."

Umberto sat in his car, watching the investors leaving the hotel. He smiled to himself at the motley crew Sarah had assembled: an old lady with an outlandish feathered hat, an elderly man walking with a stick, a young fellow in overalls, and what looked like two or three housewives, one with a baby in a carriage. Having locked his car, he entered the hotel and looked down at Sarah as she sat alone, staring into space.

"What do you think you are doing, seeing old ladies in fancy hats and trying to get money without asking me?"

"I can't be entirely dependent on you."

"Why not?"

"Because it's not in my nature. I wasn't born to be dependent. In any case, suppose you were killed in an accident. I'd be left with four-fifths of nothing and right back where I started when I arrived here with Lexy."

"How much money do you need?"

"I need the equivalent of twenty thousand pounds English for the purchase and the same again to get the place in order."

"Why are you buying a rathole! There is nothing worth having in Paris so cheap."

"The lease is only three years and not renewable, but I have to start somewhere."

"I will send my men to go over the building."

Sarah turned to face him, her voice gentle.

"I want to do this first thing on my own, Umberto. If I fail, I fail. If I succeed it'll give me confidence. You just have to let me try."

"But I love you and I am rich. I give you what you want."

Sarah sighed, conscious that he had no real insight into her thoughts. She tried to be patient.

"I want to raise this money myself, so I know I can. Next time you and I can be partners, but the first club is going to be my baby."

Umberto drove back to the apartment, glowering at his thoughts. He found it impossible to comprehend why Sarah could not simply take what he offered, why she was such a malcontent. He decided to talk about her with Mario Benedetti and then to check out everything about the owner of George's and the receipts over the past few years. Pigalle was a trash can of iniquity. How *could* Sarah consider starting there? He thought then of the ridiculously low amount of money Sarah had requested from her investors and decided to telephone the classified department of the newspaper to change her ad for the next evening. If he was right, she would have the money for the club sooner than she expected.

The following day, Sarah arrived at the Hôtel Napoléon and found Madame Nicoletti waiting for her, her red hair newly curled in a halo around her head. She was accompanied by an elderly lady, whom she introduced as her neighbor from Louveciennes.

"My dear, this is Eloise Requier. She saw your advertisement and asked me about you. I told her that if you're going into the club it must be interesting and at one hundred thousand francs a share it's cheap. She'll take one share and I'll take another. Your man said the meetings were being held here which was fine because I don't like visiting your apartment since I might run into *him*. Is something wrong, Sarah?"

Sarah picked up the newspaper and read the new advertisement, noting that the figure printed was one hundred thousand new francs instead of the ten thousand she had dictated. On calling the paper, she was told that the ad had been changed by a man with a pronounced Italian accent. She understood immediately that Umberto had made a decision for her and knew that under the circumstances he had been right. Her heart soared with relief as Madame Nicoletti continued.

"My friend Alice Kaiser also wants a share or two. She's really rich and she's always wanted to be in the business. Now, let's go and have dinner at Polka des Mandibules. I have an appointment at eight-fifteen so we'd best settle everything right now."

In the pink light of early evening, Sarah walked slowly back to the apartment, pausing to look at the glow of sunset

on the cobblestones and the silhouette of curled iron lamps
on the ancient bridge, where the statue of a boy on a winged
horse was outlined against a charcoal and amber sky. It was
springtime and she had enough money to purchase her first
club. She did a little impromptu dance and then, as she
leaned over the parapet of the bridge and stared into the
waters of the Seine, she felt the onset of doubt. The location
was a terrible risk, unless she could turn its disadvantages to
her advantage. The only other fear was that the premises
were too small. Sarah strode on, knowing what she wanted
to do with the place. It would be a ferocious gamble, but she
felt ready for anything. Thrilled to think she was at last
going to have her own place, Sarah decided to telephone her
daughter. The child knew of her ambitions and always
spoke of Umberto's club as "ours," though she knew it was
not really theirs. Sarah hurried to a phone booth and dialed
her own number, delighted when Lexy answered.

"Hello, this is Sarah Hallam's house."

"This is Mummy. I just wanted to tell you the wonderful
news that we've got a club of our own at last. It's in Pigalle
and I'm going to call it the English Club."

"Oh, Mummy, are you extra-special happy?"

"I certainly am."

"Shall I have an office there with you?"

"Of course you will. I'll give you a desk in the corner
with lots of colored pencils and your new typewriter."

"I love you ten million, Mummy."

"Goodnight, darling. I'll come in and give you a kiss
when I get home."

On the day the legal papers were signed, thirteen people
took ownership of what had formerly been George's Bar.
Then Sarah explained to her investors her ideas for the transformation. One of them ventured a question.

"Won't your idea make things rather difficult? So many
people will go away if the frontage is as you plan."

"I don't think so, not when they've seen the ads."

Sarah pulled a rough draft of the proposed first ad out of her purse, handing it to the doubtful man, who burst into peals of laughter.

"One thing's certain, Miss Hallam: We shall either make a fortune or lose every centime we've put in."

In the next few weeks the ground floor of the club was transformed into a drawing room from an English country house, all ivory and pink, with columns of fake porphyry and a ceiling painted in the style of Adam, with crosses and festoons of acanthus and honeysuckle. Sofas of rose damask were placed under a portrait of Adelina Patti by Winterhalter. Soundproofing kept out the raucous street noises and curtains the sordid view. The sounds were the gentle notes of Vivaldi and the tinkling of champagne glasses. The former kitchen had been turned into a cloakroom, the back room into an annex of the main room, its walls lined with leather-bound books. Upstairs, the apartment was gutted and the rooms converted into one large space known as the English Garden, complete with fountain, white treillage, and flowering pink roses and tree peonies. When Madame Nicoletti began to arrive for morning coffee "in the garden," Sarah realized that the club had developed an atmosphere of its own, a tiny piece of rural England in the middle of the most frenetic area of Paris.

Finally, the publicity campaign began. . . . *An English country garden in the heart of Paris with the highest prices in the city . . . Only bluebloods need apply and even blue blood won't guarantee a key to the door—if you can find the door.* The mystifying ad, the advance publicity, and the rumors as to the club's unusual status were given credence when the facade was erected. Astonished passersby gathered in the street outside to gaze up at a massive billboard that stretched from ground to roof and to either extremity of the frontage of the property. Executed in the style of billboards all over Paris, it looked perfectly at ease with its garish surroundings, the ads ranging from the Lido Show to the new spectacle at the Moulin Rouge and an old-fashioned remedy for cough mixture. The only thing no one could find was the entrance door. Locals gazed in fascination at passersby, who were touching and scrutinizing every inch of the facade in a vain attempt to find the handle. The ads had stated more than once that if clients could not find the door they would simply go away. Sarah's gamble was debated throughout the quarter, and the tone of the final advertisement was considered slightly crazy. *Only very special people have a key to the door. If you don't have one, don't come to the English Club. If you do have one and are to visit Pigalle, remember the pavements are dirty and the pickpockets superb.*

Umberto read the latest ad and the accompanying article about Sarah. The photograph made her look almost as beautiful as she really was, and he decided that he would have to increase surveillance once the club opened in order to guard her against the men who would undoubtedly fall in love. He looked across the dinner table at Sarah and began to question her.

"Why do you tell everyone the pavements are dirty?"

"Rich people like obstacles."

"And you think they like pickpockets?"

"Of course. They never carry money anyway."

"Why did you not use my people for the legal matters?"

"I want to have my own team, Umberto, that's all."

"You keep everything separate, like always."

"Not everything. You're the only man in my life. I don't keep you out of my private existence and I don't want to."

Unable to fathom or resist her, Umberto was already investigating Meteor, the shelf company given to Sarah by Vieri Aldobrandini, with dummy directors in Panama and a board of real directors in Switzerland. Impressed, he wondered how she had arranged it and why, for one little drinking club in Pigalle? What was her game and what were her real ambitions? He shook his head, awed, puzzled, and uncertain.

"I never understand you, Sarah."

"Good. That way I'll keep your interest." Her smile was brilliant, but it was obvious she would not tell him anything.

"I brought the list of the leading press people. Did you send out the keys?" he asked.

"Everything's been done."

"In a few days you will either be a success or back working for me at Le Train Bleu. I wish you come back, but I want the success for you. Always I am torn what to do. Nothing is simple and easy."

Late that night, they drove past the English Club and paused to watch the crowds outside, most of the people still trying to fathom the mystery of the missing door. Umberto was ill at ease.

"What an idea! No one will be patient enough to find how to get in."

"We'll see."

"I take you for a drink to my friend Michou. He has a bar nearby and he make a fortune in his day."

Michou was forty-eight, a plump, volatile Parisian who wore a beret and smoked Gauloises from getting out of bed to the moment when he fell asleep. He greeted Sarah with a firm handshake, his dark eyes twinkling.

"I've been reading your advertisements, Miss Hallam. You'll draw a big crowd on opening night because everyone's talking about you."

"I don't have room for a big crowd."

"Then refuse admittance to anyone whose face you don't like. That way all the best people will want to get in. If it's really that small and you have a bit of success, you could always buy the Bal Tabarin. I hear it's going cheap.''

Umberto saw the flicker of interest in Sarah's eyes and knew he must encourage her to buy, buy, buy. But could she be persuaded to borrow the money from *him?* He feigned disinterest in Michou's statement.

''I remember when that place was great. Now the Bal Tabarin is finish.''

Sarah looked from one man to the other.

''How big is it? How many does it seat?''

Umberto spoke firmly. ''You have enough debts for the moment. Don't think about it.''

''I want to see it. I'll need somewhere bigger if the English Club is successful.''

Umberto smiled, thinking that the sure way to make Sarah want something was to try to dissuade her from it. As they left the bar, he shook hands with Michou. As Sarah walked ahead to the car, the two men had a quiet word.

''I see you Friday when you come to the opening. We talk about the Bal Tabarin then. In the meantime I want to know the price and the condition of the owners.''

On the night of the opening, Sarah dressed in a sheath of black slipper satin with long gloves to match, a ''Gilda'' outfit that looked perfect with her newly fashionable long, wavy hair, glossy lips, and the crescent-shaped diamond earrings Umberto had bought for their anniversary. In her five-inch heels, she towered above everyone in the room, her face calm though her heart was fluttering like a trapped butterfly.

By five P.M. it became obvious that the bartender was not going to arrive. Sarah instructed one of the investors to take his place and then rang Madame Nicoletti to inform her of the man's disappearance. Madame promised a splendid fellow within two hours.

With minutes to go to the opening, signs of nerves were

increasing among the investors. Then Umberto arrived and made a speech that made them all laugh.

"This is the night when you lose the money or get rich. So no attacks of the nerves. You greet the clients. You tell go to hell anyone Sarah don't like and give the big welcome to special persons. If anyone complains you send to Sarah. If anyone behave bad, you send to Mario Benedetti and he throw out, even if the man is a duke or a duchess."

As Umberto left the club to pick up his wife, everyone shook his hand and promised to follow his instructions to the letter. Sarah looked around, touched that all her people were present, each one perfectly groomed and willing to do even the most menial task. There was an air of unreality about the place, as if they were all playacting at being in business— and, in truth, she knew they were.

Sarah's mind turned to the one thing Umberto did not know about the opening-night preparations, and a faraway look came into her eyes. She was thinking of the Piazza Navona, when she had worn a white dress and rosebuds in her hair. Impulsively, she took a rose from the trellis in the garden and fixed it in the blonde curls. She would wear it on this most important evening in memory of a phantom, a man who no longer existed, except in her heart.

The first guests to arrive were the influential editors of the leading Parisian dailies and the snobbish Duchesse de Griffe with a party of eleven. Photographs were taken, the finest Krug champagne was served, and the guests were shown around the club as Sarah would have shown them around her own home. The Duchess professed herself enchanted by the English Garden, took her place in the corner, and kept it against all opposition for the rest of the evening. The amber lighting and the gentle pink of the roses around her head made her look twenty years younger, and she resolved to come whenever she was in Paris and to bring all her lovers under the age of twenty-five.

As the clock struck ten, Umberto arrived with his wife. Madame di Castelli· was tall, elegant, reed slim, and beautiful in a glacial blonde fashion. Having shaken hands with Sarah and complimented her on the club's decor, she drifted to the ladies' room, where she emptied the contents of her perfume flask, which was kept permanently full of gin.

Umberto was smoking a huge cigar and talking with Sarah about the success of the evening, when there were sounds of commotion at the club entrance. Turning, he saw flashbulbs popping, newsmen calling, and the dragonlike Madame Requier hurrying in, her face uncertain.

"Sarah, there's someone outside who insists on entering without a key or an invitation. The press have gone quite mad. I think you'd best come."

"Did he give his name?"

"Yes, he did. Dear me, he's come in without permission. I shall have to dismiss the doorman!"

Umberto's face turned gray as he rose to his feet and stared disbelievingly at Vieri Aldobrandini, immaculate in a white silk dinner jacket and matching turtleneck sweater. The face was deeply suntanned and handsome, though the eyes had become harder and inured to suffering. His hair was pure white. And there was not a man or woman in the room who did not move forward eagerly to greet this phoenix, who had risen at last from the ashes of illness, anguish, and despair to take his place again in the real world.

Sarah stood quite still, her eyes on Vieri, her whole body reacting to the shock. Then she found the strength to walk toward him, her hand outstretched, a smile of sheer enchantment on her face.

"My dear Vieri, did you forget your key?"

"I'm afraid I did, but I was determined to come, so Elio gave me a lift and loaned me *his* key. He'll be joining me later."

Vieri looked at the rosebud in her hair, its innocent pink petals at odds with the shimmering black satin dress and gloves. Sarah was more beautiful than ever and more real in his eyes, the changes in her appearance subtle signs of the suffering she had endured. He was weighing every inch of her face and body, the hands with their long, thin fingers, when Umberto came and stood behind her, his black eyes challenging and full of hate.

"So, at last you come back. Where have you been all this time? Everyone thought you were dead or crazy."

Vieri gazed into the saturnine face and remembered Falco at the moment when he had amputated the finger. He showed nothing of his feelings, however, and greeted Umberto in a half-amused manner that infuriated the Sicilian.

"I've been traveling with my brother and getting fit again. It's taken a long time to get over the ordeal and to prepare myself for what must be done, but here I am."

"Now you steal all the publicity from the opening."

"On the contrary, this club will be on the front page of every newspaper in Paris and perhaps in Europe by morning. I made the effort as a deliberate tribute to Sarah, because she needs all the help she can get in the new venture. This is the first time I've been seen in public since my illness, so I think we can guarantee the English Club some sensational publicity."

"And how is your wife?"

"Mariannina is well and living with her parents in Rome. Our marriage was annulled three months ago. But here's *your* wife, Umberto. You must introduce me, as I don't think we met the last time I visited your home."

While Umberto and his wife were occupied with friends,

Sarah led Vieri to the English Garden and showed him the roses with a certain wistful pride.

"I'm so happy to see you again, Vieri. I can't find words to describe what I feel, but why didn't you write? I've heard nothing but rumors about your condition since that day in the Piazza Navona. I had no idea if you were alive or dead, sane or cuckoo, or if you and your family had decided not to contact me again."

Vieri put his champagne glass down, a mystified look on his face.

"I wrote and so did Elio. The letter to you was the very first thing I accomplished, the first stepping-stone to my recovery, and I was shocked when you didn't reply. And as the months passed, I became more and more distressed, so my brother called you in England, not just once but many times. He was told by your mother-in-law that you were out, and we finally assumed that you didn't want to speak with us. You were married, after all, and you had a child. I tried to understand, but I found it very hard and the shock slowed down my recovery."

Sarah turned pale and sat down, holding her head. Suddenly she realized what had happened. Her being moved forcibly from Thistleton House had left the way open for Mrs. James to intercept her phone calls and to confiscate or destroy her mail. Through the months of anguish, when she had longed to hear from Vieri, he had been longing to hear from her. Sarah saw Vieri motioning for a waiter to bring brandy and felt him helping her to drink.

"Stay where you are for a moment, Sarah. You've gone very pale. You must try not to take it so hard."

"I just can't believe that my mother-in-law stole my letters from you and intercepted the calls."

"What matters is the present and the future. That's something I learned since the happenings of the past year. What do *you* want for the future, Sarah?"

"I want everything and more, besides—too much, perhaps."

"I'll be in Paris for four weeks. We'll lunch together if you're free."

"Umberto has men who follow me everywhere."

"We'll send them champagne."

"You've changed; you don't mock anymore."

"Now the only person I mock is myself."

Sarah touched his hand, closing her eyes in near ecstasy at the softness of his skin.

"Oh, Vieri, what's going to happen to me?"

"You'll be a big success in business, like you always planned, and then, when your ambitions have been satisfied, you'll look for something else."

"And will I find it?"

"Haven't you found it already? You just lost it for a while."

When Sarah excused herself to circulate among the guests, Vieri went to meet his brother in the hall. The two men adjourned to the English Garden, and Elio shook his head wearily.

"Di Castelli is watching you as if he wants to shoot off your head."

"Men like him never do their own killing, so don't worry."

"What now, Vieri?"

"Now we shall see whether a Sicilian scorpion can outthink a Venetian doge in competition for an English rose."

"Scorpions sting and sometimes kill."

"True, but doges were always the most devious of men."

In the early dawn hours, Sarah bought a copy of every paper, blushing with pleasure to see her club's facade on all of them. If she had tried to buy publicity like that it would have cost a million dollars, but thanks to Vieri it was free. She gazed at the photographs of him and smiled at his statement. *Miss Hallam is a personal friend and I wanted very much to attend the opening of her club, so I came to Paris. It's time to live again. I just needed the motivation to do so.*

Sarah thought wryly that he was right. After the traumas of the past, it was time to live again. Her mind turned then to thoughts of Umberto, and she wondered what to do about him now that Vieri was back in her life. The future would not be easy. Umberto had done so much for her; she could not just throw him aside. On the other hand, Umberto would never accept her friendship with the Venetian. Older and wiser than in the early days of her love for Vieri, Sarah realized that she must not give up the substance for the shadow. If he really wanted her, Vieri was going to have to make his long-term intentions clear. For her part, she was certain of only one thing: She would never be his mistress. She wanted what she had always wanted, to be Vieri's wife. Until Vieri told her exactly what *he* wanted, Sarah decided to concentrate all her energies on working toward total independence. For the moment, that would be her aim in life, the culmination of her ambitions.

Sarah was dressing to go to view the Bal Tabarin when the doorbell rang and Mario Benedetti appeared. She rushed to embrace him.

"What a lovely surprise! Lexy'll be delighted. She's more than a bit in love with you."

Benedetti's eyes twinkled as he sat down at the table while Sarah poured him a cup of coffee.

"My congratulations on the success of the English Club."

"I hope we can sustain it. I'd hate my little people to lose their money."

Lexy appeared, kissed Benedetti soundly, and gave him a chocolate before being taken away by her nurse. Benedetti closed the door and turned to Sarah.

"I came to tell you to take care. Umberto's almost out of his mind with rage about Vieri Aldobrandini. With him, jealousy is a sickness, you know, but I never saw him like this before. Until last night he thought your friend was safely locked away in a psychiatric clinic and anyway that he was married to Mariannina. Now he's back in town, free, and in full pursuit of you. God only knows what Umberto'll do."

"If he tries to hurt Vieri I'll kill him."

Benedetti looked into the violet eyes and knew that she was capable of anything. He did his best to reassure Sarah, but he was worried and he could hide little from her.

"He won't do anything like that, but take care until he's assimilated the shock. Try not to make him completely crazy. He loves you with all his heart."

"He's done everything for me and I'm grateful."

"I know you are, but it's not gratitude he needs."

"I always told him I'd never love him, Mario. I've been honest with him from the start."

"What are your plans?"

"I want to buy the Bal Tabarin. I'm going to view it at five."

"I'll come with you. If we leave now we can have a drink at the English Club before going over there."

Umberto was in his office, sitting behind a twenty-foot-long rosewood desk and thinking of what Benedetti had told him about Sarah's visit to the Bal Tabarin. He would make sure she bought the place, and if she could not raise the necessary money from what she called her "little people" he would loan it to her. Sarah might not love him, but the combination of power, adulation, and security he could give would surely be irresistible. What had Aldobrandini to offer, after all? He would never marry Sarah. He might take

her for his mistress, but Umberto knew she wanted more
than that. Mentally and physically he prepared to declare
war against the man he longed to exorcise from Sarah's
mind. It would be hard and he would have to control the desire to have Aldobrandini and his precious Ferrari pushed
into the Seine, but he would triumph in the end or his name
was not Umberto di Castelli.

Chapter Eighteen

Arlette, Chantilly, Christmas 1973

It was Arlette's thirty-first birthday and she had been touring the ground floor of the chateau with her son, Edouard, who was three. Everywhere, staff were hurrying to get ready for an influx of visitors, including Charles's playboy cousin, René, who had just returned from a world cruise, his sister Charlotte, and her German lover, the racing-car driver Rolf Linderman. The deValois family was coming from Paris and the Hamiltons from London, all of them related by marriage to Charles.

When she had inspected the guest rooms, Arlette straightened a faded family portrait on the wall of the gallery. Impeccably dressed in dove-gray silk and pearls, she was deeply depressed, because for the first time Charles had forgotten her birthday. There had been no card on her breakfast tray, no tiny box from Cartier or Van Cleef and Arpels. Arlette thought sadly that the truth was she no longer existed for her husband. Since he had become obsessed by the maid, Ernestine, and had taken the girl as his mistress, Charles had let everything slide. He now left the management of the estate to others and no longer toured the grounds each morning as the head of the family had done for generations. Instead, at all hours of the day and night he called Ernestine to his side and could often be seen making love to her in the gazebo, the library, or in the woods behind the house. Like many aristocrats in Europe, Charles had been brought up to believe that household staff saw nothing, heard nothing, and talked of nothing, like the three wise monkeys. He appeared oblivious to the opinions of others, and the conventions of life meant nothing to him, so bewitched was he by the sensuality of the girl who had captured his body and his soul. The only time he set aside for duty was an hour each evening for his son. Even that was often shared with Ernestine, who, to her credit, adored the boy and spent most of her wages buying presents for him. Increasingly, Arlette had come to feel excluded, not only from her husband's life but from her son's. Edouard liked to play cowboys and Indians in the woods with Ernestine, instead of reading the picture books his mother bought him. When the maid went away for a holiday, Arlette grasped the opportunity, put on a pair of trousers, and joined her son in the forest, but after a few minutes Edouard put his arms around her, gave her a kiss, and led her to the lake so they could feed the swans. Arlette realized at once that she could not compete with Ernestine on even the most basic level.

Later, when the guests had been settled in their rooms, Arlette wandered the chateau, wondering where her husband was. She found him in her bedroom, pacing back and forth uneasily. It was obvious that Charles was apprehensive. She wondered what was on his mind and was shocked when he came straight to the point in his usual autocratic fashion.

"I think we should have another child, Arlette. I don't like the idea any more than you do, but if anything should happen to Edouard there would be no heir to the title."

"That's not a very good reason for having a child, Charles. People usually have children because they love each other."

"I don't love you anymore and you don't love me, either.

To tell the truth, Arlette, I have the impression that you loved my home and my title more than me from the start. You're a good wife in many ways, but you have no idea how to please a man in bed. You were born with something missing."

"Why haven't you taught me, Charles? I could learn—I *want* to learn."

"It would be a waste of time."

Arlette sighed, tears filling her eyes and starting to fall down her cheeks. "It's just that you always ask me to do such bizarre things. And sex is something no one teaches you, so if you haven't an aptitude for it it's difficult."

Charles hesitated for a moment. Then he rang the bell to summon his mistress.

Ernestine was small and dark, with long gypsy ringlets and the voluptuous curves of her Provençal heritage. She was dressed in black, with a white apron and clumsy shoes that she kicked off at every opportunity. As Charles approached her, throwing off his clothes to Arlette's astonishment, the maid licked her lips and looked with hungry eyes at his penis.

"What can I do for you, sir?"

"Get your clothes off. My wife just told me she wants a practical demonstration of the art of lovemaking."

Arlette watched, speechless with horror, as her husband placed himself astride the girl and rammed his penis inside her. Ernestine's reaction was quite different from her own, and Arlette looked on in chagrin as the maid screeched with delight and demanded more, more, more. After a while, Ernestine began to devour Charles hungrily, her mouth slurping against the rigid penis as if she wanted to provoke him to new heights of enjoyment.

Arlette moved to the bed, her fingers seeking the consolation she adored, forgetting everything and everyone as she brought herself to a climax. She saw, out of the corner of her

eye, her husband and his mistress falling back on the bed in
the final moments of passion, his howls of delight mixing
with her own self-induced cry of satisfaction and Ernestine's
squeals of triumph. Then, without a word, the maid rose,
dressed, and with a last, lingering kiss returned to her room.

Charles lit a cigar and looked in disgust at his wife.

"Your right hand is all you ever needed, my darling. A
man is superfluous in your life."

"Don't say that, Charles. I've tried so hard to find a way
to please you."

"Please me tonight at the theater. Surprise me, leap on
me—do something different, for God's sake! I can't stand
much more of this!"

"I'll try, Charles."

"Try hard. I need a woman, not a frigid fashion plate."

Arlette watched as her husband left the room, slamming
the door behind him. With eyes full of despair, she stared at
the wall and the priceless covering of Chinese silk patterned
with *strelizia*. How beautiful everything was at the chateau,
how perfect and precious. She began to sob like a child.
First, all her dreams had come true and she had married a
rich and powerful man. Then the nightmares had begun.
First, Charles had been unable to penetrate her hymen. Now
she lived with the knowledge that he preferred Ernestine's
body to her own. Everyone pitied her in her humiliation, and
everyone in the region gossiped furiously about the family.
Arlette sobbed in horror, shame, fear, and frustration, rec-
ognizing that despite all her efforts she was a failure as a
wife and that her husband regretted marrying her.

That evening at dinner Arlette showed nothing of the despair in her heart as she sat at the head of the table, her husband at the other end. While the guests talked of René's visit
to America and Charlotte's winter sports holiday, Arlette
thought that her marriage had become a mockery. Superfi-
cially, she was mistress of a chateau, mother of a fine son,

and wife of one of the richest men in France. In reality, her husband and son were both happier with Ernestine.

She knew in her heart that the fault was hers, but try as she might, Arlette could not find the key to please those she loved. She thought of the evening ahead, when she, Charles, and their guests would drive to Paris to see the ballet "La Bayadère." Arlette hoped fervently that it would not inspire her husband to rude comments and exhibitionist behavior. As he grew older, Charles seemed to be more eager to display his sexual abilities before anyone who would watch, and it had not escaped Arlette's notice that many of their former friends no longer visited the chateau, because he had begun to make improper suggestions to women whose friendship he had once respected.

The theater was packed, because Nureyev was to appear. Arlette took her place in the family box as the curtain rose on an Indian scene. When Nureyev made his entrance, there was riotous applause. Adoring the atmosphere and the Russian's magnificent presence, Arlette relaxed. Then the prima ballerina entered, her face veiled, her sinuous body alluring in an outfit of pink chiffon. As she undulated across the stage, Arlette felt her husband's hand on her back. Ignoring it, she tried to concentrate on the dancer, but the hand unzipped her dress to the waist, unfastened her bra, and then moved under her arm and took her right nipple between trembling fingers. As panic filled her, Arlette turned angrily to her husband, her cheeks scarlet, because Charlotte, René, and Rolf were watching with avid interest.

"There'll be time for all that when we get home, Charles," she hissed.

Arlette halted, shocked to see that her husband had locked the door and was removing his trousers.

"Please, Charles, have you taken leave of your senses?"

"I told you I need spice and spontaneity. Don't worry,

Arlette, the audience can't see us and our guests don't give a damn.''

Arlette began to tremble, chagrin, horror, and fear mingling with disgust. Thoughts rushed through her mind, exhausting her, and she could do nothing but sit, staring at her husband in utter stupefaction. When she made no attempt to do as she was told, Charles forced her to the ground and pushed the full skirt over her head. Then he tore off her panties and pushed his penis inside her so hard she cried out, despite her efforts to control the situation. As he penetrated her, Arlette saw Charlotte watching with interest and Rolf leaning forward, the better to see the climax of their coupling. When it was over, Arlette rose, horrified to feel the emission pouring down her legs, staining her stockings and the floor and the pristine white silk petticoat she had bought that morning. She gazed at her husband in undisguised horror.

"You are disgusting."

"And you, madame, are frigid."

"How dare you say that! You throw me down on the ground like a street whore and shower me with sperm in the middle of a crowded theater. What you want is *applause.*"

"I want a wife who'll fuck me like the biggest whore in town and who's capable of being a duchess when required. You're without doubt the biggest disappointment of my life."

At that moment something snapped within Arlette and she began to sob. She was still sobbing when Charles drove the party home through the merry Christmas streets of Paris. The woman of iron self-control had finally lost her way.

In the small hours, as dawn broke and the faint light of a winter's morning tinted the sky, Arlette telephoned Sarah, desperate to hear a friendly voice in the maelstrom of torment. Though she had written to her friend many times, they had not met since her marriage, and Arlette's hands began to tremble when she heard the familiar voice on the line.

"Sarah Hallam speaking."

"Sarah, this is Arlette. I could only find the club number. Are you too busy to talk?"

"Of course not, I'm thrilled to hear you, but tell me what's wrong. Are you crying?"

"I'm half mad, I am truly half mad. I'm losing Charles to a maid who's less than half his age. He accuses me of being unsexual and says I was born with something missing—but I've *tried*, Sarah, I've done everything he asked. It's just that I don't do it well enough."

There was a long pause before Sarah replied.

"Is Charles asking for a divorce?"

"No, he's not mentioned divorce."

"Then ignore him until he does. Charles always had a cruel streak and he'll enjoy baiting you. Until such time as he tries to get rid of you from the chateau let his comments sail over your head. You're his wife and he can say what he likes, but you'll still be his wife and still be part of his life whether he likes it or not."

"I'll try, Sarah."

"Do better than try. Ignore the bastard. Let him fuck the maid or the butler or his pet goose. To an egoist like Charles being ignored is always punishment enough. But tell me about Edouard and you—how are you? Why do you never come to see me in Paris?"

"Charles hates me to even *talk* of my friendship with you and the other girls, but when I'm feeling better I'll come to Paris and tell you all about everything. For the moment I'm not the best company; I'm just so down."

"Try not to worry too much, Arlette. Don't let your husband sap all of your confidence. No man's worth *that* much."

Arlette walked to the terrace outside her bedroom and

thought of the firm voice on the phone. She would do as Sarah suggested and see how it worked. Already she was feeling better and certain that Sarah was right. Momentarily cheered, Arlette hurried inside, put a cassette into the machine at her bedside, and began her morning exercises. She was thinking with her usual singlemindedness that she must keep her looks and figure at all costs.

Chapter Nineteen

Sarah, Paris, July 1974

Sarah was in the hairdresser's salon, having a conditioning treatment. Before her were the magazines and newspapers that had covered the opening of the Bal Tabarin. The property, which could not be demolished because of its historic interest, had taken endless time and a fortune to restore in addition to its cost of two hundred thousand sterling. Sarah had raised over half from private investors and had borrowed the rest from Umberto. She had never taken a loan in her life and had been raised not to owe money to anyone, so the enormity of what she had done prevented her from sleeping for weeks after the purchase. Now, slowly, she was becoming accustomed to the stresses of business, and the pressure of owing a fortune was receding to the back of her mind.

She had used the designer-builder team who had done the English Club to restore the interior of the property to its former glory. She had invited the Minister of Culture to the opening, along with every lobbyist for the preservation of the ancient buildings of Paris. All had been impressed by her determination to have things as authentic as possible, and the Minister had even suggested that the next time she bought a historic monument a government loan might be arranged to help with the transformation.

It had not taken long for Sarah to realize that she had another success on her hands, though she knew it would take years to recoup the investors' money and to see a real profit. For her, the Bal Tabarin was a symbol of risk and daring, and she had used all her ingenuity to ensure that the initial rocketlike send-off given it by the critics, who had heaped praise on the satirical revue she had chosen in place of the hackneyed cabaret items of Parisian nightlife, would be sustained. The previous week, she had brought off a deal whereby for the first time television cameras would bring a variety show direct from the club, using her artists and those from other cabarets in the city. She had soon realized that she needed a new source of artists and material and had also set in motion the search for an interest in a theatrical agency. Once she had that, she would be able to achieve her other current ambition, to present each Christmas a major charity performance at the Théâtre de l'Empire in aid of the Red Cross.

Sarah continued to make her plans for the future without consulting Umberto, which galled him more than she realized. He continued to be the rock on which she leaned when she was tired, the fountain from which she drank when her throat was parched, but since Vieri's reappearance their physical relationship had changed. They still made love and it was still exciting, but Sarah found herself more and more occupied with the club and less and less eager to be with Umberto. In her heart, she knew that she only let him love her because Vieri had still made no move to declare his intentions toward her. She told herself that she had played the waiting game too long, but was helpless to stop hoping and dreaming of the man she had loved for so long.

That night, at dinner, Sarah appeared in diaphanous white silk and kissed Umberto's cheeks as he delivered a bunch of tiger lilies and a compliment on her looks.

"You are a temptress in that outfit! Here, I bring you

champagne and a present to celebrate that you bought into
the International Agency. I hear you plan to put Liz Lind in
charge of the business, when she has learned all Solomon
can teach her.''

"Is there anything you don't know?''

"Sure. I don't know what Vieri write to you in the letter
he sent this morning.''

"It was a postcard of Venice with an invitation to dinner,
but I'm too busy to go.''

"You eat dinner with me, why not with him?''

"You're in Paris and he's in Venice.''

Umberto poured the champagne and raised his glass.

"To us, Sarah.''

They ate asparagus from Argenteuil and then an omelet of
sorrel and chive. Umberto watched as Sarah served a mate-
lote of eels, freshly caught on the country estate of a friend.
He thought wryly that her strange habit of visiting fellow
club owners and making friendships, even with rivals, was
beginning to pay off. There seemed to be few things she
could not arrange, and since the signing of the television
contract every club owner in Paris was trying to curry favor
in order to have his or her artists presented from the Bal
Tabarin. For her part, Sarah nurtured her friendships with
great care. When Madame Nicoletti fell ill, it was Sarah
who called at all hours of the day and night to reassure her.
When Nino Ortolani began to despair of his hotel's success,
it was Sarah who put one of her now-notorious ads in the paper and drew such a crowd to his restaurant that the chef
went on strike. Umberto sighed. He had always known that
Sarah was different, but he had not realized how unorthodox
were her ways. Despite her growing success, she remained a
mixture of innocence and sensuousness, puzzling all who
knew her by alternating between small-town neighborliness
and big-time ideas and the ruthlessness with which to carry
them out. Even Umberto had been shocked when Sarah

spoke of buying the Moulin Rouge. It would never happen, of course, but the idea was there and her audacity had taken the breath away.

Looking again at Sarah in her new dress, Umberto could not help adoring her. As they drank their coffee, he led her to the window and together they looked out at the city. The Eiffel Tower was floodlighted, its sturdy iron girders ghostly against a navy night sky. The lights of traffic twinkled red and white along the boulevards, and in apartment buildings everywhere lamps were lit and people moved in distant, silent pantomime. Umberto pulled Sarah toward him and kissed her cheeks, running his hands down her back.

"I been thinking. You need a country place to get the fresh air with Lexy. You want I look for something?"

"Not yet. I don't have time to leave the city for any length of time."

"Come to bed. I want to love you till my strength disappear."

Sarah showed nothing of the rebellion increasing daily within her. But she could not help thinking that since Vieri returned to Venice he had sent three postcards inviting her to have dinner with him at the Palazzo Aldobrandini, overlooking the Grand Canal, and that had been his only contact. She closed her eyes as Umberto unzipped her dress and kissed her shoulders with the same hunger he always manifested when they were together. Then, as he pushed her down on the wolf-fur cover, she relaxed in the familiarity of his body. Winding her legs around his shoulders, she felt him enter her with all the passionate, brute force of a fighting bull. His desire never failed to thrill, and soon she felt herself drifting to the moment before orgasm and clutching the bedposts as her body reached fever pitch. For a few precious seconds, she forgot everything but the luxury of being a woman adored.

Umberto ran his hand along the line of her chin and down to her breasts, kissing her left shoulder and the nipple exposed over the sheet as they lay together after love.

"If you agree not to see Vieri again, I buy you a chateau. There are plenty on sale at the moment and no one with enough money to buy."

"Are you trying to bribe me?"

"Of course. I give you everything if you agree."

"You don't want me to see anyone, Umberto. You even made a row when I spoke to Lord Avon at the opening of the English Club and he's sixty-five!"

"I don't like English lords, and most of all I don't like Vieri Aldobrandini."

"You're pathologically jealous."

"I *love* you! I can't bear to think of losing you. Say you don't see him again."

"Of course I shall see him. Vieri's a good friend."

Umberto sat up in bed, his face red with anger.

"I am *sick* of that man."

"Then don't think of him. Just try to enjoy the times when we're together, like I do."

"I can think of nothing but Aldobrandini. He is like a vulture who look all the time over my shoulder and write to you behind my back."

"I've had two or three letters from Vieri since he went back to Venice."

"Three, and I want that he stops writing. You belong to me. Why can he not understand?"

Sarah rose and put on a pale-gray silk kimono. Determined not to have a row on the same subject as so many times before, she spoke patiently, though it was obvious that she was angry.

"We've been together a long time, Umberto, and apart from my ex-husband I've never been with any other man. But if you keep on with this monotonous drivel about Vieri,

I promise you I'll fuck everyone who asks me. Now please go home. You're in danger of becoming a bore and I'm not in the mood for it.''

"You would rather be with him, I suppose?''

"If Vieri isn't jealous, *yes.* ''

When Umberto had gone, Sarah lay in bed thinking of what he had said. It was interesting that there were a number of chateaus on the market. She had long thought of opening a spa somewhere near Paris, to take advantage of the new craze for healthy, beautiful bodies. There, in luxurious surroundings, the super-rich could be exercised, dieted, pampered, and spoiled at exorbitant cost. The place would be easily accessible from Paris and Sarah knew in her heart that this was the moment to capitalize, but the cost would be high and she was already heavily in debt.

A few days later, Sarah was at the English Club when the Duke of Arbroath appeared, looking mournful. She ordered the bartender to send over a bottle of his favorite Glenlivet whiskey and then went to his table and asked if there was anything she could do to help.

"You look as if you lost your shirt at the races, Drum.''

"Worse than that, Sarah. Cousin Ellie was killed in a car accident in the early hours of this morning. I've been at the undertaker's half the day and at the house in Barbizon for the rest. I couldn't stand it any longer, so I came here to you.''

"I'm so sorry. If there's anything at all I can do, you only have to ask.''

"Ellie was my favorite cousin, but apart from the personal loss, I now have residential complications and so does my sister. Priscilla and I were staying with Ellie to avoid tax liability in England. As we didn't own anything here, we weren't liable, but we're his sole heirs, so now we'll have to pay French tax and that's even higher than in the U.K. for unmarried people.''

"Don't think of all that, Drum. Somehow you'll get it sorted out. There's always a way. When's the funeral?"

"You must come. Ellie and I and Sis were here on the night you opened and he did so love the English Club. It's the day after tomorrow; do say you'll be there."

"I'll drive you out to Barbizon if you want. Then, when the funeral's over, you and Priscilla must come to dinner with me."

"You're very kind, but we'll have to stay at Barbizon, so you come and dine with us. The house isn't bad and the garden's quite pretty."

Sarah walked from the club to the Bal Tabarin, pausing en route to see Nino Ortolani, who was jubilant.

"Oh, Sarah, I've just signed a three-year contract with American Express, who'll take half my rooms for forty weeks each year. Come and have a drink. It was your idea to try them and it worked. I could jump over the moon."

"You heard about Ellie d'Erlanger's death, I suppose. I'm going to the funeral the day after tomorrow."

"Umberto won't like that!"

"Why not?"

"Because Aldobrandini's sure to be there—his brother, too, and most of the clan. They were Ellie's best friends since the boys were together at Harvard."

Sarah sat in her office, looking down at the floor show of the Bal Tabarin. The satirical revue had ended, replaced by a version of the Chinese National Theater, whose artists confounded the clients with everything from masked pantomime in scarlet and gold costumes of great antiquity, to feats of balance and skill that caused a senstion when an excerpt from the show was televised. Now, as Sarah watched the finale, sixty dancers were weaving patterns on the stage, their tiny feet barely seeming to move, yet keeping them in perpetual motion. The climax of the presentation showed the dancers forming a dragon and moving with ever-increasing speed, so the animal appeared to writhe and switch its tail as the music quickened and the line receded, until only the youngest member of the troupe was left to take a final bow. Sarah watched the faces of the audience and was content that she had chosen well. For the next show, she would surprise everyone yet again and travel to Venice to take on a short-term contract the actors of a sixteenth-century play. It would be a risk, but it would be beautiful to look at and the critics would find the idea astonishing. If it was successful, Sarah planned to transfer the play to a theater after its four-week run at the Bal Tabarin.

The Erlanger funeral was attended only by family and close friends, some of whom had come from New York for the occasion. When it was over, a buffet was served, then most of the party left for their hotels in Paris or for private jets that would take them back home. As dusk fell, Drum and his sister sat with Sarah, Vieri, and Elio talking of the dead man and recalling happier days. Then Drum turned to Vieri and began to speak of the future.

"Tell Priss and me about your idea for the property, Vieri. We're desperate to know what to do with the place."

"I'm interested in buying the chateau and leaving you the upstairs section of the west wing. Elio would take the lower part of the same wing. He'll marry Vivonne soon and they need a place near Paris."

"And the rest of the house?"

"I'm open to ideas."

Sarah felt excitement rising within her and spoke of her own idea.

"What about a health spa for the rich? The chateau isn't big enough for a conference center, but it would be ideal for the other use."

Vieri turned to her with an affectionate smile.

"You could lease the place from me and run it with your

special ideas. We're all agreed you need a new partner, Sarah."

His eyes were challenging and she blushed at the suggestion, but Vieri was serious and spoke with quiet determination.

"You're someone now, thanks to good luck and your marvelous innovations. No one in Paris has shown such imagination and you'll be reaping the rewards for years. But soon you'll have to leave di Castelli behind. He's served his purpose and can only taint your reputation. Think about it, Sarah. I'm serious."

"You really think I can be that ruthless?"

"I think *he* would, so why not you?"

"You misjudge Umberto."

"Someday his moment of testing will come, as mine did in Sicily, and then you'll see what he does."

"Do you know something about him that you're not telling me?"

"Of course, but I wouldn't dream of discussing it. You're tied to him at the moment. You think you need him, and if I destroy di Castelli in your eyes it's me you'll hate and not him, but I warned you a long time ago never to become dependent on that man. He's obsessed by you and he's dangerous; that you can believe. Now think about my proposal. You want to take a five-year lease on the Chateau de Montalou if I buy it?"

"I do, Vieri."

"It's a big risk."

"Not if you're the owner."

"Well, you have a new partner. Let's shake hands on it and drink to the future."

"Have we got one?"

"That depends on you, Sarah. As long as you remain with di Castelli, I prefer to remain in the wings of your life."

Sarah drove back to Paris at one A.M. with Vieri at her side. In the darkness, he touched her hand and leaned over now and then to kiss her shoulder. There was no need to talk, no need to do anything but enjoy the moment of togetherness. Sarah wondered if he had any idea of her feelings for him, any comprehension of the love and the longing she had harbored for so long without result. She was speeding along the main highway toward the city center when Vieri spoke sharply.

"Take the next turn right and cut your lights."

She did as he said, watching as Umberto's surveillance man sped by, accelerating on the bend before disappearing from view. With a sigh of relief, Sarah drove on, happy that she and Vieri were together.

"You'll have to direct me, Vieri. I don't know this area."

"Take the first right and stop outside the farmhouse covered in ivy. I want to show you my new acquisition."

Sarah drove through the gates of the property and switched off the engine, hurrying to join Vieri as he led the way.

"This is the farmhouse where Dumas met the original lady of the camellias and fell hopelessly in love, poor fellow. I suppose you know all about that, don't you, Sarah? I'd say bewitching women were rather in your line."

She smiled at the expression on Vieri's face.

"Don't worry, you'll never fall hopelessly in love. Those are words unknown to the Aldobrandini family."

"Nonsense! You know nothing of me or my family. To tell you the truth, I fell in love a long time ago, but I didn't realize it or maybe I resisted it. It took the kidnapping and the months of being half mad in that infernal clinic to make me accept the truth."

There was a long silence while Sarah assimilated the statement. Vieri was always oblique, but tonight she was finding him almost cryptic.

"Are you talking about me? You haven't even telephoned me since you returned to Venice!"

"I'm sorry I've been out of touch. My mother died and I've been up to my neck in legal matters and arrangements for the funeral. In any case, I've been preparing to woo you in the old-fashioned style. If I'm to steal you from that awful man it's obvious I have to pander to your business ambitions as well as to the woman."

"You sound very calculating."

"Not at all. I fell in love with you when I saw you in that strange knitted dress with a posy of flowers in your hand. Now I must show you your new house and then we'll have a quick drink and get back to Paris."

"My new house?"

"I forgot to tell you, I bought it for you, Sarah. I felt sure you'd eventually realize that independence is having *everything* of your own."

The Mas de Chateaubriand was built of granite and covered in shiny green ivy with shutters painted to match. A river, overhung with willow, ran at the far end of the garden by arbors scented with lilac and laburnum. There were narrow pathways bordered by lavender and climbing yellow roses and a trellis heavy laden with honeysuckle.

Vieri paused under the trellis and turned to Sarah.

"Kiss me, my darling. Make me live again. I have not really lived since the kidnapping and I fear I may never be able to again."

She moved toward him, her face soft, her hands reaching out. As she wound her arms around his shoulders, Vieri shivered, and when their lips met he tried to move back, but Sarah drew him close and, standing on tiptoe, savored the taste of his lips against hers. Her tongue began to explore his mouth and he cried out in ecstasy, making her grow weak with desire. She wanted to rush inside to the bedroom, but she understood Vieri's anxiety and the anguish in his voice when he said he had not lived since the kidnapping. Did he really mean he had not loved? Sarah knew that suffering had robbed him of the confidence he had once had in abundance and that he was afraid of failure if they made love. She kissed him again, more tenderly this time, and ran her fingers through the white hair that shone silver in the moonlight.

Vieri pushed his body hard against hers, his whole being shuddering as they stood locked in loving combat. Finally, he began to stroke Sarah's hair and to kiss her ears.

"You make me forget that anything bad ever happened. When I'm with you, I believe I have a future, and not as a diminished version of the man I once was."

"It's going to be an augmented version of the Vieri before the kidnapping. Suffering like that either sends a man mad or makes more of him. You'll find out; you're just scared of trying the last hurdle in the race."

They walked back to the house and Sarah went to the kitchen and made coffee. On the shelf there was a bottle of liqueur distilled from herbs gathered in the countryside near Vieri's home. She poured two glasses of it and carried them out with the coffee.

"I have to get back to Paris pretty soon, Vieri. I eat my breakfast with Lexy at six each morning and I never miss."

"May I meet her?"

"Of course you can, but I'd best warn you she has very definite ideas on whom she likes and whom she doesn't."

"What kind of person appeals?"

"She adores Benedetti and Liz, but she's not too fond of Umberto."

"Obviously a child with taste, and a genius to boot."

"I love the farmhouse. I just don't know how to thank you for it. I've dreamed of owning something like this all my life."

"I bought it for you as a small thank-you for all you did

for me when I was ill. Your letters and that magic moment in the Piazza Navona were the beginning of my recovery. The Mas de Chateaubriand is yours without condition, and I hope you and your daughter will spend lots of happy times here."

Lexy was in the bathtub when they arrived, so Sarah boiled eggs and seated Vieri at the table ready for breakfast. She was cutting toast "soldiers" and feeling nervous about her daughter's reaction, when Lexy appeared and leaped into her arms.

"Hello, Mummy. I dreamed I got lost in the métro and you came to rescue me."

"I would, too."

"Shall we go to our new club this afternoon?"

"Why not, and we can stay to watch the rehearsal."

Sarah turned and introduced her daughter to Vieri.

"Lexy, this is Vieri Aldobrandini. Vieri, my daughter, Alexis James."

Vieri handed the child the bunch of scented flowers picked specially for her on the grounds of the farmhouse. He said none of the cooing things that strangers usually say on meeting children and simply stood his ground.

Lexy gazed into the cloud-gray eyes. Then, without a word, she sat at the breakfast table, pushed a plate toward Vieri, and solemnly handed him half of her toast soldiers. She did not speak, but looked at him expectantly from behind her long, dark lashes. She was used to people telling her she was pretty and offering to take her to the park, but Vieri said nothing at all. Lexy looked at the flowers he had brought her and put them into her glass of water, pleased when Vieri dipped one of the strips of toast into his egg.

When Mitzi came to take the child for a walk, Lexy insisted that they take the flowers with them. The nurse protested, but when they left the apartment, Lexy was clutching the bouquet and looking back over her shoulder to see if

Vieri was watching from the window. Sarah was satisfied that their first meeting had been a big success.

When the sale of Montalou was reported in the papers, a rumor story appeared alongside the article, saying that a new partnership had been formed, between the head of the Aldobrandini family and the young English entrepreneur many were calling Queen of the Night. The story brought two immediate results for what was already being called the most expensive spa in Europe. The first was a flood of inquiries from wealthy potential clients. The second was a phone call from Umberto, saying he would be arriving at the airport in ten minutes. Sarah thought of the article in the paper and wondered if there was going to be a row. She was pleasantly surprised when Umberto said nothing of Vieri and instead sat at the kitchen table and told her what he had been doing in the two days since their last meeting.

"I went to see Monet, the owner of the Moulin Rouge, and he tell me to go to hell when I ask if he want to sell. Then I get the results of my inquiries into his life and find he has try for forty years to buy the house where he was born and where he live with his parents till the age of fourteen. When the family lose its money the parents sell the house and he try to buy it back ever since. He long for it, because there are his roots, as mine are in Sicily. Anyway, this morning I fix everything and the owners agree to sell the house to me."

Sarah looked askance, wondering how he had changed the owners' minds after forty years.

"How did you persuade them to sell?"

"I can persuade anyone to do anything, except you. With you I can do nothing. You go your way without any thought of me."

Sarah ignored his exasperation. The news was exciting and she longed to know more.

"What are you going to do, Umberto?"

"I go to Monet and I tell him you want to buy the Moulin Rouge. If he sell, I let him have the house he has tried to buy for so long. Then he can retire in peace."

"It all sounds very easy."

"It takes months to find out his weak place and a lot of hard work to persuade the people to sell. Nothing is easy, Sarah. Only an expert can make it look so."

"How much will he want for the Moulin Rouge?"

"A lot, but this time *I* will be your partner. You don't go to your little people, you understand."

Sarah remained silent, wondering when he was going to mention Vieri, but he said nothing and with a brief kiss left her to her thoughts.

Umberto flopped down on the back seat of his car and motioned for the driver to take him to his office. Then, closing the window between the chauffeur and himself, he turned to Benedetti.

"I do it. I tell her about the Moulin Rouge and Monet and the fact that those fools decide to sell their house."

"You didn't mention Aldobrandini?"

"Not once, and the effort nearly kill me. I am not built for these deceptions you tell me I must do."

"How did she react?"

"How do I know? I am only Sarah's slave. She look at me and wait for me to talk about *him.* She listen and ask how much Monet will want for the Moulin Rouge. What she really think is impossible to know. She is a locked box I can never find the key to open."

"Try not to get so upset."

"I thought it was over with Aldobrandini. I thought he was finish forever, but he come back like a flea you cannot crush even between the shoe and the pavement. He never go away, not till I kill him and throw him in the sewers where he belong."

* * *

Sarah walked to the Moulin Rouge and stood watching the tourists passing by, all of them stopping to look at photographs of the show in cases outside. Many of them took photographs of the exterior, and all of them were unable to resist pausing to gaze at the legendary landmark. Crossing the busy road, Sarah moved to the entrance, which was locked. Inside, she could hear the sound of a rehearsal pianist thumping out the opening number and a choreographer calling in exasperation, "Oh, do *try*, dears! Getting your legs up is like trying to raise Lazarus." Hearing his words, Sarah thought how she had once been a dancer like the girls of the Moulin Rouge. Then she had met Umberto and he had transformed her life. Impulsively, she telephoned him and told him how she had remembered their early days together.

Delighted by the compliment, Umberto invited her to lunch.

"I wait for you at the Pavilion in the Bois, Sarah?"

"I'll be there."

On her way back to her apartment to change her clothes, Sarah wondered if Umberto was her addiction, a necessary dose of longed-for security without which she would be nothing. She shook her head, unable to work out the underlying reasons for her continuing need. All she knew was that his presence was comforting. When he was there, she believed that nothing could go wrong, and nothing ever had. Umberto was her safety and her protection against a hostile world and a thousand hidden fears.

Sarah was on the point of leaving the apartment when the doorbell rang. Hurrying to answer, she found a tall, robust Englishman of fifty in the corridor.

"Miss Hallam, my name's Paul Davington and I have a letter for you."

Opening the envelope she found a brief note in Vieri's hand.

Dearest Sarah,

Give this gentleman a job as your chauffeur. I leave for Verona and will then go on to Rome for a few days. I will call you as soon as I get back to Paris.

Yours, Vieri

Sarah looked at the man before her and let him into the living room.

"I can't really afford a chauffeur, so you'd best tell me what kind of salary you'll need."

"That's all been arranged with the Prince, ma'am. You simply give me my food and somewhere to stay. I first met the Prince and his brother many years ago, and he was kind enough to remember when I applied to him for a post."

"Where did you meet?"

"I was on the station in Turin when a madman tried to shoot Elio, his brother. I hit the fellow rather hard and broke his clavicle. Then the police took him away. The Aldobrandinis were grateful; they gave me a check and invited me to have a holiday in a hotel in the city. I was very proud to be remembered after all these years."

"Welcome to Paris, Davington. I hope you'll be very happy here and that we can be friends."

"I shall do all in my power to be a *real* friend, Miss Hallam."

Sarah arrived at the restaurant and found Umberto sitting alone with a bottle of white wine. He was gazing out at the lake, his face very pale, his eyes haunted. He did not see Sarah until she stopped in front of his table and spoke.

"Is something wrong? You look as if you're in a very bad mood."

"Who is the man who come to see you at the apartment?"

"That's my new chauffeur, Davington."

"I give you one of my men as chauffeur."

"I've taken Davington on because I want someone English."

Umberto scrutinized her face and saw only a merry smile.

"You smile when I am unhappy. You never want to use my people."

"You must learn to accept me how I am. I accept you how you are."

He drew a sheaf of papers from his pocket and handed them to her.

"Sign these, Sarah."

She began to read them, but could not understand the formalized legal French.

"I'd best have my lawyer go over these."

Umberto spoke sharply.

"My people have already checked everything. Sign them, Sarah. They give you and me joint ownership of the Moulin Rouge and two other clubs. The two small places you own yourself, without me. The money you owe is equal to two hundred and fifty thousand pounds English, to repay over twenty years at four and one-half percent interest. That is what a Swiss bank charges and half of what the French ones would ask. I have been very generous. Sign, Sarah. After all these years together you either trust me or you do not."

Sarah signed, apprehensive at his insistence, but eager to become joint owner of the most famous landmark in Paris by night. She knew in her heart it was a risk to own anything with Umberto, but she wanted the Moulin Rouge enough to take any risk. She told herself that if anything went wrong, there was not a bank in Paris that would not loan money on that establishment. She was moving like a bullet to her destination and she felt content. As she signed, Umberto smiled for the first time.

Chapter Twenty

Holly, Ireland, November 1974

In the still of night, as autumn leaves fell from the oak trees around the house, masked men entered the mansion of Sir James O'Malley, then bound and gagged him, his wife, the butler, and the housekeeper. In the three hours that followed, the O'Malley collection of Postimpressionist masterpieces, famous throughout Europe for its superb Gaugins, was loaded into a truck and driven away into the night. It was never seen again, and police inquiries would eventually conclude that the paintings had changed hands for a fortune only to be hidden away in the secret gallery of some Texas oil millionaire or Arab sheik with a palace on the Gulf and a penchant for the forbidden.

The aftermath of the robbery was more serious than the crime itself. Two hours after the thieves left his home, Sir James suffered a heart attack and died without recovering consciousness on his way to the hospital. The anguish of her husband's death and the delayed shock of the robbery made Lady O'Malley ill, and she succumbed to an attack of influenza that turned to pneumonia six weeks after Sir James's funeral.

Holly walked around the silent house, remembering the days of childhood, when she and her friends had run wild in the woods, galloped their ponies in the paddock, and played hide and seek on frequent rainy days in the attics. She paused to watch as members of the public inspected the furniture that would be auctioned later in the day: the Georgian dining table that seated fifty, the antique crofter's chairs that had been in the family for generations, the paintings rejected by the thieves that would probably bring a fortune. Holly had decided to keep the family home in Dublin, but to sell Ennis House because she could not afford two homes. The deaths of her parents and the mysteries connected with the robbery had gravely distressed her, contaminating the precious memories of the past; she had no desire to visit the property again.

Carlos stood at the back of the crowded room, listening to the bids. His eyes were glowing with pleasure and he was thinking hard. The house and stud had brought two hundred thousand pounds, the contents would certainly realize fifty thousand, perhaps much more if the Stubbs paintings went high. He had never had any money of his own, everything he could raise being handed over to the organization for which he worked, but now things would be different. He grasped Holly's hand as she passed by and whispered excitedly.

"That ugly old clock brought a thousand. Your father told me it was worth a lot but I didn't believe him. We shall have a quarter of a million pounds by the time the sale is over and maybe much more."

Holly's eyes flickered enigmatically, but Carlos did not notice. He was listening to the bids for the first of the Stubbs paintings, a large canvas depicting a family outing on horseback. Holly tilted her head and watched the two dealers who were in competition for the painting. Then, as tears filled her eyes, her mind wandered back to the day in early childhood when she and her sister, their parents, and Toby the groom had gone riding to the Curragh to watch the two o'clock race. They had picnicked on the heath afterward and then ridden home, at first in bright sunshine and then in a summer shower. Mother had ordered everyone to take a hot bath and afterward to come down in their dressing gowns for tea. They had feasted on scones and spicy bread, salmon sandwiches, and fresh strawberries from the garden, their scarlet color masked by sugar, cream, and a generous helping of the cook's homemade raspberry liqueur. Holly thought defiantly that she must conserve every farthing of the money from the sale of Ennis House to give her a future income. She must also renovate the property in Dublin and someday, if she married and had children, she would buy a tiny cottage in the country, where they could have tea on the lawn as she had done in the unforgettable days of innocence. As she thought of the purity of childhood, Holly felt a great wave of panic at life as she now lived it. She had felt the same emotion often of late and knew she was maturing and that soon she would have outgrown Carlos. Where the future lay, she had no idea, only the certain knowledge that she could not continue for much longer as she had in the past. Her thoughts crystallized when Carlos came out of the west-wing living room and threw his arms around her.

"Everything is bringing twice as much as the estimates! You will have three hundred thousand pounds at least. I shall buy a Lamborghini in silver or perhaps scarlet; you can choose the color. And we must look for a house near Rome, one of those small farms hidden in the countryside, perhaps. I always wanted to live there."

"Half of this money belongs to my sister, Carlos, and the rest I have to invest for my future. It's family money and I'm responsible for it as my father's chief executor."

"Your sister needs no money! Her husband is very rich."

"Legally half is hers. Anyway, you never know when you're going to be rich or poor, in good health or bad, so Eira will have half the money, however wealthy her husband might be at the moment."

"I do not understand you. You are not logical, but we can discuss all this later."

"There's nothing to discuss. This is family money and you have no right and no reason to be involved."

For days Carlos exerted every ounce of his considerable charm on Holly, puzzled because the deaths of her parents had changed her. In the past, she had obeyed his every wish, but now she was defiant. He was neither sensitive enough to her grief nor sufficiently family oriented to understand that Holly's wild personal life and her touching allegiance to her sister were separate parts of a complex personality. To her, the family was sacrosanct and no one could cross the line into that private part of her existence. Carlos tried, however. They went to the Dublin Horse Show together and then dined at Holly's favorite restaurant overlooking the bay, where the oysters were perfect and the lobsters superb. But with the passage of the years, Holly had come to know Carlos's ways; the treats were predictable, the protestations of love and proposals of marriage his way of trying to convince her that their union was forever. In a few days, she knew, he would start making demands and, when refused, would either explode in anger or sulk like a child.

Before that moment arrived, something happened that puzzled and troubled Holly and hammered the second nail in the coffin of her fading relationship with Carlos. She was in the garden cutting roses in readiness for making the potpourri with which her mother had traditionally scented the house, when she heard the telephone ringing. Holly ran to the library and lifted the receiver at the same time as Carlos picked it up in the first-floor salon. She was surprised to hear a woman speaking, the cultured voice lightly accented in a manner Holly thought either Dutch or Scandinavian. She listened wide-eyed to the cryptic conversation.

"*Fine Lady* arrives late evening at Dun Laoghaire."

"Everything's ready on my end. You'll leave at what time?"

"We arrive in Dun Laoghaire at ten and leave on the midnight tide. Does Holly suspect anything?"

"Of course not; why should she?"

"I would if I were she."

"You would suspect your own reflection in the mirror, my dear Magritte."

"Till tonight, then."

"I'll be there around nine-thirty in case you arrive early."

After Holly heard him replace the receiver, she replaced the one at her end. She wondered what it meant, what mischief Carlos was up to and who the woman was. Was his desire for a Lamborghini to impress a new mistress? And who or what was *Fine Lady?* On impulse she rang the port of Dun Laoghaire and ascertained that *Fine Lady* was a yacht en route from Rotterdam, which would return to its port of destination two hours after docking in Ireland. Holly was about to return to the garden when Carlos came into the room and spoke with unusual sharpness.

"When will the check arrive from the auction house?"

"Tomorrow or Friday."

"I need to borrow some cash, Holly. I never asked before, but I must have it immediately. Twenty thousand will do for the moment."

"I'm sorry, Carlos, I can't lend you money."

"Then give it."

"No, Carlos."

They faced each other, his dark eyes smoldering, her face pale but determined. He began to speak in his usual tough, threatening manner, obviously astonished by her obdurateness.

"If you do not give me the money you will never see me again. I wouldn't ask if it weren't important and I never asked for anything in the past other than to enjoy your body.''

"I don't wish to argue, Carlos. I won't give you money, so you must do what you think fit to do.''

"I shall pack my things, then.''

"You do that, and make sure you don't leave anything behind.''

Furious that he should make demands on the first money she had had for so long, money he knew belonged to her family, Holly found new strength and purpose. She had not worked since the film, made after the end of the Ballet Rose tour, and knew only too well that her future was insecure. She thought of the woman on the phone, surprised to feel relief instead of jealousy. It was the moment when she realized for the first time that her relationship with Carlos was doomed. She had been his puppet for long enough and it was time to grow up.

Holly was on her way to her room, when she heard Carlos talking with someone in the hall. Looking over the balustrade, she saw that the visitor was a portly gentleman from the bank. Holly called out a greeting.

"Hello there, Mr. Ackroyd. What are you doing here?''

"Mr. Hamid informed us that you wished to sign a power of attorney in his favor in case of accident or demise.''

Holly hurried downstairs. She stared from Ackroyd in his Irish tweed jacket to Carlos in his riding outfit, impatiently holding the whip with which he had so often controlled her. Keeping her voice level, Holly led Ackroyd to the salon and let him put the papers before her. When she spoke, Carlos marched from the house, slamming every door behind him.

"I'll sign the power of attorney, Mr. Ackroyd, but in favor of my sister, Mrs. Eira McMeakin. Her address is number eight, Redburn Terrace, London.''

"I'll fill in the forms and you can sign them, Miss O'Malley.''

"Half the money must be transferred immediately to my sister's account at Barclay's Bank, King's Road; the rest remains with you for the moment. If anything happens to me, Eira can withdraw the balance or give instructions without any problem, I suppose."

"Of course she can. If I may presume, Miss O'Malley, I think you are wise to keep the money in the family, though your fiancé is angry for the moment."

"He's not my fiancé."

"I beg your pardon; he said he was."

Holly led Ackroyd to the door and closed it behind him. Then she rang for the housekeeper and asked her to pack Carlos's belongings into a cabin trunk and have it delivered to the dockside at Dun Laoghaire to await the arrival of a yacht called *Fine Lady*.

An hour later, Carlos arrived with a florist's van full of roses. He was contrite and Holly hesitated, softening as he capitulated completely.

"I don't want our affair to end, Holly. We have been together too long for that. Please forgive me. I will never ask you for money again."

Carlos watched her closely, gauging her mood as he took her in his arms. He was wondering how she had known about the yacht arriving in Ireland on the night tide and thinking that for the moment he must wait until he could terminate the affair in a manner that would ensure his future safety.

Holly was wondering how best to convince this dangerous man that despite the endless incriminating business details with which he had entrusted her over the years, he was safe from reprisal in the event of the breakup of their relationship. She closed her eyes as Carlos kissed her, conscious that the rift was now inevitable, but uncertain if it could be accomplished in safety.

Chapter Twenty-One

Sarah, Paris–Venice, November 1974

Sarah boarded the Orient Express and was led to her sleeper by a uniformed attendant. On opening the door of the compartment, she found it full of pink roses. In a solid silver ice bucket, there was a bottle of her favorite Dom Perignon champagne; on a tray, two crystal glasses. Turning to inquire who had sent the roses, Sarah found herself face to face with Vieri.

"I thought as you love surprises you might want to travel to Venice with me. I'm on my way home for a few days."

She locked the door and moved into his arms.

"I thought you'd forgotten me. It's been so long."

She snuggled against his chest, closing her eyes delightedly as he replied.

"You've been busy. You now own the Moulin Rouge with di Castelli and heaven only knows what else. You're a tycoon and I've been getting more jealous by the minute. But now I'm here and I'm going to fight for your hand like an old-fashioned knight on a pure-white charger."

"Say it again—tell me you're jealous."

"Very jealous, but di Castelli's in Paris and I'm here and tomorrow I'm going to show you something that will take even the Moulin Rouge out of your mind."

"Aren't you afraid of what Umberto might do to you? He

has a man on the train with instructions to watch every move I make.''

"I have a man on the train, too, and mine can be relied on to keep di Castelli's nephew well occupied.''

They ate turtle soup with heart-shaped croutons, veal in tarragon sauce, and wild strawberries piled on Chantilly and sprinkled with *framboises*. Waiters hovered attentively as the train sped on in the darkness, their jaded faces taking in every detail of the attractive couple so obviously engrossed in each other.

Sarah explained the reason for her visit to Venice.

"I'm going to see Alfredo to discuss the costumes for the play we're putting on at the Bal Tabarin. I have to be back in Paris by Saturday for the opening of the new club.''

"What kind of place is it this time?''

"It's one of the little bars that came with the Moulin Rouge. I've decided to call it the 'Green Door,' and we've made it as Irish as we can. There's a shop attached and the Irish Tourist Board has helped put together the stock. We have everything from Waterford crystal to Arran sweaters and Irish linen embroidered with shamrocks.''

"And the Moulin Rouge?''

"We'll open for Christmas with a new show. I've decided to have the place done as it was in Lautrec's day, even down to doubles of the performers of the Belle Epoque. We're auditioning for a La Goulue, a Jane Avril, Valentine, and all the others, and for the finest cancan dancers in Europe.''

"You disappoint me; I expected innovations and you're going to do the cancan!''

"At the Moulin Rouge people expect to see the past come to life, and that's going to happen.''

"Why did you not show the purchase agreement to your lawyer?''

Sarah stared at Vieri, her heart pounding with apprehension at the unexpected inquiry.

"How do you know I didn't?"

"My dear Sarah, I've learned a great deal from di Castelli and I keep an eye on you, as he does. The only difference is that my surveillance is for your protection, while his is for your confinement within the limitations of his jealousy. That agreement contains one clause you very obviously didn't read. At any time, di Castelli can demand total repayment of the loan of two hundred and fifty thousand pounds. Default of payment within a week would oblige you to hand over ownership of everything you own in the Paris region as compensation."

Sarah shook her head in disbelief.

"I can't believe it. Umberto wouldn't do a thing like that to me—he just *wouldn't*. Anyway, I don't want to think about it. I'll deal with it when I get back to Paris."

Vieri smiled wryly as he poured them both more champagne. Evidently she had trusted the Sicilian implicitly and the trust had been betrayed. He spoke apologetically.

"I fill your compartment with flowers, prepare for a month to travel with you, and give you a wonderful surprise on arrival—and then I give you the worst one you've ever had. I'm so sorry, Sarah, but you really shouldn't trust that man. He has his price, and his price is your freedom. Anyway, I must say I admire your self-control. My brother said you'd scream like a dervish when I broke the news."

"I never scream and if Umberto's done what you say I'll never forgive him, never, ever, ever."

Vieri took her hand and kissed each of the fingers.

"I hope you'll forgive me for telling you."

"I'm glad you did and I love you, Vieri. I always did and I always will."

"Your manner of showing it is rather odd. You're another

man's mistress and you make no attempt to leave him, despite your feelings for me. What manner of love is that?''

Sarah recoiled, glowering angrily at the remark.

"You've not made much of an effort to pursue me and until you do, I prefer to keep Umberto. He's real and not a dream. I'm not a woman who lets herself dream too much.''

"Tomorrow I'll make you dream. I'll make you dream as you never dreamed before.''

He kissed her then, as he had kissed her before tragedy entered his life, his body hardening as she strained against him. Their lips were hungry and his tongue thrust deep into the warm depths of her mouth, probing, searching, titillating till Sarah cried out from the pent-up desire she had never had the opportunity to express. Vieri cradled her to his chest, enjoying the feel of her heart against his own. Her body was slim but soft and he wanted to bury himself deep inside her and never let her go, but this was not the moment. He would not start his fight for Sarah's future in the narrow confines of a train sleeper. He had made his plans and must resist her for a few more hours.

D. H. Lawrence called Venice "an abhorrent, green, slippery city,'' but in the translucent light of an early-winter morning, Sarah found it exquisite. The lagoon was milky and luminous, with opalescent shadows that reflected the buildings immortalized by Canaletto. A sundial at the entrance to the station proclaimed a typical Venetian message—*I count only the happy hours*—and all around, the sounds of the city echoed in the air: the rumble of handcarts, the creaking of bridges, the song of a gondolier, and the chug of a *vaporetto.* Sarah watched Venetians chatting outside a café, their sweeping gestures and gruff voices like no others in Italy. She heard the chiming of bells in endless campaniles and marveled at the antics of the city's cat population, who paraded near the vendors of *frittelle,* waiting for someone to drop his tasty Venetian doughnut.

The Aldobrandini launch was waiting to take them to the palace overlooking the lagoon. Sarah reminded herself sternly that she had come to Venice on business, that this was neither a holiday nor a honeymoon. But the atmosphere of romance was irresistible and she was soon lost in a dreamworld as Vieri pointed out the interesting sights. She saw the best fish market in Europe, with huge sea turtles lying on their backs next to tuna, octopus, eels, and scarlet cooked crabs. The fabulous *punto in aria* lace of Burano was draped across the top of the stalls in the general market, its cobwebby beauty in startling contrast to the melons, mushrooms, and red Treviso lettuce. Within seconds, Sarah had forgotten about Umberto and had fallen in love with the city as she had fallen in love long ago with Vieri.

The Aldobrandini palace was built in the local style, with stucco walls and ceilings by Tiepolo. The floors were of inlaid rosewood, the bathrooms walled in Carrara marble. Faded murals by Mengazzi-Colonna gave an air of antiquity, and in each of the twenty rooms crystal chandeliers held over two thousand candles to light the evening hours. The effect was one of splendor without loss of the homeliness beloved by all Venetians.

Sarah turned to Vieri, her face showing all the surprise and joy the beauty of the place had given her.

"This is a fairy-tale palace."

"I'll take you to your room and you can leave your luggage to be unpacked. Then I'll show you your surprise."

At the far end of the garden there was a glass-roofed pavilion. On three sides the walls were of crystal, the floor and fourth wall of scented cedarwood imported from the East. The pavilion had been built for the mistress of Vieri's great-grandfather, who loved Venice as if she were a true Aldobrandini. Looking around, Sarah realized that it was very small, simply furnished but in the greatest luxury. The floors were covered in handmade silk kelim rugs in shades of gold and amber. The furniture was papier-mâché inlaid with ivory and mother-of-pearl, the daybed covered in satin brocade brought from Persia in times long past by an adventuring Aldobrandini relative. Sarah looked to Vieri, waiting for him to show her the surprise.

"I think the pavilion's out of this world, but it isn't a surprise for me personally. It's part of your home."

"It's *yours*, Sarah. I made a deed of gift of it yesterday in your name."

Sarah stood in silence, wondering if it could possibly be true, that Vieri was actually giving her a part of his home. She stumbled to find words to reply.

"Does Elio know what you've done?"

"Of course. He agrees with me."

"I can't believe it. The pavilion's part of the Palazzo Aldobrandini. Why have you done this?"

"Why do you think? You can sleep here if you like. I hope you admire the bedroom as much as I do."

The walls and ceiling were of glass, the sunlight of mid-morning filtered by festooned blinds of deep cream watered silk. The bed was circular and draped in the same material as the windows. Sarah stood looking out at the swirling waters of the lagoon, imagining it as it would be at night, when the mist hung over the city. Then, the pavilion would seem suspended in space like a tiny enchanted island where love could bloom. She turned to Vieri and held him to her heart.

"Let's eat dinner there this evening."

"I'll send the chef to take your order. For the moment, I'd best drop you at Alfredo's office in the launch. You'll be late for your appointment otherwise."

"Kiss me, Vieri."

Grasping her in his arms, he kissed Sarah on the lips, his body and hers locking together like a vise as their mouths touched. To Vieri there was a dreamlike quality in the embrace. To Sarah, it was a moment of intense feeling, the promise of love to come. As he kissed her a second time, the floodgates of control opened and she wanted him to take her there and then, but knew she must wait, at least until nightfall.

Sarah spent the day at meetings with Alfredo the designer, who showed her his magnificent creations for the play. Then he took her to the factory where his partner, Fosse, executed the designs in material specially woven by their own workers. As she gazed at the rainbow silks and gilded brocades, Sarah thought that either she would have a much-applauded spectacle or the most expensive flop in recent show business history. She listened with interest when Fosse spoke of another new show being tried out at an experimental theater in the city, the cast comprised of former criminals from the Modena state prison. Their talents ranged from an operatic tenor to the finest pickpocket in Europe, who had distinguished himself by removing the brassiere of a haughty Venetian countess without the lady's realizing it. Sarah laughed delightedly on hearing about the show, certain the sophisticates of Paris would love the novelty of a spectacle composed entirely of criminals. She arranged to see the presentation the following evening, before she was due to take the night train back to Paris.

Having completed her business, Sarah walked alone around the city, enjoying scenes of Venetian life that were both curious and impressive: the children waiting at the tables and putting tips in their shoes as Venetians had since time immemorial, vistas of Byzantine towers and stone-lace balconies reflected in blue water, priests hurrying by, their black and white vestments in stark contrast to the pink and terracotta of the buildings. Once the city had been known as the greatest trading nation and liveliest brothel in all of Europe. Now it was renowned for its beauty and the honesty of its citizens, who treated with profound sympathy anyone unfortunate enough not to have been born there.

The night was misty and the pavilion, lit by a thousand candles, looked like a crystal prism suspended in space. The table was set with Murano glass and a rose lace cloth festooned with camellias. A gentle breeze made the candles flicker, and as Sarah sat facing Vieri, she knew she had never been anywhere as romantic, nor ever would be again. The meal was light, the wines superb, but she noticed little of either, because she was watching the changing expressions in Vieri's eyes, the tension in his body, and the gradual relaxing of that tension as Tizianis were followed by the amber wine of Frascati, *cappellini* by fresh pasta with smoky ham sauce.

They said little, until they were standing together on the cantilevered terrace overlooking the lagoon, their bodies hidden by the mist. Then Sarah took Vieri's hand and kissed it.

"This is an enchanted place. I won't ever forget it."

"You'll visit Venice very often, so you won't need to forget it. This is your house, remember?"

"I still can't believe it."

"I want more than anything in the world to love you, Sarah, but I don't know if I can. My body has never really been my own since the kidnapping."

"Don't try to make love if you're apprehensive. We'll go to bed and sleep until morning and eat breakfast together on the terrace."

Vieri walked with her to the bedroom, kissing her shoulders tenderly.

"You underestimate your attractions, my darling. I don't know if the man exists who could sleep at your side and feel nothing at all. Even the kidnapping didn't do that to me."

Sarah followed him, enchanted when Vieri pressed a button that made the roof disappear, revealing the dark sky of a starry Venetian night. Shivering as he untied the strap of her Grecian-style dress, she felt it fall to the ground, leaving her naked before him. She heard and enjoyed the sharp intake of his breath and began to undress him, touching the hard-muscled body in awe. How tall he was, how slim and perfect in every way. She kissed his lips, then his shoulders, then kneeled before him and tasted the tip of his penis.

Vieri's upturned face shone silver in the moonlight and he moaned softly, trying to step back as Sarah's tongue continued to provoke. She held him to her body, stroking his thighs as they tensed. He pulled back again, fearful of losing control before he had really loved her. Then he led her to the bed and lay at her side for a moment, admiring the curves of her body.

"I love you too much, Sarah. You make me afraid of my own emotions for the first time in my life."

"Make love to me. I've wanted you for so very long."

He moved above her, thrusting inside with a penis like iron and crying out in ecstasy as the warm wetness of her body enveloped him. Their movements became rapid, until in one all-consuming moment of passion Sarah's back arched as the orgasm took her strength away. Vieri felt his body dissolving into hers, the luxurious, perfect culmination of the moment he had dreamed of for so long. Fear left him and he knew only that he loved her as he had never loved any woman before, nor ever would again. Then he took her in his arms and stroked her hair, smiling at her words.

"I thought you said your body was useless and no longer under your control."

"I thought I was finished where love was concerned."

"I'm so glad you were wrong. I'm so glad you can make me dream like no one ever did before."

Outside, on the lagoon, a wedding party was homeward bound, their laughter echoing in the silence of the night. Somewhere in the far distance a gondolier sang and a dozen tabby cats began a lament to lost love in an alleyway where the feline breed of the city had lived since history began.

Vieri lifted Sarah from the bed and carried her to the balcony, putting her down at the rail to stand naked like a statue, shrouded in mist and mystery. Then he bent his head to kiss her thighs and her hips and the nipples that rose hard against his tongue. Entering her, he pushed against the railing, so her back was to the lagoon and her face looking into his. When he heard the sound of her breath quickening, he came as if he had only moments to live, seconds to achieve his personal nirvana.

In the still of night, when the only sounds were of water lapping against the post on which the pavilion had been built, Vieri woke and lay enjoying the presence of the woman at his side. Sarah was asleep, her breath coming in deep, contented sighs that made him proud. Gently, he touched her shoulder, savoring the texture of the skin and the flowery perfume she used. He kissed her shoulder and the nipples exposed as she changed position. Then, as desire filled him, he ran his hands over the stomach and pale ash of her pubic hair. Parting the hairs, he began to rotate the clitoris, his body hardening as Sarah made a tiny, contented sound in her sleep. His longing for her increased, overwhelming everything but the urgency of the moment, and he entered her, thrilled when the vagina contracted as she touched his hand and woke, realizing that he was loving her.

Like a sleepwalker, Sarah pushed him back on the bed, impaling her body on his, so Vieri could feel the cervix against his penis. As she moved back and forth above him, he marveled at the curves of her body outlined in the rose light of dawn. Then, feeling her tightening over him, milking every drop of the orgasm, he took her in his arms and told her he loved her to distraction.

"This has been the most wonderful night of my life. My dearest Sarah, I love you more than I can ever say. I'll just have to learn to show by my actions how much I feel for you."

"I want to make you happy."

"I *am* happy and I have a confession to make. I changed your ticket to Paris to give us one extra night here together. I'll drive you back and have you there at the same time, I promise. Now, let me tempt you to take a swim with me."

"The lagoon's polluted despite the lovely color. Forgive me for being unromantic!"

"True, but I've a place that's ideal for us."

Vieri pressed another wall button and part of the floor opened, revealing an ancient stone staircase. He helped Sarah down, watching her face as he turned on the lights, revealing a heart-shaped pool fed by a tiny waterfall.

"I had this put in especially for you, because you once told me you adored water. Before, it was the wine cellar of the pavilion, with a corridor leading to the main house. I suppose my great-grandfather's mistress used it when she wanted to dine with him there and I'm sure they both adored thinking no one knew about it."

"Let's swim."

"I'll go and order breakfast for afterward. We'll eat it on the terrace and watch the sun rise over the water. That's one of the most beautiful sights I've ever seen in my life."

When Vieri returned, he found Sarah floating on her back, the suntanned, statuesque body an invitation he could not resist. He dived in and swam to her side, taking her in his arms and kissing her so they sank beneath the water and emerged laughing and choking and kissing again. Vieri felt his body harden as she wound her legs around his hips, sliding slowly onto his hardness and bringing them both to orgasm. Then, exhilarated but breathless, they climbed out of the water and began to dry each other. As Sarah lay on the daybed, Vieri took some scented lotion and rubbed it into her skin, enjoying the shiver of anticipation that ran through her frame, the nipples that hardened as he covered them with the cream and circled her breasts. He closed his eyes in ecstasy as Sarah spoke.

"This is paradise."

"I agree. I've dreamed of it and feared it for so long."

"Kiss me again—I'm hungry for you."

"First we eat breakfast. I hear the maids serving it on the terrace. Then we'll spend the whole day together."

There were figs from Tuscany and tiny red strawberries from the hothouses in the countryside of the Veneto. Fresh-baked bread, currant brioche, and pungent coffee scented the air with the fragrance of home. The jams had been made in the kitchens of the palazzo, a translucent lilac jelly of violet petals and honey and a vivid yellow marmalade of orange blossom. Sarah savored the tastes and smells, longing to remember everything, so she could bring it instantly to mind once she returned to Paris. As she looked at Vieri, she knew that at last he was happy and relaxed. She stretched out her hand and held his.

"You look so at peace with yourself. I hope I'm responsible."

"You are and you know it."

The day was as near perfect as any Sarah had known, the morning spent seeing the city by private gondola, with lunch at the Cipriani, where, in a dining room hung with Fortuny curtains, they ate giant prawns and then the chef's famous raspberry tart. In the afternoon, they returned to the house and made love in Vieri's bedroom, with its dark, fourteenth-century bed and handmade cover stitched by the nuns of Santa Maria. For Sarah the lovemaking was perfect, the sudden surge of his body into her own sheer magic. As Vieri provoked her to orgasm, she felt herself giving as she had never given before and taking as she had never wanted to take before. Crying out from sheer pleasure, she fell back on the big, feather-pillowed bed, unable to think or move or do anything but savor the luxurious glow of satiation. She felt

Vieri at her side and, opening her eyes, saw him wiping sweat from his brow with a linen handkerchief. Loving him dearly, Sarah reached out and gripped his hand.

"Take me in your arms and let's sleep a while."

"Are you content, Sarah?"

"Need you ask? Can't you see it in my eyes?"

"I see, but I can't believe my luck."

They slept until five, then rose, showered, and went downstairs to drink China tea in the conservatory. The scent of orchids was heady and tea was served with muffins and cucumber sandwiches in the English style. Sarah sat back, so relaxed she was shocked to realize that she had never for a moment thought of the businesses in Paris. She looked out at the lagoon and then at Vieri, who was gazing at her with questioning eyes.

"You know something? I never thought once about my clubs and my debts and everything else I left behind when I came here!"

"And you feel guilty, I suppose?"

"I'm up to my neck in debt, so I *must* think of work. I've only recently realized that without Umberto I'm finished. I don't really own anything but a load of debts. The investors are the major owners of the English Club, and the other things depend on loans from Umberto."

"We're here, together, for the first time. If you have problems in the future we'll deal with them *together*. For the moment, don't think about Paris and the money you owe and the problems of that man."

In the smoky-gray stillness of a winter evening, they drank cocktails at Harry's Bar. Vieri chose a whiskey sour and Sarah a Bellini. From the bar, they went to dinner and then walked toward the theater, through streets full of statues, fountains, and laundry hung across narrow canals. Once, a funeral barge draped in purple and black hastened on its way to the cemetery island. Then, as they paused to embrace outside the theater, they saw the mellow glow of candles in the crystal chandeliers of a palazzo overlooking the lagoon, a sight so Venetian it would remain in Sarah's mind forever.

At eleven, they emerged from the theater with tears in their eyes, having laughed until they cried. Sarah had engaged the entire cast of the show on a three-month contract for the Bal Tabarin and was confident that she would have the hit of the season on her hands. Exhilarated by the thought of future success, she walked back to the palace on Vieri's arm, her face glowing with pleasure, her body transformed by love. She did not see the two men walking behind them, nor the one hidden opposite the gate. For the moment, she was oblivious to everything but passion.

In the morning, servants put Sarah's bags into the Aldobrandini launch and then stood back as it moved away from the jetty. Vieri put his arm around her shoulders, feeling the regret he always felt as the house he loved faded into the mist of morning. As he watched the ever-changing emotions on Sarah's face, he saw regret and sadness, apprehension and then momentary joy, when a cloud of white doves soared into the sky, a sign of good luck and future happiness to the superstitious Venetians. He touched Sarah's hand and kissed her ear.

"I'm so glad you're coming back in my car instead of on the train. At least you'll be spared the ordeal of facing di Castelli at the station."

"I'll have to face him sometime."

"He won't make a fuss in the apartment with the nurse and Lexy there."

"Who knows what he'll do. He's not the most predictable of men."

"If you need me, I'll be at the house in the avenue Foch. You only have to call and I'll come at once and bring help. Sarah, I've been patient about di Castelli, and God knows you've waited for me in the past, but now you have to find a way to rid yourself of that man. It'll take time and you'll have to be careful, but you must do it.''

"Will you wait?"

"I'm leaving for California in a week's time. I shall be away for eighteen months, perhaps more. I want you to come over with Lexy in the summer for two months, and I'll come to Venice for Christmas and Easter when she has her school holidays. My family has bought some very valuable real estate in Carmel, and it's my responsibility to see that all goes well with the development of the site. Also, to be truthful, I can't bear to stay in Paris knowing you're with that man. I'm human, you know, and I'm in love. I want all the things a man in love wants and you want the same and you always have. I'm relying on you to settle the situation with di Castelli once and for all. If you don't, we'll all be in danger and we'll never be able to have a normal family life. I'm telling you, Sarah, fix it, however long it takes, and let's start a new life together.''

"Are you proposing to me, Vieri?"

"I'm talking from the heart. When di Castelli's out of your life for good, I'll propose.''

Sarah entered the apartment and hurried to the window in time to see the taillights of Vieri's car disappearing around the corner. She had never felt so lonely, so weary and uncertain. At the same time, she was elated, because he had said he would propose when Umberto was out of her life. But how to free herself? Sarah shook her head, asking the same question she had asked a thousand times before and to which she never found an answer. To comfort herself, she walked to Lexy's bedroom, panic hitting her when she found the room empty, the bed untouched. She ran from room to room, unable to believe that the nurse and child were not there. Then, returning to the living room, she sat for a few moments, trying to still the thoughts racing through her mind. Finally, she dialed Mario Benedetti's number, terrified when he replied.

"Lexy and her nurse are at Umberto's house. Try not to be too upset, Sarah."

"What are they doing there?"

"Umberto decided to move them till your return."

"Why?"

"You know him. He's impetuous. I think he wants to show you that he can make Lexy disappear if he needs to. She's quite safe and Mitzi hasn't left her for a moment, but he's crazier than I've ever seen him. Whatever made you go and stay at Vieri's house in Venice?"

"I'm free and I love Vieri. What can I do, Mario? Umberto will know I'm back."

"Call him and just stay in the apartment till he arrives."

"I want Lexy back *now!* I won't have her used as a lever against me."

"Leave her be for the moment, Sarah. He's not in a normal state. I advise you not to make a fuss."

"Like hell I will. She's my child and I want her home with me."

Sarah ran downstairs and called a cab, giving Umberto's address in the Bois de Boulogne as her destination. She had no idea what she was going to do, only that she wanted her daughter back where she belonged. When she thought of what Umberto had done, rage filled her mind and she could only think what a shock it must have been to Lexy to be moved from her home to the house of a man she had never liked.

When the cab pulled up outside Umberto's house, it was eleven-thirty on a damp winter evening. Sarah walked to the front door and rang the bell, then hammered relentlessly to be admitted. It was some time before Umberto appeared, and his appearance shocked her. His eyes were scarlet rimmed, his face unshaven, his carriage unsteady. He looked at her in surprise and then opened the door with a mocking flourish.

"At last you come back. What happen, did he not please you in the bed?"

"He pleased me very much."

Umberto hit her without warning, one single, vicious blow to the face that carried with it all the anguish, hurt, and humiliation he had been feeling for so long. As blood poured from her nose, he rushed to her side, immediately contrite, but Sarah shoved him from her as he came to help her to a chair.

"Forgive me, Sarah. You drive me mad and then expect I act civilized."

"You have my daughter in the house. I'll give you five minutes to get Lexy downstairs and into the cab I have waiting. After that, I'll ring every newspaper and have every gendarme in the area around your neck. Now stop moaning and find my child and don't *ever* take her again."

"Sarah, I have to talk with you."

"Come to the apartment in the morning and we'll talk, but we'll do nothing till I have Lexy back. You have four minutes."

In the still of night, back in the apartment that was home, Sarah looked down at the daughter she loved above all else. Then she moved to the window, frowning at the sight of Umberto's men outside the street entrance of the building. The shock of her child's disappearance had brought the matter of Umberto to a head and Sarah had finally made her decision. In the morning, she would instruct her advisers to prepare Hallam International for launching on the Paris Bourse. On the stock exchange, the little people could buy shares, and if she was lucky, she might eventually be able to raise enough to pay Umberto back the money she owed. The total debt, after restoration of the Moulin Rouge and the other two Monet clubs, was three million, five hundred thousand francs. When Sarah thought of the alternative, the possibility of losing everything, she found herself sweating, despite the chill of the night. For as long as she could remember, Umberto had been her safety, her security and longed-for stability. Now, for the first time, she knew she was totally alone. She had been protected only for as long as she was obedient of Umberto's wishes. From this moment on, the protection and the precious feelings of safety were gone.

Sarah sat alone, wondering how to pacify Umberto, how to retain the status quo until she could find the money to remove herself completely from his life and his influence. Above all else, he was a proud man and she knew she would have to keep up the outward appearances of friendship in order not to humiliate him before his *compadres*. She also knew that she would never make love with him again and that the time would come when she might have to play a very rough game if she was to continue living with Lexy in Paris in safety. She had none of Umberto's experience of the black side of life and virtually no knowledge of how to fight a power machine, where violence was the watchword. But she would do what had to be done, just as she always had.

At dawn, Sarah went to Lexy's room and held the child tightly in her arms.

"Are you all right, my darling?"

"I'm glad to be home, Mummy. Umberto said I was having a holiday at his house and he made me eat spaghetti with *fishes* in it! He shouted at everyone all the time and smoked cigars till he was sick. Mitzi and I were scared."

"You're home now."

"Shall we go to our club for lunch? You could ask Madame Berthe to make me liver and bacon."

"I love you, my darling."

"I love you, Mummy. I don't think I'll go on holiday again for a while."

"I agree. Now get up and we'll have breakfast together. Then we'll take Bruin to the park for a bit of exercise."

Chapter Twenty-Two

Mary-Ellen, Seville, Summer 1976

Men came and removed the twenty-foot-long table from the dining room and the painting by Velázquez that had been in the family for generations. It was called "The Heads of the Drunkards," and Mary-Ellen thought that since it belonged to Luis, it should have been called "The Heads of the Gamblers." This was the third time bailiffs had come to the house to remove objects to be auctioned in order to pay off her husband's debts, and it was by far the most serious visitation. She watched in horror as a Catalan armoire followed the dining table and the Andalusian chests inlaid with silver and mother-of-pearl. The removal of goods continued for three hours, the last painting being taken away as dusk fell. It was a portrait by Pantoja de la Cruz of an original Villavicencio caballero that had graced the salon for as long as anyone could remember. All that remained, once the door slammed shut on the family, were their beds, clothes, kitchen table, chairs, and a stove too heavy by far to be removed.

Mary-Ellen wandered disconsolately about the house, gazing at the vaulted ceilings and vistas onto the courtyard full of enameled faience pots of thyme and rosemary. Antique plaster frogs surrounded the fountain, and the seats of the duennas were encircled by hedges of yew and cypress.

Hearing her husband's voice, she looked out and saw Luis arriving with half a dozen friends to drink *fino* on the terrace. As they drank the sherry, she knew they would play cards until it was time for a late lunch. She wondered if they had enough knives and forks left to feed everyone and if Luis would gamble the house away before lunch was over.

Hurrying to her room, Mary-Ellen slumped wearily on the bed, glad she had sent the children away for a few hours, so they would not have to witness the denuding of their home. For her part, she had suffered so much she felt punch-drunk, numb and incapable of tears, anger, or any normal reaction. She wanted only to run away, but Luis never gave her money, except to buy food and then it was not enough. She rose and looked at her reflection in the wall mirror, staring resignedly at the woman she had become and trying not to be bitter about the loss of her beauty or the decline in her general condition. Beaten by circumstances beyond her control, she knew that she now wandered through life like a sleepwalker, never resisting, protesting, or even reacting. She wondered if she was even capable of reaction, but knew only that she was tired, so very, very tired.

Luis entered the bedroom and looked about him.

"They didn't leave us very much."

Mary-Ellen did not reply, puzzled to see a certain satisfaction in her husband's eyes. Did Luis want them to live like this? Or did he, like many gamblers, feel he had to hit bottom before he started a new winning streak? When he spoke sharply, she continued to remain aloof.

"Make lunch for eight, nine if you intend to join us, and try to join us, and try to keep away from Ignacio."

"I can't stand your brother and you know it."

"But you flirt with him all the same. Here, take five hundred pesetas to buy food."

She looked disbelievingly at the note.

"Five hundred pesetas for food for nine? That'll buy you a plate of pasta each."

"My mother used to provide five courses for the same amount."

"That was forty years ago, but a plate of pasta is what you'll get now."

Luis threw another two hundred pesetas down on the table.

"Make that buy more than a plate of pasta."

"That'll buy a green salad and a plate of pasta and I'll do the marketing and cooking myself. After lunch we must talk, Luis. We can't go on living like this anymore."

"Not today, *Reina*. You have a serious look and I do so hate it when you are serious."

They ate a salad of anchovies and tomato, then pasta with butter and cheese. To make up for the paucity of the meal, Luis chose a fine wine from the cellars of his ancestors, ignoring completely the lack of furniture and huge empty spaces on the walls where the paintings had been. The friends asked no questions about what had happened. Everyone in Seville knew about Luis's gambling. Many hoped he would someday have to wager his wife to settle his debts. Others were waiting patiently for the moment when the hacienda would be sold over his head, and all of them agreed it would only be a matter of months before Luis lost everything he owned.

Toward the end of the day, as the sun set like a scarlet ball over the distant hills of Andalusia, Luis began to scowl at his brother, who was regarding Mary-Ellen with awe. When she carried the empty dishes to the kitchen, Ignacio followed, eager to help and caring nothing for the fact that it was contrary to the rules of Spanish male society. Finally, Luis could stand it no longer, but instead of attacking his brother, he turned on Mary-Ellen.

"Must you keep leading him on?"

She tilted her head, listening to the rattle of cicadas in the trees around the house and thinking how she had once adored all things Spanish. Now she detested the false pride and passion of the man who said he loved her above all else, but whose actions revealed the contrary. Without answering her husband, Mary-Ellen went to the kitchen and began washing up. She was almost through the pile of dirty dishes when she saw a neighboring landowner, Carlotta Hernandez, hurrying through the patio. Carlotta was dressed in a luxurious white silk dress, with a cloak of snowy fox, her vivid red hair, scarlet mouth, and enormous eyes a walking invitation that brought Luis and all the men to their feet. Mary-Ellen was furious when her husband rushed into the kitchen to take champagne from the cold store, calling out to her over his shoulder, "Bring olives and sweet biscuits for Carlotta—and *hurry!*"

She was astonished to hear herself barking a reply. "I'm not your fucking servant! Take them yourself!"

Luis stopped in his tracks and stared in bewilderment. Then, putting down the champagne, he advanced on her, gripping her by the throat so she could barely breathe. Suddenly Mary-Ellen thought how Sarah would react to similar treatment, and as Luis's fingers continued to tighten, she reached out and swung an iron pan at him, hitting him in the diaphragm and winding him, so he slumped to the ground with an anguished cry of pain.

Stepping over her husband, Mary-Ellen reached up for a gallon jar of black olives preserved in a dark mixture of herbs and spices. This she carried to the terrace, where Carlotta was holding court. Then, having removed the lid, she poured the olives and eight pints of oily black liquid over the white fox cloak and white silk dress and perfectly tinted red hair.

Carlotta screeched as if she had been stabbed. The men who had been admiring her leaped to their feet, as Luis staggered out of the kitchen, his face ashen, his legs buckling under him. Ignoring the screams and shouts of shock and horror, Mary-Ellen walked from the patio to her bedroom and locked the door, realization of what she had done suddenly dawning on her. She was sitting at the window, staring in stunned silence at the navy night sky, when Ignacio climbed in through the arch that led to the terrace.

"You had better leave. My brother is threatening to kill you."

"Stay out of this. It's not your fight, and I'm not going anywhere without my children."

Mary-Ellen was lying on the bed, staring at the ceiling, when Luis entered by the dressing-room door. She was surprised when he spoke with elaborate formality, as though to a total stranger.

"I am leaving with Carlotta for Madrid. I shall stay with her for at least one month and will be taking my sons with me. I have arranged to make over ownership of this house to her father, to clear all my debts to him, so you will have to move with Lucy to another property belonging to my family on the outskirts of Madrid. Ignacio will drive you there as soon as you have packed your things. I do not know if I will come back to you or if I shall stay with Carlotta."

Fear drummed at Mary-Ellen's temples, but she did her best to stay calm.

"I'll go to court if you try to stop me from seeing my children."

"You would not succeed. You have been a great disappointment to me. When we married you were so beautiful. Now you are nothing. No man turns to look at you in the street, because you have let yourself go, and I realize that you are a woman without quality."

"And you, what are you?"

"I am a Vidal and a grandee of Spain."

"You're a vanity-stricken prick, a lousy lover, and an

appalling father. Go join your mistress. You're exactly what Carlotta deserves."

Mary-Ellen stood watching as Luis's bags were loaded into the car. She was wondering if he could really prevent her from seeing her sons and why he had decided not to take Lucy, her youngest child. Finally, she walked through the deserted house until she reached the kitchen. There, on the table, she found a note in her husband's hand. *I shall take the boys from their aunt's house tonight. As Lucy is not my child and I do not know who the father is, I leave her in your care.*

Mary-Ellen sat on the painted chair and sobbed as if her heart would break for the years of unhappiness and anguish, the times she had tried to please her husband and failed. Outside, the sounds of a Spanish night filled the air: the song of a gypsy en route to the horse fair, the croaking of frogs in the fountain, the echo of horses' hooves as men returned from the swamps of Las Marismas. Once, these had been the sounds of home. Now all she wanted was to get out of Seville and far away from Spain before she lost her reason. She thought with longing of Paris and the Ritz Hotel, where in less than a year she would meet her friends again. She told herself she must pull herself together and get her life in order before then. The rendezvous was a dream to relieve the tensions of daily life, but for the moment she must concentrate on saving her sanity and finding the means to keep and raise the children she loved.

As the clocks struck midnight, Mary-Ellen went upstairs and waited uneasily for the dawn, when Ignacio would arrive to take her and her small child on a trip to the unknown.

Part IV

AFTER THE REUNION

There was something terribly
enthralling in the exercise of influence. No other activity was quite
like it.

—Oscar Wilde
The Picture of Dorian Grey

Chapter Twenty-Three

Madrid–Paris, July 1977

The countryside was burned-umber, as far as the eye could see. Sarah reread the letter Mary-Ellen had sent her, frowning in dismay at the contents.

> I can't call you because he's had the phone removed. He's also told me that I can no longer see my sons. Since the reunion in Paris in May, I've realized just how far I've traveled down the slippery slope. I've lost everything—my looks, my hope, and all but one of my children. I don't have enough money to take the bus even to the Spanish border. Tell me what to do, Sarah. I'm lost and I can't find the way. I don't want to sound full of self-pity, but what's going to happen to Lucy and me?

Sarah looked into the distance, at the sun-baked horizon oscillating in the midday heat. What could Mary-Ellen do? Umberto had probably been right when he said she would have to return to Paris or America, leaving her children behind. But how could she salvage her life? Exhausted by the heat and apprehensive at the thought of the emotional scenes in store, Sarah gazed ahead to the place Mary-Ellen was now obliged to call home. The house was the only property for miles around, a square, solid Spanish farm with a stunted

tree to shade the entrance. Sarah stepped out of the car and
rang the bell. There was no reply. She rang again and again,
and finally a servant came and informed her sharply that
Madame was not home. Warned that this might happen,
Sarah pushed past the woman and sat in the hall. Then, despite voluble protestations from the housekeeper, she remained where she was, ignoring the woman completely.

An hour passed; then, scowling blackly, the servant led
Sarah to an upstairs room, where Mary-Ellen was waiting
with her daughter. It was obvious that she had been crying
and Sarah was shocked to see her friend's hands shaking uncontrollably from nervous tension. She spoke gently.

"What's happened since you wrote the letter?"

"Luis still won't let me visit my sons, he's stopped it
completely because Carlotta won't let me go to the house
and she doesn't want the boys to come here. She's very rich
and as he's gambled away everything he owns, he's completely dependent on her."

"What about the boys? How are they reacting?"

"I don't know, Sarah. They're too young to telephone me
or to write."

"Why did he let you keep Lucy?"

"He's insanely jealous and he's never believed she was
his child. She *is* his child, but I can't make him see it."

Sarah took out a note pad and read from it.

"I've contacted my lawyer in London, and he's arranged
for us to see one of the leading international lawyers in
Madrid tomorrow at ten. It looks as if you'll have a choice:
stay in Spain, even though you'll probably never see the
boys again, or leave the country and start a new life."

"I can't live without my children."

"You'll have to learn to live without them, but only until
they're grown up. Then, when they're independent of their
father, they'll come looking for you."

"You really believe that?"

"Sons have a way of needing to find their mothers, no matter what the opposition."

Tears streamed down Mary-Ellen's face and she sat in silence, staring at her hands, unable to believe what had happened. She was awake, but felt as if she were in the middle of a nightmare, and panic rose within her every few seconds like a surging tide. When she thought of the meeting with the lawyer the following morning, it all seemed too much and Mary-Ellen burst into tears again. It was nightfall before Sarah could calm her.

The following morning, the two women emerged from the lawyer's office in Madrid. Mary-Ellen stood on the sidewalk, watching in silence as her husband disappeared into his mistress's car. Then she followed Sarah to the spot where the chauffeur was waiting with Lucy. During the drive back to the farmhouse, she sat like a zombie, trying not to scream from shock, hurt, and anguish. The result of the interview had been as Sarah had said, only worse. Luis would keep his sons, pending the results of the separation hearing, which could take years to come to court. She would keep Lucy, the child he had chosen to disown. He would pay no money until ordered to do so by the court. Mary-Ellen felt Sarah holding her hand and did her best to assimilate the advice of the woman who had come so far to help her.

"We'll go back to the house, pack your things, and fly to Paris right away. You can stay in my apartment till you sort yourself out. Now cheer up. It's hard but it's not impossible. You're young and in good health and you've got Lucy to look after."

When Mary-Ellen continued to sit in stunned silence, Sarah spoke firmly. "You can go one of two ways now. Either you sink or you swim, and I wouldn't give that sadistic shit the satisfaction of seeing me go down."

"You're harder than I am, Sarah. You always were. You learned to be when you were little."

"Well, you're going to learn now. Use what's happened, Mary-Ellen. In the old days you often talked of how you'd like to write songs and sing them. Well, write—put your hurt into them. Dory Previn used her hurt like that and she wrote truly wonderful things. Take music lessons, start all over again, make a fortune, and choke that bastard with envy."

"I can't even think straight, Sarah."

"Of course you can't. You've had a horrible shock and it'll take time. Just remember all the while that you can sink or swim. It's your choice and no one can make it for you."

The first thing Sarah did on arriving in the apartment was to settle Mary-Ellen and Lucy in their room. Then she took them out to lunch and on a shopping trip that ended in floods of tears. Deprived for so long of the essentials of life, Mary-Ellen sobbed like a child as Sarah helped hang her beautiful new clothes in the wardrobe. Then she dried her eyes, watching in wonder as Sarah piled boxes of spares of perfume, makeup, practice clothes, tights, and shoes into the wall cupboards in the corridor "in case you and Lucy run out." Suddenly anxious, Mary-Ellen ran after Sarah to the kitchen.

"How much did all that cost, and how the hell can I ever repay you? I may never work again."

"You'll work and I'll reap the benefit someday."

"What will I do?"

"I haven't decided yet. Now, here's a list of lessons you'll be starting on Monday. They fill ten hours of every day, six days a week."

Mary-Ellen gazed aghast at the details.

"I haven't played guitar in years. I think I forgot how."

"You were very good indeed and you'll be even better after a while."

At that moment, Lexy came past the kitchen with Lucy, and Sarah could not resist a smile of sheer pleasure at her child's turn of phrase.

"Well, that's what we do. Our clubs take up a lot of time and Mummy and I don't go out very much except on Saturdays. Then we go shopping and to lunch at the Ritz. When Mummy has an attack of economy we eat at the Boule d'Or instead—but don't worry, Lucy, the attacks of economy never last more than an hour or two. Then we go and buy some new shoes and scent."

"And will I have a club, too, Lexy?"

"If you work hard you might."

Sarah moved to the door and called to her daughter.

"I'm taking Mary-Ellen to the hairdresser and then to dinner with Arlette. What are you two going to do?"

"Mitzi's taking us to the new Italian restaurant on the ground floor to have lasagne. She's put on three kilos since it opened, you know, Mummy."

"We won't be late."

"And you'll come and kiss me like always when you come in?"

"Have I ever forgotten?"

"Never, ever, ever."

Sarah looked at her watch and picked up her purse.

"We'd best go, Mary-Ellen. Your appointment's at four and we're having dinner at six-thirty with Arlette."

"How is she?"

"Terrible. Her husband threw her out and she's drowning."

"Has Charles still got the young peasant girl as his mistress, the one who worked as a maid?"

"Ernestine doesn't work as a maid anymore. She's taken over Arlette's place completely."

"And what's going to happen?"

"Arlette's moved into one room in Montmartre and she's

trying to get back into modeling. She's too old and she knows it. When I phoned her the other day she told me she hasn't worked since she got back to Paris six weeks ago.''

"Can't you help?''

"I offered her a job at the English Club, but she says she'd get wrinkles if she didn't have twelve hours' sleep a night, so she turned it down.''

Mary-Ellen emerged from the salon, the mousy, broken hair cut, streaked, and gorgeous. A top-to-toe beauty treatment had revived her morale, and she kept pausing to look at her reflection in the shop windows, her eyes wide with wonder. She was unaware that Sarah was praying silently that the shock of this sudden change in circumstances would not result in a breakdown. Sarah had taken a gamble that her friend's inner resources were equal to the strain, but was by no means certain that she had judged the situation accurately.

They met Arlette in the bistro where they had eaten together after rehearsals in the days of the Ballet Rose. She was elegantly dressed, as always, but older and weary, as if life had suddenly become very tiring. She was obviously surprised by the transformation of Mary-Ellen's appearance and smiled with sudden pleasure as they shook hands.

"Well, Lazarus has risen from the dead! What happened to you? You look almost like you did in the old days.''

Mary-Ellen replied with a touch of her old irony. "Sarah had me transformed. Now all I need is to get a brain and nervous system to match and I'll be just fine. This place has changed a lot since we used to come and eat bananas and cream.''

Arlette smiled wryly at the memory. Then she turned to Sarah. "And how's the tycoon? They say your company is going from strength to strength on the stock exchange.''

"It's true. If it continues after the August holiday I might even be able to pay Umberto back part of the fortune I owe him. But how are you? Any luck with the agencies?''

"Nothing. No one is interested at all. I even went to see Umberto, because he owns part of Visages, but he wasn't about to help. He's never forgiven me for telling him off that night in Rome when you first went out with Vieri.''

"He has a very unforgiving nature.''

"How is Vieri? I keep reading about him in the papers. He's been away for so long. Have you seen him at all?''

"Lexy and I went over there in the summer last year and again this year, and he's been over very regularly to Venice. Now that he's coming home he says wild horses won't drive him away again.''

"Whatever are you going to do about Umberto?''

Sarah shrugged. During Vieri's absence, Umberto had calmed down. Though he and Sarah were now good friends and no longer lovers, he seemed content to be seen in her presence. When Vieri returned, things would change. Sarah felt panic edging into her mind, because she had still not managed to sever the seemingly unbreakable link between herself and the Sicilian. She knew the moment of rupture was close and wondered all the time if he would foreclose on the loan or use violence, the weapon he really understood best of all. Afraid of making Mary-Ellen uneasy, Sarah changed the subject.

"Are divorce proceedings going ahead, Arlette?''

"Of course; I shall soon be free. What I do after that is not at all clear.''

"Next year will be better.''

"No, next year I shall be a year older.''

"Start a modeling school. Age doesn't matter a damn in that business and you have all the qualifications.''

"Age matters to me. I can't stand to look at myself in the mirror.''

In the still of night, Sarah lay in bed, listening to Mary-

Ellen sobbing for the sons she loved but had lost. It was four A.M. before the sounds of grief ceased and the apartment was silent. Sarah rose and looked out at the dark rooftops of Paris. She was thinking of Vieri's return, ecstatic at the thought of seeing him again, but apprehensive because this was the moment when she and Umberto would reach the parting of the ways. Her mind turned to thoughts of Mary-Ellen and she felt a profound desire to protect her friend. She had spent a lot of money on securing Mary-Ellen's new base and symbols of security. Could she now provide her with the motivation for a return to normality? Had Mary-Ellen's personality ever really been sufficiently integrated for that?

Sarah was grinding coffee for breakfast when Mary-Ellen appeared, her face drawn, her eyes red rimmed.

"I slept a little, Sarah, but I can't sleep anymore. God, I'm dying for a cup of coffee. My brain's in a panic and my thoughts are all jumbled up. It happens often these days and it scares the hell out of me."

Sarah made the coffee, thinking anxiously that for Mary-Ellen the return to normality was going to be a very long and painful process.

Arlette walked the streets of Paris all night, trying to find a solution to the problem of what to do with her future. Charles would pay alimony, of course, but the minimum his lawyers could arrange. As she let herself into the tiny apartment on the hill of Montmartre, she wondered how she could stand being so alone, how she would suffer the inevitable slide into poverty and the loss of confidence that could not be avoided. She was about to make coffee when she found a letter on the kitchen table, with a note from the caretaker, saying it had been delivered by hand. Arlette read the contents through tears. *We have decided not to proceed with your contract for the* Vogue *session at Versailles. My regrets, Anthony Jay, L'Agence Saint Dominic.* She reread the letter, ignoring the sounds of morning as the occupants of the hill awoke and prepared for work. The *Vogue* session had been her only remaining chance to show what she could do, how beautiful she could still look, and she had prepared for it for weeks with a severe regimen of diet and exercise.

Sobbing uncontrollably, Arlette looked around the apartment, at the shabby chaise longue and hideous art reproductions. Her mind went back to thoughts of the chateau that had been her home. The scent of poplars after a shower would remind her for the rest of her life of the place she loved, and she would dream forever of her bedroom in the tower behind the massive three-foot-thick walls. At the chateau there had been Rembrandts and Titians and furniture upholstered in the finest silk brocade imported from Iran in centuries past by a thrifty ancestor. Arlette shook her head despairingly. Once married, she had thought herself safe forever, reckoning without her husband's perversity and her own dreams of romantic love in marriage, dreams that had been shattered in the constant humiliation Charles had meted out.

She remembered the rows there had been when Charles had forced her to comply with his desire in order to produce an heir to the title. She had done all she could do to satisfy him in order to be a good wife, to remain mistress of a chateau, and to be allowed the right to raise her own child. It had not been enough. She knew now that she would never again be mistress of a chateau, that she was a failure as a wife and as a mother. For her, the years to come would be years of diminishing fortune. She would live alone, on whatever pittance Charles gave her, trapped like an animal, because she had no urge or inclination to become a woman of business like Sarah. All the future held, as far as she could see, was loneliness, which she feared, and the gradual loss of looks and health that struck terror in her heart. Arlette thought grimly that the future was a nightmare to be avoided at all costs.

As the clocks struck the half hour, Arlette emptied the contents of every pill bottle in the bathroom into a glass of lukewarm water, waited until the tablets had dissolved, and swallowed the deadly cocktail without a second thought. Relief flooded through her at once, because she knew that for her the struggle was over. She remembered then that she had not written a note and ran to the bureau in the living room and scribbled a few lines.

Dearest Sarah,

Please see my son for me from time to time and tell him his mother loved him dearly. I rely on you to do this, as I have relied on you ever since our first meeting. I am so sorry for what I am about to do, but I don't want to exist anymore. Life is suddenly too hard and uncertain and full of horrible things

Forgive me,
Arlette

Having brushed her teeth and combed her hair, Arlette lay down on the green velour chaise longue, surprised to find that the approach to death was like being drunk from too much champagne. The last thing she remembered was digging her nails into the velour of the daybed, so she would not fall off and be found in an undignified position. As her eyes closed and she remembered the early days at the chateau, when she had been mistress of all she surveyed, the sun rose on the hill of Montmartre and glaziers, butchers, and vendors of newspapers hurried to their places of work. Arlette heard nothing of the hustle and bustle of morning. She had left behind her the worries of fading beauty and a husband who demanded more than she could give; she was hurrying to a new place about which she had often dreamed, where no one ever grew old.

Holly arrived for Arlette's funeral, her eyes still full of the shock that had gripped her ever since the arrival of Sarah's telegram. The intervening years had been exciting, but empty of something she could never identify, and she wondered if it had been the same for Arlette. Of late, her own life had changed for the worse. Carlos was tired of her and she knew it, and something in his manner before her departure had made Holly apprehensive. She passed through customs without incident and took a taxi to Sarah's apartment. She was thinking of Arlette, who had always been perfectly groomed and seemingly calm and who had died all alone in a dingy apartment, surrounded by cheap, cigarette-burned furniture. Of all the friends, Holly understood the despair that had provoked the action better than anyone, because she was feeling increasingly that she had lost something of the greatest importance in the intervening years. For Arlette, it had been her looks. For Holly, it was her soul.

The cemetery was deserted but for Sarah, Mary-Ellen, Holly, and the priest. Century-old yews smelled musty in the rain that fell incessantly during the service. At the graveside, as they threw scooped earth on the coffin, each one was thinking her own thoughts. Shocked, like the others, by Arlette's suicide at such a young age, Sarah resolved to do what she wanted to do in life, to see Vieri whenever she could and to hell with Umberto's threats. Life was too short for compromises. Mary-Ellen was remembering the night when she too had counted every sleeping pill in the bathroom and considered taking the lot. Now, ensconced in the security of Sarah's apartment, she felt happy for the first time in years. She vowed grimly that no husband was going to drive *her* to suicide. She would work twenty hours a day at the lessons Sarah had arranged. She would write songs till her brain got befuddled. She would learn faster and push harder than she had ever thought possible, but there would be no overdoses for Mary-Ellen Tate.

Holly was the most affected by the funeral. She knew that for years she had been traveling the wrong route in life. The relationship with Carlos had deteriorated fast ever since the death of her parents, and she knew that he had stayed with her only for two reasons: his desire to get his hands on her fortune and his fear of reprisals on ending the relationship. As she moved with her friends toward the big black-windowed car, Holly knew in her heart what she wanted to do. The problem was that after the life she had led, what she wanted to do was surely impossible.

That night, Sarah and her friends dined together. Then she drove Holly to the airport and tried to assuage her unease.

"Don't take all this too much to heart, Holly."

"There are some things we can't help taking to heart, and when I saw them bury Arlette I could barely keep from screaming. I just want to change my life, but I don't know how."

"Start slowly and move toward your goal. Never think you can't do it. Remove the obstacles carefully and you'll get what you really want in the end."

Holly was near the departure gate when she heard a curious whirring noise. Turning, she saw what looked like a cricket ball coming her way. She had no idea who had thrown the object, but when she heard Sarah's frantic scream of warning, she ran as fast as she could to a nearby office and slammed the heavy door. The device made a deafening noise on explosion, and when Holly emerged minutes later, the walls were spattered with blood and the screams of a party of children filled the air. She ran forward, horrified by the sight of sudden, violent death. It was the first great tragedy in her life and the moment that changed her forever.

Sarah hurried to Holly's side, her face ashen pale.

"That was meant for *you*. Umberto told me Carlos was tired of you and scared you'd go to the police if he dropped you."

"How did Umberto know about it?"

"They've done business together."

"But Carlos wouldn't murder me."

"The man threw the device directly at you. If you hadn't dodged into the office you'd have been killed."

When the police had taken statements and the dead had been removed, Holly walked with Sarah to her car. Too shaken to travel, she had decided to accept her friend's invitation to remain a few more days in Paris. She was getting into the passenger seat at Sarah's side when she saw her lover of many years watching through binoculars from the roof of the airport. Instead of the neat pinstriped suit he had worn since his arrival in Ireland, he was wearing the flowing robes of a man of the desert, but Holly was not deceived by the disguise. At that moment, she knew that what Sarah had said was true, that the bloody tragedy in the departure lounge had resulted from Carlos's attempt to get rid of her. She sat in silence as they drove back to Paris, looking at the blood on her hands and skirt and sleeve, where she had held a gravely injured child in her arms. On reaching the city center, she turned to Sarah with a tremulous smile.

"I want you to take me to the gendarmerie near your apartment. It's time to do what I should have done years ago, but didn't because I was too involved with Carlos. I'm going to tell them about his dealings with the terrorists in Libya."

"He'll kill you if you try that."

"My life's not worth so very much these days."

Sarah pulled off to the side of the road and telephoned Madame Nicoletti.

"Sarah here. I'm with a friend who's just come close to being murdered by a bomb thrown at her on the instructions of her ex-lover. She's going to the police to make a statement about his activities. Then she'll need a place to hide. Can you help me?"

"Of course I can; I know just the spot. Bring her to my house when you're ready, Sarah."

That night, Holly slept in an exclusive *maison de passe* on the outskirts of Paris. Used to clients who arrived incognito, no one asked questions and she retired to bed at ten after a delicious dinner of turbot poached in champagne. She did not sleep, but lay thinking of the five hours she had spent in the Paris police station with only Sarah and her lawyer for company. When the statement had finally been signed, it proved not only Carlos's guilt, but that of three of his group. It also implicated, without proof, Umberto di Castelli in the arms sale to Libya.

Holly lay back in the four-poster bed and gazed up at the ceiling, with its licentious frescoes of satyrs and naked women. She was thinking of all the beds and all the ceilings and all the wanton moments she had experienced in her life. When she asked herself why she had behaved so, there was no logical answer. She had wanted to rebel, but that was no excuse for the willful perversion of desire. Depression hit her like a bolt out of the blue as she thought of the aftermath of the explosion at the airport. She looked uncertainly about her, her gaze coming to rest on a crucifix hanging from a simple gold chain from the Louis XIV dressing table. Taking it in her hand, Holly held it close to her cheek. She was sitting quite still, her eyes closed, saying a silent prayer for guidance, when Madame Nicoletti came into the room.

"Get dressed, dear. You'll be leaving for Dublin from the old military airfield at Milly. The trouble is, Umberto di

Castelli has men looking for you everywhere and Fontainebleau is one of the places he's sure to watch. If I can get you
through the town you won't have to worry at all.''

"Are you going to drive me there?"

"I'm coming with you, but my bodyguard, Henri, will do
the driving."

Umberto was in his office, his hand on the phone, his face
enraged. Sarah had not been at home for twenty hours, and
neither had her child, the nurse, Mary-Ellen, her daughter,
or the English chauffeur he detested. His men had still found
no trace of Holly, and Umberto was worried that at last the
police might have some concrete evidence against him. He
rose and paced the room, telling himself he had been too soft
with Sarah and for too long. It was time to assert his power,
to show her who was in control, but her nature made everything difficult. She simply did not react like other people
and was impervious to threat. When he tried to discipline
her, she dug her heels in with all the stubbornness of a fighting bull. Only love made her malleable, but it was his love
for her that had made it impossible to put pressure on her until now. Umberto picked up the evening paper and looked at
the front-page photograph of Vieri and his brother returning
from a trip to America, where they had bought half of Southern California, or so it seemed. He threw down the paper in
disgust and looked again at the latest report from his men.
Aldobrandini was in the family house in the avenue Foch
with his brother, Elio's fiancée, and the staff. There had
been no phone calls and no visitors, though dinner for nine
had been ordered from Maxim's. Umberto frowned. Only
Vieri Aldobrandini would think of using Maxim's as his
takeout! He picked up the phone and called the organization's lawyer.

"You prepare the letter for Sarah Hallam?"

"You want it delivered tonight? It's ready."

"No, the morning will do. You are absolutely certain we have the legal right to foreclose?"

"She has seven days to raise what she owes the organization after receipt into her hands of the document."

"It must be into her hands?"

"Correct; otherwise, it is invalid."

"Then we wait. No one can find Miss Hallam, but when we do, we deliver."

They dined by candlelight in the Aldobrandini mansion, Lexy and her nurse, Elio and his fiancée, Mary-Ellen and her daughter, Davington and Vieri and Sarah. The food sent over by Maxim's was delicious, the wines intoxicating, and Sarah smiled as she described their flight from the apartment. It was obvious, however, that she was in a state of great tension and anxiety.

"We took a taxi to the hotel in the next street, just as you told me to do, and used the passage through their wine cellar. It went down so far that Davington said we were going to end up in the sewers."

"Elio and I have often used it when we wanted to go out without being seen by the press. That second entrance to this house was the reason we bought the hotel and then the chain we now own."

"How many people know about it? I'd hate for Umberto to arrive unexpectedly."

"My family and the man in charge of the cellar of the hotel. He used it to escape from the Gestapo in the war and he guards the secret with his life, because he's always been convinced he'll need to use it again someday."

At seven the following morning, Umberto was in his office when the telephone rang.

"Beppe here, Uncle. I don't know if it's of interest, but a

plane is due to take off in a few minutes from the old military airfield at Milly.''

Umberto frowned, conscious that the airport had not been used for twenty years or more. Still, it was worth investigating.

''Get over there, Beppe, and take Rocco with you. You have a photograph of the girl, Holly O'Malley. If she arrives, kill her.''

Holly was driven from the house to the town of Fontainebleau and quickly through the elegant streets and past the chateau into the forest, where sunlight dappled through chestnut trees planted in centuries past by the kings of France, who had hunted there. The day was warm and golden and Henri the driver, delighted to have such company, had put a flower in his peaked cap. Holly watched apprehensively as the padlock on the airport gate was unlocked. This, she knew, would be the moment of danger. Stepping out of the car, she stood tall, determined not to show any fear. On the runway of crumbling concrete, a plane was already taxiing in preparation for takeoff. Holly walked with Madame Nicoletti to the edge of the field and held out her hand.

''Thank you for everything you've done for me, Madame. Give Sarah a big kiss and tell her I'll be in touch.''

The sound of gunfire came as a complete shock, but Holly did not hesitate. With supreme courage she sprinted to the plane and disappeared from view without a backward glance.

Madame Nicoletti stood motionless like a rock, refusing to dirty her new St. Laurent gray crepe by lying down on the filthy concrete of the runway to avoid the bullets. She recognized Umberto's nephew Beppe and cousin Rocco as they ran from the shack where they had been hiding and began firing at the plane as it took off. It was at her signal that

Henri took off the flower-trimmed hat and shot both Beppe and Rocco in the back.

Henri turned to Madame and patted her shoulder.

"I told you when di Castelli had Jean-Pierre killed that you and I would await our moment to do him down. The time's come, *cherie*. Today is just the beginning."

Madame thought of the son she had loved, murdered in his prime by Umberto. She had never been able to find proof of the Sicilian's responsibility and had been obliged to watch him go from strength to strength ever since. She walked with Henri back to the car, satisfied that this was only the beginning. Soon, the moment of her revenge would arrive, and the catalyst would be Sarah Hallam.

Sarah arrived at her apartment at eleven in the morning and was drinking coffee with Davington when a letter was delivered into her hand. She opened it and read the contents in shocked silence. Then she handed the letter to Davington.

"Read it. It's in French, but there's a page of official translation into English."

Davington put on his glasses and read out loud small sections of the letter. *"In accordance with the terms of our contract, we request immediate repayment of the loans made by Umberto di Castelli and Associates and Pan-Orient, Inc. . . . Total to be repaid two hundred fifty thousand pound loan for purchasing of leases plus one hundred thousand pound loan for restoration costs. Total cost three hundred fifty thousand pounds. . . . Failure to repay within seven days will result in the automatic transfer of all assets of Hallam International. Signed Arnaldo Gezzi for Umberto di Castelli."*

Sarah went to her room and lay down on the bed, shock taking its toll at last. Umberto had chosen his time well. The French Stock Exchange was closed. All the rich people of Paris were out of town on the traditional July-August holiday, so she had virtually no hope of raising the cash. She heard Davington entering the room and watched as he put the coffee down on the bedside table, his face imperturbable, as always. Then, when the phone rang, he lifted the receiver to take the call.

"Miss Hallam's residence . . . Ah, yes, Mr. di Castelli . . . No, she is not receiving calls . . . I'm afraid that would be impossible, sir. . . . You may make threats, but I shall ignore them. . . . Oh, no, sir, that would be foolish. Come, by all means, but I shall break your jaw if you try to get in."

Davington sat on the edge of the bed and smiled down at Sarah.

"Now, you're not to give up hope, are you?"

"What do I do, pray for a miracle?"

"That would be a good idea. In the meantime, I'd best call the Prince."

"Don't tell Vieri what's happened. He'll lose all respect for me."

"He's a very practical man and he's well aware of the situation. He'll think of something."

When Umberto arrived at the apartment, he put his key into the lock. Then, realizing that it had been changed, he began to hammer at the door, infuriated when Davington appeared, his face impassive.

"What can I do for you, sir? Miss Hallam went out an hour ago."

Umberto saw suitcases and trunks everywhere in the apartment and turned furiously to Sarah's chauffeur.

"Why are you packing?"

"Miss Hallam is leaving, sir."

"I forbid it."

"With respect, sir, since the arrival of the letter this morning, I think your days of influence are over. Now, if you'll excuse me, I really must finish getting things together. There's so much to take to the country I shall need a truck.''

''Where in the country?''

''To Fontainebleau, sir, though I haven't seen the house yet.''

Umberto turned very pale. Was it possible that Sarah was responsible for the deaths of Rocco and Beppe, who had been killed at the airfield near Fontainebleau? And had *she* organized Holly's escape? Returning to his office, Umberto instructed one of his investigators to research an ancient farmhouse that had been purchased several years previously in the name of a company of nominees based in the Cayman Islands, the company owner rumored to be Vieri Aldobrandini. Umberto screamed for Benedetti to come to him. Then he sent out his chauffeur to find Sarah and bring her to him at once.

After placing ads in the Paris papers, Sarah had visited two men who had expressed interest in investing in her company and the only private bank that was open. By evening, she had raised one-third of the loan, but knew that the remainder was virtually impossible. Every merchant bank and financial establishment was closed until early September. Fellow club owners, including Madame Nicoletti, were on holiday, and the banks in Zurich and London likewise. Sarah was wandering disconsolately up the Champs Elysées when Umberto's driver stopped at her side.

''Please come with me, Madame. Mr. di Castelli wish to speak with you most urgently.''

Sarah entered Umberto's office and sat facing him across the desk. Benedetti was at Umberto's side, his face impassive. Another man was present, though he sat at a table near the window with his back to Sarah and was not introduced. Sarah opened the conversation.

''Well, what was so urgent you had to send out a search party for me?''

"I want you to tell me if you can raise the money on time. Also, where you plan to live now you leave the apartment?"

"I have seven days to raise the money, and my new house is none of your business."

"You go to the farm *he* bought you through one of his companies."

"Don't play games with me, Umberto. What do you want?"

He struggled to retain his patience in the face of Sarah's obstinacy.

"Until now, because of our friendship, your clubs have been exempt from certain expenses."

"What kind of expenses?"

"Maintenance, protection, things like that."

"Are you threatening me, Umberto?"

"I am telling you. If you default on the payment, we take over the clubs. If not, you make the payments for safety."

"I won't pay protection."

"You must be reasonable, Sarah. You have no choice in the matter."

She rose and looked down at Umberto with derision.

"I'm leaving the apartment and you know where I'll be living. If I default you get everything I own in Paris. If I find the money, you'll have back everything your organization loaned me, with interest. If you threaten me or send men to try to bleed the businesses, I'll fight you. If you touch my child, I'll have your precious son chopped up in little pieces and sent around with your butcher's order—and that's not a threat, it's a *promise!*"

"Sarah, please stay and we talk."

"There's nothing to talk about. You've made your position very clear."

Sarah walked out into the empty summer streets of Paris. She was profoundly distressed by the suddenness of her change in situation, but she felt a certain sense of relief that

Umberto was no longer her security. Now, at last, she would have to learn to survive alone. First she knew she must fight to raise the rest of the money to keep her empire, but if she lost everything she would start all over again. She thought of the man in the dark suit who had sat with his back to her throughout the interview. Was he the one who would be sent to enforce Umberto's wishes? Sarah shivered despite the heat of the day. Then she heard a familiar voice and, turning, saw Vieri in his new Ferrari.

"Get in, Sarah, and I'll take you to tea at the Ritz. After that interview with the criminal class I'm sure you need some light relief."

She did not ask how he knew where she had been, but simply got in the car and clutched his hand.

The man in the dark suit followed, watching Sarah closely. They all started by being defiant, but in the end they paid or they died. He took a seat in the hallway of the Ritz and continued to observe Sarah from the distance. Was it possible that this one might be different from the rest?

Chapter Twenty-Four

Paris, August–September 1977

On the third day of the seven days Sarah had to raise the money, Vieri took her to lunch on the Seine. It was her birthday and his gifts were surprising, as always: the paneling once used for the walls of Madame de Pompadour's bedroom in the Chateau de Champs and the bed that matched them, its headboard carved with two doves, the symbols of love and peace. He brought with him only a tiny *ciré perdue* vase by Lalique, saying that as the bed was eight feet wide it would not fit in the Ferrari.

Sarah smiled wistfully, provoking him to tease her.

"Do cheer up, darling. You're in good health, you're beautiful and successful—what more do you want?"

"I've a lot of problems at the moment."

"Nonsense! You've broken with di Castelli, so the good times are just beginning."

"He wants the equivalent of three hundred and fifty thousand pounds by Saturday morning. I've raised one hundred and twenty nine thousand from investors in three days, but I can't raise more. Umberto chose his moment very efficiently. The stock exchange is closed, and all the other financial centers too."

"To hell with di Castelli and his games."

Sarah looked incredulously at her companion, wondering if he really understood.

"Vieri, I'm going to lose all I've worked all this time to acquire. Try to understand what it means to me."

"There are times when I think you're a very intelligent woman and others when I find you incredibly stupid. Now, do drink your champagne and relax."

Two men walked into the restaurant and moved silently to the balcony over the water, where Sarah and Vieri were sitting. One handed her a note in Umberto's hand. *You have four days left to raise the loan. Tonight men will come to the Green Door to take the other payment. See you make no mistake and pay what they ask.*

Sarah pushed her plate away as Vieri read the letter and put it in his pocket.

"Don't worry, Sarah. You'll work everything out in the end. You've been associated with Umberto for so long and you must have known it would come to this in the end."

"What do I do?"

"You don't pay, but what you do is up to you. Either you sell the clubs and get out of Paris or you fight him."

"I'll not run."

"Then fight, with violence if necessary. He will and you know it, though you always gave me the impression that you believed that Umberto's mania for you would protect you, that you'd be the exception in his life. I can't believe you really thought that, that you retained the innocence that always intrigued everyone in the early days."

"I believed in love, I still do. I believe that if someone *really* loves a person the way Umberto loves me he can't just turn his back and let the sharks eat her."

"Umberto only understands violence and the traditional Sicilian way of operating. You have a choice at this moment: Either you pay, or you fight. If you fight, you have to be prepared to go to the limit."

They were drinking coffee in the garden of the inn when a

photographer appeared and snapped them. The photograph would appear in the evening papers with a caption hinting at romance: *Sarah Hallam and the Prince Aldobrandini, lunching at an inn renowned as a rendezvous for lovers.*

Sarah was having a sandwich and splitting a bottle of champagne with Madame Nicoletti at the Green Door when two men appeared and demanded the protection money. She spoke with all the authority she could muster.

"I have no intention of paying and I told that to Mr. di Castelli. Now please leave the club immediately."

Sarah and Madame continued to discuss the problem of trying to raise vast sums of money in Paris in August. They were finishing the champagne when they noticed smoke coming under the door. Madame Nicoletti leaped to her feet.

"My God, those bastards have set the place on fire!"

They ran together down the corridor leading to the basement shop, but were driven back by the flames. They retreated at once to the office, praying the phone was still working so they could call the emergency services. Madame patted Sarah's hand.

"Henri will get us out. He'll know to come and find me."

Minutes later, they heard the sound of fire-engine bells ringing and then men appeared with hoses and breathing equipment. Sarah walked through flooded corridors to the ruin of what had been an elegant rendezvous, shattered to find policemen everywhere and a body being taken out in a black plastic bag. She looked in shocked silence at the chief of the local gendarmerie, who tried to explain what had happened.

"One of your clients choked on the smoke in the women's restroom and died in a matter of seconds. I'm sorry, Miss Hallam. When people realize that di Castelli's involved, it could ruin your spotless reputation."

"How do you know he's involved?"

"I saw the photo of you and Prince Aldobrandini in the paper. I knew something like this could happen. Everyone knows di Castelli's nearly mad with jealousy."

For an hour water was sprayed on the smoldering embers, as experts checked the type of device that had been used. The press arrived and left and then Vieri appeared with his brother.

"I came as soon as I heard, Sarah. I have even worse news for you, I fear. Henri Soiron has been found shot in the back of the head a few yards from the entrance to the club. The officer in charge of the case has asked me to tell you to break the news to Madame Nicoletti."

Sarah sat on the leather chair behind her desk, her face taut with anguish. Everything stank of smoke, and Madame was looking at her with an uncharacteristically vulnerable expression.

"What is it, Sarah?"

"I have terrible news for you, Madame."

"He's dead, isn't he? I knew something was wrong when Henri didn't come to get us out."

"He was found in his car, shot in the back of the head a few yards from the door of the club. I'm so sorry. I don't know what to say or do to help you."

Tears ran down Madame's face, but she remained in control of her emotions. First di Castelli had killed her son. Now, his *compadres* had shot the man who had loved and protected her for twenty years. She was sitting at Sarah's side in stunned silence when Benedetti arrived.

"I was passing and saw the fire. What can I do, Sarah?"

"Did Umberto send you?"

"You know better than to say that."

"I know nothing anymore, except that I won't run away."

Benedetti was staring into Sarah's pale face when the man in the dark suit entered the room and introduced himself.

"I am Nicolo Magistretti, Miss Hallam. Umberto has put me in charge of your assignment. I'm sure Mario has explained the position, but in case he hasn't, you pay or one by one your clubs will be burned down and your clients killed. You have a daughter, too, and perhaps you should think of her. Accidents can happen and often do."

Sarah felt the whirring of temper in her head and the raw fury that only love for her child could provoke. She realized at that moment just how much she had trusted Umberto, how totally she had believed that his love would protect her. She thought of Vieri, who had left the club for the house at Fontainebleau, where he and Elio and some hastily summoned guards would protect the inhabitants. Sarah fought to control the panic that kept rising within her, telling herself all the while that she must stay firm and strong for her own sake and for that of her child. She had come a long way fast, but the test of her character and her business acumen was going to be whether she could hold on to what she had against the massed force of Umberto's organization. She was suddenly conscious of Magistretti looking mockingly down at her.

"Well, have you made your decision, Miss Hallam?"

"I have, and my decision is that I want you and those two men to leave the club immediately. And I don't want to see you again, ever."

"But you will see me, Miss Hallam. As I said, you are my assignment."

"Get out of my club, Magistretti."

He rose, the smile lingering on his face.

"We're thirsty, so we'll take a drink at the bar before returning to Umberto's office to report."

Madame Nicoletti watched as Magistretti left the office, followed by his *compadres*. Then she looked to Sarah for guidance.

"I'd best go and serve them their drinks. There's no one else left and I'm not sure I can find a bottle that's still intact."

"I wish I had something to put in their drinks so Mario could dump them in the river for me. Men like that don't deserve to live."

When Madame had gone, Sarah looked questioningly at Benedetti.

"Well, what's your advice now, Mario?"

He thought for a long time before replying.

"You're shocked that Umberto would threaten your child. Your faith in people never fails to surprise me. The fact is Umberto's never forgiven Lexy for calling Aldobrandini 'Papa.' "

Sarah's heart missed a beat and she rose and paced the room.

"Are you sure she said that?"

"Quite sure. Three weeks ago Umberto called at your apartment. Lexy was there with her nurse, and when Umberto reprimanded her for making too much noise she said she'd tell Papa about him. It didn't take him long to find out whom she'd chosen as her father, and he was enraged."

"Help me, Mario. I need someone to do what has to be done. Can't you leave Umberto and come and work for me?"

"I'll be more use if I stay where I am. That way I can warn you when he's planning to attack."

"Does Umberto still trust you?"

"I don't know; I think so."

At that moment Davington entered the office.

"Madame Nicoletti asked me to tell you that two gentlemen just fainted in the bar."

Sarah hurried to the spot where two of Umberto's men were lying unconscious on the ground. She looked in astonishment at Madame Nicoletti.

"Whatever did you give them?"

"I put them to sleep and now I'm going to help Mario dump the bastards in the river. You're right, Sarah. Men like these shouldn't be allowed to live."

"Where's Magistretti?"

"He left before he'd finished his drink, but the others stayed on."

Benedetti ran to the street and disappeared into the night. Davington, impassive as ever, took the feet of the first man and helped Madame Nicoletti lift him into her car. The second man went the same way, and as the clocks struck midnight, Sarah was left alone in the club, with its flooded floor and smoke-blackened walls. Though shocked by what had happened, she remained curiously calm. She had been obliged, at last, to fight Umberto on his own terms and in a manner that entailed violence, but she felt nothing except resignation to the inevitable. She had given Benedetti his instructions and could not help a grim smile at the thought of Umberto's reaction. He was accustomed to dealing out suffering and fear, but had he ever been on the receiving end of both? She could not stop a grim smile at the thought of what Umberto would do when he realized that she had declared war.

Closing her eyes, Sarah listened to water dripping from the ceiling. The noise grated on her nerves, and she checked her purse and took out her car keys in preparation for leaving the premises. Then, out of the silence of the night, she heard footsteps approaching. Looking up, she saw Umberto standing in the doorway, his face mirroring the extremes of passion that assailed him day and night. His voice was heavy with emotion.

"Why are you not home in Fontainebleau with your child?"

"Why are you here? Did you want to see what your people had done?"

"Where are they? My men do not return to my office."

"I don't know where they went."

"Aldobrandini pay guards to patrol your house in the country. He think his money buy safety, but he is wrong."

Sarah watched impassively as Umberto settled in the chair before her and looked at her with anguished, questioning eyes. When he spoke, she was conscious for the first time of the shock he too had suffered, the effects on him of friendship lost.

"I have been trying to accept that we are no longer friends, but I cannot believe it."

"It was your choice."

"Where is Nicolo Magistretti?"

"He was here with two men. He told me I was his assignment."

"Where is he, Sarah?"

"He left with the two men over an hour ago."

"Pay the money we ask. If you refuse, I cannot protect you any longer."

"I won't pay and I won't run. You'll just have to kill me."

Umberto leaped to his feet, his face livid.

"Is that what you want? You think I can afford to have you ignore me? You think in my position I need a woman who do what she like and make a fool of me?"

"I told you my position, Umberto."

Feelings of panic hit him and he looked into the pale, tense face with something close to distraction.

"Sarah, you don't understand. This is not anymore between you and me. If you pay what you owe, I can maybe give you time on the protection money. If not, you lose everything, but I let you stay at the English Club as manager. I am your friend, despite everything. I *love* you."

"Bullshit. You're my enemy and you know it. You talk of love and the words come easy, but I judge you by your actions. Your actions used to be those of a man who really loved me, but now they're the actions of a man who wants to destroy me if I don't obey him."

"What do you expect? You go everywhere with Aldo-brandini. You humiliate me before my *compadres.*"

"Why did you come here, Umberto?"

"I look for Nicolo Magistretti."

He sighed, looking appealingly at Sarah. "No, it's not true. I come because I want to see you."

"Go home, Umberto. It's over between us and we both have to accept it and do what has to be done."

"I forget the loan if you leave Aldobrandini for good."

"I *love* Vieri and I'll marry him if he asks me. I always warned you I didn't want to be one of your possessions, like your watch or your car or one of the houses you own."

"It's over, then? Are you sure this is what you want, Sarah?"

"You sent the letter. You sent the men to burn down my club and threaten my child. You're the one who decided to end the friendship."

Umberto drove through the cool stillness of the Bois de Boulogne. There was a full moon and the lake shimmered like a silver satin cloak. Owls, disturbed by his headlights, flew like phantoms past the windshield of the car, but he saw nothing, his mind in such a turmoil he felt he was in danger of going mad. He had done everything for Sarah, giving all he could give of himself and his resources. He had loaned her syndicate money on precious little interest. He had adored her, worshiped her, used his organization and his power to please her. He knew he would never again want a woman as he had wanted her. He would never *need* a woman as he needed her, either. Rage made him lose his concentration and he was forced to swerve to avoid a cyclist traveling without lights. Cursing the man, the darkness, and

his anguish, Umberto turned right and halted, speechless
with shock before the gates of his home.

The beams of the car headlights illuminated two corpses
that had been hung from meat hooks on the ornamental iron
gates of the property. Umberto leaped out of the car and
stood gazing at the faces of the men who had gone with
Magistretti to Sarah's club earlier in the evening. A thousand questions drummed through his mind, but he recovered
his composure quickly and switched off the headlights.
Then, using the automatic gate opener, he called for men to
come and cut down the bodies. Within an hour, all evidence
of their presence and untimely end would be gone. But what
had happened? Had Sarah given the order for their deaths?
And how could he obtain proof of her guilt?

Umberto walked swiftly into the house and sent out every
man he could contact to find Nicolo Magistretti. Then he
telephoned for Benedetti to come at once to the house. In the
intervening half hour he paced back and forth like a caged
tiger. He had made the decision to teach Sarah a lesson, to
show her that she was a very small cog in a very large wheel.
Now he had a war on his hands and had lost her forever. He
had also lost control of the game. When it became known
that two of his men had been killed on her instructions, there
would only be one more order to give.

Benedetti entered the office and took his usual place in the
chair facing Umberto.

"Did you really have to call me out at four in the morning? What happened?"

"The two men I send to Sarah are dead. I find them strung
on hooks from the gates of my house. I never hear of such an
insult! No one does such a thing since the Germans invade
Paris in the war. Also, Nicolo Magistretti has vanish. I have
all my men trying to find him, but still there is no news. I
went to see Sarah before I return home and she tell me I am
no longer her friend."

"That's hardly surprising."

"What do I do, Mario?"

"Why ask me? You decided to fight her when you sent that letter against my advice. What you really want is to ruin her and have her all to yourself again."

"She tell me she defy me to the death."

"She will, too. She has no fear, or perhaps she's so frightened she's capable of being heroic."

"I never met a woman like her before and I never meet another, but now she leave me no alternative. She give the order to kill Enrico and his brother, I am sure of it. She was always violent. And where is Magistretti? If *he* vanish there will be questions in Palermo and I get orders to remove Sarah at once."

"And you'll do it."

Umberto wiped the sweat from his brow.

"You are my friend. Tell me what I must do."

"I told you and you ignored the advice and now it's too late. You've left yourself no alternative but to fight your war. You always wanted to test Sarah. Now you'll have the opportunity to see what she's made of."

On the sixth day of the period of Sarah's anguished efforts to raise the money, she went to meet her daughter and Lucy at the school in Fontainebleau. Mary-Ellen usually did this, but she had stayed late in Paris for a lesson. Sarah was getting out of her car when she saw two men sitting in a car parked outside the school. They were Umberto's men and Sarah knew at once that she and her child were in trouble.

When she drove home, Umberto's men followed at a discreet distance, pausing to speak with others parked outside the local inn. Sarah put the car in the garage and ran into the house, locking all the doors behind her. Then she telephoned the inn and found out that six men from Paris were staying there at the moment, the bill for all of them to be sent to Umberto's office. She telephoned Vieri at once at his house in Paris.

"Umberto's got six men staying at the inn near the house. I think they're going to try to kidnap Lexy."

"I'll come immediately. In the meantime lock all the doors and windows, and when Mary-Ellen gets back tell her what's happening."

"I don't want to worry Mary-Ellen. She's only just beginning to recover from the shock of losing her sons."

"Tell her, Sarah, or she'll get a bigger shock if those men arrive at the house."

Sarah put down the phone and gazed out the kitchen window, wondering how to tell her friend all that was happening in her life. She was shocked when she heard Mary-Ellen's voice behind her.

"You don't have to tell me that Umberto's declared war, Sarah. I've seen the guards patrolling the house. I've watched you getting paler and more scared every day and trying not to tell me that you're in danger of your life. Tell me what I can do to help you."

"I think Umberto's going to try to take Lexy from me."

"Like hell he will!"

"Vieri's driving from Paris in half an hour to get us out of the house. Till then, he told me to lock all the doors and windows."

Mary-Ellen realized that this was the moment to show her newfound strength.

"*I'll* drive the kids to Paris, Sarah, and I'll leave right now. I can go anywhere without problem, because Umberto's men aren't interested in me and neither is he. We'll put the children in the back of the car and tell them it's a game. Then I'll register all of us at the Ritz and we'll hide out there till all this is over. Those big-footed bums'll have a hard time finding us once we're in our suite. And even Umberto di Castelli can't get past the doorman of the Ritz!"

"You could be right, but I don't like to ask you to take such a risk."

At five Mary-Ellen drove out of the farmhouse as she did each day en route to the village shop. Umberto's men looked on with disinterest, unaware that instead of returning to the property, she had taken the highway to Paris. Within an hour, she had registered herself and the children at the Ritz Hotel, as she and Sarah had arranged. Then she telephoned to confirm their safe arrival, her words almost drowned by the delighted cries of the two little girls.

"We're safe and all set up in a lovely suite with bathrooms the size of Grand Central Station. The kids think they're on holiday."

"Vieri just arrived and we'll be leaving in a couple of minutes. Wish me luck."

Vieri drove from the house down the main road and past the two men who were watching the property. Looking through the rearview mirror, he saw them turning their car and following as he took the expressway to Paris. He paused at the toll entrance to speak with the gendarmes in a police patrol car. Then, as he sped toward the city center, he watched the men accelerating behind him and the patrol car keeping pace with both. Conscious of Sarah's apprehension, he kissed her hand.

"In fifteen minutes we'll be drinking champagne at the Ritz."

Sarah's thoughts were interrupted when Vieri turned suddenly to leave the highway at the Porte de la Chapelle. She had not expected him to take this exit and neither had Umberto's men, but he had chosen well. In the heavy traffic of the Paris suburbs Umberto's men were unable to reverse to take the exit without being stopped for infringing the law by the patrol car directly behind them. For the moment Sarah and Vieri were free to proceed to their destination in safety.

In the early evening, Vieri took Sarah to the Ritz bar for a drink. When she was settled and relaxed, he began gently to question her.

"Have you managed to raise the money you owe di Castelli?"

"I have about one hundred and sixty nine thousand sterling equivalent, but that's all. I've tried everything I know, but this is the one time when it's just not possible."

"And you see di Castelli tomorrow at noon at his office. What are your plans."

"What can I do? Umberto won't take part payment, so I'll have to return the investors' money and hand over the deeds of my properties."

"Why did you never ask me for the money, Sarah?"

She thought how many times she had almost done just that, but fear of Umberto had prevented her from involving Vieri. Choosing her words carefully, Sarah tried to explain.

"I'm in love with you and I don't want you involved in all this. If I borrow the money from you, he'll either kill us both or destroy everything I own. Then I'd be unable to pay you back and I couldn't face that."

"I never loan money."

Sarah kissed his cheeks, then his lips, her heart pounding with relief and desire.

"Thank God you said that! Now let's change the subject. I've lost my shirt but I still have you."

"I never loan money, but I do give it. I've made this out to di Castelli personally. I suggest you return the money to your investors and resign yourself to having me for a partner in future. I just hope my check gives him a heart attack from rage. To the Sicilian it will be the ultimate insult."

Sarah stared uncomprehendingly at the check for three hundred fifty thousand pounds, made out to Umberto di Castelli. Her mouth turned as dry as cinders and she felt light-headed with relief. She thought with a flash of humor that if Umberto was as shocked as she when he received the check, he might well have a heart attack.

Then she tried to find something suitable to say to the man who had just given her a million dollars, but no words came to mind and she simply buried her head in Vieri's shoulder, closing her eyes when he stroked her neck and whispered, "I adore you, Sarah. Now, don't cry. You have the money you need and I shall take care of di Castelli, I promise."

"You don't understand how dangerous he is."

Vieri shook his head wearily.

"My darling, I know better than anyone what kind of man he is. Do you feel like a walk? There's something I want to show you before you go back to the hotel."

"I could do with a breath of air. It's not every day someone hands you a million dollars for nothing."

As they walked through the streets of Paris, the sounds of night echoed in the distance: the wail of a police siren, the scraping of a violin, the raucous voice of a streetwalker shouting defiance at a departing client. Sarah felt Vieri putting his arms around her and holding her against his heart. She looked fearfully behind, in case Umberto's men were following, but she saw only the familiar face of Davington, proceeding at a stately pace in the Ferrari, ignoring the impatient hooting of drivers who could not pass him.

Vieri led her to a property in the area behind the Opéra, a seemingly ordinary Parisian residence of stately gray stone. Ignoring the interior, he proceeded to the garden, which was full of scented, old-fashioned roses and verbena.

"This was my father's house in the days of his childhood. It now belongs to my aunt Cecile, who went to London for the summer."

"Imagine a garden like this in the middle of Paris!"

"I didn't bring you to see the garden. I thought the chapel might interest you most of all."

Passing under an arch covered in morning glory, Sarah

entered the tiny family chapel, with its stained-glass windows in topaz and amber and interior walls of gilded leather that glowed in the light of dozens of rose-scented candles. She listened in awe as Vieri told her about the place.

"My great-grandfather brought the tooled leather back from Saint Petersburg. It was a gift from Czar Nicholas for services rendered."

"It's a truly beautiful place."

"Would you like to get married here? I want us to have a very private ceremony."

Tears began to stream down Sarah's face and suddenly she began to sob for all the months of tension and all the years when she had longed for and dreamed of his proposal. It was a moment unequalled in her life and for a while she said nothing, but simply savored the culmination of her hopes. When she replied, Vieri sighed with relief.

"I'll marry you anywhere you like."

"That's settled, then. We'll arrange it for the last day of December and then go to the house in Venice for the honeymoon."

Under a starry sky in a garden of scented flowers, they kissed and held each other tight. For a few minutes Umberto and his malevolent *compadres* were forgotten as love ruled the night.

At eleven the following morning, Sarah walked into Umberto's office and found herself face to face with the man who had been the principal influence in her life for so many years. She saw that he was wearing a new suit with a camellia in the buttonhole. His eyes were anxious and she was well aware that he was torn between love and the masculine pride that ruled his life. She knew also that even if he wanted to, he could no longer protect her. The tension in his body and the sudden pleasure he could not conceal touched Sarah's heart. She sat down quietly opposite him, determined to try to end this important partnership in a civilized manner.

Umberto looked at Sarah, wondering how she was going to concede the game in which she had lost all she owned. Would she be polite in the true English manner, or was she in the mood to wreck the office? He gazed at her with a certain wary respect, like one dangerous animal weighing another and trying to assess the extent of the threat. He was surprised to find her calm and dignified, in an elegant Chanel suit of sugar-pink and cream, the blouse tucked like a convent girl's bodice. As he took in every detail of her body, longing weakened him and his voice shook with emotion when he spoke.

"Well, what is the news?"

"I've brought you a check, Umberto."

"How much of the money you raise?"

"The check is for three hundred fifty thousand pounds, the total amount I owe you. I need a receipt worded as it says on this paper."

Umberto sat quite still, conscious of Benedetti's sharp intake of breath and Magistretti's silent fury. Was it possible she had raised such a sum in Paris in August? Unable to believe his ears, he held out his hand for the check, losing control when he saw Vieri's signature. Speechless with rage, he looked across the desk at Sarah with a gaze of undiluted loathing. Then he began to shout.

"You think I take this! You dare to ask *him* for the money? How could you do this to me?"

"I raised one hundred sixty-nine thousand pounds from my investors, but I couldn't raise the rest. Then, last night, Vieri asked me how much I had. When I told him, he asked me to return the investors' money. He's going to be my new partner from now on and he doesn't want any outsiders in the company."

Umberto leaped to his feet, his face ashen with fury.

"Damn him! He ruin everything for me!"

Sarah rose and stood her ground.

"I'd best leave. Please ask your secretary to type out the receipt."

Umberto tore up the check, hurling the pieces in her face.

"No receipt! I do not accept this check."

Sarah's face was steely, but her voice was calm.

"Vieri said you might tear up the check and that if you did, I was to tell you he'll have the money transferred by his bank directly to your account at the Credit Suisse. Now I want my receipt, Umberto."

"Get out! I don't want ever to see you again! You ruin my life and reject my love. I give all I can give and you take all you can take. Then you say you don't want me."

Sarah walked back to Umberto's desk and stood looking down at him with such tangible fury that he rose as if to ward off a blow.

"Pick up the phone and tell Ornella to type out my receipt. You're Umberto di Castelli, not a sniveling twelve-year-old schoolboy. It's time to forget me and you know it."

He looked incredulously into the violet eyes.

"You think I forget? I told you once that I love you till the blood in my body turn to water and I *never* let you go. I mean what I say. I always mean what I say."

Sarah was almost at the door when Umberto called to her.

"Tonight Nicolo come to the English Club to collect the protection. See you have it ready."

"I won't pay. I told you before. You'll just have to do what has to be done."

He ran after her, grabbing her by the shoulder as she was leaving the room.

"You think I won't do it?"

Sarah shrugged unconcernedly.

"I'm sure you will, someday. Good-bye, Umberto.

Thank you for all you've done for me. I'm so very sorry we can't remain friends.''

When Sarah arrived at the English Club late that night, she found Nicolo Magistretti waiting for her. His eyes gleamed as he demanded the money she "owed" Umberto for protection. She looked across the desk at him, her face defiant.

"Are you going to beat me up and insist I pay? I won't."

"I shall be much more subtle than that, Miss Hallam. I am going to take you for a walk—a very small distance, I assure you."

He led Sarah from the club, through the rue Fontaine to the entrance of the new multistory parking lot being built behind her club.

Sarah felt suddenly icy calm, though aware of the danger she was in from this cadaverous purveyor of violence. As they took the elevator to the top floor of the building, she was able to gaze down on the sparkling lights of Paris by night and found strength in her love of the city and her desire to continue her life in peace. She did not flinch when Magistretti spoke.

"If you do not pay the money, I shall bring your daughter here and push her off the edge of the floor, where it has no wall. It is a very, very long drop, Miss Hallam."

When she did not reply, Magistretti grasped Sarah by the back of the neck and led her to the edge of the building, forcing her to look down.

Anger rose in her heart, anger such as she had never known before, as she thought of the child she loved and how Lexy jumped into her bed each morning and smothered her with kisses. Despite everything, Sarah smiled as she thought of how her daughter talked of "our clubs," "our TV show," and "our investors." Then, as Magistretti held her in an iron grip, Sarah thought of the innocence of her daugh-

ter, the helplessness of a child against such inhuman opera-
tors as Umberto and Magistretti. Furious, she tried to push
him from her, but he would not let go of her. Sarah roared
her anger into the darkness.

"Let go of me at once!"

"When I am ready. Come, have another look at the drop
your daughter is going to make. They will have to scrape her
remains from the pavement afterward."

Magistretti never saw the kick that hit like a sledge hammer between the legs. He felt only an obliterating pain as,
letting go of Sarah's neck, he fell like a bird shot on the wing
to the pavement below.

Sarah stepped back, terrified that someone in the street
might look up and see her. Then she took the elevator to the
ground floor and ran from the street parallel to where Magistretti had fallen back to the club. Shattered by the fact that
she had descended into the pit of violence where Umberto
had always existed and horrified by the threat to her child,
she was shaking from head to foot, her face chalk-white and
pouring with sweat. When she tried to drink a glass of
water, her hands trembled so that she spilled most of it on
the floor. When she tried to ring Vieri, to ask him to come to
her, she found herself unable to remember his number. She
was trying to settle her mind when Madame Nicoletti appeared.

"Dear God, Sarah, whatever happened?"

Madame hurried to the bar, returning with a bottle of
brandy. First she gave herself a hefty slug, then she poured
one for Sarah and insisted that she drink it.

"I don't know what you've done and I'm not asking, but
if you want to tell me I'll do my best to help."

"Magistretti was here."

"Where is he now?"

"He won't ever be coming back."

Madame poured herself another brandy and raised her

glass. Then she began to stroke Sarah's hands, speaking reassuringly, as if to a child.

"Don't think about it. I'll call Vieri in a few minutes and he'll come and take you home, and between the three of us we'll do everything that has to be done to keep you and Lexy safe."

Umberto was in his office, wondering why Magistretti had not returned from the English Club. He could barely stand the suspense and kept pacing up and down, picking up the phone and then putting it down again. Magistretti had left at midnight, saying he would be back by one. Umberto gazed out at the twinkling lights of Paris, terrified that he might have killed Sarah. His brain was paralyzed and he was ill from anger, hurt pride, and the anguish of lost love. Finally, unable to remain alone a moment longer, he telephoned Benedetti, but there was no reply at his friend's number. Without further deliberation, Umberto took the elevator to the garage and drove himself to the English Club, arriving in time to see police cars screeching to a halt at the door.

Pushing through the crowd, he saw the remains of Magistretti splattered on the pavement. It was obvious that he had fallen from a great height. As Umberto looked up, he saw the new multistory parking lot being built to the rear of the English Club. Was it possible that Nicolo had been pushed to his death by Sarah, or by the chauffeur whose life story read like a military legend? With a sigh of regret, Umberto returned to his car and drove away into the darkness. For him, the future held only loneliness and the anguish of living without the woman he loved. For Sarah, he knew now there was no future.

Chapter Twenty-Five

Mary-Ellen, Paris, December 1977

Mary-Ellen put on her makeup and then cried so hard from pent-up tension that she was obliged to wash her face, apply drops to her eyes, and redo everything. She had presented her act previously in four of Sarah's smaller clubs and had done well, but tonight was something new and awesome. She was in the dressing room of the Moulin Rouge and about to debut in the most important spectacle of her life, with a twenty-minute spot in the second half of the show—the items choreographed by Arden, lit by Colbert, with songs for the most part by Mary-Ellen Tate. She began to shake uncontrollably at the idea, despite weeks of rehearsal and months of brainwashing by Sarah, who insisted that anyone could do anything if she applied herself with sufficient determination.

Mary-Ellen was powdering her cheekbones with gold blusher when Sarah entered the room, her face jubilant.

"The journalists are here in force. You're going to be a star after tonight—I can feel it in my bones!"

"That press release of yours made me sound like Oscar Wilde via Theda Bara and Little Orphan Annie. I think I need the bucket again."

"I forbid you to be sick, Mary-Ellen. You've been sick four times in the past hour and it's time for a bit of self-control."

"Tell my stomach, will you? I've no desire to shower the front-seat tuxedos."

"Everyone's loved your act and tonight they're going to love it more. All you have to do is remember that when you get your recording contract you'll earn real money and you'll be able to see your sons again and maybe regain custody of them."

"What recording contract?"

"All the big boys are here. I told them to fight it out among themselves after the show. Liz has arrived, too—and she'll represent you when they start bidding for your services."

"Dear God!"

"Put some more blusher on your cheeks; you've gone a bit green."

"I'm not going to make it, Sarah. I'm just not built for this kind of tension."

"Tonight you sink or you swim, remember? You resign yourself to poverty and living a nothing life or you make yourself into a star. Now, we'd best go downstairs. You're five minutes from the biggest moment of your life."

Mary-Ellen stood in the wings, listening as the orchestra played her music. She felt her knees shaking uncontrollably and kept wondering what to do if she forgot the words of the songs she had written with all the desperation in her soul. Then, in the front row of the area nearest the stage, she saw Lucy, her daughter, sitting tensely between Mitzi and Lexy, all of them wide-eyed and as nervous as she. Then the curtains were drawn back and her name announced. Mary-Ellen straightened her back and thought of Sarah's words: *Tonight you sink or you swim. You resign yourself to a nothing life or you make yourself a star.* For a second she recoiled, afraid of taking the decisive step forward. Then she felt Sarah's hand on her shoulder and heard the familiar voice in her ear.

"Get out there and show them what a *real* performer is all about. Good luck!"

With that, Sarah pushed hard and Mary-Ellen felt the spotlights in her eyes and heard a little girl calling out excitedly, "That's Mummy!" As Lucy's childish voice echoed in the auditorium, Mary-Ellen took a bow to a wave of sympathetic and spontaneous applause. Then the lights dimmed and the audience fell silent. Mary-Ellen sat on her stool, tuned her guitar, and with a brief nod at the maestro began to sing the song that had charmed audiences in Sarah's clubs from her first appearance in Paris, "The Ballad of a Beautiful Child." In the vast auditorium there was a rapt silence. Mary-Ellen was on her way, unaware that Sarah and Liz were watching anxiously from the wings, each one wondering if their friend's fragile nerves would hold out, if for twenty minutes Mary-Ellen could hold the tough Parisian audience in the palm of her hand and make them her own.

Twenty minutes later, when Mary-Ellen had taken the audience through songs about the comedy of a showgirl's life, the patriotic joy of a military parade, the birth of a baby, and the loss of her sons, she rose, put down her guitar, and stood in a pinspot to sing the final number. It was called "The Survivor" and as she sang, tears fell down her cheeks and her voice grew strong, and suddenly the final notes were drowned by a wave of applause that swelled and echoed in the auditorium. Flowers were thrown, feet stamped, and sophisticated Parisian women wiped their eyes and pretended not to be crying. It was a memorable moment and an unforgettable one for Sarah and Liz as they watched their friend taking her bow. When Mary-Ellen left the stage, Sarah ran and clasped her in her arms.

"You made it! Just listen to them!"

Mary-Ellen stared from Sarah to Liz and then at Lucy, who was applauding and throwing roses. As Sarah motioned for her to take another bow, Mary-Ellen walked back on

stage and stood gazing out at the audience. Then, as she had
been taught, she took her bow, raising her arms to the count
of five, holding them widespread to the count of five, and
then clasping them before her and bowing her head to the
count of ten. The applause continued until the maestro
tapped for silence.

To end her performance, Mary-Ellen sang the encore
Sarah had insisted she prepare, "Love Song to an Unknown
Man," a haunting refrain of longing and dreams, hopes for
the future, and the image of a lover who would someday
come into her life. The reprise had been orchestrated to in-
clude tonal cadences of "The Survivor," and as Mary-Ellen
left the stage the cacophony of enthusiasm continued until
the star of the show was announced.

In the early hours of the morning, Mary-Ellen, Sarah, and
Liz walked home through the empty streets of Paris. When
they reached the Grands Boulevards, a streetsweeper raised
his cap and bade them good morning and a group of
transvestites from Chez Moune called out congratulations.
Already the news had spread that at the Moulin Rouge a theatrical event of note had happened. Mary-Ellen looked at
Sarah with a wan smile.

"My muscles ache as if I have the flu."

"You have a recording contract that'll make you as rich
as Getty if you have a hit record. You have a TV contract for
six shows and you're at the Moulin Rouge for a three-month
contract that I'll extend to six and the star spot if I can afford
you. With Liz representing you from now on, nothing's certain."

Liz paused and bought a copy of the morning paper, the
headline on the entertainment page thrilling her to the bone.
She handed it to Mary-Ellen with a smile.

"You see that, Miss Tate? *Tate Triumphs at the Moulin
Rouge*. When you get to Sarah's place you'd better get to
bed and *sleep*. I'll call a press conference for five in the af-

ternoon and we'll announce the recording contract. I'd like you to sing the theme song for the new Bond film, too, and I'll call the producers about you later in the morning. You're not known yet, but you will be by the time the film comes out. I have plans for you, Mary-Ellen, that you just wouldn't believe.''

Mary-Ellen entered the apartment, kissed her daughter, who was asleep with the velvet owls Lexy had bought her ''for company.'' Then she went to her room. Her head felt full of fog and she kept blinking to make sure she was conscious and not about to emerge from some strange dream. In her heart she knew she was not dreaming, but she could find no link with reality in the events of the evening, because the suddenness of transition from living on Sarah's charity to stardom unimaginable was impossible to assimilate. She began to shiver, terrified that she would be unable to repeat the performance of the previous night. Then she thought of Liz's words: *you have that mysterious ingredient, Mary-Ellen. Some call it charisma and some call it star quality. No one can take it from you, and it'll give you a future that's mink lined and studded with diamonds.*

If her luck held, Mary-Ellen knew she had it made. In this moment of triumph, however, her thoughts turned suddenly to the war between Sarah and Umberto, a war he was losing despite the odds. His pride had been hurt and he had lost face within the organization. Mary-Ellen thought resignedly that the rules of Sicilian life made reprisals of a savage nature inevitable.

Umberto put down the phone and gazed into space. Before him on the desk was the newspaper announcing the marriage of Sarah and Vieri the following Saturday. On the entertainment page there was an account of the triumph of Mary-Ellen at the Moulin Rouge. Umberto struggled to work out how to accept what he had to do, but he could not bear to think of it. At first the loss of Sarah had been a purely personal matter, but since her adamant refusal to pay protection on her clubs, it had become syndicate business. Her final error had been in defending herself and her property from one of his men, Renato Friulini, who had been sent to discipline the staff of the Bal Tabarin. Friulini, the son of the *capo* of Genoa, had never been seen again, and rumor had it that Sarah herself had been responsible for his death, while defending her chauffeur, Davington.

Umberto lit a cigar and gazed out over the city, where every street reminded him of the woman he adored. He was remembering the night when Sarah had jumped into a fountain and danced from sheer happiness. His eyes misted as he recalled the precious day when she had given him a handmade frame for the photographs of them both taken on the only holiday they had had together at the Palazzo di Castelli in Sicily. He took the photographs from the frame, kissed each one, and put them in his inner pocket. Then, again, he thought what had to be done, and tears began to fall down his cheeks from suffering such as he had never experienced in his life before. Sadly, Sarah had placed herself beyond the limits of his protection and must now suffer the consequences.

Picking up the telephone, he dialed a number in Rome.

"Aldo, your uncle here. Is everything ready?"

"I arrive at Orly at ten in the morning."

"I'll be there."

"When's the big day?"

"Friday, I hope. If not, within a few days either way."

"Uncle Dominic sends his compliments and invites you to Greta's wedding."

"I'll be there. I need to come home to Sicily for a while."

Umberto replaced the receiver and dialed Sarah's number, holding his breath when she replied. Then he put on his most persuasive voice.

"Sarah, I want this war to end. You agree? We were friends once and we can be friends again if you say yes."

There was no reply and he proceeded.

"I buy you a present and invite you to dine with me at Maxim's one last time on Friday, to show no bad feelings. Please say yes. Friday is my birthday, so you cannot refuse, but if you want I come all the way to Fontainebleau to beg on the bent knees."

He heard her laugh and knew he was going to have his way. Still, he was pleased when she spoke.

"I'll be at Maxim's on Friday at seven-thirty."

Sarah paused to think of the tone of Umberto's voice as he invited her to dinner and the way he had insisted so gently on the meeting. For a long time she remembered incidents in their past life together and the hours of happiness he had given her. Pity mixed with the inexorable knowledge that for both of them the moment of decision had arrived. Only one of them was going to survive this war of wills, and she hoped fiercely that she was going to be the one.

Vieri was at home in Paris when the telephone rang.

"Davington here, sir. He's made contact and will take Miss Hallam to dinner at Maxim's at seven-thirty on Friday. Your friend just rang with the warning."

"I'll be ready."

"I too, sir."

"You don't have to get involved in all this, Davington."

"I know, but I want to. I'm part of the family now."

At six on Friday, Sarah donned a St. Laurent dress of pure-white silk, with a cowl neckline that fell to the waist at the rear. She looked as calm and beautiful as a goddess when she walked downstairs, though her muscles were rigid with tension and her stomach was turning like a roller coaster. When she and Umberto had first met, she had been an inexperienced young girl with big ambitions, but in the intervening years she had learned all Umberto could teach her. Now she knew his mind and the traditions by which he lived. Would it be enough? Was she really ready for this final confrontation?

Davington spoke encouragingly.

"No need for nerves. Everything is under control. You know what you have to do and your friends know what they have to do and everyone's ready."

Umberto looked in the mirror and rearranged the white camellia in his buttonhole. Sarah did not like gaudy flowers and he was determined to impress her. Into his pocket he slipped the gift he had bought, a tiny brooch of a scorpion in diamonds, black pearls, and jet; its tail was erect and ready to strike. As he looked at the brooch, he sighed with regret, his heart heavy, his mind still struggling to find a way to avoid the inevitable.

At seven, Umberto hurried to his car and drove into the city, his heart thundering at the prospect of seeing Sarah again. He told himself he must stay calm, that she must not see how he was suffering. It was his birthday and he must try to give her a very special evening. He began to think of the past birthdays they had spent together, and his eyes filled with tears as he recalled the day when Sarah had taken over the village of Montelepre and engaged the town band to give him a big welcome home. That had been something to remember forever, and there had been many other days like it.

Entering Maxim's, Umberto was surprised by the silence. There were no diners, no one but the maître d' smiling a welcome and the waiters moving around a table where Sarah was already sitting. He realized at once that she had taken the place for the evening as a tribute to all he had done for her in the past. The orchestra was playing "Happy Birthday," and as he moved toward her table, Umberto saw that they were serving his favorite Dom Perignon. Pausing before Sarah, he bent and kissed her hand.

"You are always full of surprises. Imagine taking Maxim's for the whole evening."

"Happy birthday, Umberto."

He took a deep breath, fighting to retain control of the emotions that were almost choking him.

"I am very please to see you, Sarah. I should hate you by now, but I cannot. I love you till my blood turn to water, like I always say."

She motioned for him to sit on the pink velvet banquette at her side, her own feelings a confusing mixture of regret and remorse. She could not help thinking of the lizard Umberto had killed in Sicily and the lesson he had taught her that long-ago day. *Distract the enemy; make him watch your eyes so he does not see what the hands are doing.* Was Umberto now the lizard and she the one with the noose? Or was it the other way around? Sarah did her best to sound unconcerned.

"Let's drink the champagne. Then I ordered *tuna e fagioli* and sturgeon steaks flown in from Palermo. After that we'll have lasagna and indigestion. This is my party, Umberto."

"But you accept my invitation."

He paused to admire Sarah's reflection in the mirror, her hair pale-gold in the candlelight, her lips full and red. He longed to take her in his arms, to beg her forgiveness for any unhappiness he had caused, but he did nothing, because he knew it was too late.

When they had eaten and drunk another bottle of champagne, Umberto was provoked by the intensity of his happiness to try one last time to change Sarah's mind.

"It isn't too late, you know. If you give up that man I forget everything. He is not a real man, Sarah. He thinks like a great professor but he does nothing. After a year you will be bored with him."

"Don't spoil the evening by talking of Vieri. I'm marrying him in the morning."

Umberto shook his head in despair.

"You never change. You are like a rock."

Suddenly, exhausted by the pretense, Umberto rose and went to the telephone booth outside the men's room, returning to the table to find a birthday cake in the shape of the Palazzo di Castelli placed next to a silver coffeepot and two glasses of amaretto. When he saw the perfect outlines of the house he loved, he was overwhelmed and sat for a long time in morose silence. Then, obediently, he blew out the candles and turned to Sarah with a wistful smile.

"There will never be another woman like you. I want you to know that I never forget you. Every day, for the rest of my life, I think of you and pretend you are with me."

When the clock in the Madeleine struck ten, Umberto rose and lit a cigar.

"Come, we walk back to the garage together. I suppose you leave the car in the parking, like always."

"Of course. I'm a creature of habit."

"It is a beautiful night, full of stars like the ones in Palermo. You remember those nights, Sarah?"

She nodded, suddenly sad that the friendship that had been so dynamic and enduring should end in tragedy. Then she led the way along the rue Royale and into the cold, crisp darkness of a wintry evening.

On entering the sloping ramp of the underground parking lot, Umberto halted and lit another cigar.

"You go on alone now, Sarah. I cannot bear to say goodbye. I wait here till you drive away."

For a moment, Sarah's eyes held his. Then, without a word, she turned and walked away from him.

Umberto stood, outlined against the glow of the streetlights, his broad shoulders like those of a statue, the orange glow of his cigar a tiny dot of color in the night. As Sarah began her descent into the darkness, he took out a white handkerchief to signal to the gunman hidden below. For a moment, he hesitated, gazing after Sarah with a longing so fierce it hurt him. Then he gave the signal, as arranged.

Sarah walked tall, pausing to accustom her eyes to the dimly lit interior. Turning briefly to wave to Umberto, she saw him raising a white handkerchief and knew he was signaling to someone inside the garage. Always the traditionalist, he had invited her to a fine meal before the inevitable assassination. She walked on, knowing exactly what was going to happen, but putting all her trust in Mario Benedetti, who had promised to protect her, as he had protected her from their first meeting. Umberto had made his arrangements and she had made hers. Sarah gritted her teeth, determined not to quicken her pace or show any sign of fear. She was almost at the car when a shot rang out. Then, suddenly, she heard Umberto calling from behind.

"Take cover, Sarah! For *God's sake,* take cover!"

As the gunman fired again, Sarah heard two shots from the opposite side of the garage and saw a man falling from the rafters in which he had been hiding. Then, turning, she looked anxiously up at the place where Umberto had been standing when he called that last regretful warning, *For God's sake, take cover!* In that moment, she had realized just how much he loved her.

Sarah walked slowly toward the spot where Umberto lay on his back, a red stain marking the pristine white shirt. His eyes were open but unseeing. For him the game was over.

Vieri threw down the rifle and walked out of the shadows to Sarah's side.

"Let's get out of here."

She felt her knees turning weak and the color draining from her face.

"What are *you* doing here, Vieri? I thought Mario was taking care of this."

"Benedetti was killed by a hit-and-run driver in the Champs Elysées at seven this evening. He was on his way to the garage to protect you, as arranged. It was no accident, of course, but he knew he was in danger. There had been two previous attempts on his life in the past fortnight, but he was more stubborn than you and di Castelli put together."

"But what are you doing here?"

"Davington and I took Benedetti's place at rather short notice. Davington got rid of the gunman while I settled my score with your friend."

"What score?"

"Those years of my life in the caves of Calcelrama and the clinic in Rome. It was Umberto who had me kidnapped. I thought you knew."

"How *could* I have known? Do you think he ever confided his true business to me?"

"Don't think about it, Sarah. From this moment he's part of the past. We were lucky that Benedetti always counseled him not to kill me or have me killed, on the theory that if he did you'd make a martyr of me. You owed Benedetti your own life and mine too."

Sarah stepped over the body of the man who had loved her for so long and moved out of the garage without a backward glance. She was so weak, so shocked, so distressed by Umberto's death, despite everything, that she could barely climb the incline and was glad when Vieri put his arm around her and helped her into the street. His voice was reassuring and she closed her eyes, needing him and the peace his presence bestowed.

"It's over, Sarah. You won the game and the future's going to be a happy one. Tomorrow we'll marry and go home to Venice. Afterward, you can decide what you want to do."

"Umberto always said you were a man who knew nothing about action."

"He was mistaken. He underestimated the opposition, and it proved fatal."

In late evening, when the press were taking photographs of Mary-Ellen, Sarah left the club with Vieri and walked with him up the Champs Elysées. Neither said a word, until a familiar voice called out to them.

"Everything has been taken care of, sir. Would you like me to take you back to the Ritz now or later?"

The car sped through the dark streets of Paris to the hotel that had meant so much to Sarah and her friends. With a brief glance at the entrance of the garage, Sarah entered the Ritz and walked upstairs to her suite. She was with the man she loved and would marry in the morning and the future was golden. She thought wryly that she had come a long way from the days of childhood, when she had hurried to school on shoes padded with cardboard to keep out the rain. She was content that those days were over forever.

Epilogue

Rendezvous, Paris, May 1982

It was a beautiful spring day and Paris was sunlit and golden. Sarah was in her new Lagonda en route to the rendezvous at the Ritz. This time, only three friends would be present. She thought of Arlette, remembering in horror the depths of anguish that had brought tragedy. Then her mind turned to Mary-Ellen and the success she had had, success beyond even Sarah's wildest dreams. Sarah thought of the new apartment Mary-Ellen had bought at the summit of the hill of Montmartre. There, in penthouse splendor, in a house once owned by Degas, she and Lucy lived among the paraphernalia of a recording career. One room had been set aside for spares, and it had not escaped Sarah's notice that the spares included everything from Fortuny dresses to Russian sables, from Vuitton luggage to boxes of Mary-Ellen's favorite perfume.

Sarah thought of her own life in the intervening years and was content. She was happy with Vieri and the two sons born since the marriage. At the peak of the Arab property boom in Paris, she had sold everything she owned for a record figure, except the Chateau de Montalou. The money had been invested and the spa had prospered as the most expensive health resort in Europe. Life was good in the Venetian home she loved, and the horrors of the war that had erupted

after Umberto's disappearance had long faded from her
mind, though from time to time she recalled the day when
she had traveled to Palermo to see the man directing opera-
tions against her. The meeting had been turbulent and she
had feared for her life, until the moment when she had
handed him the urn containing Umberto's ashes and told
him that if anything happened to her, her family, or her
properties, the ashes of each of the man's three sons would
be returned to him in a similar fashion. Umberto had taught
her well to meet fire with fire, violence with violence. Even
the *capo* of Palermo had seen reason and withdrawn his opposition.

Mary-Ellen looked in the mirror and smiled. She was
wearing blue jeans made for her by St. Laurent, a silk blouse
hand-painted with daisies, and a Fendi fur in the shape of a
smock made from wild mink. She was driving an aubergine
Lamborghini and listening to her latest record on the hit parade. Content with her life, she thought of the letter received
that morning from one of her sons. Taking it from her purse,
she read it again.

Dearest Mama,
    When are you coming to Madrid? Please send twelve
photographs of yourself for the boys at school and some
of the new tapes. Alfonso got into a fight yesterday and
has a black eye. He also has a cold and keeps complain-
ing. We send our love and kisses. Please write soon.
                                        Your loving son,
                                        Fausto

They had arranged to eat in a private dining room off the
main Ritz Grill, in an attempt to avoid autograph hunters
and journalists seeking interviews. As she hurried into the
room, Mary-Ellen hugged Sarah to her heart.

"You're looking great. Being a princess suits you just fine."

"And you look a bit different from the last time you arrived for a rendezvous. Have you bought Montmartre yet?"

"Not quite, but I just bought the block next to my house. Did you hear from Holly?"

"Not a word. Perhaps she's scared of making contact. Carlos and his playmates got the longest jail sentences in French legal history for the airport explosion and they won't forget."

"I hope she comes."

"I wouldn't count on it."

Sarah ordered *fines claires,* followed by a soufflé of foie gras and asparagus. They drank a bottle of Laurent Perrier Cuvée Grand Siècle as an aperitif and were about to start the meal, despairing of Holly's arrival, when the mâitre d' appeared, a puzzled look on his face.

"Someone is asking to see you, Princess. She says she is invited to the lunch, but I am not sure it is possible . . ."

Mary-Ellen dropped her fork as Sarah turned to stare at a tall figure in black, the face almost hidden by the pristine, starched wimple of a nun of the Order of Mercy. For a moment, there was a shocked silence. Then, as Sarah recognized Holly, she ran forward and hugged her.

"That was quite an entrance! Mary-Ellen and I won't forget it in a hundred years."

Holly smiled happily and kissed them both on the cheeks.

"It's good to see you looking so well, Sarah, and you too, Mary-Ellen. I hear you're a big success as a recording artist."

Mary-Ellen stared at her friend, her eyes filling inexplicably with tears.

"What happened to you, Holly?"

"I went back to Ireland and hid for a year on the family estate in Connemara. I saw no one and did nothing but think. Then, when I got back to Dublin, I began to study in preparation for becoming a novice in the order. I take my final vows next month. After that, I won't leave the convent again."

Sarah turned Holly's words over in her mind.

"Is it really what you want?"

"Perhaps it always was, Sarah, but I fought against it for a long, long time."

Mary-Ellen found her voice at last.

"But you were the one who seemed to thrive on the way she lived."

Holly explained her thoughts as if speaking to a child.

"Sarah thought she needed power, but what she really wanted was to be Vieri's wife. You thought you needed a family and roots, but what you really needed was financial security. I needed peace of mind and I've found it at last."

In the golden sunlight of late afternoon, Vieri watched as Mary-Ellen hurried out of the Ritz and into the arms of a group of fans. Behind her, a nun moved silently away into the shadows of the Vendôme Arcade. Then, as Sarah emerged, her arms full of roses, Vieri hurried across the road to meet her.

"I thought you might like your husband to fly you home to Venice."

"What a lovely surprise."

"Mary-Ellen looked wonderful, but I didn't see Holly."

"She's a nun now. It was our last reunion with her, because she enters a closed order next month. We'll invite Liz Lind to the next rendezvous in her place."

Vieri held Sarah's hand as Davington whisked them out of the city toward the private airfield where he kept his plane. He was thinking of the young girl with the Victorian posy of flowers and the night they had met at Umberto di Castelli's house in the Bois.

Sarah was thinking that she would be glad to be home again with Lexy and the boys. Paris was too full of memories she was trying hard to forget. As Davington turned the car onto the highway, she spoke in her usual irreverent fashion.

"Keep your eyes on the road, Davington."

"Of course. I always do."

Sarah kissed the man she loved and had loved since their first meeting. The game had been hard, but she had won, and winning was what mattered in life. Winning and loving.

BESTSELLERS FROM

THE WANTON 86165-8/$3.95 US/$4.75 CAN

The things men did to her destroyed her innocence. The things she would do for the men she loved destroyed all her young notions of propriety. Trista was drawn to Blaze Devenant with a passion that shamed her, with a yearning that left her powerless to hate him for spoiling her virtue.

From her Boston finishing school to the gracious twilight of the pre-war South, from the golden land of California to the blood-soaked nightmare of the Civil War, Trista would be made to suffer the worst that men could do to her. Even the stepbrother she had worshipped was driven to possess her and hurt her. But never would she let them take her dreams. Or ruin the raging sweet love that comes but once in a woman's life.

SURRENDER TO LOVE	80630-4/$3.95 US/$4.50 CAN
CROWD PLEASERS	75622-6/$3.95 US/$4.95 CAN
INSIDERS	40576-8/$3.95 US/$4.95 CAN
LOVE PLAY	81190-1/$3.95
WICKED LOVING LIES	00776-2/$3.95
SWEET SAVAGE LOVE, STEVE AND GINNY BOOK I	00815-7/$3.95
DARK FIRES, STEVE AND GINNY BOOK II	00425-9/$3.95
LOST LOVE, LAST LOVE, STEVE AND GINNY BOOK III	
	75515-7/$3.95 US/$3.50 CAN